PASSAGES WEST

NINETEEN STORIES OF
YOUTH AND IDENTITY
EDITED BY HUGH NICHOLS

MARY CLEARMAN BLEW   RAYMOND CARVER   WALTER CLARK   H.L. DAVIS
IVAN DOIG   VARDIS FISHER   RICHARD FORD   A.B. GUTHRIE   DOROTHY
JOHNSON   WILLIAM KITTREDGE   DAVID LONG   NORMAN MACLEAN
DAVID QUAMMEN   WALLACE STEGNER

Acknowledgements

"The Snowies, the Judiths" originally published in *Four Quarters*, copyright © 1990 by La Salle University. Reprinted by permission of *Four Quarters*.

"Nobody Said Anything" from *Will You Please Be Quiet, Please?* by Raymond Carver, copyright © 1978 by Raymond Carver. Reprinted by permission of Raymond Carver.

"The Buck in the Hills" from *The Watchful Gods and Other Stories* by Walter van Tilburg Clark, copyright © 1950 by Walter van Tilburg Clark. Reprinted by permission of International Creative Management, Inc.

"The Kettle of Fire" pp. 165-189 from *Kettle of Fire* by H. L. Davis, copyright © 1959 by H. L. Davis. Reprinted by permission of William Morrow and Company, Inc.

"The Homestead Orchard" from *Team Bells Woke Me, and Other Stories* by H. L. Davis, copyright © 1953 by H.L. Davis. Reprinted by permission of Elizabeth T. Hobson.

"Flip" from *This House of Sky* by Ivan Doig, copyright © 1978 by Ivan Doig. Reprinted by permission of Harcourt Brace Jovanovich, Inc.

"Love in Idaho" from *Promised Land*, pp. 180-189, edited by Stewart H. Holbrook, copyright © 1945 by McGraw-Hill Book Co., Inc. Reprinted by permission of Opal Fisher.

"Communist" from *Rock Springs* by Richard Ford, copyright © 1987 by Richard Ford. Reprinted by permission of the Atlantic Monthly Press.

"Ebbie" from *The Big It and Other Stories* by A. B. Guthrie, copyright © 1960 by A. B. Guthrie, Jr. Reprinted by permission of Houghton Mifflin Company.

"The Gift by the Wagon" pp. 56-70 from *The Hanging Tree* by Dorothy M. Johnson, copyright © 1957 by Dorothy M. Johnson. Reprinted by permission of Ballantine Books, a Division of Random House, Inc.

"Prairie Kid" from *Hearst International-Cosmopolitan*, copyright © 1949 and © renewed 1977 by Dorothy M. Johnson. Reprinted by permission of McIntosh and Otis, Inc.

"Flame on the Frontier" from *Argosy*, copyright © 1950 and © renewed 1978 by Dorothy M. Johnson. Reprinted by permission of McIntosh and Otis, Inc.

"The Waterfowl Tree" from *We Are Not In This Together* by William Kittredge, copyright © 1984 by William Kittredge. Reprinted by permission of William Kittredge.

"Great Blue" from *The Flood of '64* by David Long, copyright © 1987 by David Long. Published by the Ecco Press. Reprinted by permission of David Long.

"USFS 1919: The Ranger, the Cook, and a Hole in the Sky" from *A River Runs Through It and Other Stories*, copyright © 1976 by the University of Chicago. Reprinted by permission of the University of Chicago Press.

"Walking Out" from *Blood Line, Stories of Fathers and Sons* by David Quammen, copyright © 1988 by David Quammen. Reprinted by permission of Graywolf Press.

"The Colt," "Chip Off the Old Block," and "The Chink" from *The Women on the Wall* by Wallace Stegner, copyright © 1943 and © renewed 1970 by Wallace Stegner. Published by Viking Press. Reprinted by permission of Brandt & Brandt Literary Agents, Inc.

ISBN 0-917652-76-2
Library of Congress Card Number 89-82162

Publication of this book is made possible by grants from the Lewis-Clark State College Foundation, the Idaho Commission on the Arts, a State agency, and the National Endowment for the Arts in Washington D.C., a Federal agency.

Cover design by Christy Hale. Typesetting and text design by Tanya Gonzales

Published by

Confluence Press, Inc.
Lewis Clark State College
8th Avenue & 6th Street
Lewiston, Idaho 83501

Distributed to the trade by

National Book Network
4720-A Boston Way
Lanham, Maryland 20706

Contents

Preface

Passages West began with the simple wish to put good stories before readers; I chose stories for this collection, first and foremost, then, because they offered a "good read." At the same time, I wanted to bring together stories that would serve other purposes, too. They would also give readers a solid sense of what I believed was a shaping literary inheritance that was slipping away from us. Even more importantly, these stories would ,appeal to capable young readers as well as to demanding adults.

My own fascination with this fiction reaches back to 1956, when I was a pre-engineering student at Idaho State College. Casting about for something more interesting than required coursework, I was attracted to a course titled, "The Literature of Western America." The course was taught by Forrester Blake, a working western novelist himself. Among a number of novels in Blake's course, two spoke to me personally: *In Tragic Life*, by Vardis Fisher, and *The Big Sky*, by Bud Guthrie. These were books rooted in the history of my part of the West, written about a land and people that I knew and cared about. And they depicted formative experiences that a boy from Boise understood.

Many years later, I started teaching some of the same novel s from Blake's course, along with a variety of short stories and poetry by other authors from the region—initially, to college undergraduates and eventually, to secondary school English teachers, at their regional gatherings. The enthusiasm was mutual. Both students and teachers spoke of the shock of recognition that I myself had felt thirty years before in Blake's class. The teachers, moreover, wanted to learn about additional short stories that they could introduce to their own students. Unfortunately, I had to tell them that much of this fiction was rapidly disappearing from print, and particularly collections of short stories. (The causes were related to the economics of the publishing industry, not the quality of the fiction.) Collections by Vardis Fisher and Walter Clark were already gone; those of A.B. Guthrie, Jr., and Dorothy Johnson soon followed. The stories of H.L. Davis were headed for oblivion, too, until they were rescued by the editorial efforts of Cort Conley and the University of Idaho Press in 1985. And Wallace Stegner's stories have only this year been collected for the first time by Random House.

This situation was further complicated, it seemed to me, by the appearance of a new generation of writers—Ray Carver, William Kittredge, Mary Blew, Ivan Doig, Richard Ford, David Long, David Quammen. Could today's readers fully appreciate the achievements of this new generation, without access to the early shapers of the regions's fiction? And without such access, wouldn't readers feel cheated out of a sense of the full scope of their literary inheritance? Wouldn't they also feel deprived of something else of inestimable value, the stories themselves? So the notion of an anthology that captured at least one strand of this inheritance was born.

All of the stories here are about *my* part of the American West, a place loosely monikered, the Mountain West. North to south, the region stretches from the Canadian border to the high deserts of northern Utah and Nevada; east to west, from the eastern slopes of the Rockies to the coastal valleys of Oregon and Washington. These stories are also written by men and women who themselves have become deeply immersed in the life of the region, either as natives or as permanent migrants. Lastly, the stories are bound together by a common theme. They all wrestle with similar questions about youth and identity in the Mountain West: How do young people from the region cope with growing up? What particular "rites of passage" do they experience? What are the tensions between youth and adulthood, and how are these either intensified, relieved, or transformed? The stories in this collection offer a spectrum of youthful experience of startling variety. Taken as a whole, the stories comprise a unique portrait of young people grappling with the perplexities in themselves and in adults.

A collection of stories with conscious geographic, cultural, and thematic boundaries does have other limitations. One of the most salient is the fact that even a prolific master of the short story like Ray Carver has published only a handful of stories dealing with young protagonists. This is typical of all the authors in the anthology, with the exception of Dorothy Johnson and Wallace Stegner. Another is the scarcity of good short fiction with female protagonists. Dorothy Johnson and Mary Blew stand virtually alone here, although there are promising new voices such as Debra Earling and Patricia Henley appearing on the horizon. Most surprising, perhaps, is the absence of short stories by Native American authors. Certainly novelists like Jim Welch and D'Arcy McNickle come to mind, but not every novelist will agree to having his work excerpted, nor does just any novel lend itself to excision. Finally, I located no strong stories from the region about young Japanese or Mexican Americans.

Any anthology editor is of course most indebted to the literature and to the writers who create it. Good stories are what make a collection like *Passages West* its own reward. Particular thanks, though, are due Norman Maclean and the University of Chicago Press for waiving the permission's fee and allowing me to reprint "USFS 1919." Also to David Quammen, special thanks for permission to be the first to reprint the long version of "Walking Out" from his book, *Blood Line*. My gratitude as well to Opal Holmes Fisher and Elizabeth T. Hobson, who continue to hold the door open to the works of Vardis Fisher and H.L. Davis for today's editors. For preparation of the text, thanks to Vana Wrigley for typing the manuscript and to Tanya Gonzales for typesetting and text design. Thanks are due the Lewis-Clark State College Foundation and the National Endowment for the Arts for grants supporting the costs of permissions and production. And finally, my profound thanks to Jim Hepworth, the publisher who took on the book out of love for the same literary heritage.

PASSAGES WEST

Mary Clearman Blew

The Snowies, the Judiths

A knock came at the door, and all eyes rose from the lesson. Mrs. Trask, looking troubled at yet another distraction, laid her book face down on the rules regarding *ser* and *estar* and went to answer it. Her first try at opening the door, however, met resistance. Had the knocker forgotten that the classroom doors opened outward into the corridor, or had he changed his mind about delivering his message, or was he merely being funny?

The students snickered, and Mrs. Trask flushed. It was hard enough for a substitute teacher to contain their excess energy during tournament season, let alone pretend to teach a lesson, without pranksters in the hall. She wrenched hard at the knob just as its resistance gave way.

The door opened so violently that the students saw Mrs. Trask lurch and almost lose her footing. Then she was taking a fast step back into the classroom. Her feet, however, in her new high heeled shoes were far from fast enough to balance the backward propulsion of her body. She landed on her back, her head bumping against the glazed oak floor. Her feet scrabbled frantically out of her shoes, as though in search of some small lost possession of great value, while her torso bucked and thrust in such a familiar and explicit way that some of the students laughed outright. But the most surprising thing about Mrs. Trask was the red flower that bloomed where her face had been, bloomed and pulsed and overflowed its petals on the oak.

Mary Dare in the back row had put her fingers in her ears to stop the vibrations. Now she took her hands away, because she knew what made ears ring the way hers were ringing. She recognized the whine and crack, too, that had run like lightning around the edges of the explosion. Impossible to mistake those sounds. Only last weekend her father had let her fire a round with the .44, and her first shot had ricocheted off sandstone and whined. What she did not recognize, never had heard before in her life, were the stacatto pips and shrills and squeals—well, yes, they did remind her of waking suddenly at night to the yammer of coyote pups, a pack of fools as her father called them, rallying for the first time in their lives with thin immature yips that chilled her and yet drew her out of her warm sleep to imagine herself walking with them through the cutbanks in the dark—the sounds that were rising now outside the classroom door and down the corridor as more shots reverberated.

Mary Dare stood up, thinking to see and perhaps comprehend. Then Ryan Novotny tackled her, big Ryan who as a senior really shouldn't have been in the first-year Spanish class at all but sat beside Mary Dare so he could copy her answers. Mary Dare found herself lying on her back between two rows of desks, looking up at the fluorescent lights burning away.

"Ho*ly*, Ryan," she said.

"Get down! Get down!" Ryan was yelling. "You crazy bastards, get your heads down!"

Now Ryan was crawling up the aisle next to hers on his elbows and knees. His rear end in his 501's was higher than his shoulders, and Mary Dare wanted to laugh at the sight he made. Somebody in the front of the room was laughing. Or hiccoughing, one or the other.

Mary Dare rolled over on her belly, wishing she hadn't worn her

good white cotton sweater and jeans. She crawled below the sur-
faces of desks, as Ryan had done, over trails of dust and forgotten
pencils and past crouching people's feet in shoes she recognized but
never had expected to see at eye level. She crawled until she
reached Jennifer Petty and took her hand and felt Jennifer's fingers
lock on to hers while Jennifer went on hiccoughing and snuffling.
Mary Dare lay with something, she thought a Spanish book, digging into her shoulder and her fingers in Jennifer's slippery grip.
She could see the dark underside of Jennifer's desk, wafered with
petrified discs of gum, and the pilling red dacron mountain that was
Jennifer in her awful sweater from Bonanza, and the inside of Jennifer's fat white wrist so close to Mary Dare's face that Mary Dare
barely could bring her eyes to focus on individual freckles. Not a
hand Mary Dare normally would be holding. Jennifer was weird.
Jennifer's fingers kept slipping almost out of hers, but at the last
second Jennifer would grab on again, so tight that Mary Dare could
see her own fingers turning as white as Jennifer's, with tiny red
lines seeping out between them and crawling down her wrist into
the sleeve of her sweater.

Mary Dare arched her back to ease it off the cutting edge of the
book or whatever she was lying on and settled down to wait for
Ryan. Nothing would happen until Ryan came back. Ryan would
be her early warning system. Mary Dare reduced the disgusting
underside of Jennifer's desk to a blur by focusing on the ceiling light
and letting all thought escape her. Nothing ever had happened to
her, nothing ever would again. Fighting this morning with Amy
and her mother over the hair dryer or Amy's endless sappy Bon
Jovi tapes, guarding her painfully acquired collection of cosmetics
and her really nice sweaters, getting on the school bus this morning
in the dark, looking forward to getting out of classes early for the
basketball tournament—none of it existed. All was reduced to the
pain in her back, and Jennifer's grip in hers, and the light endlessly
burning.

A shadow grew over the mountain of Jennifer, thrusting its head
between Mary Dare and the light. Mary Dare blinked, and the
shadow took form as Ryan.

"I can't see nothing. It's crazy out there."

Mary Dare pulled back from the brink with regret. Lint stuck in Ryan's hair and rolls of dust tracked his sweater. She felt bored with the sight of him, then sick. She rolled up on her elbow, tentatively. The line of windows was too high for her on the floor to see anything of the world outside except the fading February daylight and the distant tips of the mountains, snow-capped. For a moment she almost could breathe the freezing clean air of escape, almost feel the snow on her ankles as she ran.

"Forget it," Ryan whispered. "Them windows don't open. The bastards must of thought they was building a fucking jail when they built this place."

"Could you see him?" came a whisper behind Mary Dare.

"No, shit, couldn't see anything. I couldn't get far. All those doors and halls. He bagged Zeidel, though. I could see that."

Mary Dare closed her eyes. Ten feet away, on the other side of their wall, was the main corridor leading to the school offices. Lined with lockers, interspersed with classroom doors. After the utility dark greens and high ceilings of the old high school, the new doors painted in blues and violets had zinged at her for about the first week of school before they subsided into a familiarity as invisible as the soles of her feet.

The corridor had taken back its substance now, though. She could feel it through the wall.

"Always knew it would happen," Ryan was complaining. "Always knew it, always knew they'd pen us up like this and then take shots at us—"

"You're *paranoid*, Ryan," Mary Dare said. But she understood what he meant. She too, always had known somehow that it would come to this: the closed room, the graying windows, herself and all her classmates huddled under their desks, none daring to raise their heads while they waited for the inevitable next act. It was as though she had dreamed a thousand times about every detail. The hardwood floor, the dark underside of the desk, her knees drawn up, her arms wrapped around her skull; dreamed so many times, become so familiar that she no longer saw nor felt nor was aware of it, until now, by daylight, she recognized it at once. It was the end she always had known was coming, *and now that it's here,* unexpectedly rose her innermost voice, *we might as well get on with it.*

"Hey! Ryan! Town-ass!"

"What?" hissed Ryan.

It was Tom Barnes. She could see the blue flowered sleeve of his cowboy shirt; she remembered he usually sat in front.

"Could you see Zeidel?"

"Hell, yes. He was down. I could tell it was him by his suit."

Tom reared up on his elbows. "Oh shit, your arm."

"Yeh, her arm. And she calls me paranoid. Just because they're out to get us doesn't mean—"

Now that she was reminded of it, Mary Dare remembered how warm and wet her wrist and forearm felt. She glanced along the line of her sleeve and saw the sodden dark cuff of her white sweater and her red glistening fingers locked in Jennifer's.

"I don't think it's me," said Mary Dare. "It must be Jennifer."

To roll out from under Jennifer's desk, she was going to have to let go of Jennifer's hand. Testing, Mary Dare relaxed her fingers and felt a flutter of protest.

"Don't cry," Ryan pleaded.

"I *wasn't,*" said Mary Dare. "Oh, you mean her."

Mary Dare dug the heels of her hightops into the floor and arched her back much as Mrs. Trask had done. By squirming on her shoulders and inching herself along with her heels, she got her head clear of Jennifer's desk and rolled over and sat up without quite pulling her fingers out of Jennifer's. She glanced around. Although the desks were more or less in their rows, even with books still open at the assignment, nothing seemed quite in its usual place or even in its usual shape or color.

"Get your head *down!*"

"Hell, he ain't after us," said Tom.

With her free hand Mary Dare probed the mess of red sweater and ploughed red flesh and found the pressure point in Jennifer's arm right where in health class they had said it would be. She bore down through the fat until she felt bone. The depth of her fingers brought Jennifer's eyes popping open.

"I'm sorry," Jennifer whimpered.

"What are you sorry about?" Mary Dare asked her, fascinated.

Jennifer's eyes met Mary Dare's. Mary Dare watched the tip of Jennifer's tongue run around her lips as though she was about to explain herself.

"What makes you so sure?" Ryan was arguing.

Tom Barnes squatted in the aisle in his blue flowered shirt with the pearl snap pockets and his cowboy boots with the genuine undershot heels that had to be specially ordered. "I seen him. He ain't after us."

"Who was he?" Mary Dare wanted to know.

Ryan glared at Tom. Mary Dare, caught between them, looked from one to the other. Ryan the town-ass, really massive, as the kids here still were saying, and little Tom who wasn't embarrassed by wearing his team roping jacket to high school.

"Then how come she's laying here bleeding?" insisted Ryan.

"Hell, he was aiming at Trask, not us."

"You're being pretty fucking cool about it. For a goat roper. How come she's bleeding?"

He was glaring at Tom, as urgent as if his being called massive by everyone hung on Tom's answer. Mary Dare knew he had no idea that in Portland they wouldn't call him anything. Or Tom either, for that matter. They wouldn't know what to *do* with Tom in Portland. She never had heard of goat ropers until she moved back to Montana.

"Are you trying to tell me that ain't a fucking gunshot wound in her arm?"

"He just flung in a couple extra shots to keep us out of his way," said Tom. "He ain't after us. Petty probably just caught a ricochet."

Tom hunkered forward on his precious boot heels. Watching, Mary Dare understood what he was doing, finally understood what her dad had meant when he caught her horse for the third time last weekend and then advised her to cowboy up. It was amazing. Tom Barnes had cowboyed up.

He studied Jennifer Petty's glistening face and the raw red crater in her arm where Mary Dare was pinching off the spurt of blood. "She ain't going to die of that," he said.

"Who *was* it?" Mary Dare persisted.

"I don't know his name, but he's a kid. I've seen him around."

"I know him," came a whisper from under another of the front desks. "I mean, I seen him around, too. I don't know his name, either."

"You're saying he's after them," said Ryan.

"Well, he got Trask," said Tom Barnes. "And you say he got Zeidel."

"I said Zeidel was down."

Ryan's face worked to contain the idea of being incidental. He was on the verge of tears, Mary Dare realized; she never had seen a boy's tears before, and she didn't want to look at Ryan's, so she shut her eyes.

"Wonder where he went?" came from the whisperer.

"Or if he lost his nerve," said Tom.

Mary Dare heard Ryan snuffle hard against his arm. At least the cowboy was keeping his nerve. The floor was grinding into her hip. She remembered the pine floors in the old high school. Softwood boards, varnished a dark brown that wore away by the spring of every year, hollow as the palms of hands from receiving the feet of generations of students. Floors trodden by her uncles in turn, all of them probably wearing boots like Tom's with undershot heels, and then her dad in his turn. This year should have been Mary Dare's turn. One of the reasons her dad had wanted to move back from the west coast was so that Mary Dare and Amy could ride a school bus down the gulch into the shelter of the mountains, the way he had, and go to the old high school with kids like Tom Barnes. Her dad had recited the names of the mountains, the Snowies, the Judiths, the North Moccasins, the South Moccasins, like charms against any counterarguments her mother could raise, like the fine strings program and the languages program for the girls at Santa Angela High School. Charms for safety, the Snowies, the Judiths, the North Moccasins, the South Moccasins. Snow-capped blue mounds that ringed the town and that had offered a haven even in the long ago days before there was a town and the Blackfeet had ridden down from the north to hunt and raid the Crows. The Snowies, the Judiths, the North Moccasins, the South Moccasins, charms against this moment which, she suddenly understood, her father too must have dreamed a thousand times.

But instead of haven there was the new high school with its low maze of corridors, built and paid for by a levy her parents and the parents of practically every ranch kid she knew had voted against. The old high school wasn't even there any more. On the square block on Water Street was only an empty crater. Little kids had howled in glee when the wrecking ball had knocked its bricks to rubble, its soft floors to splinters. The charm had not worked, the moment had come when she and probably Amy had had to crouch under the futile shelter of their desks in spite of anything her parents or anyone's parents could have done to avert it, the only difference between the dream and waking reality being that another kid, apparently, had pulled the trigger.

And now Mary Dare opened her eyes and met the frozen, astonished eyes of a man in a dark brown uniform with his revolver out.

In the glazed moment in front of the revolver, Mary Dare could remember only the necessity of keeping her fingers down hard on Jennifer's arm until the very end. Then she saw the man's lips move and found with surprise that she could hear what he was saying; in fact, his tone seemed unnecessarily loud, even distorted by volume.

"Oh shit no," he was saying.

"It's not me that's bleeding but still alive, it's Jennifer," she thought to asnwer, but she could not be sure he understood her or even heard her or, although his eyes were fixed on her, even saw her. The others were rising beside her, around her. She could sense their slow unfolding, arms releasing their holds, tentative white faces emerging from under desks. Faces she could name, Tom Barnes and Ryan and Valier and Shannon and Stephen and Michael S. and Tyler and Michael J. and Ashley and Amber, like faces out of the dream, drained of life, all sockets and bones. And then, as they silently rose together, staring across the gulf at the patrolman, he seemed to recognize them with a start. He reholstered his gun.

"We'll get you out of here," his voice boomed and ebbed. He

looked from face to face, then wet his lips. "Don't worry, we'll get you out of here."

"I can't let go of Jennifer," whispered Mary Dare. She felt glued to her.

"Somebody say he got another one?"

A sheriff's deputy in a tan gabardine jacket and a gray Stetson stuck his head in the door. His gaze wandered over Mary Dare and he started to say something else. Then his gaze fell to the floor and riveted there. Other men crowded the doorway behind him, vanished, reappeared. More highway patrolmen in dark brown, city policemen in navy blue. Mary Dare saw how their eyes, too, fell first to the floor and then rose in slow surmise to her face and the other faces in the room.

Ryan nudged her, more himself. "Looks like they got all the fuzz in Montana here."

"Something here you'll have to walk by," said the patrolman. "But you don't have to look."

"I can't let go," said Mary Dare. She could feel her own pulse in her fingertips and, faintly, Jennifer's. As long as she held on to Jennifer, she could put off the walk back into the ordinary.

But men were everywhere, all the fuzz in Montana, shoving through the rows of desks, kneeling beside her, their voices thundering at Jennifer while their fingers replaced Mary Dare's in Jennifer's wound. A draught streamed over her warm sticky fingers. She was being lifted by her elbows, steadied on her feet. "You done fine, little girl. We'll take care of her now."

One of the navy blue policemen had brought in a plastic pouch of yellowish fluid and was holding it above his head. A tube dangled down from it. Noise seemed amplified; Mary Dare wanted to yell at Amy to turn down the tape. She saw Jennifer being lifted on a stretcher with a needle taped into the fat part of her arm. The policeman with the pouch and the tube followed her. Mary Dare took a step after her, as toward her last link with flesh and blood, but hands held her back and a voice flexed and roared like a distorted cassette tape over her head: "She'll be all right. Now we're gonna get you out of here."

The floor felt unstable under her, the way the ground felt after a long horseback ride. Mary Dare wobbled toward the door. She knew the others were following her in a shaky line, Valier and Shannon and Stephen and Michael S. and Tyler and Michael J. and Ashley and Amber and everybody. Police on both sides were guiding the line, not quite touching kids with their hands. The corridor ahead was hot with lights.

"A big step, now. We got a blanket down. But you don't have to look."

Mary Dare took the giant step and several baby steps and found herself in the throbbing corridor. She paused, getting her bearings by herself. She was standing in the main hall to the school offices amidst bright lights and confusion and unfamiliar smears on the floor. To her left was the north hall, to her locker, and she turned automatically in that direction. Then she stopped, fascinated. Band music was seeping through the barred doors of the gymnasium at the far end of the north hall.

Hands turned her, started her in the other direction, hovered around her as though she might dissipate through their fingers like smoke. "This way. We're taking you into the study hall for now."

"*Study* hall!" moaned someone behind her in the line.

But news somehow was in the air, crackling in fragments.

"I guess for awhile they thought he was going to shoot up the *gym*."

"He's that kid that never comes to class. Somebody said they guessed he thought it was her fault he got a pink slip."

"Maybe he thought Mrs. Trask was her."

"Wonder what happened to Zeidel."

The patrolman heard that and answered. "Mr. Zeidel took a hit in the leg and, uh, one in the lower abdomen, and they're taking him by air ambulance to Great Falls. We think he heard the shots and ran up the hall and, uh, met the kid running out."

"Wonder if he got away," said Tom Barnes low in Mary Dare's ear, but the patrolman heard that, too.

"He ran out of the school and, uh, we don't have other information as yet."

Silenced, they filed through the double doors. Mary Dare took the first desk she came to; it wasn't where she usually sat. The others were taking desks at random around her, a small cluster in the huge hall. Through the west windows she could see the last red stain of daylight.

"Wonder how the game came out," somebody whispered.

Sounds in the room were getting back to normal. A desk lid creaked.

"In here, sir," said the patrolman at the door. Everyone looked up as a man in a dark suit and a tie came in and sat down on the corner of a desk opposite them. The man's eyes moved from face to face; he looked stricken at what he saw, but that too was beginning to seem normal.

"We won't be keeping you here long," he said. He nodded two or three times, promising. "Your parents are, most of them, the ones we got hold of or, uh, heard about it, are out there waiting. They're wanting to see you, and we won't be keeping you long, but there's just a few questions, just one or two—"

He paused, and his mouth worked rapidly. Was he going to cry? Mary Dare looked away just in time. The red stain in the windows was darkening into nightfall. It must be way past the time when the school buses left.

"Did any of you see him?"

They shook their heads. Somebody, Valier, jerked a furtive finger across his eyes.

A stray voice from the hall cut in, angry—"in the middle of Montana, for chrissake, shit like this ain't supposed to go on here—" and was cut off as the patrolman pulled the door closed.

"No."

"No."

"Mrs. Trask," said Tom Barnes. "We saw her keel over."

"Yes."

"Yes."

They all had seen that, they agreed, nodding. Ryan wore a slight smile. Tom Barnes was lazing back in his desk on his spine with one leg stuck out into the aisle and the other leg crossed over it. The teachers hated it when kids sat like that. As though in the white glare of a searchlight, Mary Dare saw the downy hair on the back of Tom's neck and the bleached blue flowers of his shirt and the fragile overwashed blue of his levis. He looked like love's fading dream, Mary Dare thought. She knew she must look worse.

The man in the dark suit massaged his eyes with his hands. Maybe they all really did look like fading dreams to him. "We know you saw that," he said. "And I'm so sorry. Please believe me. I'd give anything if you hadn't had to. But did you see him?"

He was looking straight at Mary Dare.

"No," she said truthfully. "No."

He sighed and was silent. "All right," he said at last. "We might have to talk to some of you again. Just maybe. But we'll hope not. We'll hope he—"

His voice died away. They waited. Finally he sighed again and slid off the desk without explaining to them what it was he hoped for. "Anyway," he said, "I know some parents who are going to be awfully glad to see some kids."

"I wonder who won the game," said somebody else as they filed out of the study hall.

But that was one piece of news that hadn't floated down to them. Mary Dare thought the scrap of band music she had heard might have been the Libby Loggers' fight song, which might have meant Fort Maginnis was behind. She wondered if the kids had been scared to play basketball while policemen with shotguns guarded the exits of the gym, or if they had gotten used to it, or if they even had known about it.

In the adjacent classroom the faces of parents turned toward them like wet white blobs in overcoats and heavy jackets and snowy overshoes. "Oh shit," said Ryan, "the old man wouldn't—oh shit, he is here."

Mary Dare saw her mom and dad just before her mom grabbed her. She felt the crush of wool collar and a wet cheek in her neck.

"Told you she'd be all right," said her dad. He had on his good Stetson. Melted snow dripped from the brim.

Mary Dare's mother let her go, except for one tight handhold, and turned on Mary Dare's dad. "Can't you see?" she cried, picking up their argument. "She's my baby, she's fourteen, she's only fourteen, and now I'll never get her back."

"Linda," said Mary Dare's dad, and her mother stopped talking but went on crying quietly while her grip on Mary Dare's hand tightened.

"Hell, she's all right. These Montana kids grow up tough. You didn't see anything, did you, Mary Dare?"

"No," said Mary Dare. She barely could feel her fingers in her mother's grip.

They walked abreast through the double doors, her mother and father on either side of Mary Dare as though she might disappear in their hands. Someone brushed against them from behind, trying to get past the three of them in the archway; it was Tom Barnes, in a hurry, pulling on his satin team roping jacket as he went.

"You need a ride home, Tom?" called her father.

He glanced back. "No thanks, Doc. I got my truck."

"He's a good kid," said her dad. "Was he there too?"

"Yes," said Mary Dare.

Across the dark half-filled parking lot waited a school bus hung with painted banners, dieseling. Kids in Libby Logger letter jackets burst out of the double doors behind Mary Dare and her mother and father and ran yipping across the parking lot toward the bus.

"Pack of fools," said her dad angrily.

"No," said Mary Dare. "No, they're not."

You're the pack of fools, she wanted to say, but she shivered instead. In the refraction of frost under the exit lights she still could see the outline of Tom Barnes, hunching into his inadequate jacket against the freezing bite of the air and walking rapidly through the tumuli of shoveled snow toward the north lot. The sharp sounds of his boot heels on the scraped sidewalk receded as his shape faded beyond the radius of the lights, but for a moment Mary Dare followed him in her mind and faded with him into transparency in the dark. Far out in the circle of the mountains their glowing outlines fell to ash.

Raymond Carver

Nobody Said Anything

I could hear them out in the kitchen. I couldn't hear what they were saying, but they were arguing. Then it got quiet and she started to cry. I elbowed George. I thought he would wake up and say something to them so they would feel guilty and stop. But George is such an asshole. He started kicking and hollering.

"Stop gouging me, you bastard," he said. "I'm going to tell!"

"You dumb chickenshit," I said. "Can't you wise up for once? They're fighting and Mom's crying. Listen."

He listened with his head off the pillow. "I don't care," he said and turned over toward the wall and went back to sleep. George is a royal asshole.

Later I heard Dad leave to catch his bus. He slammed the front door. She had told me before he wanted to tear up the family. I didn't want to listen.

After a while she came to call us for school. Her voice sounded funny—I don't know. I said I felt sick at my stomach. It was the first week in October and I hadn't missed any school yet, so what could she say? She looked at me, but it was like she was thinking of something else. George was awake and listening. I could tell he was awake by the way he moved in the bed. He was waiting to see how it turned out so he could make his move.

"All right." She shook her head. "I just don't know. Stay home, then. But no TV, remember that."

George reared up. "I'm sick too," he said to her. "I have a headache. He gouged me and kicked me all night. I didn't get to sleep at all."

"That's enough!" she said. "You are going to school, George! You're not going to stay here and fight with your brother all day. Now get up and get dressed. I mean it. I don't feel like another battle this morning."

George waited until she left the room. Then he climbed out over the foot of the bed. "You bastard," he said and yanked all the covers off me. He dodged into the bathroom.

"I'll kill you," I said but not so loud that she could hear.

I stayed in bed until George left for school. When she started to get ready for work, I asked if she would make a bed for me on the couch. I said I wanted to study. On the coffee table I had the Edgar Rice Burroughs books I had gotten for my birthday and my Social Studies book. But I didn't feel like reading. I wanted her to leave so I could watch TV.

She flushed the toilet.

I couldn't wait any longer. I turned the picture on without the volume. I went out to the kitchen where she had left her pack of weeds and shook out three. I put them in the cupboard and went back to the couch and started reading *The Princess of Mars*. She came out and glanced at the TV but didn't say anything. I had the book open. She poked at her hair in front of the mirror and then went into the kitchen. I looked back at the book when she came out.

"I'm late. Goodbye, sweetheart." She wasn't going to bring up the TV. Last night she'd said she wouldn't know what it meant any more to go to work without being "stirred up."

"Don't cook anything. You don't need to turn the burners on for a thing. There's tuna fish in the icebox if you feel hungry." She looked at me. "But if your stomach is sick, I don't think you should put anything on it. Anyway, you don't need to turn the burners on. Do you hear? You take that medicine, sweetheart, and I hope your stomach feels better by tonight. Maybe we'll all feel better by tonight."

She stood in the doorway and turned the knob. She looked as if she wanted to say something else. She wore the white blouse, the wide black belt, and the black skirt. Sometimes she called it her outfit, sometimes her uniform. For as long as I could remember, it was always hanging in the closet or hanging on the clothesline or getting washed out by hand at night or being ironed in the kitchen.

She worked Wednesdays through Sundays.

"Bye, Mom."

I waited until she had started the car and had it warm. I listened as she pulled away from the curb. Then I got up and turned the sound on loud and went for the weeds. I smoked one and beat off while I watched a show about doctors and nurses. Then I turned to the other channel. Then I turned off the TV. I didn't feel like watching.

I finished the chapter where Tars Tarkas falls for a green woman, only to see her get her head chopped off the next morning by this jealous brother-in-law. It was about the fifth time I had read it. Then I went to their bedroom and looked around. I wasn't after anything in particular unless it was rubbers again and though I had looked all over I had never found any. Once I found a jar of Vaseline at the back of a drawer. I knew it must have something to do with it, but I didn't know what. I studied the label and hoped it would reveal something, a description of what people did, or else about how you applied the Vaseline, that sort of thing. But it didn't. *Pure Petroleum Jelly*, that was all it said on the front label. But just reading that was enough to give you a boner. An *Excellent Aid in the Nursery*, it said on the back. I tried to make the connection between *Nursery*—the swings and slides, the sandboxes, monkeybars—and what went on in bed between them. I had opened the jar lots of times and smelled inside and looked to see how much had been used since last time. This time I passed up the

Pure Petroleum Jelly. I mean, all I did was look to see the jar was still there. I went through a few drawers, not really expecting to find anything. I looked under the bed. Nothing anywhere. I looked in the jar in the closet where they kept the grocery money. There was no change, only a five and a one. They would miss that. Then I thought I would get dressed and walk to Birch Creek. Trout season was open for another week or so, but almost everybody had quit fishing. Everybody was just sitting around now waiting for deer and pheasant to open.

I got out my old clothes. I put wool socks over my regular socks and took my time lacing up the boots. I made a couple of tuna sandwiches and some double-decker peanut-butter crackers. I filled my canteen and attached the hunting knife and the canteen to my belt. As I was going out the door, I decided to leave a note. So I wrote: "Feeling better and going to Birch Creek. Back soon. R. 3:15." That was about four hours from now. And about fifteen minutes before George would come in from school. Before I left, I ate one of the sandwiches and had a glass of milk with it.

It was nice out. It was fall. But it wasn't cold yet except at night. At night they would light the smudgepots in the orchards and you would wake up in the morning with a black ring of stuff in your nose. But nobody said anything. They said the smudging kept the young pears from freezing, so it was all right.

To get to Birch Creek, you go to the end of our street where you hit Sixteenth Avenue. You turn left on Sixteenth and go up the hill past the cemetery and down to Lennox, where there is a Chinese restaurant. From the crossroads there, you can see the airport, and Birch Creek is below the airport. Sixteenth changes to View Road at the crossroads. You follow View for a little way until you come to the bridge. There are orchards on both sides of the road. Sometimes when you go by the orchards you see pheasants running down the rows, but you can't hunt there because you might get shot by a Greek named Matsos. I guess it is about a forty-minute walk all in all.

I was halfway down Sixteenth when a woman in a red car pulled onto the shoulder ahead of me. She rolled down the window on the passenger's side and asked if I wanted a lift. She was thin and had little pimples around her mouth. Her hair was up in curlers. But she was sharp enough. She had a brown sweater with nice boobs inside.

"Playing hooky?"

"Guess so."

"Want a ride?"

I nodded.

"Get in. I'm kind of in a hurry."

I put the fly rod and the creel on the back seat. There were a lot of grocery sacks from Mel's on the floorboards and back seat. I tried to think of something to say.

"I'm going fishing," I said. I took off my cap, hitched the canteen around so I could sit, and parked myself next to the window.

"Well, I never would have guessed." She laughed. She pulled back onto the road. "Where are you going? Birch Creek?"

I nodded again. I looked at my cap. My uncle had bought it for me in Seattle when he had gone to watch a hockey game. I couldn't think of anthing more to say. I looked out the window and sucked my cheeks. You always see yourself getting picked up by this woman. You know you'll fall for each other and that she'll take you home with her and let you screw her all over the house. I began to get a boner thinking about it. I moved the cap over my lap and closed my eyes and tried to think about baseball.

"I keep saying that one of these days I'll take up fishing," she said. "They say it's very relaxing. I'm a nervous person."

I opened my eyes. We were stopped at the crossroads. I wanted to say, *Are you real busy? Would you like to start this morning?* But I was afraid to look at her.

"Will this help you? I have to turn here. I'm sorry I'm in a hurry this morning," she said.

"That's okay. This is fine." I took my stuff out. Then I put my cap on and took it off again while I talked. "Goodbye. Thanks. Maybe next summer," but I couldn't finish.

"You mean fishing? Sure thing." She waved with a couple of fingers the way women do.

I started walking, going over what I should have said. I could think of a lot of things. What was wrong with me? I cut the air with the fly rod and hollered two or three times. What I should have done to start things off was ask if we could have lunch together. No one was home at my house. Suddenly we are in my bedroom under the covers. She asks me if she can keep her sweater on and I say it's okay with me. She keeps her pants on too. That's all right, I say. I don't mind.

A Piper Cub dipped low over my head as it came in for a landing. I was a few feet from the bridge. I could hear the water running. I hurried down the embankment, unzipped, and shot off five feet over the creek. It must have been a record. I took a while eating the other sandwich and the peanut-butter crackers. I drank up half the water in the canteen. Then I was ready to fish.

I tried to think where to start. I had fished here for three years, ever since we had moved. Dad used to bring George and me in the car and wait for us, smoking, baiting our hooks, tying up new rigs for us if we snagged. We always started at the bridge and moved down, and we always caught a few. Once in a while, at the first of the season, we caught the limit. I rigged up and tried a few casts under the bridge first.

Now and then I cast under a bank or else in behind a big rock. But nothing happened. One place where the water was still and the bottom full of yellow leaves, I looked over and saw a few crawdads crawling there with their big ugly pinchers raised. Some quail flushed out of a brush pile. When I threw a stick, a rooster pheasant jumped up cackling about ten feet away and I almost dropped the rod.

The creek was slow and not very wide. I could walk across almost anywhere without it going over my boots. I crossed a pasture full of cow pads and came to where the water flowed out of a big pipe. I knew there was a little hole below the pipe, so I was careful. I got down on my knees when I was close enough to drop the line. It had just touched the water when I got a strike, but I missed him. I felt him roll with it. Then he was gone and the line flew back. I put another salmon egg on and tried a few more casts. But I knew I had jinxed it.

I went up the embankment and climbed under a fence that had a KEEP OUT sign on the post. One of the airport runways started here. I stopped to look at some flowers growing in the cracks in the pavement. You could see where the tires had smacked down on the pavement and left oily skid marks all around the flowers. I hit the creek again on the other side and fished along for a little way until I came to the hole. I thought this was as far as I would go. When I had first been up here three years ago, the water was roaring right up to the top of the banks. It was so swift then that I couldn't fish. Now the creek was about six feet below the bank. It bubbled and hopped through this little run at the head of the pool where you could hardly see bottom. A little farther down, the bottom sloped up and got shallow again as if nothing had happened. The last time I was up here I caught two fish about ten inches long and turned one that looked twice as big—a summer steelhead, Dad said when I told him about it. He said they come up during the high water in early spring but that most of them return to the river before the water gets low.

I put two more shot on the line and closed them with my teeth. Then I put a fresh salmon egg on and cast out where the water dropped over a shelf into the pool. I let the current take it down. I could feel the sinkers tap-tapping on rocks, a different kind of tapping than when you are getting a bite. Then the one tightened and the current carried the egg into sight at the end of the pool.

I felt lousy to have come this far up for nothing. I pulled out all kinds of line this time and made another cast. I laid the fly rod over a limb and lit the next to last weed. I looked up the valley and began to think about the woman. We were going to her house because she wanted help carrying in the groceries. Her husband was overseas. I touched her and she started shaking. We were French-kissing on the couch when she excused herself to go to the bathroom. I followed her. I watched as she pulled down her pants and sat on the toilet. I had a big boner and she waved me over with her hand. Just as I was going to unzip, I heard a plop in the creek. I looked and saw the tip of my fly rod jiggling.

He wasn't very big and didn't fight much. But I played him as long as I could. He turned on his side and lay in the current down below. I didn't know what he was. He looked strange. I tightened the line and lifted him over the bank into the grass, where he stared wiggling. He was a trout. But he was green. I never saw one like him before. He had green sides with black trout spots, a greenish head, and like a green stomach. He was the color of moss, that color green. It was as if he had been wrapped up in moss a long time, and the color had come off all over him. He was fat, and I wondered why he hadn't put up more of a fight. I wondered if he was all right. I looked at him for a time longer, then I put him out of his pain.

I pulled some grass and put it in the creel and laid him in there on the grass.

I made some more casts, and then I guessed it must be two or three o'clock. I thought I had better move down to the bridge. I thought I would fish below the bridge awhile before I started home. And I decided I would wait until night before I thought about the woman again. But right away I got a boner thinking about the boner I would get that night. Then I thought I had better stop doing it so much. About a month back, a Saturday when they were all gone, I had picked up the Bible right after and promised and swore I wouldn't do it again. But I got jism on the Bible, and the promising and swearing lasted only a day or two, until I was by myself again.

I didn't fish on the way down. When I got to the bridge, I saw a bicycle in the grass. I looked and saw a kid about George's size running down the bank. I started in his direction. Then he turned and started toward me, looking in the water.

"Hey, what is it!" I hollered. "What's wrong?" I guessed he didn't hear me. I saw his pole and fishing bag on the bank, and I dropped my stuff. I ran over to where he was. He looked like a rat or something. I mean, he had buck teeth and skinny arms and this ragged longsleeved shirt that was too small for him.

"God, I swear there's the biggest fish here I ever saw!" he called. "Hurry! Look! Look here! Here he is!"

I looked where he pointed and my heart jumped.

It was as long as my arm.

"God, oh God, will you look at him!" the boy said.

I kept looking. It was resting in a shadow under a limb that hung over the water. "God almighty," I said to the fish, "where did you come from?"

"What'll we do?" the boy said. "I wish I had my gun."

"We're going to get him," I said. "God, look at him! Let's get him into the riffle."

"You want to help me, then? We'll work it together!" the kid said.

The big fish had drifted a few feet downstream and lay there finning slowly in the clear water.

"Okay, what do we do?" the kid said.

"I can go up and walk down the creek and start him moving," I said. "You stand in the riffle, and when he tries to come through, you kick the living shit out of him. Get him onto the bank someway, I don't care how. Then get a good hold of him and hang on."

"Okay. Oh shit, look at him! Look, he's going! Where's he going?" the boy screamed.

I watched the fish move up the creek again and stop close to the bank. "He's not going anyplace. There's no place for him to go. See him? He's scared shitless. He knows we're here. He's just cruising around now looking for someplace to go. See, he stopped again. He can't go anyplace. He knows that. He knows we're going to nail him. He knows it's tough shit. I'll go up and scare him down. You get him when he comes through."

"I wish I had my gun," the boy said. "That would take care of him," the boy said.

I went up a little way, then started wading down the creek. I watched ahead of me as I went. Suddenly the fish darted away from the bank, turned right in front of me in a big cloudy swirl, and barrel-assed downstream.

"Here he comes!" I hollered. "Hey, hey, here he comes!" But the fish spun around before it reached the riffle and headed back. I splashed and hollered, and it turned again. "He's coming! Get him, get him! Here he comes!"

But the dumb idiot had himself a club, the asshole, and when the fish hit the riffle, the boy drove at him with the club instead of trying to kick the sonofabitch out like he should have. The fish veered off, going crazy, shooting on his side through the shallow water. He made it. The asshole idiot kid lunged for him and fell flat.

He dragged up onto the bank sopping wet. "I hit him!" the boy hollered. "I think he's hurt, too. I had my hands on him, but I couldn't hold him."

"You didn't have anything!" I was out of breath. I was glad the kid fell in. "You didn't even come close, asshole. What were you doing with that club? You should have kicked him. He's probably a mile away by now." I tried to spit. I shook my head. "I don't know. We haven't got him yet. We just may not get him," I said.

"Goddamn it, I hit him!" the boy screamed. "Didn't you see? I hit him, and I had my hands on him too. How close did you get? Besides, whose fish is it?" He looked at me. Water ran down his trousers over his shoes.

I didn't say anything else, but I wondered about that myself. I shrugged. "Well, okay. I thought it was both ours. Let's get him this time. No goof-ups, either one of us," I said.

We waded downstream. I had water in my boots, but the kid was wet up to his collar. He closed his buck teeth over his lip to keep his teeth from chattering.

The fish wasn't in the run below the riffle, and we couldn't see him in the next stretch, either. We looked at each other and began to worry that the fish really had gone far enough downstream to reach one of the deep holes. But then the goddamn thing rolled near the bank, actually knocking dirt into the water with his tail, and took off again. He went through another riffle, his big tail sticking out of the water. I saw him cruise over near the bank and stop, his tail half out of the water, finning just enough to hold against the current.

"Do you see him?" I said. The boy looked. I took his arm and pointed his finger. "Right *there*. Okay now, listen. I'll go down to that little run between those banks. See where I mean? You wait here until I give you a signal. Then you start down. Okay? And this time don't let him get by you if he heads back."

"Yeah," the boy said, and worked his lip with those teeth. "Let's get him this time," the boy said, a terrible look of cold in his face.

I got up on the bank and walked down, making sure I moved quiet. I slid off the bank and waded in again. But I couldn't see the great big sonofabitch and my heart turned. I thought it might have taken off already. A little farther downstream and it would get to one of the holes. We would never get him then.

"He still there?" I hollered. I held my breath.

The kid waved.

"Ready!" I hollered again.

"Here goes!" the kid hollered back.

My hands shook. The creek was about three feet wide and ran between dirt banks. The water was low but fast. The kid was moving down the creek now, water up to his knees, throwing rocks ahead of him, splashing and shouting.

"Here he comes!" The kid waved his arms. I saw the fish now; it was coming right at me. He tried to turn when he saw me, but it was too late. I went down on my knees, grasping in the cold water. I scooped him with my hands and arms, up, up, raising him, throwing him out of the water, both of us falling onto the bank. I held him against my shirt, him flopping and twisting, until I could get my hands up his slippery sides to his gills. I ran one hand in and clawed through to his mouth and locked around his jaw. I knew I had him. He was still flopping and hard to hold, but I had him and I wasn't going to let go.

"We got him!" the boy hollered as he splashed up. "We got him, by God! Ain't he something! Look at him! Oh God, let me hold him," the boy hollered.

"We got to kill him first," I said. I ran my other hand down the throat. I pulled back on the head as hard as I could, trying to watch out for the teeth, and felt the heavy crunching. He gave a long slow tremble and was still. I laid him on the bank and we looked at him.

He was at least two feet long, queerly skinny, but bigger than anything I had ever caught. I took hold of his jaw again.

"Hey," the kid said but didn't say any more when he saw what I was going to do. I washed off the blood and laid the fish back on the bank.

"I want to show him to my dad so bad," the kid said.

We were wet and shivering. We looked at him, kept touching him. We pried open his big mouth and felt his rows of teeth. His sides were scarred, whitish welts as big as quarters and kind of puffy. There were nicks out of his head around his eyes and on his snout where I guess he had banged into the rocks and been in fights. But he was so skinny, too skinny for how long he was, and you could hardly see the pink stripe down his sides, and his belly was gray and slack instead of white and solid like it should have been. But I thought he was something.

"I guess I'd better go pretty soon," I said. I looked at the clouds over the hills where the sun was going down. "I better get home."

"I guess so. Me too. I'm freezing," the kid said. "Hey, I want to carry him," the kid said.

"Let's get a stick. We'll put it through his mouth and both carry him," I said.

The kid found a stick. We put it through the gills and pushed until the fish was in the middle of the stick. Then we each took an end and started back, watching the fish as he swung on the stick.

"What are we going to do with him?" the kid said.

"I don't know," I said. "I guess I caught him," I said.

"We both did. Besides, I saw him first."

"That's true," I said. "Well, you want to flip for him or what?" I felt with my free hand, but I didn't have any money. And what would I have done if I had lost?

Anyway, the kid said, "No, let's not flip."

I said, "All right. It's okay with me." I looked at that boy, his hair standing up, his lips gray. I could have taken him if it came to that. But I didn't want to fight.

We got to where we had left our things and picked up our stuff with one hand, neither of us letting go of his end of the stick. Then we walked up to where his bicycle was. I got a good hold on the stick in case the kid tried something.

Then I had an idea. "We could half him," I said.

"What do you mean?" the boy said, his teeth chattering again. I could feel him tighten his hold on the stick.

"Half him. I got a knife. We cut him in two and each take half. I don't know, but I guess we could do that."

He pulled at a piece of his hair and looked at the fish. "You going to use that knife?"

"You got one?" I said.

The boy shook his head.

"Okay," I said.

I pulled the stick out and laid the fish in the grass beside the kid's bicycle. I took out the knife. A plane taxied down the runway as I measured a line. "Right here?" I said. The kid nodded. The plane roared down the runway and lifted up right over our heads. I started cutting down into him. I came to his guts and turned him over and stripped everything out. I kept cutting until there was only a flap of skin on his belly holding him together. I took the halves and worked them in my hands and I tore him in two.

I handed the kid the tail part.

"No," he said, shaking his head. "I want that half."

I said, "They're both the same! Now goddamn, watch it, I'm going to get mad in a minute."

"I don't care," the boy said. "If they're both the same, I'll take that one. They're both the same, right?"

"They're both the same," I said. "But I think I'm keeping this half here. I did the cutting."

"I want it," the kid said. "I saw him first."

"Whose knife did we use?" I said.

"I don't want the tail," the kid said.

I looked around. There were no cars on the road and nobody else fishing. There was an airplane droning, and the sun was going down. I was cold all the way through. The kid was shivering hard, waiting.

"I got an idea," I said. I opened the creel and showed him the trout. "See? It's a green one. It's the only green one I ever saw. So whoever takes the head, the other guy gets the green trout and the tail part. Is that fair?"

The kid looked at the green trout and took it out of the creel and held it. He studied the halves of the fish.

"I guess so," he said. "Okay, I guess so. You take that half. I got more meat on mine."

"I don't care," I said. "I'm going to wash him off. Which way do you live?" I said.

"Down on Arthur Avenue." He put the green trout and his half of the fish into a dirty canvas bag. "Why?"

"Where's that? Is that down by the ball park?" I said.

"Yeah, but why, I said." That kid looked scared.

"I live close to there," I said. "So I guess I could ride on the handlebars. We could take turns pumping. I got a weed we could smoke, if it didn't get wet on me."

But the kid only said, "I'm freezing."

I washed my half in the creek. I held his big head under water and opened his mouth. The stream poured into his mouth and out the other end of what was left of him.

"I'm freezing," the kid said.

I saw George riding his bicycle at the other end of the street. He didn't see me. I went around to the back to take off my boots. I unslung the creel so I could raise the lid and get set to march into the house, grinning.

I heard their voices and looked through the window. They were sitting at the table. Smoke was all over the kitchen. I saw it was coming from a pan on the burner. But neither of them paid any attention.

"What I'm telling you is the gospel truth," he said. "What do kids know? You'll see."

She said, "I'll see nothing. If I thought that, I'd rather see them dead first."

He said, "What's the matter with you? You better be careful what you say!"

She started to cry. He smashed out a cigaret in the ashtray and stood up.

"Edna, do you know this pan is burning up?" he said.

She looked at the pan. She pushed her chair back and grabbed the pan by its handle and threw it against the wall over the sink.

He said, "Have you lost your mind? Look what you've done!" He took a dish cloth and began to wipe up the stuff from the pan.

I opened the back door. I started grinning. I said, "You won't believe what I caught at Birch Creek. Just look. Look here. Look at this. Look what I caught."

My legs shook. I could hardly stand. I held the creel out to her, and she finally looked in. "Oh, oh, my God! What is it? A snake! What is it? Please, please take it out before I throw up."

"Take it out!" he screamed. "Didn't you hear what she said? Take it out of here!" he screamed.

I said, "But look, Dad. Look what it is."

He said, "I don't want to look."

I said, "It's a gigantic summer steelhead from Birch Creek. Look! Isn't he something? It's a monster! I chased him up and down the creek like a madman!" My voice was crazy. But I could not stop. "There was another one, too," I hurried on. "A green one. I swear! It was green! Have you ever seen a green one?"

He looked into the creel and his mouth fell open.

He screamed, "Take that goddamn thing out of here! What in the hell is the matter with you? Take it the hell out of the kitchen and throw it in the goddamn garbage!"

I went back outside. I looked into the creel. What was there looked silver under the porch light. What was there filled the creel.

I lifted him out. I held him. I held that half of him.

Walter Van Tilburg Clark

The Buck in the Hills

I left the peak about two o'clock, drank the very cold, shale-tasting water coming from under last winter's snow in the notch, went on down, and then south through the marshy meadow, already in shadow from the col, the grass yellowing and the sod stiffening from the fall nights, so that I could walk straight across and feel only the first solidity and then a slight give which didn't spring back. It was strange in the meadows, walking in the shadow, but with the sky still bright blue, as in the middle of the afternoon, and the sunlight, when I stopped to look back at the peak, just beginning to look late. It was chilly in the shadow too, but I didn't hurry. The peak was sacred to me, the climb was pilgrimage, and five years is a long time. I had been very happy all day, climbing with the sun on my neck and shoulders, and I was very lonely happy now. I took my time, and looked at everything, and remembered a lot, and would have yodelled sometimes, but the quiet was better.

I climbed over the big rock barrier, which a million winters had cracked into terraces, saw the dry, shriveled clumps of leaves and single dead stems in the cracks, and remembered times I had come up there in the summer, which is spring at that height, and seen it pouring with green, like cascades, and lighted by flowers. I remembered the dark girl who knew all the flowers, and who, when I bet her she couldn't find more than thirty kinds, found more than fifty. I remembered how we had eaten our pocket lunch dry, in a niche on the east side of the peak, out of the strong wind we could hear among the rocks and more heavily in the notch below. We couldn't see it then, but the image was new in our minds of the big basin to the west, with its rolling of dark green to pale blue, heavily timbered hills, and the wide, dark-blue flat of Tahoe, rough with wind and jointed exactly into all the bays and coves, and the little lakes at different heights around it, also fitted like single pieces into a relief puzzle. In front of us, way down, squared with fields and pencilled by the straight roads, was the chain of ranching valleys, and then the lesser, burned mountains rolling to the east, and in the far northeast just a sky-colored sliver of Pyramid Lake showing through the last pass. I remembered that the cloud that day had gone all around the horizon in a narrow band, flat underneath, all at exactly the same level, with clear sky between them and the mountains, and with their tops standing up in little, firm bosses and domes, and not a single cloud in the field of sky above them, so that we sat high up in the center of a great circle of distant cloud. This seemed to mean something, and gave our thoughts, and the big arch of world we looked at, a different quality that made us uneasy but happy too, the way I was now.

I went on through the sparse trees and the rocks over two ridges, and could see from them, and from the little valley between, the rock castle at the end of the high col to the west, where I had eaten at noon another time, when I was alone, and then stayed for two hours to watch a hawk using the wind over the hollow to the west of me, feeling myself lift magnificently when he swooped toward me on the current up the col, and then balanced and turned above.

I was feeling like that when I got back to the little, grassy lake where I'd left my pack. The pack was still there all right, under the bench nailed between two of the three trees on the hump at the farther side. Beyond the three trees, which were stunted and twisted by wind, I could see the wall of the col, very dark now, with a thin gold sky above it. Besides the bench, there was a pine-bough bed and a rock fireplace in the shelter of the trees. I hadn't made them, just found them there, but in the dusk the place gave me the hawk lift again. I had the night here alone, and another day in the mountains. That was a lot. And I had already stacked my firewood; brought it down that morning from the east slope.

I went around to the camp side and stood looking at the lake, thinking about swimming before I made a fire and ate. It was cold, and the water would be cold too. The lake was really just a pool of snow water, with no outlet, and no regular inflow, shallow enough so the dead grasses showed up through at the edges. But I like that kind of clean, cold feeling, and it had been warm climbing in the middle of the day. I peeled off, and stood liking the cold on my body, and the frozen, pebbly earth under my feet, and then, when I went nearer the edge, the wiry grass. It was very still in the valley, and the water reflected, exactly and without break, the mountains and the last of that thin, yellow light. I got that lift again. This time I would take it out. I ran splashing till I was thigh deep, and then rolled under. The water was even colder than I had expected, and hardened my whole body at once. For a minute or two I swam rapidly in circles in the small center that was deep enough. Then I was all right, and could roll easily, and even float looking up. The first stars were showing above the ridge in the east. I let go a couple of bars of high, operatic-sounding something. It came back at me from under the col, sounding much better, sweet and clear and high. God, I was happy. This was the way I liked it, alone, and clean cold, and a lot of time ahead. I rolled over to dive and start one more fast turn, when I heard the yodel that wasn't an echo.

I stood up, feeling the cold rim of the water around my chest, and even in the dusk could see the shape of the man coming over the hump and down toward the lake. When he was part way down, I could tell by the walk, a little pigeon-toed and easy, giving at the knees all the time, that it was Tom Williams. He had his pack on, and his rifle over one shoulder, with a thumb in the sling, the way Tom always carried it. The remainder of ecstasy went out of me. I'd rather have Tom than almost anyone I know for outside company, but I didn't want anybody now. And Tom meant Chet McKenny, and I didn't want Chet now or any other time. Chet was a big-boned, tall Scotchman, probably ten years older than either Tom or I, with gray in his stiff hair. He had a kind of stubborn originality that wouldn't use a joke somebody else had told, but he couldn't make a good one, so he was laughing all the time over bad jokes of his own. But that wasn't what I disliked, though it got tiresome. What I didn't like about McKenny was deeper than stupidity. You saw it when you saw that his eyes were still watching you when he laughed; you were always on guard against McKenny.

The three of us had come up in Tom's car, and they'd left me at the summit meadows. They were going on over to the flat to start a deer hunt. I was supposed to have today and tomorrow and then be back out at the meadows by sunset to wait for them.

Tom came down to where I'd dropped my clothes and unslung his rifle and pack and put them down.

"Cold?" he asked. He didn't have to speak loudly.

"Plenty," I said.

I kept looking for Chet to come over the rise too.

Tom peeled off and came in, but slowly, and then just lying out and letting himself sink under. He came up slowly too, as if the water weren't cold at all, and just stood there, not even rubbing himself. There was something wrong.

"Where's Chet?" I asked. It would even be pleasant, with a fire after supper, to have Tom to talk to, if he was alone.

"That bastard," Tom said. Then he let himself down into the water again, and came up a few feet farther off, his thin, blond hair streaming down and the springy blond mat on his big chest holding a few drops.

"He won't be here, anyway," he said, "so you don't have to worry."

He began to swim hard, and I took another turn, to get the blood stirring again. Then we walked up out of the water. Tom didn't say anything more, and I didn't either. I knew it would come. Tom doesn't often talk much, except about engines, but this was different. It was working in him, hard. He went up to his pack, and I could see the muscles in his heavy white shoulders working while he hunted in it. He got out a towel and threw it to me. Then he went back down to the water, and I saw he had a cake of soap in his hand. But he didn't bathe. I stood there wiping off and watching him, and he just bent over in the shallows and washed his hands. He washed them hard, three or four times, rinsing them between. That was queer for Tom. He was an auto mechanic, ran a little shop of his own, and he'd long ago given up hoping to have his hands really clean. Often on trips like this he'd go two or three days without washing them at all.

He still didn't say anything, though, when he came up; just took the towel from me and began to wipe himself slowly.

It felt good to be in the warm flannel shirt and cords again, and shod heavily. Maybe that's even the best feeling, the cold that makes you feel thin and single, with no waste matter, but beginning to get warm. I lit a cigarette with stiff fingers, and saw against the match flame how dark it was getting. The cigarette tasted very good too. I was all set to be happy again, if Tom was right.

Tom didn't talk while he was dressing, or while we went up to the camp, or while he was cooking and watching the coffee and I was putting some new boughs and the sleeping bags on the bed. The bed was a good one, wide enough for three, and in a pit a foot deep. I went down to the lake to get two cans of beer out of the water. They're a lot of weight to carry in a pack, and I'd thought maybe I was pampering myself when I'd put them in, one for each evening. Now I was glad I'd brought them. When I came back up with them, he was just letting the things cook, and standing away from the fire, looking at the stars over the valley and in the little lake.

"This is a swell place," he said in an easier voice. "Gee, I haven't been in here for years. I'd forgot what a swell place it was."

Then I knew it was going to be all right, once he got around to telling me, and I had to sing a little while I put the beers between roots and took the eggs and beans off the fire; not loudly, but just about like the crackling of the fire.

When he came back and sat down on the bench, the light on his face with its fine mouth and big, broken nose and blue eyes, and its hard weather lines, he looked at me because I was singing, and I could see he was still thinking, but not feeling the same way about it.

When we'd started to eat, I asked, "How did the hunting go?"

"Don't you worry," Tom said. "I didn't get anything. I didn't even get a shot. I didn't see a thing."

He looked closed up again, as he had when he came into the water. He finished his beans, staring into the fire. Then he said suddenly, "That McKenny is a first-rate bastard."

"What's he done now?" I asked.

Tom looked right at me for a moment, as if he'd start, but then he said, "Oh, hell, let it go."

He got up and went down to the edge of the lake slowly, and after a moment I saw his match flare, and then, every now and then, the fire point of his cigarette moving.

I'd never seen Tom let anything eat in him like that before. He made up his mind very hard about what was wrong and what was right, especially about people, but he did it carefully, and he was usually gentle about it, even afterwards. It was the first time I'd heard him speak out like that. Whatever had happened, it must have been pretty bad.

Well, I was sure now that McKenny wasn't coming. I stopped thinking about it, put more wood on the fire, and lay on my back where the light wouldn't be in my eyes. Then I could see the silhouette of the col, where it walled out the stars, and the big peak glimmering in the starlight in the north. The size of the place, and the cold quiet, came back on me, and I was happy again.

I'd forgotten about Chet when Tom came back up and sat down on the bench. He stared at the ground for a moment. Then he looked across at me.

"You always thought so, didn't you?"

"Thought what?"

"That Chet McKenny was a first-rate bastard?"

I didn't like to say so.

"All right," Tom said. "I guess he is, at that."

He didn't say anything more, so I sat up.

"Have a beer?"

"No, thanks."

I had to get him started.

"Did Chet get anything?" I asked.

Tom looked at me hard.

"Yeah, he got one, all right, a good big buck, better than two twenty, I'd guess. Ten points." He looked down.

Then he looked up again, and said suddenly and loudly for that place, "You know what that bastard did? He—" but stopped.

"He what?"

"No," Tom said. I'll tell you the way it was. Maybe I'm wrong.

I worked down south, toward the lake meadows. I didn't see a thing all day; not even a doe; not even a fresh track or droppings. I figured it had been worked over and got disgusted and went back to the flat in the afternoon to get some sleep. I was washing up at the brook, and when I stood up and turned around, there was this big buck, a mule, on the edge of the trees across the flat. Even from there I could tell he was a big one, and I cussed, because there was my rifle up against a tree thirty yards from me, and the buck had spotted me. You know, his head was up and right at me, and those big ears up too. He was trying the wind. I figured if I moved he'd be back in those trees before I could take a step. So I held it. After a while he let his head down, way low, and began to go along the edge of the flat toward the pass. Then I saw there was something the matter with him. He wasn't using his left front leg; just bucking along on the other one, in little jumps. He was tired out, too, stopping every few jumps and taking the wind again, and then letting his head drop that way, like he couldn't hold it up. I figured somebody'd made a bad shot. I started for the gun. He saw me then, but he was so far gone he didn't even care, just kept hopping and resting. Then I didn't know whether I wanted him or not. Only I might as well, if his leg was really busted.

I was standing there on the edge of the flat, wondering, when I heard this yell. It was Mac, coming down through the trees. He yelled at me to head the buck off. Your lousy shot then, I thought.

"When I went right out at the buck, it tried to hurry. I yelled at

Mac did he want me to finish it, and he yelled at me, hell no, it was his buck. The buck stood there with his head up when we yelled; he didn't try to do anything.

"I don't know. It made me mad. But it was Mac's buck. I started to work around so as not to hurry it any more than I had to. Mac was working along in the timber to get right above him. When I got around in front, we worked in closer, and then the buck saw us both, and just stopped and stood there. He was shivering all over, and didn't have any fight left in him. I could see now that he'd been hit in the leg, right up against the body. The blood was mostly dried on black, but there was a little fresh blood coming out all the time too. The bad leg was all banged up from being dragged on things too, and he was soaked with sweat on the hind quarters and under the throat, and making cotton at the muzzle."

Tom stopped.

Then he said, "It's funny the way they look at you like that. I don't know. There wasn't anything, no fight, no panic, no hope, no nothing. He just looked at you. But you couldn't move. They got such big eyes. I don't know."

Tom kicked at a stone with his boot.

"Well, anyway, I couldn't move. But Mac could. He came up close behind. He had his cap on the back of his head and he was grinning. He said wasn't it a nice one. Ten points, he said.

"When he talked, the buck got going again, that same way. It was headed across the meadow toward the camp. I got ready to finish it, but Mac yelled at me to mind my own damn business and let it go or he'd damn well lather hell out of me. You know the way he does, grinning, but mad as the devil. I asked him what he thought he was doing, but he said that was his business, and to mind my own.

"The buck was going so slow you could pass it walking; had to wait on it. And it stopped two or three times. Mac could have killed it a long time before it got to the flat; I was sure of that. I began to think he wanted to take it in alive, or something. But it wasn't that."

Tom stopped talking and sat there.

"No?" I said.

"No," Tom said. "When the buck stopped, near where we'd had the fire, Mac said that was good enough, like he was pleased, and unslung his rifle and took mine too, and stood them up against a tree. Then he told me to hold the buck's head."

After a moment Tom went on again.

"I don't know why I did it. I just did. I never felt that way before. I guess I thought he was going to operate, as near as I thought anything. He just said to hold it, and I did, like I was in a daze. The buck kind of backed a little, and then, when I had hold of his antlers, he stood still; didn't make a move. Holding onto the antlers, I could feel him shivering all over, you know, like putting your hand on a telephone pole. Mac had his skinning knife out.

"'Hold his head up,' he said.

"He was kind of leaning over and looking at the bullet hole when he said it, and I did.

"Then all of a sudden he leaned down on the buck's neck with one hand, and slit its throat wide open with the knife in the other. Leaning on it that way, he put all his weight on the buck's one leg, and the buck fell over front, and I didn't get out of the way fast enough. It knocked me onto my knees too, and the blood came out all over my hands and arms. It kept coming, in big spurts; there was an awful lot of it. I don't know."

Tom got out a cigarette and lit it. I didn't have anything to say. The story made a difference though, as if it were a lot darker all at once, and we were farther away from other people than before, and there were things alive in the rocks, watching us. I noticed there was a wind coming up too, but didn't think about it, just heard it in the trees as if it had been going all the time.

"It's funny," Tom said. "When the buck got pushed down, it stretched way out; you know. Its muzzle was right in my face, and it blew. It made a little spray of blood, but it had a sweet-smelling breath, you know, like a cow's. And then all that blood came out, hot."

Finally he asked me, "You know what Mac said?"

"No."

"Well, he laughed like hell when the buck pushed me over, and then he said, 'I never take more than one shot,' and then he laughed again.

"I was mad enough, I guess. I told him it was a hell of a shot, and he said two inches to the right would've killed him, and pointed at the hole, and laughed again and said hell, it was perfect. The bullet had busted the joint all to pieces. There was splinters sticking out where they'd worked through."

I was looking at Tom now.

"You mean he meant to?" I asked.

"That's right," Tom said. "He thought he was real clever. He boasted about it. Said he'd spotted the buck way up in that little meadow under the castle rocks; what's its name? The buck was on the north edge of the meadow, and up wind of him, what wind there was. He said he figured it all out, that it was eight miles back to camp, and the buck was a big one. He couldn't see carrying it all that way, so he just laid down there on the edge of the timber, to make his shot good, and waited till the buck was broadside to him, and then busted that foreleg. Said he'd never made a better shot, that it was a hundred and fifty yards if it was an inch, and uphill. He was set up about that shot."

"Well," I said, letting out my breath.

"Yes," Tom said.

"He told me all about how he drove it, too," he said angrily. "How it kept trying to run at first, and falling over so he had to laugh, and then how it tried to turn on him, but couldn't stand it when he got close, and what a hell of a time he had driving it out of a couple of manzanita thickets where it tried to hole up. Then he figured that if he stayed off it, it would keep going steadier, and it did.

"So, I guess you were right," Tom said, making it a question.

"I didn't think he was that bad," I said. "You have to keep it up a long time to do a thing like that."

"He was still going strong," Tom said. "Only excited and talking a lot."

"Like I am now," he added.

I didn't want to ask. I figured anything he'd done wasn't enough. But I still looked at Tom.

"No," he said. "You don't have to worry. I didn't touch him."

"I don't know," he said doubtfully. "I wanted you to know the way it was, first."

"He had it coming to him," I said. But I was scared, so I nearly laughed when Tom told me.

"I told him if he'd been saving himself so careful, he could damned well carry his buck home, and I left him there."

"I'd like to have seen his face," I said.

"I didn't even look at him," Tom said. "I just put my things into the car and got out.

"He knew better than to say anything, too."

"Well," I said finally, "I wouldn't say you were too hard on him."

"No," Tom said. "But he'll try to bring that buck out."

"Sure," I agreed, "but he wouldn't let it go if it was killing him."

Tom heeled his cigarette out carefully and said, "You wouldn't care to go up the mountain again tomorrow, would you?"

"Sure I would," I told him. "Now *you* quit worrying. He had it coming to him."

Tom said he was going to take another swim, and we undressed by the fire, and went down together, and came back up wet. It felt very cold then, and the wind was stronger. But we piled more wood onto the fire, so it threw shadows of the three trees way up the hump, and when we'd dried off it felt so good we didn't get dressed, but just put on our shorts and stayed close to the fire.

"I'll have that beer now," Tom said. He was cheerful.

In the morning the wind was down, but it was snowing. We couldn't even see the mountain. I felt worse about the buck than I had when Tom told me, and kept thinking about it. We packed up and went back down trail, single file and not talking. Snow makes a hush that's even harder to talk in than the clear silence. There was something listening behind each tree and rock we passed, and something waiting among the taller trees down slope, blue through the falling snow. They wouldn't stop us, but they didn't like us, either. The snow was their ally.

H. L. Davis

The Kettle of Fire

THE kettle of fire story was told to me at different times during the summer when I was eleven years old and working at typesetting for a patent-inside weekly newspaper in Antelope, Oregon, though it didn't end with the telling and, I think, has not ended even now. The man who told it to me, a rundown old relic named Sorefoot Capron, held the post of city marshal except when there was somebody loose who needed to be arrested, and also managed the town water system, because he was the only resident who had been there long enough to know where the mains were laid. He used to drop in at the newspaper office sometimes when things were dull around town, which was often, to borrow a couple of dollars to get drunk on, and he would kill time by digging up experiences from his youth while he waited for the editor to show up and open the safe.

As he told it, he had run away from a respectable home in Ohio in the early eighteen-sixties, out of disgust with his parents because, after he had beaten his brains half out winning some prize in school, they had merely glanced coldly at it and reminded him that he was almost a half-hour late with his milking. The war was beginning then, but the enlistment boards turned him down because he was only fourteen and slight of build even for that age. He castigated his itinerary on west to St. Louis, where he supported himself during the winter by gambling at marbles and spit-at-a-crack with the colored youngsters around the stockyards, and by running errands for a Nevada silver-mine operator named Cash Payton, a heavy-set man with a short red beard, a bald spot on top of his head like a tonsure, and a scar across the bridge of his nose from having mistimed a fuse, who was hanging around waiting for the Overland Mail route to reopen so he could freight some mining machinery west over it.

He had two partners who were waiting in St. Louis with him, one a blocky little Cornishman with bow legs who talked in a chewed-up kind of bray, the other a long-coupled German with a pale beard and gold earrings, which in those times were believed by some people to be a specific against weak eyesight. They were both pleasant-spoken men, though hard to understand most of the time, but Cash Payton was not the kind of man to let his good nature stop with mere pleasant-spokenness. He took a special liking to young Capron, believed or let on to believe all the lies he told about being homeless and an orphan, and made plans to take him west with the mining machinery as soon as the road got opened up. When it turned out that the road was apt to stay closed for several months longer, he arranged to sign young Capron on as a herder and roustabout with a train of emigrants from Illinois and Missouri who were organizing to sneak past the frontier outposts and head west for a new start in unspoiled country, and also, though none of them brought the point up, to get themselves somewhere out of reach before they got picked up in the draft.

Travel across the plains to Oregon was forbidden at the time, because the military posts along the emigrant route had been abandoned and there was no protection against Indian raids, but the train managed to work its way out into open country while the border garrisons were busy with some rebel foray, and it rolled along on its westward course without any sign of trouble until it struck the Malheur Desert, not far from the line between Oregon and Nevada. It had moved slowly, and summer ends early in that part of the country, so it struck bad weather and had its horse-herd stampeded by Snake and Bannock Indians, who also killed a couple of night-herders by filling them full of arrows. The emigrants had hired some mountain man to steer them through the bad country, but the killings made them scared and suspicious, and they talked so loud and pointedly about hanging him for treachery that he picked up and pulled out in the night, leaving them stalled without any idea where they were or any draft-animals to haul them anywhere else.

It was a doleful place to be stuck in with bad weather coming on: merely a little muddy water-hole at the bottom of a rock-gully with nothing in sight anywhere around it but sagebrush and greasewood and rocks. They had vinegar to correct the alkali in the water, but several of the women got sick from drinking it, the dead sagebrush that they picked up for fuel was so soggy they couldn't get it to burn, and when they tried starting it by shooting a cotton wad into it they discovered that all their powder had drawn damp and got unusable except what was in the guns. They didn't dare squander that, and some of them opposed shooting of any kind for fear of drawing more Indians down on them, so they held a meeting and decided, since young Capron was not of much use to them and had nobody depending on him, to send him down toward the Nevada mining settlements for help, if he could find any. In any case, and whatever he found or did, he was to bring back an iron kettle full of live coals with which they could start a fire in damp wood.

It was a risky mission to put off onto a youngster, and several of the men, all elderly and in no danger of being let in for it themselves, dwelt with some sarcasm on the idea of selecting anybody so young and inexperienced for a job that they were all willing to offer advice about but not to undertake in his place, but nobody came up with anything better, and as far as young Capron was concerned he didn't in the least mind being picked for it. He was tired of the whole pack of them by then, and would have welcomed anything, dangerous or not, that could serve as an excuse to get away from them. He was not especially uneasy about the risks, or about the chance of finding any fire to bring back. His only difficulty, all through the time when they were arguing back and forth about sending him, was trying to decide whether to come back and expose himself to them again even if he did find it.

The strain and solemnity of starting settled that for him. He knew, even before he had finished saddling up and had climbed on the saddle-pony they had caught up for him, that he would have to come back. They had made him wait till after dark to start, and he couldn't see any of the men around him, though he knew that they were all there. From the ground, he had been able to make out their figures against the sky, but looking down at them from the saddle was like trying to keep track of a foam-streak after it had been swept under in a deep rapid. One of them reached out and clattered the kettle-bale over his saddle-horn, and he heard them all draw back to leave the way open for him. Except for that, they were all silent. There was no sound in the camp except for the herd-ponies shifting to keep warm, and a child blubbering listlessly in one of the wagons, and the choking sound of a sick woman trying to vomit. A curious apathy comes over people facing death when they know it and know what form it will take, even when they still go through the form of refusing to admit that they know anything about it. Afterward, when the reality begins to show itself, they are likely to fall into a panic and do things too disgusting to bear telling or thinking of. Young Capron knew that he had to get back with the fire, and that if he failed to get back with it before they reached that point it would be useless. Saving the lives of people who had made themselves unfit to live would be work wasted, and possibly worse than wasted. It would not help merely to keep on going, either: that would mean carrying the sounds of the camp along with him, the woman choking, the child blubbering, the silent men shuffling as they drew back in the dark, through all the years that he could reasonably expect to live, and maybe even beyond them. He had to find fire, and he had to get back with it while they were still able to hold themselves together. They might have been wrong and selfish in picking him, and they might be hard to like or live with, but there was nothing else for it. With that in his head, and with the kettle on his saddle-horn and a sack of food strapped on the cantle, he rode out between the wagons into the sagebrush.

Getting out of the gully into open country was slow and precarious work. The Indians turned out to have an outpost line drawn all the way around the camp a half-mile back from it, and he had to keep to the draws and move cautiously, leading the pony and inching along in places a step at a time, to dodge them. The pony saved him once, by balking and refusing to move even when spurred. He got off and crawled ahead to investigate, and discovered that he had been riding straight into a watch-post at the top of the ridge. The Indians had dug a hole and covered it with a blanket to keep the warmth in, with a head-slit cut in the middle to look out through. It took him an hour to back-track, find the pony in the dark, and circle around it. Afterward he heard dogs yapping in the Indian camp, and he put in another two or three hours edging around that, dismounting and putting his ear to the ground every dozen yards or so to keep from running into squaws out rummaging firewood.

Toward daylight the desert around him looked clear, and he dropped down into a creek-wash and slept in a little thornberry thicket while the pony filled up on salt-grass around a mudhole, but when he got saddled up to start off again he saw mounted Indians casting around in the sagebrush for his trail a couple of miles away, so he kept to the draws, crawling and hauling the pony along by main strength where the thorn-bush grew heavy, until almost noon. Then he mounted and struck up a long lope and held it, stopping only to rest for an hour when he struck a water-hole, all day and most of the night and all through the next day, with no sleep except when he forgot and dozed in the saddle and no food except a sage-hen which he knocked over with a rock and ate raw. Toward nightfall he made out some scattering pine timber with shadows that looked palish blue as if smoke were coloring them. He headed for it, hoping to find some camp that was burning charcoal for the Nevada mines, or possibly a dead tree smoldering from being struck by lightning. Night came while he was still a couple of miles away, but he kept going because, in the darkness, he could see that it was a real fire, and that the reddish pine trunks lit up and darkened as it flickered back and forth across them.

He dismounted, playing it safe, tied the pony to a boulder and hung the kettle from his belt, and crept forward on his hands and knees, keeping the sagebrush clumps between him and the light and stopping behind every clump to sight out the ground before inching on ahead. It was a good thing he did, for he saw when he got close that the fire had men around it. The light was too fitful and uneven to show what they looked like, but he could make out a wickiup behind them, a round-topped basketwork structure covered half-way down with skins and tattered pieces of old canvas. It was enough to make him hug the ground and peer through the tangle of sagebrush instead of looking out around it. Only Snake Indians built basketwork wickiups, and the Snakes were the most warlike of all the tribes in that part of the country. He felt pleased at being able to remember about wickiups at such a time, and started looking for more signs that the men really were Indians, ignoring whatever evidence there was that might have hinted at anything else.

The fire itself was a clear sign that they were Indians. It was not the kind of towering holocaust that white travelers always set going when they were camped for the night in wild country, but a wan little flicker of only three or four small sticks, so puny and half-hearted that he wondered how its light could have been visible so far out in the open desert. It was not nearly big enough for the men to keep warm by, but it seemed what they wanted, for they kept piling ashes on it to hold it down, and once one of them picked up a stick that was beginning to blaze up and quenched it by sticking it into the dirt. Only Indians would have gone to so much trouble to keep a campfire low, and when the man who had quenched the stick stood up to rake the coals back together young Capron saw that he was wrapped in a blanket and that there was a gleam of something whitish as he turned his head that looked like an Indian headband.

There might have been other signs if he had looked for them, but they were not needed, and he didn't dare wait any longer. The smallness of the fire had led him to miscalculate his distances, and his pony was tied close enough so that they might hear it if it started stamping or pawing. There was nothing to hold back for, anyway. Indians were Indians.

They had not wasted their time arguing about killing the emigrant train's two night-herders and running off its livestock, and the train needed fire worse than they had needed wagon-horses. He rummaged out his pistol, poked it carefully through the middle of the sagebrush clump, and waited till the man with the blanket stood away from the fire so he would have the light to sight against. He drew for the center of the blanket a handbreadth below the man's shoulders, leveled up till the foresight filled the back notch, and let go. The smoke of the black powder filled the tangle of sagebrush like gray cottonwood-down settling from a wind, but he lay and glared through it and through the smoke still dribbling from the pistol muzzle without even noticing it.

The man stood motionless for a long second while the blanket slid from his shoulders and piled up around his feet. Then he swayed, flapped his elbows and tipped his head back as if getting ready to crow, and fell face-down across the fire and plunged the whole camp into pitch darkness. He must have died falling, by the slack-jointed thump his body made when it hit in the ashes. If he had still been conscious he would have tried to avoid the fire, and he didn't; he merely let go all holds and whopped down and gathered it to his bosom like a hen covering her chickens from a hawk.

The other men jumped up and legged it for cover. Young Capron could hear brush cracking and dead branches ripping at their clothes as they galloped off into the timber. He waited till the light from the dead man's clothes taking fire showed him that he had the camp all to himself. There was something faintly worrisome about the smell of the clothes burning. It was like wool, and Indians never wore anything except cotton cloth and buckskin. Still, it might be from a corner of the blanket burning, and there was no time to speculate about it, whatever it was. He scrabbled in the dead sagebrush needles for the kettle, had an awful moment of thinking he might have lost it, and then found it by the clatter it made against his pistol, which was still clutched in his hand. He grabbed it and scrambled up and ran in, flubbing the pistol into his holster between strides, and rolled the body clear of the ashes and stirred the blackened embers together and began scraping dead pine needles from the ground to pile on them. They were almost out. He had to pile on small twigs and fan up a glaring blaze to keep them from dying on him, knowing that every twig that caught would make him an easier target for the men who had taken to the timber, and not daring to stop feeding in more sticks to make it flame up stronger.

Ministering to the flame and strained between dread when it gained and panic when it sank, he did some wondering about what the dead man looked like, but when it finally took a solid hold and burned high enough to see by, he decided that he would rather not know, and moved back into the shadows and sat with his back to it, except for one moment when some sound, possibly of tree limbs rubbing together, made him glance around to see if it had moved. There was no sign that it had, but he didn't turn away quite fast enough to keep from noticing that what he had taken for an Indian headband was a bald spot and that a stiff beard down one side of the face had been burned to a pale gray ash that the draft from the fire kept crumbling into powder so that it looked, in the slanting light, as if it was twitching.

The sight was unnerving, though he had hard work to hold back from looking at it again, and its significance was not much help, either. Indians did not have beards or bald spots. The smell of wool had been the man's flannel shirt scorching. He had been white: possibly some Indian trader, or gun-peddler, or mining promoter; possibly somebody with political influence, and friends, and relatives; even possibly—

There was no use running possibilities all the way up the string. It was done, and there was no help for it and no use in thinking about it. It was not even certain that there was anything about it to regret. There were white men in the country who needed salting worse than most of the Indians, and a man shacked up in a Snake Indian lodge in that remote corner of the desert must have had some business in hand besides organizing classes in Bible study or quilt-piecing. Still, shooting him had been overhastiness, and young Capron was sorry about it, and scared. He scooped half the fire into the kettle, though the bigger pine sticks in it had not yet burned down to coals, and hung it on a dead tree-limb and ran for his pony. He was thankful that he had his errand to hurry for. Without it, his excuse for hurrying would have had to be something less dignified: fear that the two men might be creeping up through the trees to bushwhack him, fear that if he stayed any longer he would not be able to hold out against looking once more at the dead man's face.

The fire on the ground had burned low when he rode back, but the pitch-knots in the kettle were flaring up so the pony refused to edge within reach of it, even with spurring. Finally he got down and covered the kettle with a piece of bark, and then rode past at a trot and grabbed it from the limb before the bark had time to take fire. He moved up in the saddle, raked the pony down the ribs, and lit back into the desert with the kettle held out at one side and the flame from the bark caressing his hand and arm as vengefully as if the dead man had prayed it on him for a parting retribution.

When he got a couple of miles out, he reined up to let the flame burn down, but he heard hoofbeats from the trail behind, so he merely dumped a couple of the hottest knots out into the sagebrush and shoved on. Afterward, looking back at the glare they were making, he could have kicked himself for leaving so plain a marker for the men to steer by, though the truth was that it didn't matter much. Uncovering the coals he had kept made them flare high enough to be visible two miles away, and when he tried holding the kettle low they scared the pony into a paroxysm of rearing and pin-wheeling that threatened to scatter all the fire out of it.

He had to go back to holding the kettle at arm's length before the pony would move ahead at all. It looked like trying to flag a steamboat, and the foolishness of it started him to reflecting bitterly on the things he should have done and had lacked the sense to think of till too late. He should have hunted out and stampeded the men's saddle-horses while he was waiting for the fire to get started. He should have picked greasewood for the fire instead of pitch-pine.

He should have covered the kettle with dirt instead of bark. He should have used his brains instead of letting them run to imagining things that merely scared him. He should have kept his nerve, figured things out ahead, made himself into something steadier and more far-sighted than he ever had been. He should not have been in such a hurry to play the hand Providence had dealt him to establish his future on. It would have been better if he had held back and tried to change the spots on the cards by making faces at them, or possibly by crying over them. A man had to live up to what he was, weaknesses and all. Finding out what they were was probably not worth shooting a man for, but it was a gain. The kettle had returned him that much for his trouble, at least.

He held the pony to a high trot for a couple of miles, and then pulled up to let it catch its wind. He could no longer hear hoofbeats back of him, so he took time to pull off his coat and wrap it around his hand as a protection against the heat from the coals. Then a rock clattered back in the distance, and he knew the men were still coming, and closing the range. The pony heard it too, and he had to rein back hard to keep it from breaking into a run and getting wind-broken. It would have been easy to lose them if his hands had been free: he could merely have walked the pony down into some gully and laid low till they passed. The kettle killed that possibility; they could line him in by the light from it, no matter which way he turned or what track he took. He thought of covering it with gravel, or with a sod from some mudhole, but decided against that for fear of smothering the fire completely.

At the end of six or seven miles more, he realized that it was not far from going out all by itself. The coat wadded over his burned hand had kept him from noticing how much the kettle had cooled down. One welcome part of it was that the light had got too weak to be visible at a distance, but he was too much afraid of losing the fire to take comfort in its debility. He slowed to a walk for awhile, and then turned sharp away from his course down a long draw, dismounted and tied the pony in a thicket of giant sagebrush, and felt his way down the slope hunting for dead roots that could be used for kindling. There was nothing dry enough until, in the low ground where the draw widened out, he bumped into some stunted junipers. Juniper wood is too light and porous to be much use as fuel, but the trunks were run through with dead streaks from which, by gouging with his knife, he managed to pry loose a handful of splinters that would take fire easily, even if they didn't hold it long.

The kettle was cool enough to touch by the time he finished collecting them, but with careful blowing they condescended to flicker up so that he could lay on heavier fuel from the dead branches. When that caught, he rammed the kettle down into a badger hole, piled whole branches over it to make sure the fire would last, and went on down the dry watercourse to find hardwood that would burn down into coals. The light from the branches glared like a haystack burning, and he had no trouble finding greasewood roots and a dead chokecherry tree and loading himself up with chunks from them. The flame behind him filled half the sky by then, so he circled back cautiously and hid under a low-branched juniper fifty or sixty yards from it, in case it drew anybody to come investigating.

It happened quicker than he had counted on. He had got himself settled among the juniper boughs, which smelled bad, and was smearing his face with wet dirt to blend with the shadows when two men came down the slope from his trail, stopped where the sagebrush thinned out, and stood watching the fire and shading their eyes against it. They were a hundred yards away, and they looked unearthly tall in the sheeting glare of the fire, but he could see that they were white men. They had on ordinary work clothes, and they wore hats and had their hair cut short. That was nothing much; he had expected that they would turn out to be white, and he was not afraid of them except for a slight feeling of strain inside him. It gouged harder to see that one of them was blocky and reddish and bowlegged, and that the other was tall and thin and pale-bearded, with earrings on which the light sparkled when he moved his head. Young Capron would not have noticed the earrings at such a distance if he had not been expecting them. The men were the sawed-off Cornishman and the tall German who had been Cash Payton's partners. He had liked Cash Payton better than both of them—better than anybody else, as far as that went—but he had liked them. Because he had shot Cash Payton, he dared not move for fear they would pick out his hiding place and kill him. They stood peering across the firelight into the junipers, the German wagging a long army cap-and-ball revolver and the Cornishman holding a rifle as if he were fixing to rake hay with it, all primed and set to open up on anything that moved.

They loomed up against the shadows like clay pipes in a shooting gallery. If they had been strangers, if the firelight had not outdone itself to show who they were beyond the possibility of a mistake, he could have cleared his way back to the emigrant train with two cartridges, besides acquiring possession of two unjaded saddle-horses which he could have used very handily. What they had been doing camped in the timber so far from anywhere he didn't try to guess. Nothing to their credit, likely, or they would not have gone to so much trouble to run him down. Catching Indian children to sell as slaves in San Francisco was a flourishing business then, and if it was that, they deserved shooting for it. So did Cash Payton, except that points of ethics no longer counted. All that did count was knowing that the man who had befriended him and kept him alive over a whole winter was lying dead back in the pine timber with half his face burned off, all because of a scary young squirt's clubfooted foolishness. Bad or good, right or wrong, he had deserved better than to be shot down from cover when his back was turned. Young Capron shut his eyes and buried his face in the dirt, wondering, to end a painful trail of reflection, whether he could ever smell juniper boughs again without getting sick, as in fact he never could, in all the years afterward.

When he looked up, the men were leaving, probably having realized the sappiness of standing in the full glare of the fire when the man they were hunting might be lurking somewhere close enough to take advantage of it. The tall German stopped at the edge of the sagebrush and examined the caps in his revolver to make sure they were all in place. That meant that they were not giving up, and that they would probably post themselves somewhere along his trail, figuring to knock him over when he came back to it. If it had not been for the shooting they would have been glad to see him and, if they could, to help him. If it had not been for the fire kettle there would not have been any shooting. Of course, he could leave it where it was and ride after them and let on not to know anything about it, so they would blame the shooting on somebody else. They would probably take his word for it: foreigners were trustful about things they didn't understand very well, in contrast to Americans, who were always the most suspicious in matters they knew the least about. He could go with the two men and be safe, and be rid of the emigrants and their sniveling and domineering for good.

The only trouble was that he couldn't bring himself to do it. It would mean that Cash Payton had died for nothing, for mere foolishness, because a streak of light hit him in the wrong place. The only way to make his death count for anything was to get the fire back to the train. He shook loose from his seesawing and went into the tall sagebrush for his pony.

The fire had burned down when he came back with the pony, and the juniper boughs were falling into coals that the stir of air fanned into flaky ashes. It was hard to lose time building them back, but he had to have some kind of fire that would last, and the pony would hold up better for being left to graze and rest a little longer. He piled on the greasewood and wild cherry, waited to make sure it caught, and then lay down upwind from the junipers and slept until the glare of the new fire woke him. He fished the kettle out with a forked tree-limb, left it to cool while he caught and bridled the pony, and scooped it full of new coals and tried to mount with it.

The pony had recuperated too well. It shied back and fought so that he had to put the kettle down to keep from being yanked off his feet. He tried covering the coals with ashes, but the glow still showed through, and the pony fought back from it till he set the kettle back on the ground and climbed aboard without it. He rode past it and tried to pick it up from the saddle, but the pony shied off so he couldn't reach it. Finally he found his forked tree-limb, circled back, and hooked the kettle at long range and hauled it in. Even then it took all his strength on the reins to keep the pony from pinwheeling and running away from the heat and light following along even with its off-shoulder.

He had held his feelings back too long, probably. He was crying by the time he got the kettle hoisted up and felt the heat on his burned flesh again. He got angry with himself for crying, and his anger made him forget about the two men waiting for him somewhere along the trail ahead. He remembered them after he had ridden a few hundred yards, and swung back along the draw on a wide circuit to keep clear of them. Half the coals in the kettle had got spilled out in his manipulations with the forked tree-limb, and he had no idea how he would manage about renewing them when they burned low again, but there was no use killing snakes till they stopped hibernating. He put it out of his mind, along with what seemed a lifetime of other useless reflections and apprehensions, and rode on.

The coals burned low about daylight, when he was crossing a long level plain on which even the sagebrush grew so thin that he was in plain sight of anybody two or three miles away in any direction. Sagebrush roots burned out almost like wadded newspaper, but there was nothing else, and he got down and gathered an armload of them and nursed the fire back to life. They were damp, and the smoke from them rose in a whitish column that could be seen for miles, but at least the open plain made it impossible for anybody to sneak up on him. It was about fifteen miles across, and he could see anything that moved on it. A man on horseback would have loomed up like a steeple, even at the edge of it.

Nothing came in sight. The plain was lifeless except for horned toads. With the daylight, the pony had got over its fright of the kettle, and it struck up a trot when he remounted, as if it were as anxious to see the last of the place as he was. The plain broke into a long ridge, speckled at its base with little rusty junipers and with a tangle of mountain mahogany marking the line of a dry gully. He halted and broke some of its dead boughs for fuel, since they were hot and slow-burning. They took away his anxiety about the fire for the moment, and it began to be brought home to him that he had circled into country where nobody had ever been before. A herd of antelope came out of the junipers as he passed, looked after him with their back-tufts twitching with inquisitiveness, and then followed along after him, edging downwind to catch his scent and then moving in to gawk at him from such close range that he could have hit them with a rock. The pony watched them uneasily and stumbled over so many rocks and roots trying to keep out of their way that he was halfway tempted to do it, except that it would have meant having to stop and dismount to find something to throw.

Beyond the ridge, he lost them. The ground leveled off into a long expanse of naked earth, pocked and honeycombed with sage-rat burrows. It must have been a mile across, and the country around it for a half-dozen miles was stripped as bare as if it had been plowed and harrowed. There were sage-rats all over it. Some sat up and stared at him as he passed, and then dropped almost under the pony's feet and went on about their business, whatever it was. Some scurried for their holes as if scared, but then they sat up and stared too, and finally sauntered back where they had come from, evidently feeling that whatever was happening at the pony's level was no concern of theirs, and that, when all was said and done, the proper study of ratkind was rats. There was nothing anywhere near the ground that could be used for fuel to keep the fire up, and the ground itself was treacherous because the pony kept breaking through it where they had tunneled it for their nests.

They were not much company. The worst of it was not their strangeness and preoccupation with themselves, it was the loneliness of the country that made young Capron adapt himself, without being aware of it, to their values and scale of living. A few more miles of them, he felt, and he would find himself growing feeler-whiskers, squeaking, and rearing up on his hind-legs to watch himself ride past and try for a second or two to figure out what he was. He turned down a dry gully to get clear of them and the waste they had created, and came to a long scarp of low gray cliffs, broken into rifts and ledges for its entire length. Every rift and every ledge was occupied by great pale-gray owls. None of them moved as he rode past. They sat straight and impassive, hooting to each other briefly sometimes with a hollow sound like blowing into an empty jug, their blank yellow eyes staring past him into the sun without seeing it or him and without knowing or caring what he was. They could see objects only in the half-dusk or in the dark. Nothing that passed in the sunlight made any impression on them.

The cliffs fell away, and the gully spread out into a wide flat covered with stubby clumps of old weatherstained rye-grass. The ground between the clumps was dark and water-soaked, but it was covered so densely with jackrabbits that it looked gray and moving like a spread of water. The jackrabbits moved sluggishly, some of them waiting till they were almost under the pony's feet and then dragging themselves barely out of the way and settling down again. Their trouble was one that usually hit jackrabbits in the years when they had run themselves down by overbreeding. They were swollen with wens from bot-flies, and so weakened by them that they couldn't have moved fast if they had wanted to.

A curious thing about it was that though disease had undermined their instinct for self-preservation, it had left their appetites unimpaired, or only a little slackened. They were still able to crop all the green sprouts out of the dead rye-grass clumps, and they had not lost their interest in copulation, whatever might have happened to their ability. They were not noticeably energetic about it, but they stayed with it faithfully, working as the pony picked its way among them at the absorbing task of perpetuating their kind, bot-flies and all, and regarding nothing else as deserving of notice.

The flat fell away into a long rise and fall of stony desert, and then to a broad grass-slope that reached down to a bright-green little alkali lake, with dark wire-grass in the shallows and patches of willow on the damp ground back of them. The slopes and the shallows were covered solid with wild geese, mottled like a patched quilt with their different colors--brown Canada geese, white snow-geese, dark little cacklers, blue honkers, ringnecked black brant--rocking placidly on the bitter water or crowded solid along the swell of short grass overlooking it. Young Capron would have liked to avoid them, but the fire was low in the kettle, and there was dead wood among the willows that would make good coals and no way of getting it except to ride straight through them.

Of all the forms of life the country had put him up against, they were the worst. They held their ground till he could have reached down and touched them, and then rose with a horrible blast of screeching and banging of wings, darkening the sky overhead and spattering him and the pony and the kettle and the fire in it with filth to show how much he had upset them by turning out to be something they had not been expecting. Then, as the next flock went squalling and clattering up with a new shower, the one behind him settled back onto the grass as unconcernedly as if nothing at all had happened, as, no doubt, in the tablets of their memory, nothing at all had.

They should have quieted down and gone back to resting when he dismounted and went to work preparing the dead willow limbs for his fire, but they seemed unable either to stand him or to let him alone. Every few minutes, though he moved as little as he could and the pony scarcely stirred out of its tracks, some of them would stalk close to him, rear up and look him over again, and then let out a horrified squawk and put the whole flock up to spatter him with filth all over again. It was not hostility so much as indignation. They were outraged with him for being there, without having the ghost of an idea what he was doing or the slightest interest in finding out.

Getting clear of the wild country took a long time. He had circled farther than he realized, and crossing the long swells of ground beyond the lake took up the whole afternoon, counting two or three times when he had to skirmish up dead limbs of cottonwood and service-berry to stoke the kettle. There was one more small flurry of wild life, a little creek bordered with short grass that was being stripped off by huge wingless Mormon crickets. They were slippery for the pony to step on, but there was nothing else to them except appetite. Some little darkish rattlesnakes picked languidly at them around the edges, without any great show of interest in doing it. Young Capron spurred away from the place, feeling with some self-pity that a man had to fall low to be siding with rattlesnakes, but wishing them well even in wanting to be rid of them for good.

He would have liked to keep going when it got dark, but the pony was sunken-flanked and laboring on the slopes, so he turned into a little stand of cottonwoods and unsaddled and turned it out to graze. He found some half-dead wild plum and dumped the coals from the kettle and built up a fire with fuel from it, first dead sticks and then bigger green ones, which burned slower but made long-lasting coals. When the fire took hold, he ate some salt pork that the emigrants had given him, downing it raw because cooking wasted it, and spread out on a patch of dampish ground and slept.

Something brought him awake along in the night. He didn't know what it had been, but he could tell by the wandering fire that he had slept for several hours, and he noticed that the silence around him was deeper than it had been when he was going to sleep. Building the fire back, he realized that what he missed was the sound of the pony grazing. He piled kindling into the kettle for a light and went out to see what had become of it. The grass showed where it had been grazing, but it was gone. He tried farther out, remembering gloomily that Indians always ran the horses off from a camp that they were getting ready to jump, and found a shallow mudhole that had been trampled all around by horses. The tracks were fresh, which disturbed him for a minute, but a smoothed-down place in the mud where they had been rolling showed that they were running loose. Not all of them were Indian horses either; some of them were shod, and the calk-marks were big enough to have been made by wagon-teams, possibly from the emigrant train, not that it mattered. The pony might have been scared off by some cougar stalking the herd, and it might still be hanging around. That didn't matter either. All that mattered was that the pony had gone with a loose horse-herd, and that there was no use trying to get it back on foot and burdened with a kettle of fire that it had been scared of from the beginning. One from one left nothing, no matter what had been responsible for it.

He ate salt pork again, hung his saddle and bridle from a tree limb, filled the kettle with new coals and cut a stick to carry it by, and started on afoot without waiting for daylight. In some ways, traveling was easier with the pony gone. There was no worry over having it snort or stamp or whinny at the wrong time, or over having to find grass or water at the stopping places, or having it shy and fight back when he tried to mount, and being able to carry the kettle close to the ground made it less easily seen at a distance. More than that, he was freed from the temptation to throw it away and head out for himself. Without a horse and without food enough for another day, the emigrant camp was the only place he could go. Having to concentrate on one thing instead of see-sawing between lurking alternatives made everything simpler: not easier, but easier to summon strength for.

In the afternoon, plodding down a wide valley that opened into draws where there was small wood and water, he found the first sign that he was nearing human beings. It was not a brightening one, merely a dead horse spread out on a patch of bare ground with some buzzards lined up waiting for the sun to burst it open, but it did show that he was headed right and that he was making distance. It turned his thoughts to the emigrant camp, and he began to notice, thinking of the emigrants waiting for him, that the dead sagebrush tops were drying out and that the ground underfoot was strewn with little chips of black flint. He refired the kettle and hurried on, driven by fear that the emigrants might have run into the same thing near their camp, that they might have found dry kindling and lighted a flint-and-steel fire for themselves.

Thinking of that possibility and discovering what his own feelings about it were opened a new area of self-knowledge to him, and not an especially comforting one. He tried to think how much suffering and fear and despair they would be spared if they had thought of trying it, and could get no farther than the reflection that it would make his own suffering and fear and despair useless: a man dead, and his pain, terror, weariness, humiliation and hunger all gone for nothing. He took more consolation from thinking that, if his knowledge of the emigrants was a sign of anything, they wouldn't have sense enough to think of hunting for flints to start with, even if they had the courage to venture far enough out to find them.

It was humiliating to realize that his values had all been turned upside down, when he could welcome seeing a dead horse with buzzards around it and be downcast to think that people he knew might be keeping warm and cooking food and drying out their gunpowder, but the fear held on in spite of him. When he looked down from the last rise of ground on the Indian camp he had skirted around in starting out, he saw a smoke rising from beyond it that appeared to come from the emigrant train, and it set him shaking at the knees so that he had to sit down to keep from collapsing. It was near sundown by then, and when it got dusk he crept on through the sagebrush and discovered that it was not from the wagons at all, but from the hole where the Indian watch post had been on the night he left camp. The hole had been abandoned, it appeared, and the Indians had made a smudge of damp sagebrush roots in it to scare the emigrants into staying where they were. He took time to pile wet earth on the smudge, to keep the emigrants from finding out how easy it would have been for them to get fire if any of them had thought of it, and he felt relieved and uplifted in spirit to think that none of them had.

The camp seemed dead when he came stumbling down into it, but after a few minutes he began to hear sounds from the wagons: children whimpering with the cold, a man praying in a loud monotone under a wagon, the sick woman still trying to vomit. He remembered that the sounds were the sweetest music he had ever listened to. No ninety-eight-piece orchestra in the land could have come within flagging distance of them. Even after so many years and so many changes, remembering it still stirred him inside, something like jumping off a barn-roof after swallowing a half-dozen humming jew's-harps.

That was all of the story. He used to build up different parts of it at different times while he sat waiting in the printing office for the editor to arrive, but at the first telling he told it all straight through, and he ended it, as he was right to do, with the concluding emotion instead of stringing it out into the subsequent events that dulled it all down. I asked what had happened afterward, and he said nothing worth telling about. The emigrants had scraped up nerve enough to go out and run in their teams, or most of them, and they were so pleased with themselves for doing it that they forgot all about his fire that had given them the necessary courage. Then they had moved on, and finally they had come out at a river-crossing that took them into the old Barlow Road. They were not worth much, on the average, any of them.

"They made me pay for the pony I lost," he said. "And the saddle and bridle, too. Took it out of my wages, what little there was of 'em."

"It don't sound like you'd got much out of it," I said. At the time, it didn't seem to me that any story with such a frazzled-out ending was worth spending all that time on. "It sounds like everybody had come out ahead except you."

"That was what they all thought, I guess," he said. "They're welcome to their notions. None of 'em come out as far ahead as they thought they had, and it's the only thing I've ever done that I got anything out of that was worth hellroom. It's the only thing I'd do over again, I believe, if I had to. Not that I'll ever get the chance. Things like that don't happen nowadays."

He was wrong about that, of course. Such things change in substance and setting, but they go on working in the spirit, through different and less explicit symbols, as they did through the centuries before emigrations West were ever heard of, and as they will for men too young to know about them now and for others not yet born. There will always be the fire to bring home, through the same hardships and doubts and adversities of one's life that make up the triumph of having lived it.

H.L. Davis

The Homestead Orchard

THE patch of sagebrush which young Linus Ollivant's charge of six hundred lambed ewes had selected as a bed ground for themselves and their progeny was an old starved-out homestead halfway down the slope of Boulder River Canyon, with a few broken-down sheds, a naked slope of red conglomerate that had once been plowed, and a slow trickle of water, small, but holding its flow steady in spite of the drying wind that had driven most of the country's water supply off into the unknown, and a considerable proportion of the country along with it.

It lacked a good deal of being an ideal location for a range camp, being altogether too far from pasture. The sheep, in the three days they had been there, had put in most of their waking hours plodding out to feed and trudging back to water, but they refused to omit either end of the circuit; and Linus, trying to handle them alone until an extra herder could be raked loose from a boxcar and sent out from town, shoved his old herding horse along behind them in the hard glare of a windy twilight and pulled up on the slope above the bed ground to count them into camp before going down into the shadows after them.

The intense blackness of the shadows in that clear air made the camp so dark that even the white tent looked ghostly against the gloom. There was one clear patch of light where the sky reflected in the pond of water, and the mass of dark-wooled old ewes and white-fleeced and inquisitive lambs trailed down into it and stood patterned against it clear and distinct as they drank and crossed to their bed ground for the night.

When they had all crossed, Linus strained his eyes back over the naked rock ridges of the canyon, hoping, because he was too inexperienced at sheepherding to know that it contained no pleasant surprises, that some tail-end bunch of late feeders might still come moseying along in time to bring his count up somewhere near where it belonged.

As might have been expected, he saw nothing except the ridges, ranked one behind another, as frail-looking as if they had been shadows in the pale red sky, darkening to gray at the edges where they touched it. The country's lifelessness was a new thing to Linus. His family had homesteaded on the divide back of that river canyon in his childhood, and one of his few pleasant recollections from that time was of standing on high ground at dark and counting the lights of other homesteads where families had settled to grow up with the country. Now there were no signs of life visible anywhere except in the range camp, where the sheep fidgeted themselves into position for the night and where Linus' father, suffering from a case of dust blindness from the alkali flats back in the desert, fumbled matches into a pile of greasewood in an effort to get a fire started for supper.

His fire building didn't make much headway. His eyes were so inflamed that they were not only useless but so agonizingly sensitive that they had to be kept heavily bandaged against the least light or wind or irritation. Most of his matches blew out while he fumbled around for fuel to touch them to, and Linus, seeing that he was about to run a fit of temper over his own helplessness, gave up hopes of the stray sheep and hurried down to help him out. The fire started easily enough, with a little coddling, and old Ollivant settled gloomily back against the tent pole, hauled his bandage down into place as if he were conferring a favor on society by tolerating the thing, and supplied what entertainment he could by offering conversational leads as Linus got their cooking under way.

"It ain't right for you to have all this work put on you," he said. "It looks like them people in town could have raked up some hobo herder to ship out here, if they had any consideration for a man. How did the sheep handle today? It didn't sound to me like there was as many come in as usual. Did you get a count on 'em?"

Linus raked the fire, clattered buckets and said he had counted them in carefully. He didn't mention what his count had come to. He thought of owning up to it, and then reflected that it would be better to hold back until daylight, when he could make sure that the strays were actually lost and not merely yarded up in the brush, waiting to be sent for.

"They pulled in too tired to make much noise, I expect," he said. "They had a long lug in from pasture tonight. Three or four miles, anyhow."

Side-stepping one disturbing circumstance, he ran squarely into another. His father picked on his estimate of the distance to pasture as if it were a dynamiting he had confessed to.

"We can't carry these old pelters where they've got to trail four miles to pasture," he said. "They'll wear themselves to death on it. If I could trust you to stay out of trouble with people, I'd be about in the notion to hold the whole bunch here in camp for a day or two, till you could scout up some better place to bed 'em. You'd probably land up in some fight, though. Blame it, what does a man have to depend on sheep for, anyhow?"

That was something of a dig; it was Linus' fault that he had been reduced to depending on sheep. Ordinarily, he wouldn't have made a point of that, but enforced inaction made him short of patience. Linus knew enough to humor him.

"It wouldn't do any good to scout around here," he said. "There ain't any other place around here where we could camp sheep at all. You'd see that if you could see what this country looked like."

"If I ever get these old buzzard baits sheared and turned off to ship, I'll kill the next man that says 'sheep' to me," old Ollivant said. "There ain't a jury in the land that would cinch me for it, the provocation I've had." He stopped and lifted one hand for silence for a minute. "I heard horses," he said. "If them people in town have sent out a herder, I'll never complain about my luck again."

It was a handsome offer, and Linus hated to sound as discouraging about it as he felt obliged to.

"It can't be anybody to see us," he said. "We've moved camp five times since you sent for a herder, and the people in town wouldn't know where to send one. You heard some bunch of wild cayuses. Maybe it's Indians out to dig camass."

"It was a shod horse I heard," old Ollivant said.

They both listened, saying nothing and even taking care not to rattle the dishes as they ate supper. Neither of them heard a sound, and Linus fell to thinking over their homesteading days up on the ridge, and of the long string of accidents that had led him back to it against his will. His father had come to that country to homestead a likely quarter-section of sagebrush and find out whether high-altitude soil and climate couldn't be adapted to raising domestic fruits, and he had been obliged to give that up, the orcharding and the homesteading together, through a run of misfortune for which Linus was a good deal to blame.

Afterward he worked around a feed yard in one of the river towns long enough to figure that it led nowhere, and finally he allowed himself to be tempted into taking a half interest in a flock of rickety old ewes, on a chance that, given a decent year and careful handling, they might bring in a crop of lambs worth three times his original investment in them, with the wool figuring at enough extra to cover incidental expenses, taxes, and possibly even day wages for his work.

It had been a tempting project, with little risk showing on its exterior, to begin with. But there had been enough risk about it to make it a gamble, and, like most gambles undertaken by people who couldn't afford to lose, things had gone wrong with it almost from the outset.

The roster of bad luck began with a feed shortage and a rise in hay prices, proceeded onward into an outlandishly protracted dry spell and a shortening of the country's water supply, and held on into a failure of all the spring pastures at the exact time when the entire country had counted on them as a last hope to keep going on. A vast invasion of cast-off scrub horses used up what little coarse grass the land had managed to hold on to, and old Ollivant's dust blindness had topped off the whole structure of calamities and left, as far as Linus could see, scarcely any possibility of their pulling through to shearing time with any sheep at all.

He had done his best to keep going singlehanded, and though he had been forced to several emergency measures that his father would not have approved of, he had kept the herd up better than most professional herders would have bothered to do.

He hadn't wanted to pasture back so near the scene of his father's abandoned experiments with dry-country orcharding. That was one of the emergency measures he had not been able to avoid. The sheep had wandered down from the alkali desert with no notion in their heads except to move where they could find something to eat, and the line of grass had led them, almost as if it had been set out for the purpose, straight down into Boulder River Canyon and through it to the water hole where they were bedded. It wasn't a good place for them, but it was the only water in the neighborhood where sheep could be held without running into opposition from the resident landowners.

One of the few useful things Linus had got out of his homesteading years on the ridge over Boulder River was a knowledge of the country and its limitations and prejudices. He knew the region well, and he knew there were no open camping places in it that had even as many advantages as the one where they were. One of the points about it was that there were thirty head of his father's sheep running loose somewhere around it, and he couldn't leave until he had taken some kind of a stab at finding them. He roused out of his train of reflections and remarked that it was a cold wind to be sitting out in with a case of inflammation of the eyes. Old Ollivant said morosely that he wasn't responsible for the temperature of the wind.

"It's a blamed funny thing we don't hear any coyotes," he

remarked. "This is the first night since we've been out here that there ain't been a dozen of 'em on the yip all around us. They couldn't all have left the country in a day."

"You can't tell about coyotes around these blamed rock piles," Linus said vaguely. The coyotes had not left the country, and he knew the reason they weren't making themselves heard as they usually did. With thirty head of sheep wandering at large, they had something better to while away their time on than hunkering on a cold rock to howl.

He tried to decide whether to own up about the strays, and heard metal grate on rock somewhere up on the ridge. He held up his hand for silence, heard it again, and let the strays slip out of his thoughts with a feeling of relief at not having to make up his mind about them.

"Somebody with horses," he said. "You'd better fetch out the gun. It might be some of these neighborhood busybodies come to drag us out of here in a sack."

"Guns can make more trouble for some people than draggin' in a sack," old Ollivant said, without moving. "I told you I heard shod horses fifteen minutes ago. It's somebody from town come out to see what's happened to us, I expect."

The wind shifted, and for a long time they heard nothing more at all. Then the hoofs clattered on the ridge above them, and they could tell that it was several horses in charge of one man who was humming a loud mixture of three or four different tunes as an indication that he was not trying to sneak up on anybody. Linus stirred the fire into a blaze, and he stopped his humming, shaded his eyes against the glare, and rode down into the full light, so they could look him over before he offered to dismount.

"They told me in town that some people named Ollivant wanted a herder," he said. He was a large-built man with a saddle a couple of sizes too snug for him, and he had three pack ponies strung, head and tail, behind him. He kept yanking their lead rope to keep them from trying to lie down.

"My name is Dee Radford. I'm a herder, and I ain't ever worked this country before, so I come out to see what your layout looked like. They had this order of groceries made up for you, so I brung it along. This place ain't fit to camp sheep on. I'll bet you've lost a couple of dozen head in the last two days, if you'll count."

Linus didn't consider it necessary to mention what the correct statistics on his shortage were. "How did the people in town know where to send you?" he asked.

"They didn't. I had to work out your trail from the scenery," Dee Radford said.

He dismounted so heavily that he almost pulled the weary animal over on top of himself, and proceeded to unsaddle and unpack in the dark, working as confidently as if nobody had ever told him what a lantern was for.

"When you've been in this business as long as I have, you don't need to know where people are to find 'em," he explained, unraveling a complicated four-way hitch from a pack. "A man that can't find what he wants without help ain't entitled to call himself a herder. This ain't any place to camp a band of sheep like these of yours. They walk off their feed gittin' to water, and they dry out thirsty trailin' back to feed, and they're too old to stand it. I picked out a place up on the ridge where they'll handle better. There's an old homestead with a patch of run-down orchard around it, and there's water enough to make out on if we're careful. You can git your camp struck and packed, and we'll move up there the first thing in the morning."

To Linus, it seemed a little high-handed for even a skilled herder to drop into the middle of a strange camp and start issuing orders as if it belonged to him.

Old Ollivant was less touchy and more interested. At mention of a ridge homestead surrounded by an old orchard, he sat up and said he had been agitating to have their camp moved, and that Linus had assured him the thing was impossible.

"It is," Linus said. "That ridge country ain't open land. It belongs to people that use it to feed cattle on. If we move in with sheep, they'll throw us out, and maybe run the sheep to death for good measure. I know the people around here. I know how they act with pasture thieves, and I don't blame 'em for it."

"We won't be pasture thieves, because there ain't any pasture on that ridge to thieve," Dee Radford said. "There's been cattle over every foot of it, and they've cleaned the grass right down to the roots. The only thing about it is that there's a big scatter of grass seed blowed around into horse tracks and under rocks where the cattle couldn't reach it. Sheep can, and there ought to be enough of it to run us for three weeks or more anyhow. We won't be trespassers, because the place don't belong to anybody. I asked some men in the road about that. I told 'em I was a mind to buy it, and they said it hadn't ever been proved up on. We'll move up there in the morning, if it's all right with both of you."

It was not all right with Linus and he said nothing, but his father said there was no use palavering around about a move so plainly commendable and necessary.

"We'll move any time you say, and don't pay any attention to anything this boy says," he said. "He's always balky at the wrong times, and there ain't much you can do with him. He's done well to handle the sheep by himself without any losses, but he's got to learn to listen to other people sometimes, and he can't start any younger."

Linus still remained silent, so he fumbled his way inside the camp tent and began rattling small articles into his war bag to save having to pack them in the morning. They heard his boots thump and the blankets rustle as he spread down in them, and then the noises subsided as he went to sleep.

Dee Radford remarked that they had better be thinking about rest themselves, if they were to make it up to the ridge homestead in a day's trailing. Linus replied that he didn't plan to make it to any ridge homestead, and that he would rest when he felt like it. He tried to sound chilling, but Dee Radford merely sat back and studied him thoughtfully.

"I've seen young squirts act like this when I've pulled into some camp to help through a bad season," he said. "You're a different cut from that, if looks is anything. You don't look like a squirt, and you ought to know that you'll lose all your sheep if you try to handle 'em down here. You don't think I'd be in this business if I didn't know anything about it, do you?"

"You know your business, I guess," Linus conceded, a trifle sullenly. "What you don't know about is this country. You've got it fixed to land us all in trouble with the people in it. That old ridge orchard you've picked for us to move to ain't open land. If any men told you it was, they lied. It used to be our homestead. My old man planted that orchard, and I took care of it, and I could draw you a picture right now of every tree in it. We'd be there yet, but I got into a rumpus, so the old man had to sell out his homestead rights and leave to get away from lawsuits. I shot a man, if you want to know what it was. Maybe that homestead ain't been proved up on, but it ain't ours, because we sold the rights to it. If we take sheep onto it we'll have trouble, and people around here will swear I started it to show off. That old man don't know about that, because he don't know what part of the country we've drifted back to. He'll probably claim I sneaked back here to hunt up some more cussedness, if he ever finds it out."

Dee Radford stirred the fire and said that cleared up two or three points that he hadn't understood at first. He added that old Ollivant's dust blindness had looked serious, and that they might manage to get the sheep sheared and off their hands and get clear away from the Boulder River country before he cured up enough to realize that they had been there.

"It would be playin' underhanded with him, but that ain't any business of mine," he said. "Sheep is all I claim to know anything about, and there ain't but one thing to do with this bunch of yours. We can keep 'em alive on that ridge homestead, and we'll try to handle 'em so people won't find out we're there. If they have to stay here they'll die, and if you'd sooner they done that, say so and I'll leave you to handle 'em. You'll go broke, but that ain't any of my put-in. How many head have you lost since you've been here that you ain't told your old man about?"

That was a sharp surmise, and Linus took no risks in replying to it. He nodded toward the tent, and stated in clear tones that he had lost no sheep at all. Then he opened and closed the fingers of his hands three times, traced the course of one setting sun down the sky, and waited to see if Dee Radford had ever stopped long enough in one place to know what Indian sign talk was.

Dee indicated his comprehension with a nod, and remarked cautiously that he would have expected the shrinkage to have run higher and sooner. If they had dropped out only that afternoon, they might still be alive. Having turned in that reflection, he got up, got his horse out of the corral, and reached down his saddle.

"I'm goin' to show you that a man don't need to know a country to handle sheep in," he said. "You show me which direction you pastured today, and I'll find them strays for you. You git packed and line the sheep for the ridge the first thing in the morning, and quit this shiverin' around for fear of trouble. People ain't fools enough to fight us over a place as worthless as that homestead. If they do, I'll tend to 'em, and if we damage the premises, I'll stand good for it. We won't hurt your old man's orchard, if that's what you're uneasy about."

"I don't care what you do to the orchard," Linus said. "I put in four years' hard work on it, and all I ever got for it was a pile of trouble, and all I want is to make sure we won't get into any more. Trouble ain't easy to dodge out on in this country."

"Trouble ain't easy to dodge out on in any country that you spend too much of your time in. You ought to learn your trade and travel around with it, like I do, and then you wouldn't have to bother about what people thought of you."

Linus and his father packed camp an hour or so before sunup. Linus getting everybody's personal belongings together into one of the packs, and reflecting that it did look as if Dee Radford's system of short-staking around had paid better than any protracted residence in one place.

Dee's outfit included such show pieces as a leather-faced bed roll, double-lined goatskin chaps, and a hand-carved rifle scabbard, all of which were expensive and none of which either Linus or his father possessed at all. His rifle was a new flat-shooting rig with box magazine, oiled stock, peep sight with micrometer scale, buckhorn tips, and all the trimmings. Linus' father had a common little saddle carbine with iron sights and a squared-off butt, and Linus not only had no gun at all but wasn't even supposed to handle one except under his father's personal supervision.

Except that it showed what he had missed by staying too long in the shadow of his youthful reputation, the contrast in the rifles didn't bother Linus much. The old piece of momentary

recklessness that had ended his residence on the ridge homestead
had also destroyed most of his interest in guns, and the sight of one
was generally enough to bring the whole unlucky episode back to
him clearly and painfully.

Its beginning cause had been the old homestead orchard. He had
put in an entire spring on it, pruning, cultivating, whitewashing
and spraying for insects, and, as he was applying a few final touches
against twig borers, a contingent of old Lucas Waymark's cowboys
pulled in and camped a herd of starved-out old cows right against a
weak place in the fence where they were certain to break through
the minute they were left to themselves.

Linus was alone on the place at the time and, not feeling disposed
to let a pack of scrub cows grab what he had barely finished
rescuing from all the other pests in the country, he forted up behind
some baled hay with the family musket and ordered the Waymark
minions to begone.

The minions hadn't kept up with their reading sufficiently to
realize that they were supposed to slink away in baffled rage, so
they offered to spank him if he didn't take the gun straight indoors
and put it back where it belonged. One of them straddled the
orchard fence to illustrate how they would go at it, and Linus
tightened down and cut loose, intending to hit the post under his
hand as a final warning. The fore sight of the old gun had got
knocked out of line and, instead of jarring the post, he spread the
Waymark man across the top wire of the fence with a smashed
collarbone.

There was never any general agreement in the country over
which of the parties to the incident had been most to blame for it.
The homesteaders blamed old Waymark for running his cattle
around the neighborhood as if he owned it. The Waymark men
blamed their stricken co-worker for trying to walk down a gun in
the hands of a frightened youngster. Linus blamed the gun for not
shooting straight, Linus' father blamed Linus for pointing it at a
man he didn't intend to shoot, and several people blamed Linus'
father for keeping a firearm on the premises without making sure
the sights were lined up properly.

All the bestowals of blame were probably partly justified, but none of them could clear Linus of the responsibility for injuring a fellow man with a deadly weapon, and old Waymark played that fact for all there was in it. He worked up claims for doctors' bills, wages for the wounded man's lost time, physical suffering and mental anguish, and complaints against Linus for everything from juvenile delinquency to attempted manslaughter. In the end, Linus' father gave up, sold him the homestead relinquishment, and moved away.

The change was no particular misfortune, but Linus' mismanagement in bringing it on was something he never liked to be reminded of. The old gun that had done the shooting was so painful a momento that he stuck it back of a rafter in the homestead cabin, out of sight, and neither he nor Linus thought enough of it to get it down when they moved. They never mentioned the shooting afterward, and there was always a little strained note in their conversation with each other, because they so painstakingly avoided any subject that seemed likely to lead into it.

They both steered around handling the two herding rifles while they were packing up. After Linus had got them wrapped in some bedding and stowed quietly on one of the packs, his father went out and felt carefully over the horses to make sure where they were. It wasn't that he suspected Linus of having stolen them; he merely wanted to see that they hadn't been overlooked, and he preferred to hunt them out rather than open a subject which neither of them took anything but distrust and uneasiness in thinking back over.

Trailing the sheep was slow, but not troublesome. The cold kept them well bunched, and since there was not enough grass to tempt them to loiter, they moved along without needing any encouragement beyond a little rock throwing to keep them pointed right.

Old Ollivant dragged along behind with the pack horses, holding his eye bandage down against the wind with one hand and his reins, trail rope and saddle horn with the other.

Linus pulled into the homestead about an hour past sundown, and found Dee Radford waiting. Dee sat beside a fresh-banked pond, watching it fill up from the spring. He had turned the little quarter-inch trickle of water away from the sink back of the orchard where it disappeared into the ground, and he was storing it for the sheep to drink.

"We may have to ration it out, the way it's runnin'," he said. "We'll know about that after they've watered a couple of times. You notice I collected your strays."

There was probably not another man in the country who could have found those strays in that river canyon in the dark. Linus paid his respectful acknowledgements to the feat, and looked doubtful about the arrangements for conserving the water. The thing that came into his mind, in spite of him, was that the trees must have come to depend on the flow of water into the ground. They looked so wild and worthless, all broken and tangled and killed down by cattle and heavy snows and freezing, that he kept his thoughts to himself, for fear of sounding sentimental. He did remark that the trees belonged to somebody, and Dee took him up hard on that.

"You've got a patch of fruit trees that ain't worth anything, and a band of sheep that'll bring your old man ten thousand dollars if they stay alive," he said. "You've got an old orchard that nobody thinks enough of to prove up on, and you've got sheep that your old man has run himself alkali-blind over, besides the work you've put in on 'em yourself. I don't see how you can even argue about turnin' this water. I'd be ashamed to be that big a fool about any place I'd ever lived."

"I ain't any fool about this place," Linus said. "You may have to answer a claim for damages to these trees before you're through here, that's all. Don't think you'll be able to argue yourself out of it, either. There's harder outfits around here than you might think."

Old Ollivant drew up with the pack horses, and Dee searched his box-magazine rifle out from under the bedding and hung it ceremoniously on a fence post.

"If anybody shows up to be fought, he's mine," he said. "I don't notice any signs of heavy travel around here, so it ain't likely that anybody will. You don't need to look that far ahead for anything to worry about, anyhow. When you've stood a week or two of feedin' sheep on grass seed in these rocks, you'll wish you had a good quiet fight to rest up on. We'll make a herd camp here where we can take turns standin' guard over the bed ground, and we'll put the tent off yonder in the orchard where your father can be out of the wind.''

Old Ollivant didn't think much of that arrangement, insisting, with a stubbornness of conviction that turned out to be almost clairvoyant, that Linus would land in some trouble if he stood guard over the bed ground without somebody to stand guard over him. He gave in only when Dee, having pitched the tent in the cove, helped him down from his horse and led him into it, with instructions to stay there until his eyes felt better.

The ridge was not so abundantly supplied with either grass seed or water as it had looked to begin with. It had barely enough of both to keep the old ewes from bawling loud enough to be heard clear down to the road, and even that frugal measure of sustenance didn't last well.

Trouble started one evening when Linus brought the herd in by himself; Dee having gone down to the road to put up a flag for the shearing crew. Instead of bedding down quietly, the sheep milled, changed ground and collected in little bunches, blatting tunelessly and persistently. Linus was too tired to hear them, and Dee, getting back late, didn't discover till daylight that they had run short of water. Some animal—a skunk or a sage rat, by the signs—had burrowed into the ditch between the spring and the catch pond, and the entire night's supply had seeped out into the ground behind the orchard.

He patched up the break, but that was no immediate help. The ditch and pond basin had dried out so deep that getting them primed and getting the pond filled afterward took the entire day. The sheep waited and continued their blatting, and, to get out of listening to them, Linus went out and cut bundles of willow and wild-cherry sprouts as something for them to practice eating on, even though it couldn't be considered food.

Coming back through the high sagebrush behind the camp with his harvest of shrubbery, he heard men talking and Dee's voice rising in an argument which, to judge by the sound of horses moving restlessly, didn't seem to be commanding much attention. He dropped his brush and crept up behind the old homestead cabin for a look, knowing beforehand who the visitors were and what they had come for.

Old Waymark's bad-news committee hadn't changed its membership in the years that Linus had been away. There was old Waymark himself, undersized and savage-looking. Behind him was his foreman, a sandy-haired man with red eyes who kept fiddling with his rope; back of him were a couple of ordinary herders, and off to one side was old Slickear Cowan, who would have classed as an ordinary herder, except that he was the man whom Linus had rimmed with the shot heard round as much of the world as old Waymark could command a hearing from.

The injury hadn't damaged Slickear Cowan's vitality much. He carried a long jute woolsack on his saddle fork, and he kept working his horse sideways, getting, as if accidentally, between Dee and the post where he had hung his rifle. Linus' father was asleep in the tent, out of range of the conference, and Dee was so absorbed in handling the case for the defense that he didn't notice the maneuver being organized against his peace and dignity.

He proved that he was not stealing pasture, pointed out that, instead of damaging the homestead, he had kept it from falling apart, and touched on various phases of the land-title question with so much authority that old Waymark acted apologetic about being there at all. His sandy-haired foreman shook out a turn of his rope and looked thoughtful, Slickear Cowan gathered in his reins and sat forward in his saddle, and old Waymark studied the tent in the orchard as if half wondering whether there was anybody in it who ought to be invited to see the fun.

It was clear enough what they were up to. Dee Radford was about to be taken through the rural ceremony known as a sheepherder's sleigh ride. Slickear Cowan would make a run and snatch his rifle; when he turned to see what was up, the foreman would hang a rope on him and dump him. The woolsack would be yanked over him and tied shut, and he would be dragged behind a horse over the rugged countryside, with special attention to those portions of it that would bounce him highest.

That was the standard treatment for men who ran sheep on somebody else's land, and there was only one way to head it off. Linus tiptoed inside the old homestead cabin, noticing, with a little half-homesick feeling, that a worn-out pair of his own shoes were still on the kitchen floor where he had dropped them on leaving, and how woebegone they looked with the strings trailing loose and the dust heavy on them.

He had not been tall enough to reach the rafters the day his father hid the old rifle back of them. Now he put his hand up to it without even having to stretch. The rifle was dusty and the action was rusted shut, so it wouldn't work, but that didn't disturb him. He didn't intend to shoot, and it added something to his confidence to know that he couldn't, even if he felt tempted to. He tiptoed to the back door, kicked it open and stood in it with the rifle trained, in involuntary deference to the past, on the fork of Slickear Cowan's collarbone.

"Pull up that horse and drop them reins," he ordered. "Put your hands under your belt and take your feet out of the stirrups. Now move out of here, the whole bunch of you."

If he had appeared draped in a sheet and clanking a chain, he couldn't have quenched the delegation's high spirits more completely. Everybody stared, and nobody moved. Linus motioned Dee Radford toward the rifle on the post, and Dee roused himself, got it and backed off, still staring.

"Where in creation did you find that gun?" he asked. "You ain't robbed any Indian graves, have you?"

"It didn't come out of any Indian grave," Linus said. His voice, with the empty house backing it up, sounded so spooky that he hardly recognized it himself. "We left this gun here when we moved away, and I remembered where it was." He turned apologetically to old Waymark. "I don't want to shoot any of your men. All I want is for you to let us alone. We'll pay for any damage we've done here."

Old Waymark edged his horse sideways, picking up his spirits a little.

"You're that young Ollivant hoodlum that like to killed one of my men once before," he said, as if he expected Linus to deny it.

"You ought to have gone to jail then, and I'll see that you do go now. I bought this place from your father, and I want these men to witness that you've ordered me off of it at the point of a gun. You'll hear from it, you and your father both."

He picked up his reins, and Dee asked him to hold on a minute.

"There's a point or two about this trespass business," he said. "This boy has told me that his father moved out of here before he got this homestead proved up on. What you bought was his relinquishment, wasn't it?"

Old Waymark conceded that it was, and said that had nothing to do with the main issue. "One of my men went down and filed on it. You'll find that out plenty soon, if you've got any doubts about it."

"I've got a few," Dee said. "There's a residence requirement about homesteads, and your man ain't ever lived here. This boy's father left that gun in the house when he moved out, and it ain't been touched till now."

Old Waymark's whiskers pointed slightly astern again. It was not unusual for people in remote districts to be a little neglectful about residence on their homesteads. The fact that his man had followed the general custom was the main reason he had come there. There was nothing on the homestead worth squabbling over, and he wouldn't have cared how many sheep camped on it if his title had held a little closer to legal standards, but a counterentry on the place was worth going to some trouble to head off. He said an old gun being overlooked in some hiding place meant nothing, and picked up his reins again.

His men were all staring down into the orchard. The tent had come open, and Linus' father came slowly up from it, holding his bandage clear of one tortured eye, so he could see his way between the tangle of neglected old trees that he had set out to be a light and a beacon to horticultural expansion in the sagebrush. He drew up and fixed Linus with a glare that was all the more expressive because it was so obviously agonizing to him.

"This is the kind of high-handed thuggery you've sneaked in on me, is it?" he demanded. "You tore loose with a gun once, and got yourself in trouble till I had to sell out and leave here to get you

79

clear of it. A man would think that would have been enough to last you, but here you're back for more. You wait till I get my eyesight crippled, so I can't see what you're up to, and then you gallop straight back to the same place to do the same trick all over again. You promised me never to touch a gun unless I was around to watch you, and you know it. You know we ain't got any right to be here too. You know this old skunk bought this place off of me, and you've got no right to order him to leave it. Put that gun down."

Linus leaned the gun against the wall outside the door. The Waymark men watched thoughtfully as he stood back from it, and Slickear Cowan lifted his hands clear of his belt. Dee Radford advised him to avoid rashness, jiggled the safety catch on his rifle to indicate that he was serious and told Linus' father to cover his eyes from the light and show a little sense.

"You didn't sell anything to this outfit but your homestead rights," he said. "Nobody has ever used 'em, and we can prove it. This homestead is open to anybody that wants to live on it the legal time. This boy of yours has got a right to occupy it and he's got a right to use a gun on anybody that tries to run him off of it. He may intend to file a contest on it himself, how do you know?"

"It was on his account that I sold it to start with," old Ollivant said. He did cover his eyes from the light. "How would it look if he come back and took it away from the man I sold it to? It wouldn't be honest."

"You didn't sell his rights to it, because he was too young to have any," Dee said. "He's old enough now to file on any open land he wants to, and it ain't anybody else's business. It ain't even yours."

Old Waymark started to say something about principles, and Linus put in ahead of him, seeing that the argument was reaching a little too far into metaphysics to be practical.

"I don't want to file on any homestead and I wouldn't file on this one if I did," he said. "I've put in too much time in one neighborhood already, and I don't aim to do any more of it."

That was a sentiment that Dee Radford had done a good deal of arguing in favor of, and yet he seemed disappointed.

"I'll be blamed if I'll see this place go back to this outfit, after the way they've acted," he said. "I'll file on it myself, if I have to. I want you men to take notice that there's a contest to be entered on this claim and you can keep off of it till the law settles it. Now move, before I shoot up a few of your horses for you." He watched them until they were a little distance away, and then turned to Linus. "Pick up that old pacifier of yours and touch it off somewhere over their heads. I'd like to hear what it sounds like, and I'd like to see how they take it."

"It won't touch off," Linus said, feeling a little foolish over having to admit it. "The breech is rusted shut. I didn't bring it out to shoot with. Them men was about to drag you in a sack, and all I wanted was to head 'em off till you could get clear of 'em. It come out all right."

Linus' father pulled his bandage clear of one eye, looked the old gun over and tried unsuccessfully to budge the hammer. He put it down again and looked at Linus. The light and wind must have been agony to him, and yet he didn't appear conscious of any particular pain.

"It did come out all right," he said. "Not but what it took a blamed long time to it. I've distrusted you all these years, and the Lord knows how much longer I'd have kept on at it if you'd got a hold of a gun that would shoot. You've turned out dependable in spite of me, it looks like. If you've got a mind to take this homestead for yourself, I've got no right to forbid you. It used to be a sightly place, when it was kept in shape."

"I don't want it," Linus said. "There never was anything to it except that patch of orchard, and the trees is all killed out. I whittled into some of 'em, and they're as dry as a wagon spoke."

"Not any more," his father said. "That was what I started up here to tell you, and then I heard them men. There's been a funny kind of a noise outside that tent ever since the sheep blat let up. It got so loud I couldn't rest, so I went out to see what it was. It was bees. Them old fruit trees has all come into bloom. You didn't waste all the work you put into 'em, after all."

"I wouldn't call it wasted, even if them trees all dried up and fell down," Dee Radford said. "If you hadn't recognized them men and remembered about that old rifle, we'd have lost them sheep sure. It would have been the first herd of sheep I ever lost in my life, and I wouldn't want that on my record.''

The breaking up of that drought was not especially beautiful in itself, but it ended the long monotony of dust and dry wind and cold sun, and its contrasting mildness and silence made it seem one of the most beautiful things imaginable. A night rain laid the dust, the sky clouded over, the air was so still that the sheep shearers didn't even bother to anchor their burlap corral panels down, and the sheep, having come through their pasturing season, turned from a care and a burden into a salable asset that strange workmen labored over and strange buyers bid for and strange feed yards were almost embarrassingly gratified to advance wagonloads of hay on.

Dee Radford knelt outside the old herding tent, packing up to leave the sheep he had half killed himself to save from the buzzards. That was an old ceremony for him, and he took it tranquilly. Linus couldn't feel quite so lighthearted about it. He detested sheep, but there seemed something unnatural about working so hard over something that had to be given up afterward, with nothing left to show where his work had gone. There were wages, but they were the same for bad work as for good.

He walked down into the orchard, thinking about that, and saw, in the scrubby tangle of old trees in bloom, something he had worked hard on that had not disappeared afterward, but had lived and developed courage to bring forth its clumps of perfect flowers, pink apricot and apple, green-white plum and white pear and cherry, through all the tangle of dead and broken and mutilated limbs that showed how hard it had been to live at all. That much of his work had not been wasted, since it had helped to bring into life a courage and patience and doggedness in putting forth such delicate beauty against all the hostility of nature and against even the imminence of death.

Linus' father was sitting under one of the trees with his bandage lifted from one eye, and Linus sat down beside him. "I've decided to try this old homestead for a while," he said. "It's—"

He didn't bother to finish.

His father nodded. "I know how you feel," he said. "I know how it feels to have something you've raised turn out better than you expected."   July 29, 1939

Ivan Doig

Flip

LET me call her Ruth here.

She came to the ranch on one of the first pale chilly days of an autumn, hired to cook for us for a few months, and stayed on in our lives for almost three years. Her time with us is a strange season all mist and dusk and half-seen silhouettes, half-heard cries. There is nothing else like it in the sortings of my memory. Nor is there anything now to be learned about why it happened to be her who became my father's second wife and my second mother, for no trace of Ruth—reminiscence, written line, photograph, keepsake—has survived. It is as if my father tried to scour every sign of her from our lives.

But not even scouring can get at the deepest crevices of memory, and in them I glimpse Ruth again. I see best the eyes, large and softly brown with what seemed to be some hurt beginning to happen behind them—the deep trapped look of a doe the instant before she breaks for cover. The face was too oval, plain as a small white platter, but those madonna eyes graced it. Dark-haired—I think brunette. Slim but full breasted. And taller than my mother had been, nearly as tall as Dad. A voice with the grit of experience in it, and a knowing laugh twice as old as herself.

Not quite entirely pretty then, this taut, guarded Ruth, but close enough to earn second looks. And the mystery in her could not be missed, the feeling that being around her somehow was like watching the roulette wheel in the Maverick make its slow, fanlike ambush on chance.

Even how Ruth came to be there, straight in our path after Dad turned our lives toward the valley, seems to have no logic to it. Never before or since did I see anyone quite like her on a ranch. Ranch cooks generally were stout spinsters or leathery widows, worn dour and curt by a life which gave them only the chore of putting meals on the table for a dozen hungry men three times a day. So alike were cooks usually that the hired men seldom bothered to learn their names, simply called each one *Missus*.

But Ruth didn't fit Missus, she was Ruth to everybody. Those eyes were the kind which caught your glance on the streets of Great Falls or Helena, where young women went to escape to a store job and the start toward marriage and a life they hoped would be bigger than the hometown had offered—city eyes, restless eyes. Yet here Ruth was in the valley, passing the syrup pitcher along the cookhouse table, and for all anyone could tell, she seemed ready to stay until she came upon whatever she was looking for.

Her first reach had been badly out of aim—a marriage, quickly broken, to a young soldier. *He was home on a furlough one time*, a voice from his family tells it, *and met her and married her in such short time; really they weren't even acquainted.* Dad must have known about that jagged, too-quick marriage; the valley kept no such secrets. But living womanless had left us wide open for Ruth. To me, an eight-year-old, she was someone who might provide some mothering again. Not *much* mothering, because she kept a tight, careful mood, like a cat ghosting through new tall grass. But the purr of a clever voice, fresh cookies and fruit added to my lunchbox, even a rare open grin from her when I found an excuse to loiter in the kitchen—all were pettings I hadn't had. And for Dad, Ruth must have come as a sudden chance to block the past, a woman to put between him and the death on the summer mountain.

It happened faster than any of us could follow. This man who had spent six careful years courting my mother now abruptly married his young ranch cook.

Ruth, Dad. They were a pairing only the loins could have tugged together, and as with many decisions taken between the thighs, all too soon there were bitterest after-thoughts.

I remember that the drumfire of regret and retaliation began to echo between them before we moved from the ranch in early 1948, only months after the wedding. The ranch itself had plenty of ways to nick away at everyone's nerves. Any sprinkle of rain or snow puttied its mile of road into a slick gumbo, the pickup wallowing and whipping as Dad cussed his way back and forth. Yet the place also was too dry for good hay or grain, and too scabbed with rock up on the slopes where the cattle and sheep had to graze. Dad had begun to call it *this-goddamn-rockpile*, the surest sign that he was talking himself into dropping the lease. For her part, Ruth likely was ready to leave after the first night of howling coyotes, or of a cougar edging out of the Castles to scream down a gulch. Working as a cook on the big ranches out in the open expanse of the valley was one thing, but slogging away here under the tumbled foothills was entirely another. Ruth's mouth could fire words those soft eyes seemed to know nothing about, and the ranch primed her often. I can hear her across the years:

Charlie, I don't have to stay here, I didn't marry this hellforsaken ranch . . . I got other places I can go, don't you doubt it. . . . Lots of places, Charlie.

And Dad, the jut notching out his jaw as it always did when he came ready for argument: *Damn it, woman, d'ye think we can walk away from a herd of cattle and a band of sheep? We got to stay until we get the livestock disposed of. You knew what you were getting into . . .* And always at the last, as he would hurl from the house out to another of the ranch's endless chores: *Will-ye-forget-it? Just-forget-it?*

But nothing was forgotten, by either of them. Instead, they

stored matters up against one another. *The time that you . . . I told you then . . .* There came to be a full litany of combat, and either one would refer as far back as could be remembered.

If they had fought steadily the marriage might have snapped apart before long and neither would have been severely hurt. But they bickered in quick seasons. Weeks, maybe a month, might pass in calm. Saturday nights, we went to dances in the little town of Ringling. Dad and Ruth whirled there by the hour. Often my Uncle Angus called the square dances, and I would watch Dad in a circle of flying dances while a burring voice so close to his cried: *Swing your opposite across the hall, now swing your corners, now your partners, and promenade all!* Sometime after midnight, I would stretch on a bench along the dancehall wall with a coat over me and go to sleep. I would wake up leaning against Ruth's shoulder as the pickup growled down the low hill to the ranch buildings. The murmurs I heard then between Dad and Ruth would go on for a day or two. But eventually, a blast of argument, then no talking, sulking. Sometimes Ruth would leave for a day or two. Sometimes Dad *told* her to leave, and she wouldn't. At last, one or the other would make a truce—never by apology, just some softened oblique sentence which meant that the argument could be dropped now. Until Ruth felt restless again; until Dad's unease twisted in him once more.

I watched this slow bleed of a marriage, not yet old enough to be afraid of exactly what might happen but with the feeling creeping in me that the arguments in our house meant more than I could see. Joking with me as she sometimes did, Ruth would grin and her face come down close to mine: *If your hair gets any redder, you're gonna set the town on fire, you know that?* Dad talked in his usual soft burr when I rode in the pickup with him: *Son, let's go fix that fence where Rankin's cows got in. There's not enough grass on this place for our own without that honyocker's cows in here, too. Hold on, I'm gonna give her snoose to get up this sidehill . . .* But when they were together, I so often heard a hard edge in what they said to each other, a careful evenness as they talked over plans to leave the ranch as soon they could.

For what was happening, I can grasp now, was the misjudgment greater by far than their decision to be married: their mutual refusal to call it off. Each had a fear blockading that logical retreat. Dad would not admit his mistake because he wanted not to look a fool to the valley. On that he was entirely wrong; the only mystification anyone seemed to have was why he kept on with a hopeless mismatch. *I couldn't see that, going on with that marriage, with that little child you in the midst of it,* a woman of the valley once cried to me. *Ruth thought every thing should come in a cloud for her. But she had hate in her, she was full of hatefulness . . . What was Charlie thinking of to let that go on?* For her part, Ruth would not face up to another split, would not let another broken marriage point to her as an impossible wife. Since neither could see how to call a halt to the mismarriage, it somehow was going to have to halt itself. But before it did, the pair of them would make two mighty exertions to stay together.

Perhaps because this arrival of Ruth in our lives is a riffle of time which everyone around me later tried to put from mind, memory hovers stubbornly here. Memory, or the curious nature, perhaps, that keeps asking exactly what the commotion was about. For on the edge of this fray between Dad and Ruth I began to see myself, and here at the age of eight and nine and ten I was curiosity itself. If I inscribe myself freehand, as Dad did with the unfading stories he told me of his own young years, the words might be these: *I was a boy I would scarcely know on the street today. Chunky, red-haired, freckled—the plump face straight off a jar of strawberry jam. Always wearing a small cowboy hat, because I seared in the sun. Under that hat, and inside a name like no one else's. Ivan: EYE-vun, amid the Frankie-Ronny-Bobby-Jimmy-Larry-Howie trill of my schoolmates. Dad was amazed with himself when he at last discovered that he had spliced Russian onto the Scottish family name; he and my mother simply had known someone named Ivan and liked the sudden soft curl of the word—and besides wanted to show up Dad's least favorite brother, who had recently daubed 'Junior' onto a son.*

The name, together with the hair and freckles, gave me attention I wasn't always sure I wanted. At Dad's side in the saloons I sometimes met men who would look down at me and sing out: 'Now the heroes were plenty and well known to fame/Who fought in the ranks of the Czar/But the bravest of all was a man by the name/Of Ivan . . . Skavinsky . . . Skavar!' I consoled myself that it was better than being dubbed Red or Pinky, which I also heard sometimes in the saloons. And once in a great while, in his thoughtful mood as if remembering a matter far away, Dad would call me 'Skavinsky.' It made a special moment, and I prized it that way.

People who remember me at this age say I was something of a small sentinel: 'You always were such a little sobersides.' 'You was always so damned bashful it was hard to get a word out of you.' All right, but how jolly was I supposed to be, with a mother dead and the next one in a sniping match with my father? I believe that much of what was taken to be my soberness was simply a feeling of being on guard, of carefully watching life flame around me. Of trying not to be surprised at whatever else might happen.

I can tell you a time, as my father storied so many of his into me: Dad and Ruth and I are walking toward the movie house, on some night of truce in the family. We are at the end of the block from the building when I notice Kirkwood coming down the street. Kirkwood is a school classmate, but a forehead taller than I am, and with that head round as a cannonball and atop square shoulders you could lay bricks on. Kirkwood can never be counted on to behave the same from one minute to the next, and now he bears down on us, yelps 'Hullo, Ivy!' and takes a swipe at my hat.

The worst prospect I can think of is coming true: the great given rule of boyhood is not to make you look silly in front of your grownups, and Kirkwood is toe-dancing all over it. Now he has put on a hyena grin and falls in step with me. He glances toward Dad and Ruth, then skips at me and knocks the hat from my head.

'Kirkwood-I'll-murder-you!' I rasp as lethally as I can and clap the hat down over my ears. It sends his delirium up another notch, and he skips in for another whack at the hat. Dad and Ruth no longer can pretend not to notice and begin to glance back at the sniggering and muttering behind them.

Kirkwood giggles; this time when I hear him scuffling close, I swing around with my right arm stiff in what I now understand was a right jab. Kirkwood runs his round jaw into it and bounces flat onto the sidewalk. He wobbles up, looks at me dazedly, then trots off in a steady howl. I hustle toward the movie house where Dad and Ruth are waiting and watching. Both are grinning as if they have mouths full of marshmallows.

But I was less sure of my feelings. It was as if I had been through a dream that I knew was going to happen. Not in every detail—who could foresee even Kirkwood gone that batty?—but in its conclusion: that from the instant Kirkwood rambled into sight, he was aimed onto my fist. It somehow seemed to me there ought to be an apprehension about such certainty, some questioning of why it had to be inexorably so. But it was a questioning I could not handle, and what I felt most was the curious intensity of having seen it all unfold, myself somehow amid the scene as it swept past me. Somehow a pair of me, the one doing and the one seeing it done.

It was exactly that twinned mix—apprehension and interestedness—that I felt all during Ruth's startling time in our lives.

Now the awaited move, when we at least would put the ranch and its zone of combat behind us. Put them behind us, in fact, in a way as wondrous to me as it was unexpected, for Dad and Ruth faced toward White Sulphur Springs and undertook the last livelihood anyone could have predicted of either of them: they went into the cafe business.

The Grill, across the street from the Stockman, had come up for rent. It was the third and smallest eating place in a town which had not quite enough trade for two. There was the barest smidgin of reason to think of Ruth coping with such an enterprise; with her years of cooking for crews, she at least could handle a kitchen. But for Dad, the notion had all the logic of a bosun's mate stumping ashore to open up a candy shop. Yet somehow Dad and Ruth, this pair who had never been around a town business of any sort and who already were finding out that they flinted sparks off each other all too easily—somehow they talked one another into trying to run the Grill together, and somehow they turned out to have a knack for it.

The knack, of course, was nine-tenths hard work. *Those two took on that place like a house afire.* But when Dad sorted through his savvy, there was use there, too. From all the ranches behind him, he knew enough about purchasing provisions, and better yet, he knew the valley and its people. He put up new hours for the Grill. It would stay open until after the last saloon had closed.

There at the last of the night and the first hours of morning, the Grill found its customers: truckers on their runs through the pitchy dark, ranchers heading home from late business in Helena or Great Falls, some of the Rainbow crowd trying to sober up on black coffee and T-bone. Steaks and hashbrowns covered Ruth's stove, and Dad dealt platters of food until his arms ached. Saturday nights I was allowed to stay up as late as I wanted—on Dad's principle of fathering, that I might as well have a look at life sooner than later—and I looked forward to the pace of that last night of the week like a long, long parade coming past.

Just at dusk, ranch hands would begin to troop in for supper, minutes-old haircuts shining between their shirt collars and hat brims, because *Well, I gotta go in and get my ears lowered* was the standard excuse to come to town for a night of carousing. As the dark eased down and the war-whoops from the crowds in the Maverick and the Grand Central came oftener, the cafe would begin to receive the staggerers who had decided to forget the haircut after all and get right on with the drinking. They were a pie crowd, usually jabbing blearily at the fluffiest and most meringue-heaped possibilities in the countertop case. Sometime in mid-evening, Lloyd Robinson would arrive, suspiciously fingering down a coin for a cup of coffee and demanding to know if my freckles weren't from a cow's tail having swiped across me. Soon after him, as if the town's two prime bellies couldn't be long apart, it would be Nellie crashing in, chortling with delight and spinning a joke off the first item he spotted: *That jam jar, now—did you hear about the Swede at the breakfast table?* 'Yiminey,' he says, 'I yoost learn to call it yam and now they tell me it's yelly.'

Then if there was a dance in the hall behind the Rainbow, the night would crest with two tides of customers: one which filled the cafe as soon as the dance ended, and a second made up of those who had gone off to drink some more until the first wave cleared out. And at last, sometime after two in the morning, would come the phone call from Pete McCabe thirty yards across at the

Stockman: *Save us three, Charlie.* Dad would put aside a trio of T-bone steaks, and before long, Pete and his night's pair of bar help would be straddling in to the counter and trading the night's news with Dad. A few hours before Sunday dawn, the Grill would close and we would step out the door into the emptied town.

A quieter flow of eaters presented themselves too, I was to notice—the town's oldtimers, the pensioners, the sheep-herders and cowpokes hanging on from yesteryear. As I have told, the Stockman, where Pete McCabe was known to be the kind of a fellow who would set up a drink even when the pension check hadn't yet come to pay for it, drew most of these oldtimers, some-time in the night, sometime through the week. Now, over across the street, Dad was good for an emergency meal as well. How many times I heard one or another of them, joking so as not to seem begging, ask Dad for a meal *on account*— on account, that was, of being broke. Weeks and months and even years afterward, one or another of them might stop him on the street and say, *Charlie, here's that Grill money I've been owing you.*

Ruth, I think, never objected to those meals Dad would jot on the tab. They might fight over a spilled holder of toothpicks, but not that long apologetic rank of "accountants." Out on the valley ranches, she had seen in the crews clopping to her supper table the men who were growing too old for the work they had done all their lives, and soon too old for anything but those lame rounds of the saloons along Main Street.

Age was making that same wintry push on the one person Ruth seemed steadily to hold affection for, too. She had been raised by her grandmother—her family so poor and at war with itself it had shunted her off there—and regularly she went across the Big Belts to the next valley to see the old woman. Several times, on an after-noon off from the cafe, she took me on those visits.

Creased and heavy, stiff in the knees and going blind, the grand-mother was the most ancient woman I had ever seen, and her house the shadowiest and most silent. The grandmother spent her days entirely in the dim kitchen, finding her way by habit through a thickening haze of cataract webs. When we stepped in past the black kitchen stove and the drab cabinets lining the walls, the grandmother would peer toward us and then begin to talk in a resigned murmur, eyes and legs giving way above and below a body not yet quite willing to die, and Ruth, listening, would be a different person, softer, younger, seeming to feel the grandmother's aches as her own.

But whatever Ruth took from those visits seemed to stop at our own doorsill. Time and again, she and Dad faced off, and then they would go full of silence for a day or more. Or worse, one would be silent and the other would claw on and on.

If nothing else set them at each other, there always was the argument about our small herd of cattle, which Dad had kept after all when we left the ranch and which he was pasturing now in the foothills of the Big Belts. He drove out each morning to pitch hay to the cattle, then came back to work in the cafe from mid-afternoon until closing. On weekends, I went with him to the cattle, and only then would hear out of him the few tiny snatches of music he knew, his absentminded sign of contentment. A forkful of alfalfa to the cows, then *But the squaws* ALONG *the Yu* KON . . . . *are-good-enough-for-me*; a tuneless minute of whistling and looking out across the valley to the pinnacles of the Castles, then *When it's SPRINGtime in the ROCKies . . .*

Whether or not Ruth knew he was out there singing and whistling amid the cows, she did suspect that Dad had not given up intentions of ranching. Dad suspected, just as rightly, that neither of them could keep up the day-and-night pace of the cafe work for long, and that our income soon was going to have to come from livestock again.

In the meantime, we had become town people, and I had the time to myself to roam White Sulphur. Once, in one of the off-balance tributes I would get used to in the valley, someone beside Dad in a saloon caught me studying up at him and blurted: *That kid is smarter than he knows what to do with.* Which was right enough, and yet I did know enough to keep my eyes moving through the town, reading whatever of it showed itself. The rememberings from that have lasted as a kind of casing which goes into place over the earlier odyssey with Dad through the saloons, a second and wider circle across undefined territory, and this time on my own.

The plainest fact I found, so plain that it seemed to me then it never could change, was that White Sulphur totally lived on livestock. All the places I liked best had the sounds and smells and feels which came one way or another from the herds and flocks out on the leathered slopes of grassland. In the creamery where Dad bought milk and butter for the cafe, the air hung so heavy with the dampness of processing that it was like walking against pillows, and everyone talked loudly out of the sides of their mouths to be heard over the rumble of churns. Nearby, the grain elevator took a noise like that and tripled it, the roaring clank of conveyors carrying off wheat and barley and oats somewhere into the high box of tower. At the railroad shipping pens, the noises came directly from the livestock. In their best of times sheep go through life in a near-panic, and their frenzied bleating as they were wrangled up to the chutes into boxcars grew to a storm of sound. And the cattle, when they were pastured near the pens a day or so before shipping could be heard all across town—a constant choir of moaning, like wind haunting into ten thousand chimneys at once.

White Sulphur was as unlovely but interesting as the sounds of its livelihood. A teacher who had arrived just then to his first classroom job would remember to me: *The town didn't look too perky. It had been through the Depression and a world war, and obviously nobody had built anything or painted anything or cleaned anything for twenty years.*

Sited where the northern edge of the valley began to rumple into low hills—by an early-day entrepreneur who dreamed of getting rich from the puddles of mineral water bubbling there, and didn't—White Sulphur somehow had stretched itself awkwardly along the design of a very wide T. Main Street, the top of the T, ran east and west, with most of the town's houses banked up the low hills on either side of the business area at its eastern end. To the west lay the sulphur slough, the railroad and shipping pens, and the creamery and grain elevator. The highway, in its zipper-straight run up the valley, snapped in there like the leg of the T onto Main Street. Much of the countryside traffic, then, was aimed to this west end of town, while all the saloons and grocery stores and cafes—and the post office and the druggist and the doctor and the two lawyers, since it took two to fight out a court case—did business at the east end.

This gave White Sulphur an odd, strung-out pattern of life, as if the parts of the community had been pinned along a clothesline. But it also meant there was an openness to the town, plenty of space to see on to the next thing which might interest you. Even the school helped with this sense of open curiosity, because it had been built down near the leg of the T where two of the town's main attractions for a boy also had ended up—the county jail, and the sulphur slough.

Since the nine saloons downtown fueled a steady traffic of drunks, the jail was kept busy, and most schooldays we had a fine clear view of the ritual there. It was only a few dozen yards from the diamond where we played work-up softball to where the brick jail building perched atop a small embankment. Just in from the edge of this embankment, a wire clothesline had been looped between two fat posts. Right there, the prisoners often had a morning recess at the same time as ours. They were sent out to pin their bedding on the clothesline and beat some cleanliness into it—and, I suppose, to huff some of the alcohol out of themselves. Sheepherders who had come in from the mountains for their annual binge, the regular winos from the Grand Central who were tossed in jail every few months to dry out, once in a while a skinny scuffed-up cowboy from one of the Rankin ranches—there they would be, on the enbankment before us like performers on a stage.

Most of the men I could recognize from my nights downtown with Dad. But one morning a single inmate came out, a slender man I didn't know but whose face I seemed to have seen before. The softball game stopped as we all puzzled at that strange familiar face. The instant before any of us figured it out, one of my classmates rushed to get his words into the air first: *Hey, that's my dad!* His face the replica of the man's, he looked pleadingly from one to another of us. Desperation knowing only bravado to call on, one more time he cried it - *That's my dad!* - before we faced around, shame fixed in the air, toward the next batter.

At the bottom of the slope from the school grounds, as if it had seeped down from the overflow off the prisoners' bedding, lay the sulphur slough which gave White Sulphur its name. On cold days, the slough steamed and steamed, thin fog puffs wisping up from the reeds, as if this was where the entire valley breathed. Any weather, the water stewed out an odor like rotten eggs. At the slough edge nearest the school stood a tiny gazebo, a rickety scrap from the town days when it had tried to be a resort. Either as decoration or a roof against bird droppings, the gazebo sheltered a small hot spring. A corroding cup hung on one pillar of the gazebo, and if you dared to touch it, then you could dare the taste of the sulphur spring water.

One of my classmates—of course, Kirkwood—downed the water as if it were free lemonade. His grandfather, a nasty-faced character who indeed gave every sign that he might live forever, had convinced him that the stuff was a positive elixir for a person's insides. After Kirkwood had slurped down a cupful, I would reluctantly sip away. What bothered me even worse than the taste was the rancid look of the spring. The sulphur water had layered its minerals into a kind of putty on stones and clay and even the underwater strands of grass, and the spring always was coated with this sickly whitish curd, as if something poisonous had just died there. And yet, nowhere else had anything like this steaming place, and so the slough and its baleful water drew us.

White Sulphur had other lures I thought must be the only ones of their kind in the universe—the giant carcasses of buildings to be poked into. Late in the last century, when the town had figured it might grow, a few grandoise buildings had been put up, and they had not yet fallen down entirely. Near the sulphur slough stood the remains of the Springs Hotel, a long box of gingerbread-work and verandas which had been built for resort-goers who came to take the waters. I seem to remember that whatever was left of this building was so treacherous none of us would go out on its floor more than a few feet from the wall; you could fall through the sagging floorboards to some black awfulness below. Another awfulness clung to the Springs Hotel's past. The story was that someone had been killed diving into its swimming pool, that White Sulphur dwindled away from being a resort after that. The public death of that diver was epitaphed in the hotel's blind gape of windows and the broken spine of ridgepole. A boy stepped uneasily here, and stepped away not quite knowing what it was that brought him back and back.

Across town loomed a huger wreck, cheerier and much more inviting. This one was called the Old Auditorium—a sharp comedown from its original name, the Temple of Fun. It had been built in the 1890's by an earnest group of local businessmen—a magazine writer who happened through town described the type as *exerting every nerve to prosper*—who totally misjudged the town's need for a structure of that size. Probably there never had been enough people in the entire county to fill the place, even if they all had been herded in at gunpoint for culture's sake.

Built of brick, with a shingled dome rising from the middle of the roof like a howdah on the back of a great red elephant, and a forest of chimneys teetering unevenly around the edge, the temple had never been finished by its exhausted backers, although it was complete enough to use for school recitals and graduation ceremonies by the time the 1925 earthquake shook it onto the condemned list. A dozing dinosaur of a building, it had been collapsing little by little ever since the earthquake. Now the remains stood over us, roofless, ghostlike, magical as a wizard's abandoned castle.

I think it must have been not only the size and gape of the place, but the glacial spill of red brick that attracted me. Oddly, since in the early days White Sulphur had its own brickyard and a number of substantial buildings besides the Temple of Fun had been put up, the town had come through the years into a clapboard, take-it-or-leave-it appearance which made brick-built respectability seem very rare. And here was the largest stack of the reddest brick I could imagine. I could prowl in—windows and doors had vanished long since—and amid the clattering emptiness walk the old stage, study out from the dilapidated walls where rooms had been. Echoes flew back to me as if the auditorium had stored all the sounds from its prime years. It stood as a kind of cavern of history for a few of us, a place where you could go off into an expanse of both space and time.

One other large brick building graced White Sulphur, and if the old auditorium was a cave to be sought out, this next was a man-made mass you could not avoid. You came to it—the Sherman Hotel—as you walked up Main Street: three massive stories of brick and cornicework snouting out into the thoroughfare as firmly as a thumb crimping into a hose.

At the very start of White Sulphur's history there had been a dispute about where Main Street ought to run. The doctor who held the land at the west end of town banked too heavily on the notion that some judicious slough drainage and timber roadbedding would draw the route along his holdings. A rival laid out a plat to the east of him, complete with a 25-foot jog away from the direction of the slough and directly out into the path mapped out for Main Street. In some wink of confusion or bribery, the rival survey was accepted by the authorities, the town grew up along the misjointed plat lines, and for the next sixty years, the big brick hotel built at the boundary of the muddle squatted halfway into Main Street.

In the hotel lobby, a wide high window had been installed near the outer edge of this prowlike jut to take advantage of the outlook. Sitting there in a leather chair you could watch the cars come, straight as fence wire, until suddenly they had to angle off. Old men hobbled into the hotel to lobby-sit the afternoon hours away and watch the cars do their surprised swerve around them. It made a pastime, and the town didn't have many.

For some reason I can't summon back, once in those years Dad and I checked into the Sherman Hotel for a night. The room was worse than we had expected, and worse even than the hotel's run-down reputation. A bare lightbulb dangled over a battered bed; I think there was not even a dresser, nightstand, or chair. The bedsprings howled with rust. Sometime in the skreeking night, Dad said: *Call this rattletrap a hotel, do they? I've slept better in wet sagebrush.*

And yet, dismal as it was, the cumbersome hotel did some duty for the town. The teacher arriving to his job stepped from the bus there and went in to ask the clerk if there were lockers for his baggage for a day or two. *Just throw it there in the corner,* he was told. *But I'd like to lock it away, everything I own is in there. . . .* The clerk looked at him squarely for the first time: *Just throw it in the corner there, I said.* When the teacher came back in a day or so, all was in the corner, untouched.

One last landmark from those years, the gray stone house called the Castle. It speared up from the top of the hill behind the Stockman, a granite presence which seemed to have loomed there before the rest of the town was ever dreamed of. Actually, a man named Sherman had built it in the early 1890's, with bonanza money from a silver lode in the Castle Mountains. He had the granite blocks cut and sledded in by ox team from the mountains, and from a little distance, the three-story mansion with its round tower and sharp roof peaks looked like one of the sets of fantasy pinnacles which poke up all through that range. So in name and material and appearance, all three, old Sherman built for himself an eerie likeness of the Castles which had yielded up his fortune.

If the outside was a remindful whim, the inside of the Castle showed Sherman's new money doing some prancing. It was said he had spared nothing in expense—woodwork crafted of hardwoods from distant countries, crystal dangles on every chandelier, a huge water tank in the attic which sluiced water down to fill the bathtubs in an instant, a furnace which burned hard hot anthracite coal shipped all the way from Pennsylvania. All this was known only by rumor as I would circle past, because Sherman had been in his grave for twenty years and the Castle now stood with boards across its windows and swallows' mud nests clotted onto the fancy stonework.

Those were the relic faces of White Sulphur, the fading profiles of what the town had set out to be. Other features presented themselves to me, too, off the faces of the thousand people who lived in White Sulphur then, and a second thousand dotted out on the ranches from one far end of the county to another. Of all those twenty hundred living faces, the one clearest ever since has been our madman's.

What had torn apart Hendrik's brain—defect of birth, some stab of illness or accident—I have never known. But he hung everlastingly there at the edge of town life, gaping and leering. His parents, old and made older by the calamity which had ripped their son's mind, would bring Hendrik to town with them when they came for groceries. Slouched in their pickup or against the corner of the grocery, Hendrik grimaced out at us like a tethered dog whose mood a person could never be entirely sure of.

He was able to recognize friends of the family, such as Dad, and make child's talk to them—innocent words growled out of a strongman's body. And somewhere in the odds and ends of his mind he had come up with the certain way to draw people to him. He would gargle out loudly what could have been either plea or threat: *YOU god uh CIGuhREDD?*

No one would deny this pitiful spectre a cigarette, and Hendrik would puff away with a twisted squint of satisfaction, his eyes already glowering along the street for his next donor. Dad, who was uneasy around any affliction but was fond of Hendrik's family, always lit the cigarette carefully and said a few words, while I peeked up at the rough man. If he happened to look down at me, it was like being watched by the hot eye of a hawk. All through this time, I can pick out again and again that scene of poor clever lunatic Hendrik, and a town uneasy under his glare.

In that time I puzzled up into three other faces which were strange to me—the black faces of Rose Gordon, Taylor Gordon, and Bob Gordon. The Gordons, I know now, were one of the earliest and most diligent families of White Sulphur. The parents of Rose and Taylor and Bob had come in during the town's short heyday of mining wealth, and Mother Gordon had become the town's laundress: *Momma's back-yard looked like a four-mast schooner comin' in.* But to me, the three Gordons could have been newly set down from the farthest end of the world, where people were the color of night. They were very black—Rose in particular had a sheen dark as ink. Their faces were unlined, not crinkled at the corners of the eyes as Dad's and the other ranch men's were. And their voices chimed amid the burrs and twangs of everyone else downtown.

Taylor Gordon was a singer. Every so often he would perform at the high school auditorium, singing the spirituals he had heard from his mother as she worked at her wash tubs. His tenor voice could ripple like muscle, hold like a hawser across the notes: *Swiiing low, sweet chaaaariot. . . .* The strong, sweet sound had carried him to New York, where he sang in concert halls and on the radio and had been declared by a national magazine as "the latest rival to Paul Robeson." He also had gone through money as if he were tossing confetti into the streets of Harlem, and when the Depression hit, he promptly ended up back in the valley herding sheep.

But he brought with him New York stories such as no one in the valley had ever heard or dreamed of. Of his writer friend Carl Van Vechten: *He was a big Dutchman, he had very buck teeth, rabbit teeth like, and weighed about two hundred pounds, let's say, and was six feet tall. But he wasn't what they called a potbellied six. . . . He liked sometimes to wear a phantom red shirt, reddest red I ever saw. He wore rings, y'know, exotic rings, something that would stand out, or a bracelet, somethin' like that. Bein' a millionaire he could do those things. I remember one night we went to a party. Carl and I was dressed as in Harlem, dressed in kind of satire. Some man gave both of us sam hill. He said, 'You got somethin' to offer the world. You don't have to do anything out of the ordinary, just be yourselves.' Carl laughed and said, 'Well, can't we have a little FUN?'* Of a black man who Taylor said had a magic with words and deeds: *When everybody was broke, a lot of people would go to Father Divine and get the best meal in the world for thirty-five cents, see. And you'd be surprised—white, black, blue, green and the other, they'd eat in Father Divine's because you could get a meal you couldn't pay two dollars for downtown for thirty-five cents, including ice cream dessert. And he had 'em lined up, you'd thought a baseball game was goin' on.* Of how people in Harlem could tell where a man was from just by the scar on his face: *By the brand that was on him, y'see. They could tell where he'd been in a fight. If you were shootin' craps, you more or less would be bendin' down when you got cut and that way you'd get it across the forehead here. Whereas if you were playin' poker, you were more apt to be settin' up, then you'd be apt to get this one here across the cheek. Then if you were playin' what they called 'skin,' why you'd apt to get this other. So y'see, if a fella was cut here, he was from Greechyland, if he was cut this other way he was from Selma, Alabama, and so on and so on.*

Now, either Taylor or Bob owned the building the post office was in, and the pair of them lived on the second floor. Taylor came and went in a bold erect style, always with some new plan for singing in New York again or making a fortune from some gadget he had invented. He also took pride in being the one writing man the valley had ever had. Taylor was a talented storyteller—it was as if his voice put a rich gloss on anything it touched—and while he had been in New York singing at society parties, white writers such as Van Vechten urged him to make a manuscript of his stories of early-day White Sulphur. They steered him to a publisher and illustrator, and shepherded his guesswork grammar into print as a memoir with the title *Born to Be.*

The book with his name on it naturally impressed Taylor into thinking he could do another. This time there was no help, and no publisher. The failure worked on his mind for years; eventually he saw conspirators. The man who published his first book had become John Steinbeck's publisher as well, and for the rest of his life, Taylor told anyone who would listen that Steinbeck and the publisher had pirated his second book idea and made it into *The Grapes of Wrath.*

While Taylor built that phantom swindle in his mind, Bob Gordon crashed back and forth between street and room, a desperate drinker even by White Sulphur standards. I would see him sometimes when I went to the post office for the mail, off somewhere in his plodding stagger. I remember that he wore suspenders, one of the few men in town who did, and the straps made a slumping X across his big back as they slid down his shoulders. Brothers indeed, Taylor and Bob, in desperation as well as in skin, the one daydreaming of New York and second fame, the other fumbling for his next bottle of whiskey.

Rose Gordon lived apart from her brothers, both in place and behavior. She was the one in the family who had chosen to be courtly toward the white faces all around, and a time or two a week she came along Main Street, a plump dark fluff of a woman, with her constant greeting, *How do you do? And how are you today?* Rose had extreme faith in words and manners. The death of any old-timer would bring out her pen, and a long letter to the

Meagher County News extolling the departed. She was especially fond of two groups in the valley's history, the Scots who had homesteaded in the Basin and elsewhere around the valley, and the Indians who had worn away before the tide of settlement.

Her passion for the Indians, fellow sufferers for the dusk of their skin, was understandable enough. *They were the first ladies of this land,* she would declare of the Indian women she had seen when she was a girl, and the saying of it announced that Rose Gordon knew ladyship from personal experience. But the transplanted Scots, my father's family and the others who had never seen black faces before and in all likelihood didn't care for them when they did? It was their talk. The lowlands burr, the throaty words which came out their mouths like low song, captivated Rose.

She was as entranced with the spoken word as Taylor was with the written, and the oration she had given when she was valedictorian of her high school school class of five students in 1904—that oration given from a rostrum in the old auditorium, a large American flag fastened square and true along the back stage wall—had been the summit of her life. When I had become a grown man, she astonished me once by reciting word-for-word the climax of that oration sixty years before: *I gave my address on the progress of the Negro race. I ended, I said: 'The colored soldiers have earned the highest courage, and they won unstinted praises by their bravery, loyalty and fidelity. They have indeed been baptized into full citizenship by their bloodshed in defense of their country, and they have earned the protection of that honorable emblem, the Stars and Stripes!'*

While Rose held those words in her memory as if they were her only heirloom, other street voices plaided White Sulphur life for me as well. The twang which gritted out of Lloyd Robinson and the other Missourians: *You could of talked all day long and not said that . . . Seen anything of that long-geared geezer who was gonna break that gelding for me? . . . That Swede don't know enough to pound sand in a rat hole . . .* In June, mosquitoes would come in a haze off the Smith River, and the mosquito stories would start: *Bastards're so big this year they can stand flatfooted and drink out of a rainbarrel . . . saw one of 'em carry off a baby chick the*

*other day . . . yah, I saw two of 'em pick up a lamb one at each end
. . .* Any time of year, the muttering against Rankin and his vast
holdings in the valley: *That goddamn Rankin's so crooked he
couldn't sleep in a roundhouse . . . so tight he squeaks . . . so mean
the coyotes wouldn't eat him . . .* One rancher or another proud of
a new woven-wire fence: *Horse-high, bull-strong, and hog-
tight. . . .* Another, defending himself against the notion that his
saddle horse was the color and quality of mud: *No, by God, she's
more of a kind of tansy-gray, the color of a cat's paw . . .* Nellie in
the Grill, shaking over early morning coffee: *I got lit up like a
church last night . . . Went home and threw my hat in the door
first. It didn't come back out, so I figured I was safe. . . .*

And always, always, the two voices which went at each other
just above my head, *Ruth, where the hell you been? If you think
you can just walk off and leave me with the cafe that way, you got
another think coming . . . Mister, I didn't marry you to spend all
my time in any damn cafe. Where I go is my business . . . .* The
look in my direction, then: *Better leave us alone, Ivan. . . .* But the
voices would go on, through the walls, until one more silence set in
between my father and my second mother.

The silences stretched tauter until a day sometime in the autumn
of 1948, when the Grill and our town life came to an end. Dad and
Ruth could agree on one thing: the tremendous hours of cafe work
were grinding them down. They gave up the lease, and now
bought a thousand head of sheep and arranged to winter them at a
ranch on Battle Creek in the Sixteen country, not far from the
Basin where Dad had grown up.

There seemed to be no middle ground in the marriage. Not
having managed to make it work while under the stare of the entire
town, now the two of them decided to try a winter truce out in
what was the emptiest corner of the county, just as it had been
when Peter and Annie Doig came there to homestead a
half-century before and as it is whenever I return now to drive its
narrow red-shale road. Gulch-and-sage land, spare, silent. Out
there in the rimming hills beyond the valley, twenty-five miles
from town, Dad and Ruth would have time alone to see whether
their marriage ought to last. *Could* last.

And I began what would be a theme of my life, staying in town in the living arrangement we called *boarding out*. It meant that someone or other, friend or relative or simply whoever looked reliable, would be paid by Dad to provide me room-and-board during the weekdays of school. It reminds me now of a long visit, the in-between feeling of having the freedom to wander in and out but never quite garnering any space of your own. But I had some knack then for living at the edges of other people's existences, and in this first span of boarding out—with friends of Ruth, the Jordan family—I found a household which teemed in its comings-and-goings almost as the cafe had.

Indeed, *We call it the short-order house around here,* Helen Jordan said as deer season opened and a surge of her out-of-town relatives, armed like a guerrilla platoon, swept through. Ralph Jordan himself came and went at uneven hours of the day and night, black with coal dust and so weary he could hardly talk: he was fireman on the belching old locomotive called Sagebrush Annie which snailed down the branch-line from White Sulphur to the main railroad at Ringling. Ralph with a shovelful of coal perpetually in hand, Helen forever up to her wrists in bread dough or dishwater—the Jordans were an instructive couple about the labor that life could demand.

And under their busy roof, I was living for the first time with other children, their two sons and a daughter. The older boy, Curtis, thin and giggly, was my age, and we slept in the same bed and snickered in the dark at each other's jokes. Boarding out at the Jordans went smoothly enough, then, except at the end of each week when Dad was to arrive and take me to the Battle Creek ranch with him. Friday night after Friday night, he did not arrive.

Whatever Dad or Ruth or I had expected of this testing winter, the unlooked-for happened: the worst weather of thirty years blasted into the Sixteen country, and Dad and Ruth found themselves in contest not so much with each other now, but with the screaming white wilderness outside.

As bad winters are apt to do, this one of 1948-49 whipped in early and hard. Snow fell, drifted, crusted into gray crystal windrows, then fell and drifted and crusted gray again. Dad and his hired man pushed the sheep in from the pastures to a big shed at the ranch buildings. Nothing could root grass out of that solid snow. The county road began to block for weeks at a time. Winter was sealing the Sixteen country into long frozen months of aloneness, and I was cordoned from the life of Dad and Ruth there.

At last, on the sixth Friday night, long after I had given up hope again, Dad appeared. Even then he couldn't take me to the ranch with him; he had spent ten hours fighting his way through the snow, and there was the risk that the countryside would close off entirely again before he could bring me back to town Sunday night. *Tell ye what we'll do, Skavinsky. Talk to that teacher of yours and see if you can work ahead in your schoolwork. If she'll let you, I'll come in somehow next Friday and you can come spend a couple of weeks out at the ranch.*

All week, whenever the recess bell rang I stayed at my desk and flipped ahead in one text or another, piling up lesson sheets to hand to the bemused teacher. Before school was out on Friday, Dad came to the door of the classroom for me, cocking his grin about clacking in with snowy overshoes and a girth of sheepskin coat.

The highway down the valley was bare, a black dike above the snow, as he drove the pickup to the turnoff toward Battle Creek. Then the white drifts stretched in front of us like a wide storm-frothed lake whose waves had suddenly stopped motion to hang in billows and peaks where the wind had lashed them against the sky.

The very tops of fenceposts, old gray cedar heads with rounded snow caps, showed where the road was buried. Between the post tops, a set of ruts had been rammed and hacked by Dad and the few other ranchers who lived in the Sixteen country.

Dad drove into the sea of snow with big turns of the steering wheel, keeping the front wheels grooved in the ruts while the rear end of the pickup jittered back and forth spinning snow out behind us. Sometimes the pickup growled to a halt. We would climb out and shovel away heavy chunks like pieces of an igloo. Then Dad would back the pickup a few feet for a running start and bash into the ruts again. Once we went over a snowdrift on twin rows of planks another of the ranchers had laid for support, a bridge in midsea. Once we drove entirely over the top of a drift without planks at all.

Where the road led up to the low ridge near the old Jap Stewart ranch, we angled between cliffs of snow higher than the pickup. Near Battle Creek, with our headlights fingering past the dark into the white blankness, Dad swerved off the road entirely and sent the pickup butting through the smaller drifts in a hayfield. It had started to snow heavily, the wind out of the Basin snaking the flurries down to sift into the ruts. I watched the last miles roll up on the tiny numbers under the speedometer as Dad wrestled the wheel and began his soft Scots cussing: *Snow on a man, will ye? Damn-it-all-to-hell-anyway, git back in those ruts. Damn-such-weather. Hold on, son, there's a ditch here somewhere . . .* The twenty-fifth mile, the last, we bucked down a long slope to the ranch with the heavy wet flakes flying at us like clouds of moths. Dad roared past the lighted windows of the ranch house and spun the pickup inside the shelter of the lambing shed. *Done!* he said out into the storm. *Done, damn ye!*

To my surprise, Battle Creek was not living up to its name, and Dad and Ruth were getting along less edgily there than they ever had. It may have been that there simply was so much cold-weather work to be done, feeding the sheep, carrying in firewood, melting snow for water because the pump had frozen, that they had little stamina left over for argument. Or perhaps they had decided that the winter had to be gotten through, there simply was no route away from one another until spring. Whatever accounted for it, I slipped into its bask and warmed for the days to come.

Each morning, Ruth stood at the window sipping from a white mug of coffee, watching as Dad and the hired man harnessed the team to the hay sled. Then, if Dad had said they needed her that day, she would pull on heavy clothing and go out and take the reins while the men forked hay off to the sheep. Dad helped her in the house, the two of them working better together at the meals and dishes than they had when they were feeding half the town in the Grill. The pair of them even joked about the icy journey to the outhouse which started each day. Whoever went first, the other would demand to know whether the seat had been left good and warm. *It damn well ought to be,* the other would say, *half of my behind is still out on it.* Or: *Sure did, I left it smoking for you.*

The ranch house had been built with its living quarters on the second floor, well above the long snowdrifts which duned against the walls. A railed porch hung out over the snow the full length of the house, and from it the other ranch buildings were in view like a small anchored fleet seen from a ship's deck. The lambing shed, low and cloud-gray and enormously long, seemed to ride full-laden in the white wash of winter. Most of the time, the sheep were corralled on the far side of the shed, their bored bleats coming as far as the house if the wind was down. Not far from the lambing shed stood the barn, dark and bunched into itself, prowing up out of the stillness higher than anything else in sight. A few small sheds lay with their roofs disappearing in drifts, swamped by this cold ocean of a winter. Battle Creek flowed just beyond those sheds, but the only mark of it was a gray skin of ice.

In this snow world, Dad and his hired man skimmed back and forth on the hay sled, a low wide hayrack on a set of runners pulled by a team of plunging workhorses. I rode with the men, hanging tight to the frame of the hayrack prowing above where the horses' hooves chuffed into the snow. When the men talked, their puffs of breath clouded fatly out in front of their faces. Our noses trickled steadily. Dad put a mitten against my face often to see that my cheeks weren't being frostbitten.

The winter fought us again and again. Our dog crashed through the ice of Battle Creek, and the wind carried the sound of his barking away from the house. We found the shatter where he had tried to claw himself out before the creek froze him and then drowned him. A blizzard yammered against the back wall of the house for two days without stop. Outside the snow flew so thick it seemed there was no space left between the flakes in the air, just an endless crisscross of flecks the whiteness of goose down. When Dad and the hired man went to feed the sheep, they would disappear into the storm, swallowed, thirty feet from the window where Ruth and I watched.

An afternoon when the weather let up briefly, I climbed the slope behind the house, to where a long gully troughed toward

Battle Creek. Snow had packed the gulch so full that I could sled down over its humps and dips for hundreds of feet at a time. Trying out routes, I flew off a four-foot shale bank and in the crash sliced my right knee on the end of a sled runner as if I had fallen against an axe blade.

That moment of recall is dipped in a hot red ooze. The bloody slash scared out my breath in a long *uhhhhh*. A clench ran through the inside of me, then the instant heat of tears burned below my eyes. The climb from the gulch was steep. Now the burning fell to my leg. Blood sopped out as I hobbled to the house with both hands clamped over my wound, and Ruth shook as she snipped away the heavy-stained pants leg. The cut, she quickly told me, did not live up to its first horrific gush; it was long but shallow and clean, and dressings easily took care of it. In a few days, I could swing my leg onto the hay sled and again ride with the men above the horses' white-frosted heels.

The two weeks passed in surges of that winter weather, like tides flowing in long and hard. On the last morning, no snow was falling, but Dad said so much had piled by then that we could get to town only by team and sled. Ruth said she wanted to go with us. Dad looked at her once and nodded.

Dad and the hired man lifted the rack off the hay boat and fixed a seat of planks onto the front pair of sled runners. Inside that seat, blankets piled thickly onto the heavy coats we wore, we sat buried in warmth, almost down in the snow as the horses tugged us along on the running bob. Harness buckles sang a *ching-tink, ching-tink* with every step of the horses. Dad slapped the reins against the team's rumps and headed us toward the hayfields along Battle Creek. The road would be no help to us, drift humped onto drift there by now. We would aim through meadows and bottomlands where the snow lay flatter.

The grayness stretching all around us baffled my eyes. Where I knew hills had to be, no hills showed. The sagebrush too had vanished, from a countryside forested with its clumps. One gray sheet over and under and around, the snow and overcast had fused land and sky together. Even our sleigh was gray and half-hidden, weathered ash moving like a pale shadow through ashen weather.

Dad headed the team by the tops of fenceposts, and where the snow had buried even them, by trying to pick out the thin besieged hedge of willows along the creek. I peeked out beside Ruth, the two fogs of our breath blowing back between us as the horses found footing to trot. More often, they lunged at the snow, breaking through halfway up their thick legs. Dad talked to the horses every little while: *Hup there, Luck, get your heft into it. . . . Pull a bit, damn ye, Bess . . . Up this rise, now, get yourself crackin' there* . . . Their ears would jab straight up when they felt the flat soft slap of the reins and heard Dad's voice, and they would pull faster and we would go through the snow as if the sled was a running creature carrying us on its back.

The twin cuts of our sled tracks, the only clear lines the snow had not yet had time to seize and hide, traced away farther and farther behind us. Except for the strides of the horses and Dad's words to them, the country was silent, held so under the weight of the snow. In my memory that day has become a set of instants somewhere between life and death, a kind of eclipse in which hours did not pass and sound did not echo, all color washed to a flannel sameness and distance swelling away beyond any counting of it. We went into that fog-world at one end of Battle Creek and long after came out at the other, but what happened in between was as measureless as a float through space. If it was any portion of existence at all, it did not belong to the three of us, but to that winter which had frozen all time but its own.

After that ghostly trip, I went back to my boarding family and Dad and Ruth went on with the struggle against the winter. It was another month or so before Dad arrived to take me to the ranch again. This time, we drove across the drifted world inside a plowed canyon, the slabs and mounds of frozen snow wrenched high as walls on either side of the thin route. *We've had a D-8 'dozer in here, the government sent it out when it looked like we were all gonna lose the livestock out here. I had to get a truckload of cottonseed cake sent in for the sheep, the hay's goin' so damn fast. They put the bumper of that truck right behind the 'dozer and even so it took 'em sixty-six hours to make it to the ranch and back, can ye feature that? That load of cottoncake is gonna cost us $2500 in* transportation, but we had to have 'er. I looked at him as if he'd said the moon was about to fall on us; $2500 sounded to me like all the money in the state of Montana. But Dad grinned and talked on: *You should of been out here to see all the snowplowin'. After they 'dozed out our haystacks, the crew was supposed to go up and 'doze out Jim Bill Keith's place. I was the guy that was showin' them the way, ridin' the front end of that Cat. Hell, I got us lost on the flats up here—same damn country I grew up in, ye know—and we 'dozed in a big circle before we knew what was goin' on. Plowed up a quarter of a mile of Jim Bill's fence and didn't even know it. Blizzardin', boy it's been ablowin' out here, son. They came out in one of those snow crawlers to change Cat crews—changed 'em with an airplane when they first started, but the weather got so bad they couldn't fly—so here they come now in one of these crawlers, and the guy drivin' is drunker'n eight hundred dollars. I thought he was gonna bring that damned crawler through the window of the house . . .* I laughed with him, but must have looked worried. He grinned again. *We're doin' okay in spite of it all. Haven't lost any sheep yet, and that high-priced cottoncake gives us plenty of feed. If this winter don't last into the summer, we're even gonna make some pretty good money on the deal.*

Then in the next weeks came an afternoon when Dad saddled a horse and plunged off through the below-zero weather to the neighboring Keith ranch. *He came up here wanting to borrow some cigarettes, and some whiskey.* Probably the truce with Ruth was wearing through by then. Dad idled in the kitchen, talking and drinking coffee with Mrs. Keith while waiting for Jim Bill and his hired man to come back from feeding their cattle. *I remember, yes, your dad had ridden up on a little sorrel horse and he was sitting in the kitchen with Flossie, and he kept looking out at this kind of a red knob out here on the hill. He looked and he looked, and pretty soon he jumped up and yelled: 'It's broke, it's broke!' and he ran outside. And that winter was broke. The hired man and I came riding home with our earflaps rolled up and our coats off, and our mittens stuck in the forkhole of the saddle. Just like that.*

The chinook which had begun melting the snowdrifts even as

Dad watched did signal the end of that ferocious winter, and somehow too it seemed to bring the end of the long storm within our household. Before, neither Dad nor Ruth had been able to snap off the marriage. Now they seemed in a contest to do it first, like a pair tugging at a stubborn wishbone.

Near the start of summer, Ruth announced she was leaving, this time for all time. Dad declared it was the best idea he'd ever heard out of her. Alone with Ruth sometime in the slash and swirl of all this, I asked why she had to go. She gave me her tough grin, shook her head and said: *Your dad and me are never gonna get along together. We're done. We gave it our try.*

Why it was that the two of them had to endure that winter together before Ruth at last could go from Dad, I have never fathomed. Perhaps it was a final show of endurance against one another, some way to say *I can last at this as long as you can.* But that long since had been proved by both, and it is one of the strangenesses of this time that they had to go on and on with the proof of it. A last strangeness came over these years even after Ruth had vanished from us, and the divorce been handed down, one last unrelenting echo of it all. Dad no longer would even refer to Ruth by name. Instead, he took up something provided by one of the onlookers to our household's civil war. Naturally, the valley had not been able to resist choosing up sides in such a squabble, and a woman coming to Dad's defense reached for anything contemptible enough to call Ruth. At last she spluttered: *Why, that . . . that little flip!* For whatever reason, that Victorian blurt rang perfectly with Dad, put him in the right in all the arguments he was replaying in his mind. From the moment the surprising word got back to him, he would talk of Ruth only as *Flip, that damned Flip.*

Ruth went, and Flip stayed, one single poisoned word which was all that was left of two persons' misguess about one another. I have not seen Ruth for twenty years, nor spoken with her for twenty-five. But for a time after those few warring years with my father, her life straightened, perhaps like a piece of metal seethed in fire for the anvil. She married again, there was a son. And then calamity anew, that marriage in wreckage, and another after that, the town voice saying more than ever of her *She thinks everything*

should come in a cloud for her but she has hatefulness in herself,
until at last she had gone entirely, *disappeared somewhere out onto
the Coast, nobody's cared to keep track of her.*

The son: I am curious about him. Was he taken by Ruth to see
the grandmother blinking back age and blindness? Did Ruth stand
with him, white mug of coffee in her hand, to watch snow sift on a
winter's wind? But the curiosity at last stops there. When Dad and
Ruth finally pulled apart, the one sentiment I could recognize within me—have recognized ever since—was relief that she had gone,
and that the two of them could do no more harm to each other.

Once more Dad had to right our life, and this time he did it simply by letting the seasons work him up and down the valley. He
went to one ranch as foreman of the haying crew, on to another to
feed cattle during the winter, to a third for spring and the lambing
season.

When school started and I could not be with him, he rented a
cabin in White Sulphur and drove out to his ranch work in the
morning and back at night. During the winter and in spring's busy-
ness of lambing, I usually boarded with Nellie and his wife in their
fine log house. Nellie's wife was a world of improvement from
Ruth—a quiet approving woman, head up and handsome. In the
pasture behind their house she raised palomino horses, flowing
animals of a rich golden tan and with light blond manes of silk. The
horses seemed to represent her independence, her declaration away
from Nellie's life of drinking, and she seemed to think Dad was
right in letting me be as free and roaming as I was. It occurs to me
now that she would have given me her quiet approving smile if I
had come home from a wandering to report that I'd just been down
at the Grand Central watching a hayhand knife a sheepherder.

And after her season of calm, Dad began one for us together.
When the summer of 1950 came, he bought a herd of cattle, and
we moved them and ourselves to a cattle camp along Sixteenmile
Creek.

There our life held a simpler pace than I could ever remember.
The two of us lived in a small trailer house, the only persons from
horizon to horizon and several miles beyond. Dad decided to teach
me to shoot a single-shot .22 rifle, using as targets the tan gophers

which every horseback man hated for the treacherous little burrows they dug. We shot by the hour, rode into the hills every few days to look at the cattle, caught trout in the creek, watched the Milwaukee Railroad trains clip past four times every day.

Then I had my eleventh birthday—five years since my mother had died—and it seemed to trigger a decision in Dad. Something had been working at him, a mist of despond and unsteady health which would take him off into himself for hours at a time. One evening in the first weeks after my birthday, after he had been silent most of the day, he told me a woman would be coming into our lives again.

His words rolled a new planet under our feet, so astonishing and unlikely was this prospect. Ruth had come and gone without much lasting effect, except for the scalded mood Dad showed whenever he had a reason to mention her. But the person he had in mind now cast a shadowline across everything ahead of us, stood forth as the one apparition I could not imagine into our way of life. My mother's mother.

Vardis Fisher

Love in Idaho

JUNE Weeg upon knees and elbows was studying her image in a clear pool. She could see her face lying darkly under and her ears like a small shadow on either side, strangely luminous and very queer. Her pale hair was a bushy wet darkness and her green eyes were alluringly dark and deep. She smiled—because more than one person had said she had a lovely smile. It was a wonder, it was a very great wonder, that there was anything lovely about her; for look at her round face there with its funny little nose! She turned her head and looked across her cheek, trying to see her profile, but she could make out only the blurred foolishness of a girl who was striving to seem beautiful when she was not. . . .

She struck the water with an open palm.

Then she drew near and looked intently at her face, now elongated in weird distortions or dimpling in the hills and valleys, with her hair flowing in the waves like a shadow, with her eyes dancing in odd shapes, in grotesque and terrible shapes. Changing her position, she reclined on the bank in one way and another, now resting her face on one hand, now stretching her legs, seeking some attitude that would be irresistible and sweet. She held her head at one angle and another, to soften the angry thrust of her chin or to diminish the roundness of her face; or she strove to reduce the full-ness of her breast and hips, to give slenderness to her waist. Her free arm she rested at her side and then across her breast and then be-hind her. She wanted to be a picture of voluptuous unconcern: alluring and a little sinister and splendidly unique.

She wanted to be like the heroine of a novel who, upon a day like this, had reclined on a sofa before a startled and worshipful hero. And as she changed her position and studied her image, she remem-bered the scene. The hero had called her a tyrant and had said she was driving him mad. He had shaken, the book said, and had clutched his hair and muttered with woe; and the heroine had smiled with gentle and charming pity, with an incredulous lift of her brows, as June was smiling now. She had raised a lovely bare arm in protest, her red mouth scorning him, her mocking eyes as-king him to repeat. And the poor fellow had gone to his knees and had sobbed with anguish and devotion. Very softly then, the heroine had said, "How you weary me!" and had raised a naked arm to her dark hair.

June sat up and pulled a sleeve to her shoulder and looked at her stout arm. She looked around to see if anyone watched; and then, with a gesture of sensuous weariness, she raised her arm and murmured: "Oh, how you weary me!" Her voice faltered a little, but she felt that she had done very well. She rose to her feet and looked down at the monstrous simpleton. "And now, if you will excuse me—I am expecting Lord Vick-Lullendale any minute. . . ." She walked against the sun: when it was high to the zenith she never gave it her back because it threw a short shadow from her heels and reminded her that she was short and stout. She loved the morning and evening sun; for in the morning and the evening her shadow was long and slender and made her feel taller than she was.

Once, years ago, when she was very foolish, she had set a pole in the earth, measured exactly to her height; and when, in afternoons, the post threw a shadow five feet and eight inches long, then she walked, looking at the shadow going before her. Sometimes, when the earth rose sharply before her, diminishing the shadow, she would stop, bewildered by what she saw; but after gaining the crest, her shadow lengthened down the slope and she almost wept to see it grow. But all that was when she was seventeen. Of her mother she once asked:

"Don't people grow any taller after they're twenty?" And Kitty had cried:

"I'd wonder now! Aren't you tall enough?"

"Tall enough! I'm not even five feet, and I want to be five feet eight."

"Nonsense!" Kitty had said.

"Don't they?" June had persisted. "Anywhere in the whole world?"

"Oh, what a silly question!"

But that was four years ago. She asked no such questions of her mother now.

In the shade of a fir she sat and took off her shoes. They were ugly shoes—proletarian shoes, she decided, remembering another book; and she wondered if she could give them higher heels. If she had heels like those worn by ladies of fable and fashion: in catalogues the women wore many kinds of high heels, curved and tapering; and at dances too. You could judge a lady by her heels and her eyebrows and by little else. At dances here, or in the valley, the girl with costly shoes was a popular girl, no matter how unlovely her face. . . . Or wasn't it true? She wondered, and made a face. A girl on high heels, a novel said, was alluringly poised but a girl on low heels seemed to be pushed back, pushed down into herself, with her legs grotesquely shortened. She looked as if she would fall over backward any minute. And as women grew old and stout they settled like a snowbank and walked on their heels as if the forward half of their feet had been worn away. . . .

Filling the inside heel of her shoes with earth and tamping it in, she pondered the matter of height and poise; and then she slipped her feet into her shoes and rose, her breath coming deep as she felt her tallness. Her height could not be, she knew, more than five feet now—not much more, anyway—but she felt almost as tall as a queen. She took a few steps, with difficulty keeping her shoes on:

walking with her breast rounded and her head lifted so that her throat, she hoped, was a lovely curve. Then she studied her poise and strove to let her arms hang naturally from proud shoulders and to feel that her whole body was eager and awake. She liked the firmness in her thighs now, the easy gracefulness of her waist. . . . Then she took her shoes off and walked in her stockings, alert to every new pull of muscle and to every change. She now seemed to settle earthward, her shoulders pressing down upon her hips as if she had no waist at all, her legs feeling heavy and burdened. . . .

Yes, the novel was right.

She put her shoes on again and drew herself slowly erect so that she could measure the full change. Now her breast and thighs came forward; her abdomen vanished into the suppleness of her waist; her shoulders came to poise and life. She stood a little while with one arm akimbo, one shoulder raised; and upon her face there was a scornful smile for Sol Incham who was upon his knees, imploring her love. "You bore me," she murmured, walking away from him and looking back. . . .

Twilight was entering the world now. From a graveyard of dead aspens rose the smoke of her home fire, lifting like blue mist into the sky. Inside the house her mother would be reading a novel, her two fat hands holding the book, her great bosom pausing a moment in its rise and fall if she came upon words of love; or she would be in the kitchen, lazily preparing supper and bending now and then over the book to read a few lines. The book would be flattened upon the table, its ardor smudged with grease and dough. . . . And her father, the big incalculable dreamer, would be heaven knew where, with pain in his eyes and a song on his mouth. And after they all ate supper, Kitty would sit by a window and read until darkness fell and Jon would go out into the night, whistling his tunes. And June Weeg, the homeliest girl in Antelope, the most unloved little squab in ten counties—what would she do? What, indeed, had she ever done! She ought to be in a circus, one wag had said. "What a mug you got, Juney, anyhow!"

But Sol Incham, she reflected, had not always been a sight to look at. He had probably been handsome long ago, before accident set upon him and spoiled his face. Beyond these mountains, beyond the lonely changelessness of these hills, he had perhaps danced and loved and dreamed dreams. He had lived in New York and in Georgia and in Hollywood. Behind his face lay a long life—and memories of things done; but behind her face with its pert little nose and its solemnly round silliness there were only twenty-four monotonous years. She had been a fat babe—oh, a monstrous little dumpling; and then a girl, round and plump and growing plumper; and then a young woman at whom men winked and smiled.

And nowhere in all her days had she seen another girl as homely as herself. All other girls were lovely in one or in many ways: one had large teeth but she had deep lustrous eyes and a loveliness of dark hair. Another's chin was a little short, her face a little long but her hair lay upon her in waves of gold and her complexion was a wonder to look at. There was Virgin Hill, loveliest thing in the whole world here, with a mouth for kissing and a body so perfect you could not believe your eyes. There was Lucille Reade whom no man could look at without stopping dead in his tracks. Yes indeed: every other girl had been given some beauty, some irresistible charm; and you could hunt the earth over, search until you were old and blind and lame, and you could never find another June Weeg.

"Never!" she said, and made an awful face.

Even Japanese girls were lovelier, with their queer eyes, or those almost naked ones whom she saw in Sol's magazines, with rings in their noses or ears. There was fire in them, grace and meaning and curve. And in novels there was never a person like herself. Even the kitchen drudges had lovers; the female slaves often stood in the moonlight on back stairs or eloped into fairyland. . . . No; in the whole world there was only one June Weeg; a squimp of a girl who read novels and wanted to be an actress and talked to herself. . . .

And on the next day she was again in the woods, making contemptuous faces at the riddle of her life. She was thinking of her father, too: a large man with bushy uncombed tangle of hair and strange sad eyes. The folk in Antelope were a little afraid of the towering size of him and his unmannered ways. He had eyes that looked with paralyzing directness and they were full of grim amusement or passionless cold lights or the shadows of an old wrath. But his laugh was a thundering burst of good will. One day, years ago, he had taken the *h* from the name John and had thrown it away; whereupon, as if he had kicked a mountain out of his path, he disappeared for a week.

She went to the house, and Kitty looked up from her book. "Where you been?" she said. "Out to gab?" She stared at her daughter for a long moment and asked: "I say, where you been?"

"Just out and around."

Kitty was reading again, her full red lips moving over the words as if she were tasting them. "You been down to Sol's. Don't you know you'll be talked about from sunup to sundown?"

"And do you think I care?"

"Of course you will," said Kitty, still reading. "You'll be ready to care about any man soon has two good hands and a farm—" For a moment she was breathless, and when she turned the next page her dimpled hand trembled.

And June was wondering if, in twenty years, she would be like her mother: with fat in a plump mound under her chin—a woman lost in a mattress of flesh, covered over, buried, save for two bright eyes that peered at the legends in books. Perhaps she would be. Perhaps the years would add layer to layer until she would shake when she walked or sink into a great soft cushion of flesh when she lay down. There would be no bones, no bones to feel or see: nothing but dewlaps as large as her arm, trembling excess upon her, hide stretched until it was pink, and dimples in which she could bury a saucer.

"You think you don't care," said Kitty, looking up with blue untroubled eyes. "Well, why don't you? I'd wonder!"

"It's none of your business."

"Now, ain't that a way to talk! You twenty-four, and I was married at seventeen. Twenty-four and you don't care." She stared at her, gently perplexed. Then she turned to her novel and left June to wonder what Kitty had been like at seventeen.

In their old red album was a photograph of Kitty, taken twenty-odd years ago. Kitty Beal had been a slender girl with a sweet mouth and lovely blue eyes, with hungry red cheeks. Giants had fought over her and threatened to die for her: John Weeg and Sandy McGinnis and Ole Humbersum—titans all. There was one fabulous tale of a rejected suitor who shot his head off. And while reflecting on her mother, June wondered if she herself might grow lovelier as she grew older. Some women did. Some of them—most of them, of course—passed into middle age with beauty going out of them and with ugliness seeking them out of the years; but some—only a very few—seemed to discover beauty as they looked more around them, and to make of it their own.

And such a woman she would be. She would look only at lovely things and she would take them into herself with her breath and her eyes and her words. She would look at sunsets until their flame was in her cheeks, smell of wild flowers until they sweetened her breath, and walk in the beauty of these mountains and grow with them in their ways. In such manner lived one heroine in a book. This girl twisted wild flowers into her hair until it was as fragrant as a garden and danced until she was as light on her feet as a wind. . . .

Jon entered now. He went over and looked at the book Kitty was reading and turned it over to see its title. He grunted with contempt. For a moment he hesitated, and Kitty looked up at him, her eyes guilty and frightened; and then he seized the book and hurled it so savagely against a wall that the story of passionate love fell out of its cover. Swinging, then, he entered the night.

"Well, I'm a horse and buggy!" cried Kitty, staring across the room at her fable. "What's the matter of him?"

"You ought to know," June said.

Kitty recovered her novel and sat at the table. She moved close to the table and let her heavy bosom sink upon it, spreading within her blouse like a mound of dough; and after another long moment of troubled thought she opened the book and read.

An hour later June lay in bed, wondering fiercely about herself and life. Somewhere out in the darkness was her father, doing heaven alone knew what. Years ago he had been madly in love with Kitty and he was gentle and tender then; but later, for some dark reason, he had abused her and cursed her out of the house. And now, feeling himself growing old, he loved life with such gloomy intensity, with such impetuous, triumphant joy, that often his daughter was a little terrified. Some folk said he was crazy, but June knew better than that. She understood his fierce loves and his great vagabond heart and his hatred of age and death. She understood his impatience with books and the hunger in his hands and heart—for she was like him and she was not like Kitty at all. How a woman could sit day after day, serenely stuffed with food and dreams, and read and read without being lifted to her feet and driven to seek life; how she could sit week after week, year after year, reading of passionate matings and then go to bed and sleep and snore: who could understand a thing like that? Who could understand the lazy, purring indolence of a woman with a husband like Jon? And some night, if she dared, she would go with her father and see what he found and learn what he did. And she would dare. She hoped for a lover like him: a giant who would come up over the world's rim as one had come in a book: he would stand on the edge of earth, limned against time and eternity, and then he would come to her, over the mountains and tablelands of the world. All things would leave a wide path to his coming and the earth would shake under his feet. Perhaps Willie Argyll, the new hired man, would be such a lover: tall and strong, and with his eyes full of incredible things. Up over the western mountains out there, asleep now like a pile of shadow, with their upper edge stripped like a sword against the stars, he would come to look for her; up a hill and down, up another and down, lost now in a valley of darkness, now bright and vivid on a peak. She could hear him breaking the trees from his path and throwing the mountains out of his way. Or was he a small fellow who slunk through underbrush, with a feeble little chin hiding under a weak mouth? Was he pinched in his shoulders and did he have thin arms that were lost in their sleeves? Were his eyes pushed together with a timid nose between and had fear gathered unimportant wrinkles around his mouth? Or did he bellow with a sudden oath and reach up into the sky and shake the stars down like raindrops?

Wondering what Willie would be like, she turned to sleep. She awoke suddenly and sat up, believing that a man was in her room; and she peered around her, hoping that a man was. Then she left her bed and dressed and went into the night. It was a lovely night, with mountains piled in magic and gloom and with trees standing like the shadows of trees. Down in a canyon to the east everything was in a sleep that was like death, and northward upon the Antelope hills the pale light was golden. The aspen leaves around her fluttered like black butterflies held by their feet.

She went down the mountain and came to a fir and leaned against it, with its bark rough and strong on her skin. She liked to think of the bark as the palm of a man's hand and of the waving branches as arms reaching to take her. She closed her eyes on the wonder of it and her breathing was slow and deep. . . .

"How sweet it would be to love!" she thought. "How sweet, how sweet!"

Richard Ford

Communist

MY mother once had a boyfriend named Glen
Baxter. This was in 1961. We—my mother and I—were living in
the little house my father had left her up the Sun River, near
Victory, Montana, west of Great Falls. My mother was thirty-two
at the time. I was sixteen. Glen Baxter was somewhere in the middle between us, though I cannot be exact about it.

We were living then off the proceeds of my father's life insurance
policies, with my mother doing some part-time waitressing work
up in Great Falls and going to the bars in the evenings, which I
know is where she met Glen Baxter. Sometimes he would come
back with her and stay in her room at night, or she would call up
from town and explain that she was staying with him in his little
place on Lewis Street by the GN yards. She gave me his number
every time, but I never called it. I think she probably thought that
what she was doing was terrible, but simply couldn't help herself. I
thought it was all right, though. Regular life it seemed, and still
does. She was young, and I knew that even then.

Glen Baxter was a Communist and liked hunting, which he

talked about a lot. Pheasants. Ducks. Deer. He killed all of them, he said. He had been to Vietnam as far back as then, and when he was in our house he often talked about shooting the animals over there—monkeys and beautiful parrots—using military guns just for sport. We did not know what Vietnam was then, and Glen, when he talked about that, referred to it only as "the Far East." I think now he must've been in the CIA and been disillusioned by something he saw or found out about and been thrown out, but that kind of thing did not matter to us. He was a tall, dark-eyed man with short black hair, and was usually in a good humor. He had gone halfway through college in Peoria, Illinois, he said, where he grew up. But when he was around our life he worked wheat farms as a ditcher, and stayed out of work winters and in the bars drinking with women like my mother, who had work and some money. It is not an uncommon life to lead in Montana.

What I want to explain happened in November. We had not been seeing Glen Baxter for some time. Two months had gone by. My mother knew other men, but she came home most days from work and stayed inside watching television in her bedroom and drinking beers. I asked about Glen once, and she said only that she didn't know where he was, and I assumed they had had a fight and that he was gone off on a flyer back to Illinois or Massachusetts, where he said he had relatives. I'll admit that I liked him. He had something on his mind always. He was a labor man as well as a Communist, and liked to say that the country was poisoned by the rich, and strong men would need to bring it to life again, and I liked that because my father had been a labor man, which was why we had a house to live in and money coming through. It was also true that I'd had a few boxing bouts by then—just with town boys and one with an Indian from Choteau—and there were some girlfriends I knew from that. I did not like my mother being around the house so much at night, and I wished Glen Baxter would come back, or that another man would come along and entertain her somewhere else.

At two o'clock on a Saturday, Glen drove up into our yard in a car. He had had a big brown Harley-Davidson that he rode most of the year, in his black-and-red irrigators and a baseball cap turned backwards. But this time he had a car, a blue Nash Ambassador. My mother and I went out on the porch when he stopped inside the olive trees my father had planted as a shelter belt, and my mother had a look on her face of not much pleasure. It was starting to be cold in earnest by then. Snow was down already onto the Fairfield Bench, though on this day a chinook was blowing, and it could as easily have been spring, though the sky above the Divide was turning over in silver and blue clouds of winter.

"We haven't seen you in a long time, I guess," my mother said coldly.

"My little retarded sister died," Glen said, standing at the door of his old car. He was wearing his orange VFW jacket and canvas shoes we called wino shoes, something I had never seen him wear before. He seemed to be in a good humor. "We buried her in Florida near the home."

"That's a good place," my mother said in a voice that meant she was a wronged party in something.

"I want to take this boy hunting today, Aileen," Glen said. "There're snow geese down now. But we have to go right away, or they'll be gone to Idaho by tomorrow."

"He doesn't care to go," my mother said.

"Yes I do," I said, and looked at her.

My mother frowned at me. "Why do you?"

"Why does he need a reason?" Glen Baxter said and grinned.

"I want him to have one, that's why." She looked at me oddly. "I think Glen's drunk, Les."

"No, I'm not drinking," Glen said, which was hardly ever true. He looked at both of us, and my mother bit down on the side of her lower lip and stared at me in a way to make you think she thought something was being put over on her and she didn't like you for it. She was very pretty, though when she was mad her features were sharpened and less pretty by a long way. "All right, then I don't care," she said to no one in particular. "Hunt, kill, maim. Your father did that too." She turned to go back inside.

"Why don't you come with us, Aileen?" Glen was smiling still, pleased.

"To do what?" my mother said. She stopped and pulled a

package of cigarettes out of her dress pocket and put one in her mouth.

"It's worth seeing."

"See dead animals?" my mother said.

"These geese are from Siberia, Aileen," Glen said. "They're not like a lot of geese. Maybe I'll buy us dinner later. What do you say?"

"Buy what with?" my mother said. To tell the truth, I didn't know why she was so mad at him. I would've thought she'd be glad to see him. But she just suddenly seemed to hate everything about him.

"I've got some money," Glen said. "Let me spend it on a pretty girl tonight."

"Find one of those and you're lucky," my mother said, turning away toward the front door.

"I already found one," Glen Baxter said. But the door slammed behind her, and he looked at me then with a look I think now was helplessness, though I could not see a way to change anything.

My mother sat in the backseat of Glen's Nash and looked out the window while we drove. My double gun was in the seat between us beside Glen's Belgian pump, which he kept loaded with five shells in case, he said, he saw something beside the road he wanted to shoot. I had hunted rabbits before, and had ground-sluiced pheasants and other birds, but I had never been on an actual hunt before, one where you drove out to some special place and did it formally. And I was excited. I had a feeling that something important was about to happen to me, and that this would be a day I would always remember.

My mother did not say anything for a long time, and neither did I. We drove up through Great Falls and out the other side toward Fort Benton, which was on the benchland where wheat was grown.

"Geese mate for life," my mother said, just out of the blue, as we were driving. "I hope you know that. They're special birds."

"I know that," Glen said in the front seat. "I have every respect for them."

"So where were you for three months?" she said. "I'm only curious."

"I was in the Big Hole for a while," Glen said, "and after that I went over to Douglas, Wyoming."

"What were you planning to do there?" my mother asked.

"I wanted to find a job, but it didn't work out."

"I'm going to college," she said suddenly, and this was something I had never heard about before. I turned to look at her, but she was staring out her window and wouldn't see me.

"I knew French once," Glen said. "*Rose*'s pink. *Rouge*'s red." He glanced at me and smiled. "I think that's a wise idea, Aileen. When are you going to start?"

"I don't want Les to think he was raised by crazy people all his life," my mother said.

"Les ought to go himself," Glen said.

"After I go, he will."

"What do you say about that, Les?" Glen said, grinning.

"He says it's just fine," my mother said.

"It's just fine," I said.

Where Glen Baxter took us was out onto the high flat prairie that was disked for wheat and had high, high mountains out to the east, with lower heartbreak hills in between. It was, I remember, a day for blues in the sky, and down in the distance we could see the small town of Floweree, and the state highway running past it toward Fort Benton and the Hi-line. We drove out on top of the prairie on a muddy dirt road fenced on both sides, until we had gone about three miles, which is where Glen stopped.

"All right," he said, looking up in the rearview mirror at my mother. "You wouldn't think there was anything here, would you?"

"*We're* here," my mother said. "You brought us here."

"You'll be glad, though," Glen said, and seemed confident to me. I had looked around myself but could not see anything. No

water or trees, nothing that seemed like a good place to hunt anything. Just wasted land. "There's a big lake out there, Les," Glen
said. "You can't see it now from here because it's low. But the
geese are there. You'll see."

"It's like the moon out here, I recognize that," my mother said,
"only it's worse." She was staring out at the flat wheatland as if she
could actually see something in particular, and wanted to know
more about it. "How'd you find this place?"

"I came once on the wheat push," Glen said.

"And I'm sure the owner told you just to come back and hunt
anytime you like and bring anybody you wanted. Come one, come
all. Is that it?"

"People shouldn't own land anyway," Glen said. "Anybody
should be able to use it."

"Les, Glen's going to poach here," my mother said. "I just want
you to know that, because that's a crime and the law will get you
for it. If you're a man now, you're going to have to face the conse-
quences."

"That's not true," Glen Baxter said, and looked gloomily out
over the steering wheel down the muddy road toward the
mountains. Though for myself I believed it was true, and didn't
care. I didn't care about anything at that moment except seeing
geese fly over me and shooting them down.

"Well, I'm certainly not going out there," my mother said. "I
like towns better, and I already have enough trouble."

"That's okay," Glen said. "When the geese lift up you'll get to
see them. That's all I wanted. Les and me'll go shoot them, won't
we, Les?"

"Yes," I said, and I put my hand on my shotgun, which had been
my father's and was heavy as rocks.

"Then we should go on," Glen said, "or we'll waste our light."

We got out of the car with our guns. Glen took off his canvas
shoes and put on his pair of black irrigators out of the trunk. Then
we crossed the barbed wire fence, and walked out into the high,
tilled field toward nothing. I looked back at my mother when we
were still not so far away, but I could only see the small, dark top of

her head, low in the backseat of the Nash, staring out and thinking what I could not then begin to say.

On the walk toward the lake, Glen began talking to me. I had never been alone with him, and knew little about him except what my mother said—that he drank too much, or other times that he was the nicest man she had ever known in the world and that someday a woman would marry him, though she didn't think it would be her. Glen told me as we walked that he wished he had finished college, but that it was too late now, that his mind was too old. He said he had liked the Far East very much, and that people there knew how to treat each other, and that he would go back some day but couldn't go now. He said also that he would like to live in Russia for a while and mentioned the names of people who had gone there, names I didn't know. He said it would be hard at first, because it was so different, but that pretty soon anyone would learn to like it and wouldn't want to live anywhere else, and that Russians treated Americans who came to live there like kings. There were Communists everywhere now, he said. You didn't know them, but they were there. Montana had a large number, and he was in touch with all of them. He said that Communists were always in danger and that he had to protect himself all the time. And when he said that he pulled back his VFW jacket and showed me the butt of a pistol he had stuck under his shirt against his bare skin. "There are people who want to kill me right now," he said, "and I would kill a man myself if I thought I had to." And we kept walking. Though in a while he said, "I don't think I know much about you, Les. But I'd like to. What do you like to do?"

"I like to box," I said. "My father did it. It's a good thing to know."

"I suppose you have to protect yourself too," Glen said.

"I know how to," I said.

"Do you like to watch TV," Glen asked, and smiled.

"Not much."

"I love to," Glen said. "I could watch it instead of eating if I had one."

I looked out straight ahead over the green tops of sage that grew to the edge of the disked field, hoping to see the lake Glen said was there. There was an airishness and a sweet smell that I thought might be the place where we were going, but I couldn't see it. "How will we hunt these geese?" I said.

"It won't be hard," Glen said. "Most hunting isn't even hunting. It's only shooting. And that's what this will be. In Illinois you would dig holes in the ground and hide and set out your decoys. Then the geese come to you, over and over again. But we don't have time for that here." He glanced at me. "You have to be sure the first time here."

"How do you know they're here now," I asked. And I looked toward the Highwood Mountains twenty miles away, half in snow and half dark blue at the bottom. I could see the little town of Floweree then, looking shabby and dimly lighted in the distance. A red bar sign shone. A car moved slowly away from the scattered buildings.

"They always come November first," Glen said.

"Are we going to poach them?"

"Does it make any difference to you," Glen asked.

"No, it doesn't."

"Well then, we aren't," he said.

We walked then for a while without talking. I looked back once to see the Nash far and small in the flat distance. I couldn't see my mother, and I thought that she must've turned on the radio and gone to sleep, which she always did, letting it play all night in her bedroom. Behind the car the sun was nearing the rounded mountains southwest of us, and I knew that when the sun was gone it would be cold. I wished my mother had decided to come along with us, and I thought for a moment of how little I really knew her at all.

Glen walked with me another quarter-mile, crossed another barbed wire fence where sage was growing, then went a hundred yards through wheatgrass and spurge until the ground went up and formed a kind of long hillock bunker built by a farmer against the wind. And I realized the lake was just beyond us. I could hear the sound of a car horn blowing and a dog barking all the way down in the town, then the wind seemed to move and all I could hear then and after then were geese. So many geese, from the sound of them, though I still could not see even one. I stood and listened to the high-pitched shouting sound, a sound I had never heard so close, a sound with size to it—though it was not loud. A sound that meant great numbers and that made your chest rise and your shoulders tighten with expectancy. It was a sound to make you feel separate from it and everything else, as if you were of no importance in the grand scheme of things.

"Do you hear them singing," Glen asked. He held his hand up to make me stand still. And we both listened. "How many do you think, Les, just hearing?"

"A hundred," I said. "More than a hundred."

"Five thousand," Glen said. "More than you can believe when you see them. Go see."

I put down my gun and on my hands and knees crawled up the earthwork through the wheatgrass and thistle, until I could see down to the lake and see the geese. And they were there, like a white bandage laid on the water, wide and long and continuous, a white expanse of snow geese, seventy yards from me, on the bank, but stretching far onto the lake, which was large itself—a half-mile across, with thick tules on the far side and wild plums farther and the blue mountain behind them.

"Do you see the big raft?" Glen said from below me, in a whisper.

"I see it," I said, still looking. It was such a thing to see, a view I had never seen and have not since.

"Are any on the land?" he said.

"Some are in the wheatgrass," I said, "but most are swimming."

"Good," Glen said. "They'll have to fly. But we can't wait for that now."

And I crawled backwards down the heel of land to where Glen was, and my gun. We were losing our light, and the air was purplish and cooling. I looked toward the car but couldn't see it, and I was no longer sure where it was below the lighted sky.

"Where do they fly to?" I said in a whisper, since I did not want anything to be ruined because of what I did or said. It was important to Glen to shoot the geese, and it was important to me.

"To the wheat," he said. "Or else they leave for good. I wish your mother had come, Les. Now she'll be sorry."

I could hear the geese quarreling and shouting on the lake surface. And I wondered if they knew we were here now. "She might be," I said with my heart pounding, but I didn't think she would be much.

It was a simple plan he had. I would stay behind the bunker, and he would crawl on his belly with his gun through the wheatgrass as near to the geese as he could. Then he would simply stand up and shoot all the ones he could close up, both in the air and on the ground. And when all the others flew up, with luck some would turn toward me as they came into the wind, and then I could shoot them and turn them back to him, and he would shoot them again. He could kill ten, he said, if he was lucky, and I might kill four. It didn't seem hard.

"Don't show them your face," Glen said. "Wait till you think you can touch them, then stand up and shoot. To hesitate is lost in this."

"All right," I said. "I'll try it."

"Shoot one in the head, and then shoot another one," Glen said. "It won't be hard." He patted me on the arm and smiled. Then he took off his VFW jacket and put it on the ground, climbed up the side of the bunker, cradling his shotgun in his arms, and slid on his belly into the dry stalks of yellow grass out of my sight.

Then, for the first time in that entire day, I was alone. And I didn't mind it. I sat squat down in the grass, loaded my double gun and took my other two shells out of my pocket to hold. I pushed the safety off and on to see that it was right. The wind rose a little, scuffed the grass and made me shiver. It was not the warm chinook now, but a wind out of the north, the one geese flew away from if they could.

Then I thought about my mother, in the car alone, and how much longer I would stay with her, and what it might mean to her for me to leave. And I wondered when Glen Baxter would die and if someone would kill him, or whether my mother would marry him and how I would feel about it. And though I didn't know why, it occurred to me that Glen Baxter and I would not be friends when all was said and done, since I didn't care if he ever married my mother or didn't.

Then I thought about boxing and what my father had taught me about it. To tighten your fists hard. To strike out straight from the shoulder and never punch backing up. How to cut a punch by snapping your fist inwards, how to carry your chin low, and to step toward a man when he is falling so you can hit him again. And most important, to keep your eyes open when you are hitting in the face and causing damage, because you need to see what you're doing to encourage yourself, and because it is when you close your eyes that you stop hitting and get hurt badly. "Fly all over your man, Les," my father said. "When you see your chance, fly on him and hit him till he falls." That, I thought, would always be my attitude in things.

And then I heard the geese again, their voices in unison, louder and shouting, as if the wind had changed again and put all new sounds in the cold air. And then a *boom*. And I knew Glen was in among them and had stood up to shoot. The noise of geese rose and grew worse, and my fingers burned where I held my gun too tight to the metal, and I put it down and opened my fist to make the burning stop so I could feel the trigger when the moment came. *Boom*, Glen shot again, and I heard him shuck a shell, and all the sounds out beyond the bunker seemed to be rising—the geese, the shots, the air itself going up. *Boom*, Glen shot another time, and I knew he was taking his careful time to make his shots good. And I held my gun and started to crawl up the bunker so as not to be surprised when the geese came over me and I could shoot.

From the top I saw Glen Baxter alone in the wheatgrass field, shooting at a white goose with black tips of wings that was on the ground not far from him, but trying to run and pull into the air. He shot it once more, and it fell over dead with its wings flapping.

Glen looked back at me and his face was distorted and strange. The air around him was full of white rising geese and he seemed to want them all. "Behind you, Les," he yelled at me and pointed. "They're all behind you now." I looked behind me, and there were geese in the air as far as I could see, more than I knew how

many, moving so slowly, their wings wide out and working calmly
and filling the air with noise, though their voices were not as loud
or as shrill as I had thought they would be. And they were so close!
Forty feet, some of them. The air around me vibrated and I could
feel the wind from their wings and it seemed to me I could kill as
many as the times I could shoot—a hundred or a thousand—and I
raised my gun, put the muzzle on the head of a white goose, and
fired. It shuddered in the air, its wide feet sank below its belly, its
wings cradled out to hold back air, and it fell straight down and
landed with an awful sound, a noise a human would make, a thick,
soft, *hump* noise. I looked up again and shot another goose, could
hear the pellets hit its chest, but it didn't fall or even break its pattern for flying. *Boom*, Glen shot again. And then again. "Hey," I
heard him shout. "Hey, hey." And there were geese flying over
me, flying in line after line. I broke my gun and reloaded, and
thought to myself as I did: I need confidence here, I need to be sure
with this. I pointed at another goose and shot it in the head, and it
fell the way the first one had, wings out, its belly down, and with
the same thick noise of hitting. Then I sat down in the grass on the
bunker and let geese fly over me.

By now the whole raft was in the air, all of it moving in a slow
swirl above me and the lake and everywhere, finding the wind and
heading out south in long wavering lines that caught the last sun
and turned to silver as they gained a distance. It was a thing to see, I
will tell you now. Five thousand white geese all in the air around
you, making a noise like you have never heard before. And I
thought to myself then: this is something I will never see again. I
will never forget this. And I was right.

Glen Baxter shot twice more. One he missed, but with the other
he hit a goose flying away from him, and knocked it half falling and
flying into the empty lake not far from shore, where it began to
swim as though it was fine and make its noise.

Glen stood in the stubby grass, looking out at the goose, his gun
lowered. "I didn't need to shoot that one, did I, Les?"

"I don't know," I said, sitting on the little knoll of land, looking
at the goose swimming in the water.

"I don't know why I shoot 'em. They're so beautiful." He looked at me.

"I don't know either," I said.

"Maybe there's nothing else to do with them." Glen stared at the goose again and shook his head. "Maybe this is exactly what they're put on earth for."

I did not know what to say because I did not know what he could mean by that, though what I felt was embarrassment at the great numbers of geese there were, and a dulled feeling like a hunger because the shooting had stopped and it was over for me now.

Glen began to pick up his geese, and I walked down to my two that had fallen close together and were dead. One had hit with such an impact that its stomach had split and some of its inward parts were knocked out. Though the other looked unhurt, its soft white belly turned up like a pillow, its head and jagged bill-teeth, its tiny black eyes looking as they would if they were alive.

"What's happened to the hunters out here?" I heard a voice speak. It was my mother, standing in her pink dress on the knoll above us, hugging her arms. She was smiling though she was cold. And I realized that I had lost all thought of her in the shooting. "Who did all this shooting? Is this your work, Les?"

"No," I said.

"Les is a hunter, though, Aileen," Glen said. "He takes his time." He was holding two white geese by their necks, one in each hand, and he was smiling. He and my mother seemed pleased.

"I see you didn't miss too many," my mother said and smiled. I could tell she admired Glen for his geese, and that she had done some thinking in the car alone. "It *was* wonderful, Glen," she said. "I've never seen anything like that. They were like snow."

"It's worth seeing once, isn't it?" Glen said. "I should've killed more, but I got excited."

My mother looked at me then. "Where's yours, Les?"

"Here," I said and pointed to my two geese on the ground beside me.

My mother nodded in a nice way, and I think she liked

everything then and wanted the day to turn out right and for all of us to be happy. "Six, then. You've got six in all."

"One's still out there," I said, and motioned where the one goose was swimming in circles on the water.

"Okay," my mother said and put her hand over her eyes to look. "Where is it?"

Glen Baxter looked at me then with a strange smile, a smile that said he wished I had never mentioned anything about the other goose. And I wished I hadn't either. I looked up in the sky and could see the lines of geese by the thousands shining silver in the light, and I wished we could just leave and go home.

"That one's my mistake there," Glen Baxter said and grinned. "I shouldn't have shot that one, Aileen. I got too excited."

My mother looked out on the lake for a minute, then looked at Glen and back again. "Poor goose." She shook her head. "How will you get it, Glen?"

"I can't get that one now," Glen said.

My mother looked at him. "What do you mean?"

"I'm going to leave that one," Glen said.

"Well, no. You can't leave one," my mother said. "You shot it. You have to get it. Isn't that a rule?"

"No," Glen said.

And my mother looked from Glen to me. "Wade out and get it, Glen," she said in a sweet way, and my mother looked young then, like a young girl, in her flimsy short-sleeved waitress dress and her skinny, bare legs in the wheatgrass.

"No." Glen Baxter looked down at his gun and shook his head. And I didn't know why he wouldn't go, because it would've been easy. The lake was shallow. And you could tell that anyone could've walked out a long way before it got deep, and Glen had on his boots.

My mother looked at the white goose, which was not more than thirty yards from the shore, its head up, moving in slow circles, its wings settled and relaxed so you could see the black tips. "Wade out and get it, Glenny, won't you, please?" she said. "They're special things."

"You don't understand the world, Aileen," Glen said. "This can happen. It doesn't matter."

"But that's so cruel, Glen," she said, and a sweet smile came on her lips.

"Raise up your own arms, 'Leeny," Glen said. "I can't see any angel's wings, can you, Les?" He looked at me, but I looked away.

"Then you go on and get it, Les," my mother said. "You weren't raised by crazy people." I started to go, but Glen Baxter suddenly grabbed me by my shoulder and pulled me back hard, so hard his fingers made bruises in my skin that I saw later.

"Nobody's going," he said. "This is over with now."

And my mother gave Glen a cold look then. "You don't have a heart, Glen," she said. "There's nothing to love in you. You're just a son of a bitch, that's all."

And Glen Baxter nodded at my mother, then, as if he understood something he had not understood before, but something that he was willing to know. "Fine," he said, "that's fine." And he took his big pistol out from against his belly, the big blue revolver I had only seen part of before and that he said protected him, and he pointed it out at the goose on the water, his arm straight away from him, and shot and missed. And then he shot and missed again. The goose made its noise once. And then he hit it dead, because there was no splash. And then he shot it three times more until the gun was empty and the goose's head was down and it was floating toward the middle of the lake where it was empty and dark blue. "Now who has a heart?" Glen said. But my mother was not there when he turned around. She had already started back to the car and was almost lost from sight in the darkness. And Glen smiled at me then and his face had a wild look on it. "Okay, Les?" he said.

"Okay," I said.

"There're limits to everything, right?"

"I guess so," I said.

"Your mother's a beautiful woman, but she's not the only beautiful woman in Montana." And I did not say anything. And Glen Baxter suddenly said, "Here," and he held the pistol out at me. "Don't you want this? Don't you want to shoot me? Nobody thinks they'll die. But I'm ready for it right now." And I did not know what to do then. Though it is true that what I wanted to do was to hit him, hit him as hard in the face as I could, and see him on the ground bleeding and crying and pleading for me to stop. Only at that moment he looked scared to me, and I had never seen a grown man scared before—though I have seen one since—and I felt sorry for him, as though he was already a dead man. And I did not end up hitting him at all.

A light can go out in the heart. All of this happened years ago, but I still can feel now how sad and remote the world was to me. Glen Baxter, I think now, was not a bad man, only a man scared of something he'd never seen before—something soft in himself—his life going a way he didn't like. A woman with a son. Who could blame him there? I don't know what makes people do what they do, or call themselves what they call themselves, only that you have to live someone's life to be the expert.

My mother had tried to see the good side of things, tried to be hopeful in the situation she was handed, tried to look out for us both, and it hadn't worked. It was a strange time in her life then and after that, a time when she had to adjust to being an adult just when she was on the thin edge of things. Too much awareness too early in life was her problem, I think.

And what I felt was only that I had somehow been pushed out into the world, into the real life then, the one I hadn't lived yet. In a year I was gone to hard-rock mining and no-paycheck jobs and not to college. And I have thought more than once about my mother saying that I had not been raised by crazy people, and I don't know what that could mean or what difference it could make, unless it means that love is a reliable commodity, and even that is not always true, as I have found out.

Late on the night that all this took place I was in bed when I heard my mother say, "Come outside, Les. Come and hear this." And I went out onto the front porch barefoot and in my underwear, where it was warm like spring, and there was a spring mist in the air. I could see the lights of the Fairfield Coach in the distance, on its way up to Great Falls.

And I could hear geese, white birds in the sky, flying. They made their high-pitched sound like angry yells, and though I couldn't see them high up, it seemed to me they were everywhere. And my mother looked up and said, "Hear them?" I could smell her hair wet from the shower. "They leave with the moon," she said. "It's still half wild out here."

And I said, "I hear them," and I felt a chill come over my bare chest, and the hair stood up on my arms the way it does before a storm. And for a while we listened.

"When I first married your father, you know, we lived on a street called Bluebird Canyon, in California. And I thought that was the prettiest street and the prettiest name. I suppose no one brings you up like your first love. You don't mind if I say that, do you?" She looked at me hopefully.

"No," I said.

"We have to keep civilization alive somehow." And she pulled her little housecoat together because there was a cold vein in the air, a part of the cold that would be on us the next day. "I don't feel part of things tonight, I guess."

"It's all right," I said.

"Do you know where I'd like to go?"

"No," I said. And I suppose I knew she was angry then, angry with life, but did not want to show me that.

"To the Straits of Juan de Fuca. Wouldn't that be something? Would you like that?"

"I'd like it," I said. And my mother looked off for a minute, as if she could see the Straits of Juan de Fuca out against the line of mountains, see the lights of things alive and a whole new world.

"I know you liked him," she said after a moment. "You and I both suffer fools too well."

"I didn't like him too much," I said. "I didn't really care."

"He'll fall on his face. I'm sure of that," she said. And I didn't say anything because I didn't care about Glen Baxter anymore, and was happy not to talk about him. "Would you tell me something if I asked you? Would you tell me the truth?"

"Yes," I said.

And my mother did not look at me. "Just tell me the truth," she said.

"All right," I said.

"Do you think I'm still very feminine? I'm thirty-two years old now. You don't know what that means. But do you think I am?"

And I stood at the edge of the porch, with the olive trees before me, looking straight up into the mist where I could not see geese but could still hear them flying, could almost feel the air move below their white wings. And I felt the way you feel when you are on a trestle all alone and the train is coming, and you know you have to decide. And I said, "Yes, I do." Because that was the truth. And I tried to think of something else then and did not hear what my mother said after that.

And how old was I then? Sixteen. Sixteen is young, but it can also be a grown man. I am forty-one years old now, and I think about that time without regret, though my mother and I never talked in that way again, and I have not heard her voice now in a long, long time.

A.B. Guthrie, Jr.

Ebbie

EBONY, the Gordon setter, was in heat again, and a bunch of dogs were always hanging around the Bostwick house. From the window Charlie could see the Jacksons' yellow cur, Tip, and the bulldog that the Johnsons had sent east for and the Bowmars' little Sprite and four or five others, some of which he wasn't sure of. Sometimes they fought, but not often. Mostly they were friendly and patient, lying with their tongues hanging out and their eyes on the back door, or one after the other cocking their legs against the old cottonwood tree or the axe-marked chopping block that Father cut the firewood on.

Because old Eb was in heat, Father was out of humor with her. Coming home from the office and seeing all the dogs lying around, he walked stiff and kept his eyes on the ground as if Eb was bringing shame on the house. It was the same in the morning when he set out for work and maybe found Tip lying just outside the door. He would aim a sudden kick at him and go on while words sounded in his throat.

Charlie didn't know what made Father feel that way.

Grown-ups had reasons of their own that you wouldn't understand until you were grown up yourself. Until then you didn't ask and you didn't object; you just wondered, like wondering why Father sometimes was full of play and tricks, and it was like the sun shining inside the house, and then at other times, for no cause that a boy could understand, he was touchy and short-tempered, and it was like a thundercloud had come across the sun.

Charlie sat down on the floor and let his hand run over the thick, silky curl of Eb's coat. She was tipped with gold, but most of her was watered black. She looked at him out of her good eye, and her tail made a slow pat on the floor. The other eye had been put out by birdshot long ago, before Charlie could remember. There was just the hole there and the lids half closed and the meat showing a little behind them and always a little wet streak down her muzzle where the eye drained. Father said he had tried to dust her, when they were out hunting, because she ranged too far, and one of the shot had happened to get her in the eye.

Eb loved Father, maybe understanding him better than a boy could. She loved the smell of his hunting jacket and the sound his shotgun made as he tried the pump before setting out for prairie chickens or mallards or geese. She would prance crazily around him and whine almost like talking, and he would smile and say, "All right, old girl. All right."

Father said maybe Eb didn't have the best nose in the world, but he would like to see her equal at retrieving. She would go any-where to get his birds and bring them and lay them at his feet with-out a tooth mark on them. Charlie thought she must have a pretty good nose at that or she wouldn't find anything at all, not with just one good eye. He would try her out himself as soon as he was old enough to carry a gun. He felt old enough now, at nine years, but Mamma said he would have to wait until he was twelve at least. So all he could do was play with Eb. He had broken her to lead and to pull a wagon, and she would scratch like everything for him, trying to dig a gopher out. He bet that next to hunting she liked to be with him best, tagging at his heels or retrieving the sticks he threw or just lying with him behind the big range in the kitchen where the slow warmth sometimes put them both to sleep.

Outside, the day was dimming off toward dark. The dogs were all lying down, some of them with their eyes closed but with their ears alive and listening. Father was probably on his way home by now.

Charlie got up and put on his sweater and went to the kitchen to go outside. His mother turned from her work board, the ends of her fingers lumpy with dough, and smiled at him. She said, "Don't go far. It'll be suppertime before long."

"I'm just going out."

"What for?"

"Well, I thought—you see, Father doesn't like the dogs in the yard, and I thought—"

She turned back to the board, and it was a little time before she spoke. Then she said, "I see, dear. Watch Eb doesn't go out with you."

Eb tried to follow him, her heavy brush of tail wagging hopefully, but he kneed her back and closed the door. He had stored a handful of rocks by the step, and now he picked them up, yelled, "Get out of here!" and began pegging the stones at the dogs, throwing easy and not very straight. The dogs slid out of range and stopped and grinned at him.

Father was silent at the supper table, thinking thoughts and feeling things Charlie couldn't guess. Once he asked, "Where's Eb?" and Mamma answered, "On the back porch. I latched the door," and Father went on eating and thinking. The porch was boarded up for three feet or so and screened the rest of the way to the top.

It had grown darker, so dark you couldn't see out the window from the lighted room, but Charlie knew the dogs had come back. He knew it even before he heard the sounds of the fight. Father's face clouded. "Those dogs!"

It was Mamma who found later that Eb had got out. She opened the door to the porch and turned back and stood with a still and startled look on her face, and the knowledge of what had happened leaped up in Charlie and clutched his insides. He started to whisper, "I'll find her," but Father came into the kitchen just then and caught the still and startled look, too, and asked, "What's wrong?" and looked outside and saw where Eb had made a hole through the screen.

Father went over to the corner where Charlie had leaned his ball bat and picked it up and said, "Come along, son! You can help locate her."

Two up-and-down lines marked Mamma's forehead, between the eyes. "Please, Harold," she said, and added, "It's just natural," but Father acted as if he didn't hear her. He slammed through the screen door with the bat held tight in his hand.

They found Eb right away, at the rear of the vacant lot next to their house. To Charlie it seemed there must have been a hundred dogs around. Some of them were just shapes at the edge of darkness. One was on top of Eb. Father ran up, waving the bat. It was the Jacksons' dog, Tip, that was on top. Father swung at him and missed, and Tip leaped off and jumped away and stood waiting, his eyes sharp and his mouth open and his hanging tongue looking dark in the half-dark.

Father grabbed Eb by the collar and started jerking her back toward the house. When his back was turned, Tip ran up again and rose on his hind legs and began hugging Eb with his front ones. Eb hung back, and Father turned and saw what was happening and swung the bat at Tip and, after he had missed again, raised it high and brought it down on Eb's head. The solid whack of it was drowned out by the howl that burst out of Eb. It was a high, shrill, wavy howl that hurt the ears like a whistle, and it went on and on, not stopping even for a breath.

Father jerked her ahead again and dragged her up the steps and flung her toward the rag rug on the porch. Then he moved the woodbox over so that it covered the hole she had made in the screen. "She won't want to be getting out again this night, I'm thinking," he said in a voice that made Charlie's stomach draw up.

Mamma looked at him when they came in the house, and Father said, still in that hard, ungiving tone, "I made a dead dog out of my dog, almost." Eb's crying reached inside the house. It sounded a little weaker here, but it still hurt the ears and it still went on and on as if the pain in her never let up even for a swallow or a gulp of air. Mamma's voice was so quiet it made Charlie look at her. "I don't know why you let yourself get into these blind rages. You've made a dog out of yourself, I'm afraid." Charlie saw that her face was white and that the hands over the dishpan trembled. He never had heard her speak to Father that way before, and he drew back inside himself, expecting a fierce answer, but Father didn't say a word. He turned and walked from the room.

"You get ready for bed, son," Mamma said, not looking at him.

Before he went to school the next morning, Charlie found what had made Eb howl. He had gone to tell her good-by, and her tail thumped on the floor for him, and she raised her old head. He held still, unbelieving, and the breath in him held still, too, while the fact beat against him. He saw the blind eye and the glimmer of red behind the lids, but what he couldn't believe he saw was the other eye, blind now, too, and empty-socketed, and the seepage from it making an unclean furrow down her nose.

He didn't cry. There were no tears in him, only a feeling of emptiness, only the feeling of unbelieving. He dropped down and brought her head into his lap and couldn't look at the eye again. "Oh, Ebbie," he whispered, "why did you have to do it? Why did you have to go and do it, Ebbie?" She let her head rest in his lap, and her tail wagged on as always, but slower, Charlie thought, than he had ever seen it.

Mamma called from inside, "You'll be late for school, Charlie," and he got up, not answering, and picked up his books and made his feet take him away. He couldn't tell anyone what had happened, not even Mamma. He had to hold it tight inside himself, a cold secret that lay in his stomach like a weight all day.

Coming back after school, he saw the dogs in the back yard again, and a sudden fury came on him. He gathered up a big handful of rocks and sneaked up and began throwing hard and straight as he could, feeling a fierce biting inside his chest when one of the stones brought a yelp from Tip.

Inside, he still couldn't tell Mamma about Eb, though he

wondered if the knowing of it wasn't what made her quiet and gentler, even, than usual. He refused the cookies she offered and afterward stole out to the porch. It was true. The secret was still true. He got Eb's head in his lap again.

Father was late getting home. The sun had gone beyond the mountains and the light was fading out of things before Charlie heard his step. Charlie slipped into the bathroom, leaving the door open just a crack, not wanting to see Father now, not wanting Father to see his face and read the secret in it. The front door opened and closed, and Charlie heard the rustle of clothing as Father took off his topcoat. He heard Mamma coming from the kitchen and then her voice, sounding low but not sharp, sounding low and gentle. "Ebbie's blind, Harold. Her other eye's out. I don't know what to tell Charlie. Maybe he knows already." The voice faltered before it got through.

There was a long silence. In his mind Charlie could see Father, standing with his head bent and his mouth set while he thought. The silence grew into a ringing in the ears, and then Father's step broke it, lagging toward the kitchen.

Mamma's voice was just above a whisper. "What are you going to do?"

"There's only one thing." Father's steps went on.

Charlie flung open the bathroom door and ran out. Mamma wasn't to the kitchen yet. She turned and said, "Charlie."

He cried out, "I know. I know. I've got to see!"

"I wish you wouldn't go."

"I've got to."

Her hand, uplifted in a little movement, stayed him for an instant. Her eyes searched his face. "Don't be angry, Charlie. Don't feel hard toward Father. Try to understand. He's sorry, sorrier than you can know."

"Why'd he do it then?"

"He couldn't help himself. Don't you see, he couldn't help himself?" He saw tears shining in her eyes and her mouth trembling.

"I got to go," he cried out again, and dodged her and ran to the kitchen.

Father was on the back porch. He had his shotgun in one hand

and Eb's head held up in the other, looking to make sure, Charlie guessed, that the good eye wasn't good any more. He let the head down and took hold of the collar and said, "Come on, girl," and, turning, saw Charlie. "You stay back, son!"

"I got to see, I tell you. I got to see."

Father didn't say any more. He just breathed deep and started leading Eb off the porch. She bumped against the door frame as they went out. The dogs lying in the back yard got up and backed off, watching.

Father took Eb over to the vacant lot, almost to where they had found her yesterday. The dogs trailed after them, Tip in the lead.

Father's hand worked the pump, throwing a shell in the chamber, and Eb's tail waved at the sound of it. Charlie thought if she could see she would be prancing.

"Sit down, girl. Sit down."

She let her hindquarters down and looked up at Father out of her blind eyes, and her tail waved again. In the dusk Charlie could see the ugly furrow that the matter from her hurt eye made.

Father stepped back. The shotgun was a long time coming up. Charlie couldn't look when it was leveled. He couldn't believe he stood there in the dark waiting for the shot, waiting for Eb to be killed, waiting for this cold and awful end.

The roar of the gun shook him. It brought his head around. Eb had sunk to the ground. A little twitching was running over her body. After a minute it stopped, and Eb didn't stir at all except for one curl of hair moving to a breath of air.

Father went over to her and stooped and put his hand out and rested it on her side. He didn't speak, not for a long time, but just stooped and let his hand lie soft and kind on her side. He moved his head a little, and Charlie saw the side of his face downturned to the ground, and of a sudden it seemed to the boy he had never seen the face before, never seen the sadness there and the kindness, too, and the marks of wild, dark angers that he couldn't help.

Father's voice sounded tired. "Run to the woodshed and get the spade, will you, son?"

When Charlie hesitated, Father said, "We'll dig a grave under the Balm of Gilead. I think she'd like to lie there."

Charlie turned and ran for the woodshed, and a great sob formed in his stomach and tore at his throat and burst out of him. He got around the corner of the shed, where Father wouldn't see him, and his legs let him down on the chopping block. He thought that all his life he would see Eb sinking to the ground and Father's sad, dark face downturned on her and the tears in Mamma's eyes. He didn't know for whom he cried, for Eb or Father or Mother or himself. He only knew, while sobs racked him and the tears streamed down his cheeks and put the taste of salt in his mouth, that now he had to cry.

Dorothy M. Johnson

The Gift by the Wagon

AFTER a while, Caleb understood that he was sick, that he had been sick quite a long time. The simmering pain in his shoulder had been a boiling pain, he remembered dimly. So he must be getting better. And someone had been looking after him, but he did not know who it was or why they should be doing it or how he was going to pay for it.

There was a medicine smell, but that was on himself. Beyond it was the smell of horses, and he was bedded down on hay. He worried for a while and then wavered dizzily back to sleep.

Later he heard a girl's voice: "I could look after him if you'd move him to the house."

And a man's: "It wouldn't be fitting. Anyhow he's too sick to be moved yet."

"Did he say anything about who he is or who shot him?"

"I don't know any more than you do. A ragged stranger without a dollar in his pocket."

Ragged, yes. But rich, too. The shock of realization made Caleb start and hurt his shoulder. Then the gentle warmth of knowledge crept over him: I've got $15,000 banked with Wells Fargo. That's why I was dry-gulched back there somewhere. The men figured I was taking the gold out myself.

When the man came again and put a hand on Caleb's forehead to test the fever, Caleb asked, "Where is this place?"

"Livery stable in Fenton," the man answered. "Fort Fenton, it used to be. My boys found you in the pasture. Thought you were dead."

Caleb murmured, "I came a long way, then, after I was shot."

A long way I rode—must be ninety miles—with the fever blazing. And what brought me in this direction in the first place? I wanted to go back ten years and prove to somebody that I amounted to something after all. Somebody who probably isn't here any more, and I hated her anyway because I was a coward and she wasn't.

He wanted to call out to the man, You needn't think you have to give me charity. I can pay you well.

But he knew that was not true. You cannot balance a debt of kindness with a poke of gold any more than you can subtract three pigs from five applies. He was in debt to this man whose name he did not know, and the thought angered him.

The man did not know him, either; the man looked after him, that was all. Charity, Caleb thought. It's a burden to me.

He found out the man's name, Pete Wilson; he ran the livery stable. He had two half-grown sons who hung around sometimes. The girl's name was Fortune.

When she came with a pitcher of lemonade (pretending she did not know Pete was away just then), Caleb said, "You don't look old enough to have boys as big as they are," and she answered with a laugh, "They're not mine, except I'm raising them. I'm Pete's sister."

She was a pretty girl, calm and easy to talk to.

When Caleb was well enough, he moved to the hotel. But first he called on the local banker and made some arrangements and paid the doctor. After that, the hotel keeper was cordial, although Caleb wore the same clothes he had come in. They were clean now, and no longer ragged but nicely mended by Fortune. Even when Caleb lived at the hotel, he spent much time at the livery stable, talking to Pete or anybody, because he wasn't yet able to do anything else.

Pete asked no questions, but he was willing to answer them.

"How long you been here?" Caleb inquired, just passing time.

"Came right after the war. Some of my folks was here before me."

"I came by here once, to the old fort, with a wagon train on the way west," Caleb volunteered, hating to remember that but having a need to mention it. "Things have changed."

And with me they've changed, he assured himself. Gold banked with Wells Fargo now. I can have just about anything—but what do I want? Why, just to prove to somebody that was here once that I amount to something. A fool reason for heading this way, but a man's got to head somewhere.

Pete's boys went into the house across the road, and Caleb asked lazily, "What makes the younger one limp?"

"Got hurt when he was a baby. Don't mention it to him—he hates that limp."

"How old is he?"

"Twelve. Wesley's fourteen. . . . What you shivering for? Got a chill?"

"Goose walked over my grave. I'm all right."

But they could be the same boys who had howled with fear ten years ago. Fortune could be the little girl he remembered with envy and distaste, the little girl he wanted to prove something to and still wanted never to see again.

But they can't be, Caleb decided. Those folks must have moved on.

When he had been at the hotel for a week, he got up courage enough to ask if he might accompany Fortune to church.

"Why, I'd be pleased," she answered, looking as if she meant it. "There's preaching next Sunday. The circuit rider comes once a month."

"I figure to dress up a little better than I am now," Caleb promised.

"A person can go to church in whatever clothes they've got," Fortune said stoutly.

He bought new clothes and a black scarf to make a decent, inconspicuous sling for his left arm, which couldn't stand being moved much.

Sunday morning lasted about a month, he calculated, until it was time to call for Fortune at the house across from the livery stable.

Fortune's nephew Basil, who walked with a limp, said, "She ain't ready yet," and Fortune called from somewhere, "I am so!" but didn't come for a few minutes.

Basil and his brother Wesley had found Caleb in a field, face down and bloody, with his horse standing over him because he had tied the reins to his good arm before he fainted. They took it for granted he was dead, but Basil had dared to touch him so as to boast that he had touched a dead man. Basil was still a little edgy with Caleb because of that.

Fortune came into the kitchen, walking rapidly with small steps, neatly slim in a gray dress. She said, "Good morning, Caleb," in a businesslike fashion, and he answered, "Good morning, Miss Fortune," and wished he hadn't, because she dimpled and young Basil haw-hawed.

"I mean, Miss Wilson," he corrected, embarrassed. He had not called her anything before that day.

"You may call me by my first name," she said, "without any Miss on it."

Basil remarked, "She says it's a misfortune to be Miss Fortune."

"It is my good fortune to take her to church," replied Caleb, feeling better about everything.

This is a more important day, he thought, than any day there ever was. More important than the day I found colors in the pan at Greasy Gulch or the day I sold my mine.

And he thought—he hoped—it was important for her too. She seemed breathless, as he was. It was a wonderful thing that had happened. One day he was a sick stranger lying in a stable, and another day he was almost well and Fortune was glad of his company.

My life is twisted with hers for good now, he realized. Forever, even if we part forever. For no reason except that we have met and she likes me.

In church she made sure nobody bumped his arm, and he wanted to protect her from dragons. But there were no dragons, unless you counted the inquisitive good women, and they attacked Caleb, not Fortune, with their questions.

"You're getting better, I see. Just how did it happen?"

"Three men dry-gulched me, ma'am, and thought they finished me off."

"At Greasy Gulch, we heard?"

"A little this side of there, ma'am. I didn't aim to go back there and run into the same robbers, so I rode this way."

Ninety miles of pain and horror, of increasing fever and increasing fear that he wasn't going to make it.

"And Pete Wilson's boys found you. How fortunate!"

"Yes ma'am. It was indeed."

They eyed him closely, pretending not to. If he could wear good clothes now and stay at the hotel, why had he come in rags?

He had headed out of Greasy Gulch silently, by night, alone, but the road agents guessed it and ambushed him. They got maybe a hundred dollars in dust for their trouble. The rest of it had gone out on Wells Fargo's treasure coach and was safe. But all that was none of the good ladies' business.

"You were prospecting?" one of the women inquired.

"Lately I was mining, ma'am," he answered, and the woman didn't know the difference between seeking for gold and digging it out after you'd found where it was.

Someone asked, "Do you plan to stay here for a while?" but Fortune interrupted that they'd have to go now to see whether the boys had put the potatoes on as instructed. So he didn't have to answer that question.

On the way to the Wilson house they were breathless again—"It's a lovely day, isn't it? . . . A fine day indeed. Sun's bright but not too warm. . . . How pretty the light is on the cottonwoods! . . . Sure is pretty. Yes, it is."

Being together was so splendid, so important, that they could not speak of anything that mattered.

The boy had put the potatoes on and kept the fire going. Fortune tied on a starched apron and busied herself with Sunday dinner while Caleb watched. Watching Fortune mash the potatoes was as fine a sight as he'd ever seen, he thought. As pretty as flake gold showing yellow in a pan of gravel.

Fortune told the boys, "Now go get your father. We'll be ready soon as he washes up."

When Pete Wilson sat down with them at the table, he guessed the situation, and Caleb saw his face change, sag into weariness.

Fine way I'm treating the man who saved my life, Caleb thought. He's got two motherless boys to raise, and now he figures to lose his sister that's raising them. Maybe, on account of that, she wouldn't go away with me if I asked her. Fortune is a girl that wouldn't shirk her duty.

But we needn't go away! he realized. A man that's got fifteen thousand dollars put away with Wells Fargo can live anywhere he wants to.

Caleb was so recently rich that the idea still shocked him. He hadn't yet got any pleasure out of it to speak of, except buying a fine chestnut horse in Greasy Gulch and now he had new clothes.

"Shall I cut your meat, Caleb?" Fortune asked. "With your sore arm, you can't."

"You cooked it so tender it don't need a knife," he said, and she looked pleased.

"Wouldn't be interested in selling your horse?" Fortune's brother suggested. "A man was in, asking."

Caleb shook his head. "If you had a real good horse for the first time in your life, would you sell him?"

"Not if I didn't have to."

"I don't have to. I never had any luck till lately," Caleb explained. "Worked at one thing and another since I was a young kid. I struck pay dirt at Greasy Gulch. Enough so the road agents figured I was worth robbing."

Fortune was not startled at the news that he had found gold. She beamed approval, because she was sure that so remarkable a man as Caleb naturally would find what he was looking for.

Her brother commented without jealousy, "Struck it rich. Well, I'm glad to hear it."

"And all the gold in the gulch wouldn't have helped me if you hadn't taken me in," Caleb reminded him. Then he made a mistake. He added, "I aim to pay you for what you did."

"No," Pete said, offended. "I make out all right with my business."

One of the boys yelled from the yard, "Hey, Pa, Mr. Hendrickson wants the sorrel."

Pete got up, grumbling, "He can't have it when it's out, can he?" and went across the road to his place of business.

So Caleb and Fortune were in the kitchen by themselves, and Caleb longed to say something memorable, but Fortune became very housewifely just then.

"Just you sit," she advised, "while I pick up the dishes."

"Please," he said, "I'd like to help with them."

She glanced at his arm in its sling and answered, with the sweetest smile he had ever seen, "Some other time you can."

And he knew that she had said something memorable, if he hadn't. It was a hint of a promise. There would be other times. He wanted to yell with jubilation, but he only smiled instead and they understood each other perfectly.

"Smoke if you want to," Fortune invited, so he lighted a cigar and admired her domesticity.

There was quick movement outside—he only glimpsed it, without understanding. But Fortune said, "I declare!" and ran out, dropping her dish towel. Caleb waited, puzzled, for it seemed to him that nothing had happened except that one of the boys had run past, and why should that upset her?

She mothers those kids, he thought. She mothers everybody.

He remembered a little girl of whom he had thought the same thing, a gaunt, serene child who had once been near this fort.

It can't be the same, he told himself. They surely didn't stay. She had two little brothers—or were they her brothers? They could have been nephews. He hadn't been concerned with relationships that day ten years before when he himself was fourteen.

He did not want Fortune to be that little girl grown up. He remembered the time and the girl with horror. He was so disturbed that he got up and walked back and forth across the floor while he waited for Fortune to come back.

"What's wrong?" he demanded.

Something certainly was wrong. He thought she had been crying.

"It's Basil. Some new boys teased him because he's lame. It's a terrible thing; it happens too often. And he gets mad and cries, and that makes him madder."

"But you made him feel better."

She shook her head. "Not unless it helped him to take his mad out on me. He said it's my fault he's lame, and it is. I—I hurt him when he was two years old."

Then she was crying, with her hands over her face, and Caleb yearned toward her, wanting to touch her but aware that he had no right.

"It wasn't your fault," he insisted. "It couldn't have been. You wouldn't hurt anybody."

"But I broke his leg," she sobbed. "I should have managed better."

Caleb put his good hand on her arm firmly, whether he had any right or not.

"Look at me, Fortune, and stop crying."

He knew now that she was that little girl he remembered.

"Was it when the Indians came and you hid the children in a tree?" he demanded.

She gasped and stared at him, trembling. She didn't say yes. She didn't have to.

So Caleb would be no hero to Fortune now. He would kill no dragons for her. Because he had been a coward when he was fourteen years old, and she had kept her head in the midst of danger—and remembered, when it was over with, to come and comfort him.

Caleb thought bleakly, Well, I can partly pay Pete back. Pete's charity and mine can sort of balance out.

"Call Basil in here," he commanded. "I want to tell him something. What have you been telling him all these years?"

"Why, what could I tell him? I never meant to hurt him, but I did, and he's lame for life."

There was, Caleb thought, a dragon he could kill for Basil at least, and then he would ride on somewhere away from the old fort that was called a settlement now. Maybe the truth would help Fortune too, but it would do no good for Caleb.

She didn't have to call the boy. He limped in and went to the kitchen pump for a drink.

"Go tell your pa I want a rig and a horse," Caleb ordered. "Mine's not broke to harness. You and I and Fortune are going for a drive."

"What for?" the boy challenged, snuffling.

"I want to show you a place and tell you what happened there." Caleb turned to Fortune. "How far is it? Ten, eleven miles?"

She was trembling. "I won't go. I've never been back there. I won't go."

"Yes, you'll go," he said gently. "Because you have to."

She would not sit next to him in the buggy but put Basil between them. Caleb talked about the sun and the trees, but nobody answered.

It was a long drive to the place, and ten years since he had seen it, but he found the overgrown wagon road. He had gone that way on foot the other time—first, mile by slow mile with the wagon train westward, and then alone into a meadow, looking for a lost cow. He could have recognized now any landmark in the hundreds of miles he had trudged ten years before.

"We'll leave the horse here," he said when he found the old wagon track. "From here we'll walk."

Basil whined, "I don't want to. This is where the Indians came."

Caleb tied the horse to a tree. "Do you remember anything about it?"

The boy shook his head. "I was only two."

"Did you ever stop to think you're lucky not to remember it?" Caleb asked.

He led the way along the traces of a rough road.

I am fourteen years old, he thought, and I am looking for Mr. Forsyth's cow. Not that his lost cow is any concern of mine, but I want the people in the wagon train to know how useful I am. Maybe some of them will take me in when we get to Idaho. Because my sister Elsie is going to marry that man Hankins, and he doesn't like me. There'll be no place for me in their house when they get one.

Fortune spoke piteously behind him: "Why do we have to go to—this place?"

"To see that it is only a little meadow with nothing in it. And to tell Basil some things he doesn't know."

There was no menace there. No menace had whispered the first time he walked that wagon track, either. But he had smelled smoke that other time and had seen the charred, ruined cabin and a dead man, bloody, lying on the ground.

Caleb turned to Fortune and asked, "Will you tell your nephew what happened here, or shall I do it?"

She would not answer except to shake her head.

"All right. I will, as far as I can. Basil, see that old broken snag to the right of the cabin. She hid inside that snag with you boys. There's a window at the back of the cabin. You can't see it from here. I guess she went out that window while the Indians were busy with the man out in front.

"I never found out who he was," Caleb said, feeling faintly surprised. "I never asked." Or cared, either, he admitted to himself. The man was dead and didn't matter.

Fortune said in a strained voice, "My father's brother. He went out and they killed him. It gave me time to go out the back window with the boys."

She looked at the ground before her feet, but she did not turn her back on the place of horror.

"She could have run and saved herself," Caleb told the boy. "But she took the two of you out with her, and she put you both in that hollow snag before she climbed in to hide. Remember that, boy. When the Indians were killing a man not twenty feet away, she didn't run and save herself and leave you. And she wasn't more than twelve years old, I judge."

Basil's head was bent, but he kept stealing glances at the ruined cabin and the hollow snag, crumbling now with rot.

I've given him something to think about, Caleb told himself. Something nobody bothered about before. They never talked about all this any more than they had to. It was something they would rather not think about at all.

Basil demanded, "And where were you?"

"Way on beyond by the river with a wagon train when this happened. Nobody knew it was happening. We were stopped for Sunday by the river so the women could do their washing and we could go on to the fort next day. I was traveling with my older sister and her kids. I came this way on foot, looking for a lost cow.

"First I smelled smoke. Then I saw the meadow with the cabin in it. And a man lying there."

Basil was seeing those things too, identifying himself with that other boy who had become a man named Caleb Stark.

Basil asked in a hushed voice, "Why didn't you run?"

"Why, because—" Why didn't I? Caleb wondered. "I guess because I didn't believe it, what I was seeing. The meadow was so quiet, so peaceful, not even a bee buzzing. It was as quiet as—death. You know," he said earnestly, "you can't believe death either, first time you see it close."

The boy blinked. "Like I saw you, lying in the field. I thought you were dead."

"And you touched me so you could boast you had touched a dead man. You didn't want to. You were afraid. But you did it. It didn't matter one way or another. Except then you saw the dead man was breathing, and you went for your pa."

Basil nodded, feeling himself something of a hero.

"It was something like that with me here at the edge of the meadow. After I could believe what had happened, then I was scared. I wanted to run, I was going to run and get out of here. But there was a little sound from over to the right there, a faint little sound in the deathly quiet. I thought it was a wounded Indian, and

I thought if he was wounded I could kill him. And have something to boast about back at the wagon camp.

"Because God knows," Caleb burst out, "I never had had anything to boast about or be proud of, and it was time I did. So I yelled something, some kind of challenge. I don't know what it was."

Fortune spoke quietly, "You said, 'Damn you, I'll shoot!' and I couldn't hold my hand over Basil's mouth any longer because he'd bitten me, and he screamed and then you came and got us out of the hollow snag."

Caleb said to the boy, "How many hours did she stay in there, cramped in there with you two kids, holding your mouths so you couldn't scream and bring the Indians back to kill the lot of you? She was so cramped she couldn't climb out.

"I found an axe with the handle half burned off and chopped out the side of the snag before any of you could get out. I was so scared I couldn't even see good. It's a wonder I didn't chop you with that axe."

He felt bathed with shame, as always, remembering how scared he had been, how witless. And how cool and sensible that little girl was, telling him what to do as she lay on the ground where she had fallen out of the snag. She was trying to move her cramped legs, and her face was contorted with the pain, but she wasn't crying, she never cried once. And she thought of everything.

Caleb said, "First thing she said was, 'Get the kids some water.' I didn't want to stop for that. I wanted to get out of this place to where it was safer. But she said, 'Get the kids some water,' and told me where the spring was, so I carried water in my hat, and she didn't drink till after you boys did."

Every step of the way, he remembered, I hated her for delaying me. I hunched my muscles, expecting a bullet from somewhere in the brush, or an Indian yell and death right behind it.

"And I wanted to go then, just grab one of you kids and run for it—or leave you there, for that matter. I didn't care. But she said, 'Basil's hurt,' and I saw your leg looked crooked. You were trying to crawl but couldn't, and you and your brother were howling blue murder. I thought you'd bring the Indians for sure.

"She said, 'You'll have to brace his leg someway to carry him. Get a stick or something and tie onto it.' She thought of that, even, and told me, while she was still working the cramps out of her legs. So I got a straight stick and then couldn't think of anything to tie it with, but she tore the shirt off your brother and we tied the splint that way. She got blood on the cloth, you'd bitten that deep into her hand.

"When she could walk, she dragged your brother by the hand and I carried you and my rifle, and we went as fast as we could along the wagon track to get out of here."

Fortune whispered, "Then we had to hide."

That was another thing that Caleb hated to remember—and to have her remember.

"I was so scared," he said slowly. "We heard men's voices ahead of us on the wagon track and I couldn't move any more. I was so big a coward I couldn't move or think. I just stood there, hanging onto you and waiting for someone to kill me."

Fortune said sharply, "Nonsense! I was the scared one. I said, 'Let's hide,' and we did, in the brush. But it wasn't Indians, it was men from the wagons."

"I was a coward," Caleb repeated. "But after that it didn't matter much because they hustled us out of there.

"That's all, kid. You can be glad you don't remember anything about it."

Caleb turned abruptly and led the way back along the grass-grown ruts, away from the quiet meadow where death and terror had been a long time ago.

On the way back to the old fort, Fortune was willing to sit beside him in the rig, with her hands in her lap. After a while she said, "That wasn't all. You gave me your coat. And I think it was the only one you had."

Caleb shrugged. "My sister fixed me another one."

He remembered that makeshift coat with shame. It was made of a torn patchwork quilt. He wore it when he had to, the rest of the way to Idaho, and many a time he shivered in the cold rather than put it on. Some of the people laughed and some tried to comfort him, which was worse. They called it Caleb's coat of many colors;

they said the lilies of the field were not arrayed like Caleb.

I've got fifteen thousand dollars banked with Wells Fargo, he reminded himself. But that did not erase the bitter memory of the gaudy coat that took the place of the one he gave away.

Fortune said suddenly, "Basil, he didn't tell you the straight of it. That boy that rescued us—I never knew his name till today—he was no coward. He was the bravest boy I ever knew. He could have run away. Nobody would have known. Nobody but him, anyway. But he stayed and got us out.

"Some people took us in their wagon for overnight, and a man who did some doctoring fixed your leg as well as he could, and they fed us. My father was coming from the fort; we met him on the way. He and Uncle Will used to sell hay there. That's why we were at the meadow.

"Just before the wagon train moved on to the fort, Caleb saw I was cold, and he gave me his coat."

"I still have it."

Caleb said, "What!"

"I wore it out, because we didn't have much in those days. But I've still got it, what there is left. It was something—to remember you by."

Caleb said gently, "Why, Fortune!"

And then nobody said anything the rest of the way to the settlement that had once been a fort.

That chilly morning long ago, cold before the sun came up, he wore his ragged brown coat while he harnessed the horses. The whole camp was stirring, getting ready to move on, and he felt that everybody stared at him. He was no hero, he was only an unwanted boy who had brought in some other unwanted, desperate children that somebody had to look after, at least temporarily.

The people felt that he had just about brought the Indians down on them. Men had been on guard all night, and nobody got much sleep.

Mr. Forsyth slouched up to him and asked with a long face, "I don't suppose you found my cow?"

"Never saw her," Caleb admitted.

Forsyth sighed and slouched away, not saying thanks for your trouble, just giving the impression that nobody expected Caleb to succeed even at a simple thing like that.

Caleb wondered, as he worked, what he would do in Idaho. There would be no place for him in his sister's home, and Caleb had a poor opinion of his own abilities. Nobody had ever suggested that he had any abilities. He was small for his age, hadn't got his growth, and that would handicap him in getting work.

He was as miserable as he had ever been in his life when the little girl came to him from behind a wagon. Her face was clean, and her hair was combed and braided, but she wore the same stained, torn dress, and she shivered, hugging herself with her arms but not saying anything about being cold. Someone had tied a clean rag on her hand, the hand the baby had bitten.

Caleb looked at her with distaste. The people in the wagons blamed him because they were worried about Indians. He had nobody to blame but the girl whose name he didn't know and didn't want to know.

She said politely, "I wanted to say thank you."

He shrugged, not knowing any better answer. He detested her because her need was so great and her future so bleak and she wasn't afraid of anything.

In the growing light of dawn she stepped toward him. Before he could guess her intention, she took his scowling face between her hands and lightly kissed his cheek.

He jumped back, angrily, scrubbing at his face, and demanded, "What's that for?"

"I don't know," she said, and turned away.

That was when he couldn't stand her shivering any more. He shucked off his old brown coat and threw it at her.

"Put that on," he growled.

She nodded and kept on walking away while she thrust her thin arms into the sleeves.

"I'll show you!" he muttered. "I'll come back some time and show you."

Show her what? Why, that he amounted to something, even if

she didn't think so, even if she had come and kissed him as if he were a baby to be pitied.

In the settlement that was a fort no longer, Caleb pulled up in front of the Wilson house. He helped Fortune down and ordered, "Basil, take the outfit back to your pa."

Then he stood looking into Fortune's quiet face.

"Why," he asked, "did you kiss me long ago?"

"It was all I had to give you," she replied. "Like the coat was all you had to give me."

Caleb nodded. He should have understood that all along.

"The years gone by were bad ones," he said. "The years to come will be better."

He was almost sure of that, but he was completely certain when she put both her hands into his outstretched hand and answered, "Why, yes, Caleb. Of course they will."

Dorothy M. Johnson

Prairie Kid

When Elmer Merrick was eleven years old, he
marched an outlaw off the Ainsworth place at the point of a
gun.

They still talk about it in Montana, telling the story with a
proud chuckle, implying that in the old days all the boys were
men, and all the men were tough as saddle leather. After Elmer
grew up, he was as tough as he needed to be, but when he held a
gun on Buck Saddler on that summer night in 1888, he was a
frightened, desperate child.

Except for size, he didn't look like a child. He walked like a
tired old man, with his shoulders drooping; when he rested, he
sagged with patient weariness, not fidgeting. He looked sullen
and puzzled and hostile, and he felt hostile toward just about
everybody except Lute Kimball. Lute was his idol, for two good
reasons: Lute treated him like an equal, and Lute could do well
everything that Elmer was still learning. But Lute lived up in
Miles City in those days, close to two days' ride on a good
horse, so they did not meet often.

In one respect only, Elmer doubted Lute's judgment. Lute was courting Charlotte Ainsworth, and Elmer considered her a fool and a tenderfoot. A tenderfoot she certainly was, for she had come out from the East only that summer to keep house for her brother, Steve. She had to be told the most elementary things, such as the rule that all comers had to be offered food, unless they were Indians.

More visitors came to Steve's place during her first month there than ordinarily passed in a year, so pretty Charlotte Ainsworth spent a great deal of her time cooking quick meals for staring, bashful cowboys, who pretended they hadn't known she was there.

That summer, while Charlotte Ainsworth was enjoying the privileges of being the only single white girl in almost a hundred miles, Elmer Merrick, on his father's ranch three hours' ride to the westward, was learning to live with fear. Waking or sleeping, it stalked him, and sometimes it leaped and took his breath away, and a jeering voice in his own mind demanded, If your pa dies, what are you going to do about Varina?

His sister Varina was six years old, sunny and carefree, unreliable and perverse. She did not know she was lonely, because she had always lived on the prairie. She played with a stick doll and sang to herself and carried on long, murmured conversations with a couple of entirely imaginary little girls named Beauty and Rose. Varina was of no use to anyone, and she worried about nothing except her chances of getting over to Steve's place fairly often to visit Miss Charlotte.

Miss Charlotte, she said, had a little rosewood melodeon that she had brought out in a trunk; Miss Charlotte was teaching her to play it; Miss Charlotte washed Varina's fair hair and made it hang in curls. Elmer, sick with his own worries, sometimes shouted, "Aw, shut up about Miss Charlotte!" but Varina would answer smugly, "Miss Charlotte likes me."

Once Elmer snapped, "Aw, she pretends she likes everybody," and then was ashamed of himself because Varina cried so hard.

He had enough to worry him. More than half his father's cattle starved in the snow in the terrible winter of 1887, his mother died the following fall, and his father, old Slope Merrick, was crippled with a gnawing pain in his belly. Slope had arranged with three cowboys, who were following the roundups for other outfits, to brand and tally his remaining scattered cattle, and sell them if anyone wanted to buy, but that meant putting a lot of trust in frail human nature. He and Elmer, between them, had found and branded only twenty head of calves.

If Slope had any plans for the future, he did not confide in his son, and Elmer confided in nobody. He wanted to talk to Lute Kimball, but Lute spent his time shining up to Miss Charlotte.

The fear pounced at Elmer more than once that summer; he sent it slinking back by ignoring it. He could forget about it if he worked hard enough, and there was work enough to do, with Slope lying in his bunk a good share of the time. Even when Slope decided, one morning before dawn, that he had to get to a doctor, the boy still did not quite face his problem. He was too busy to think about it for a while, after his father groaned, "Elmer! Elmer, git up! We're going to Steve's."

The boy sat up in his bunk, demanding with numb lips, "You want the wagon?"

Slope turned his head back and forth and groaned, "Of course! Of course!" as if they had discussed the whole matter in detail, and his son had forgotten.

Elmer woke his sister by giving her tangled blonde hair a jerk. Varina whimpered and slapped at him blindly.

"We're going to Steve's place for a while," he snapped. "You want to go along, you pile out and git ready!" He was wide awake now and planning. "You're going over ahead of us, by yourself."

Slope groaned, "No! Not alone."

But Elmer had his first taste of mastery. "She kin do it," he answered, and his father did not argue.

Elmer pulled on his pants and the boots he had outgrown, wrapped his moccasins in his other shirt, and grabbed his throw-rope off its peg by the door. By the time Varina was dressed and had her extra dress rolled up, Elmer had roped and saddled three horses and tied a rope halter on the cow. It did not occur to him to help his sister mount her horse; she scrambled on with what

Lute Kimball, smiling, had called a flying clamber. It was the same system Elmer used himself.

"Hurry up!" Elmer barked. "Tell 'em to git the team and wagon ready to take Pa up to town. We'll be coming along directly."

It was midmorning when Steve Ainsworth helped Slope down from the saddle and into the hay-filled wagon bed.

"I'll take good care of the children, Mr. Merrick," Miss Charlotte promised. "Don't you worry about them for a minute." She held Varina by the hand.

Slope lay back on the blankets and the hay. "Elmer!" he said. "Look after the women."

Elmer answered, "Yuh, sure." He stood with his hands in his pockets, his shoulders hunched.

"My old Colt," Slope said between his teeth. "You can carry it."

Elmer said, "All right," as calmly as if a dream had not suddenly come true. The old cap-and-ball .44 was in Pa's saddle bag with its belt and powder flask and the leather sacks of lead bullets and caps.

Steve Ainsworth let go the brake on the wagon. "You'll be all right," he told his sister with what he hoped sounded like conviction. "We'll be back as soon as we can make it. Maybe I can send Lute Kimball down ahead."

"Take good care of Mr. Merrick," she cautioned. "Children, don't you want to wave good-bye?"

Varina obediently waved, but Elmer stood with his hands in his pockets, thinking, Children, huh!

The cow lowed, recalling him to duty.

"I gotta milk," he announced, turning his back as the wagon dropped out of sight beyond the first low bridge. "You could cook us some breakfast. We ain't et yet."

Miss Charlotte was off in a flurry of skirts, exclaiming, "Oh, dear, when will I remember that visitors have to be fed! Come, Varina—you may play the melodeon."

Elmer scowled. "Don't you let her fool around with that!"

he ordered. "Make her do something useful. She's got a lot of things to learn."

Miss Charlotte turned, looking puzzled and amused. "She's just a little girl, Elmer. What should she be learning at her age?"

"If I knowed," he burst out in exasperation, "I'd learn her myself. Start her off with cooking. She won't pay no attention to me."

As he plodded with the bucket toward the cow, the fear came right up to meet him, and for the first time he faced it. It said, What you going to do about Varina if your pa dies? and he answered, I'm gonna leave Miss Charlotte look after her.

And what for would Miss Charlotte or anybody want to have her around? How you going to fix that, eh?

He answered honestly, I ain't got that quite figured out yet.

Then he milked the cow and started looking after the women, as he had been told to do.

Three days up by wagon, a day to see the doctor, and three days back, if all went well. A week before Steve could get back to the cabin. But Lute could make the return trip in less time: If Steve located him, he might get back late on the fifth day. If Steve met a rider, someone he could trust, there would be a man on the place sooner than that. But the wagon was not likely to meet anyone, because riders came by the horse trail.

The first day Elmer kept busy cutting firewood down by the river, annoyed because Miss Charlotte was pampering Varina, letting her waste time playing the melodeon, although when he came in for meals, Varina industriously peeled potatoes and wiped dishes. Varina helped Miss Charlotte spread the blankets smooth in the bunks. The two of them slept in the lean-to, and Elmer had Steve's bunk in the main room, the kitchen.

The second day, seven Indians came by. Elmer sent them on their way—an old buck, four squaws, a young girl, and a boy about his own age—but he was embarrassed at having let them get clear to the cabin. He did not go back to cutting wood by the river.

After that, when the water buckets needed filling, he made the women go with him down to the river. Miss Charlotte obviously thought he wanted her for protection and made quite a show of being gay to let him know she wasn't scared. Elmer didn't tell her any different. He was learning the patience a man has to have with women.

When she wanted to help carry water, he growled, "I'd rather carry the both buckets. It's easier." Even Varina knew that. One bucket pulled you down sideways. The old Cavalry Colt, sagging along his right leg, already did that.

Miss Charlotte was slightly amused about his wearing the Colt. With what Miss Charlotte didn't know about guns, you could win battles. She didn't even suspect the Colt was loaded; the bright copper caps were plain to see, but she didn't notice. Elmer felt a little guilty about having all six chambers charged; Lute played safer than that, and he had a Frontier model—a Peacemaker—that took regular cartridges. Lute kept the hammer on an empty chamber. But Elmer Merrick preferred to take chances on shooting himself in the foot accidentally, as long as he could convince himself that he was ready for six kinds of trouble. Reloading took a lot of time; many a man had been killed and scalped, in the old days, while he fumbled with powder and ball.

The third day, Elmer chopped the wood into stove lengths, and on the day after that he started to dig post holes for Steve's horse corral. Steve planned to drive a bunch of horses in from Oregon the following spring.

When Miss Charlotte saw what he was doing, she came flying out, exclaiming, "Elmer, now you stop that!"

Everything she said or did annoyed him, so he answered. "Digging's got to be done, don't it? Steve wants a corral, don't he?"

"Let him go on building it himself, then. I don't want you working so hard as you've been doing, Elmer Merrick. I want you to settle down. My goodness, don't you ever play?"

He had not played for a long time; his spare time he had usually spent in practicing things he needed to learn, like roping, or pulling his gun fast. But while he was affronted by her insistence that he was a child, he was pleased that she had noticed how hard he worked.

"When there's things to be done, someone's got to do 'em," he told her.

"But not heavy work like that!" she insisted. "You're liable to stunt your growth."

That was enough to stop him. Maybe, he thought, she was right. But he could not admit that he was going to take her seriously. He said doubtfully, "Well, I'll find something else."

He set out to chink the cracks of the lean-to, built that spring for Miss Charlotte's bedroom. While he worked at it, he solved part of his problem: What he was going to do if his father did not come back. Somewhere there must be an outfit that needed a wrangler on the home place, a helper to bring in the cavy for the cowboys and chore around for the cook. He dreamed about an imaginary boss saying, "That boy ain't very big for what I had in mind," and Miss Charlotte assuring him, "Oh, but he's a very hard worker. Elmer just works all the time."

And what are you going to do about Varina? his conscience nagged.

I'm figuring about that, he answered patiently. I'm figuring how to get Miss Charlotte to keep her.

That was on the fourth day. On the fifth, Lute Kimball might have come, but a fair-haired stranger got there first, a wary man with quick-darting gray eyes. It was Miss Charlotte's fault that he stayed instead of riding on. She convinced Elmer all over again that she was a tenderfoot and a fool. But it was Elmer's fault that the stranger ever had a chance to feel so much at home.

When the man came, Elmer was in sight, but he was down at the edge of the river grove, with Steve's deer rifle, scouting around where he had seen deer signs. In the back of his mind was the thought, If she was to tell it around, "That Elmer is a good hunter; he got us venison," that would sound good to the boss, I guess.

He did not hear the stranger's horse, but a tingling on the back of his neck made him aware that something was going on. When he saw the buckskin horse and the buckskin-shirted rider, he set out for the cabin at a run.

But Miss Charlotte was already making the stranger welcome.

And the man was saying, "Well, now, if you're sure it ain't too much trouble, I could eat all right, and that's a fact."

He whirled when he heard Elmer's pounding feet on the hard earth but the steel-spring tension went out of him when he saw only a boy and not a man. He turned back to Miss Charlotte and took off his dusty hat with a flourish.

"Buck Saddler, ma'am, and pleased to make your acquaintance."

"I am Miss Charlotte Ainsworth," she answered, smiling, "and these are the Merrick children, Elmer and Varina. If you'd like to wash up, Mr. Saddler, there's the basin."

The man hesitated for just a moment. "Thank you kindly. I'll just look after my horse first." He loosened the saddle cinch and walked around the horse, frowning and shaking his head. "Poor boy!" he murmured, slapping the animal's shoulder. "Plumb beat, ain't you?" Then he turned to Elmer and commented, grinning, "You sure carry a lot of artillery."

Elmer glanced at the man's sagging gunbelt and loaded saddle and answered, "So do you." Buck Saddler carried a rifle and a shotgun on the saddle, and two belts of cartridges slung over the horn—not unreasonable armament for a long journey, but impressive.

The stranger glanced at the hog leg that pulled Elmer's belt down and smiled with unwise condescension. "I gollies, one of them old cap-and-ball Colts! Let's look at it, kid."

Elmer backed off, scowling. "Nobody touches my gun but me."

"If you was to show it to me," the stranger offered, teasing, "I might let you see mine."

"I kin see it," Elmer informed him. "It's a Peacemaker." In the old days before he had so many other things to worry about, he had dreamed of owning a Peacemaker himself, and money enough to buy all the ammunition he wanted, and hands big enough to handle a man-sized gun easily.

Miss Charlotte called, "I've got the griddle heating for pancakes. It's close to suppertime, so we'll all eat."

"You'll be wanting to go on before dark," Elmer told the

stranger, hinting strongly. "We better git in there and eat, so's you won't be delayed."

Buck Saddler looked down at him through half-shut eyes. "I might have to delay anyway," he said deliberately. He walked toward the cabin and left Elmer worrying.

Miss Charlotte worried him more. She fussed as if Buck Saddler were a welcome guest. "Now, if you'll sit here, Mr. Saddler! You prefer the other side of the table? Of course, of course. Varina, Elmer, did you wash?"

Buck Saddler, Elmer noted, preferred to sit facing the window. You got some good reason for that, Elmer decided. And there's nothing wrong with that horse you're so cut up about.

Miss Charlotte raised her eyebrows at Elmer. "Young man, you can't come to the table with that gun on." Elmer kept his mouth shut, but it required effort. Never before in his life had he wanted so much to have a gun handy. But Buck Saddler stood up, grinning, unbuckled his own belt and hung it ostentatiously on a peg on the wall. Elmer did the same and sat down at the table without appetite.

Where's Lute? he fretted. It's time you come, Lute Kimball!

Lute Kimball was riding as hard as he dared on a spent horse, but he was also dreaming, as he often did, of being a hero for Miss Charlotte. No one would have suspected so stern-faced a man of dreaming about anything. He was a dark and silent man, thoughtful and practical. He had never stayed very long in any territory or on any job, but he had never quit any job so long as the boss needed him. He had made two trail drives up from Texas, and for most of his life had been looking for greener pastures. When Steve Ainsworth's sister came West, he saw them for the first time—green pastures, full of flowers, wherever Miss Charlotte was. Lute Kimball was twenty-seven years old that summer, and ready to settle down.

He missed his chance to be a hero for Steve's pretty sister, after all. He reached the cabin a few minutes too late.

Elmer had to admit that Miss Charlotte didn't make any more

fuss over Buck Saddler than she did over anybody else; she always seemed delighted to see anyone who happened to come. But the stranger, following her quick movements with his darting eyes, assumed that he was a favored guest. He turned courtly and affable.

"That there pretty little organ," he commented; "that's a mighty nice thing to have. I bet you play it mighty pretty, Miss Charlotte."

"Only a few tunes," Miss Charlotte fibbed modestly. "But Varina, my goodness, Varina is learning to play it very nicely." To Elmer's disgust his little sister piped up, "I sure do play it good."

Charlotte beamed and did not reprimand her for boasting.

If Miss Charlotte wanted to bring the little girl into the conversation, the stranger was willing to play along. He said fatuously to Varina, "You're a real smart little girl, ain't you? And all fixed up with your hair in curls, anybody'd think it was your birthday, maybe."

"When is your birthday, dear?" Charlotte inquired.

Varina looked puzzled. Elmer answered, "Fifteenth of August. She don't know nothing."

Miss Charlotte glanced up at the calendar. "I declare," she cried, "that's today! If I'd known, I'd have baked a cake!"

Birthdays had never been of much account in the Merrick cabin; Varina would never have thought of making a fuss if she hadn't been encouraged. But Buck Saddler encouraged her.

"By George, a nice bright little girl like that, and she ain't got no cake or no presents! Now that sure is a shame!"

Varina's eyes flooded with tears. She began to cry, with her face in Miss Charlotte's lap.

Elmer growled, "Shut up, Foolish!" Embarrassed, he explained, "She don't howl like that when she falls off a horse."

Miss Charlotte patted the child's shoulder. "We'll have a present for Varina. I know just the thing—a pretty ribbon I brought in my trunk. Would you like a ribbon for your hair, Varina?"

Varina heard that, in spite of her squalling, and nodded emphatically.

The stranger said, "I can't have a lady beating my time with this here little girl. I'm gonna give her a present, too." He dug in his pocket, fished around a little, and brought out a coin. He opened Varina's hand and closed her fingers over the gift. Tear-stained, she stared at it.

Miss Charlotte cried, "Mr. Saddler, you can't do that! Why, it's a double eagle!"

He said with reproach, "Wouldn't want me to take back what I give her, would you, Miss Charlotte? No sir, that's for the little lady." He looked so smug that Elmer wanted to hit him.

And then he said the thing that scared Elmer: "Plenty more where that came from," said Buck Saddler.

For a few seconds Elmer forgot to breathe. A man might possibly have one gold piece or a couple. But if there's plenty more where that come from, Elmer realized, he never earned it. Was it a bank or a stage?

Miss Charlotte's face had colored, and she looked even a little scared, Elmer thought. Glowering at her, he could suddenly tell what she was thinking: Go away, you man! We don't want you here!

Never before had he been able to see so clearly what was in an adult's mind. The revelation startled him so much that, for a moment, he was dazed by his own cleverness. And then, with desperate cunning, he arrived at the answer to that dismal question: What are you going to do about Varina?

If it was so Miss Charlotte owed me a debt, he thought, might be she'd take Foolish and raise her. Might be she'd be that grateful. Well, how can I get rid of this man?

That was how Elmer got on the track of saving Miss Charlotte—for cold, calculating reasons of his own. Lute Kimball, who had another reason for wanting to do the same thing if he ever had a chance—no less selfish a reason, but very different—still had nine miles to ride.

Miss Charlotte was not one to depend on someone else if she could do a thing herself. She started in a business-like way to pick up the dirty dishes. Pointedly she remarked, "It'll be dark in no time. You'll be wanting to go on, Mr. Saddler."

The stranger frowned. "I don't rightly like to leave you all here without no menfolks," he objected. "No telling what might come along."

"How true," Miss Charlotte murmured. "Don't give it a thought, Mr. Saddler. Elmer is our menfolks, and we are entirely confident that he will look after everything."

Elmer stared, for the first time thinking that Charlotte Ainsworth was, though still a tenderfoot, not actually a fool.

He began to figure: If I do this, he'll do that, but maybe he won't. Well, if I do that, what'll he do? Elmer was eleven years old and scared silly. But he was a prairie boy, and if he had not been self-reliant, he would not have lived to be eleven years old. He would have drowned at ten, when his horse threw him while fording a river, or he would have frozen in the blizzard that got him lost the year before that.

Buck Saddler gave him time to think. Buck wiped his mustache on his sleeve and strolled over to look at the melodeon. To the entranced Varina he suggested, "How'd you like to play me a little tune, girlie?"

Miss Charlotte said, "Varina is going to help me with the dishes," but Varina did no such thing. She started to pump the melodeon; she had to stand up to reach the keyboard, and pump the little metal pedal with one foot. Looking very well pleased with herself, she began picking out notes, making soft, pale-colored tones that you could almost see—silken ribbons of sound.

In the midst of figuring about Buck, Elmer thought, Oh, Lord, how would Miss Charlotte or anybody want to raise her, when she don't mind no better than that?

But he got his problem solved. If I do that, he will do this. There were only a few maybe's this time. Almost everything depended on: If I do that.

When he reached up to get his gun belt, Buck Saddler was instantly alert, but he only watched. He was within reaching distance of his Peacemaker. Elmer removed the old .44 from its holster, but left the belt and holster hanging on the peg. He walked over to Steve's small box of tools on the window sill and began to rummage.

Charlotte, scraping plates, asked tensely, "What are you looking for?"

"Worm," he muttered. "Think Steve's got a worm here. I want to unload my gun."

She looked so sick and helpless Elmer was afraid she would cry out and give everything away.

"This'll do it," Elmer remarked.

Buck watched him, slit-eyed, not moving. Elmer took his own sweet time. Never once did he move quickly; he kept the old Cavalry Colt carefully pointed at the wall while he worked, with the casual carefulness of one who had always handled firearms and had not pointed a gun at anyone since he got his ears boxed for it at the age of four. Delicately, he pried five caps off their nipples and let them lay on the table in plain sight. Painstakingly he reamed the powder and ball from five chambers, and Buck could count if he chose.

Buck relaxed enough to comment, "Mighty pretty tune you're playing, girlie." Miss Charlotte did not relax at all.

Elmer, on the far side of the table, put the gun down on the bench where he sat, with enough force to make it sound believable—and almost enough force to make his heart stop, because one chamber was still charged, and the cap was on the nipple. He sat for a little while, yawning, while he slid the long weapon down through his torn pocket and along his leg. The hole in his pocket was just right to catch and hold the hammer. When he stood up, yawning, Buck Saddler demanded, "Where do you think you're going?"

"A person can go outside, can't they?" Elmer answered with elaborate dignity. "Maybe I'm gonna hunt rabbits."

Buck grinned. Hunting rabbits was what gentlemen passengers were invited to do when stage coaches with lady passengers made a comfort stop. Ladies "picked flowers."

When Elmer Merrick went outside to start to rescue Miss Charlotte, Lute Kimball was still two miles away.

"You was gone quite a while," Buck commented a little later.

"I come back," Elmer pointed out. "Your horse is down," he

announced, as if he didn't care one way or the other. "I'll get the lantern if you'd like to take a look."

Buck scowled. "There wasn't nothing wrong with that horse!"

He was cornered and puzzled. But how could he be cornered by a small boy who had just unloaded his gun in plain sight? Buck Saddler relaxed and grinned.

"We'll be right back," he promised Miss Charlotte. "And the little girl can play me another tune." So complete was his disdain that he did not even reach up to the peg for his gun belt. Elmer came close to choking, because he wanted to draw a deep breath of relief and could not. That had been one of the maybe's.

He lighted the lantern and held it in front of him so that his shadow was in Buck Saddler's path. Buck grunted and snatched the lantern. Beyond the saddle shed he held the lantern high.

"There's nothing wrong with that horse!" he growled.

"Not a thing," agreed Elmer. "He's all cinched up and ready to travel."

Saddler laughed. "I ain't traveling nowhere. Not till I get ready."

"You're ready now," Elmer told him softly. "And this gun says so."

Saddler sneered. "I seen you unload it."

"You seen me unload five chambers. I got one charge left—and that's all it takes. You want to find out for sure, mister?" he demanded with tense urgency. "You ever get hit with a ball from a .44 not ten feet away from you?" Buck glanced toward his saddle. "Your other artillery is on my saddle," Elmer told him. "You'll get it back, but not just yet. Hold the lantern nice and steady, Buck."

Getting on his horse was another of the maybe's, but Saddler was wise enough to make no false moves. Elmer went up to his saddle like a flying bird, and when he got there, he cocked the hammer.

He heard Buck's grunt at the triple click, as the stranger realized that the gun had not been ready for action until that moment. Buck had been a man for too many years; he had forgotten that a boy's hand might not be big enough to cock and fire a single-action revolver with one quick motion.

"Git on your horse, mister," Elmer told him.

They rode away from the cabin. And Lute Kimball, coming over a hill, saw the lantern on the ground.

Half an hour later, several hills away, Elmer said, "You kin stop now. I'm gonna drop your guns and cartridge belts. You can pick 'em up, and I'll be watching, still with my gun in my hand, Buck. Still with my gun in my hand. Your rifle and shotgun are plumb empty."

The cabin was dark when Elmer got back to it. He could feel the waiting silence. Lute Kimball called, "Elmer, anybody with you?"

Elmer went limp in the saddle as the strength went out of him along with the tension. "Nope," he croaked.

Miss Charlotte called, "Are you all right?"

"Aw, sure," he answered. But when he slid from the saddle, his knees went limber. He landed in a heap.

Lute said, "Come in the cabin. We're not going to have a light any more." He was standing in the doorway with his rifle ready, watching into the darkness.

Miss Charlotte said, "Varina is asleep in the lean-to. She doesn't know anything special happened."

Foolish is the lucky one, Elmer thought. All hell could bust loose, and she'd never know it.

He remarked, "I don't think he'll come back."

Lute laughed, one short laugh. "I don't think he will. Getting run off by a runt of a boy with an empty gun."

"It wasn't empty," Elmer explained. "I had one chamber loaded."

"Did you now?" Lute sounded half smothered. "One charge, so you was all ready for bear!" He moved aside as Elmer entered the cabin, but he stayed near the doorway watching into the night with the rifle over his arm.

Elmer took three deep breaths and asked, "How's Pa?"

Lute cleared his throat, and Miss Charlotte said softly in the darkness, "Elmer, come over here to me. Please?" She put her arms around his shoulders, and he tried to stop shivering. "Lute?" she prompted.

Lute told him then. "Your pa died just before Steve got him to town. Steve stayed to see he got a good funeral. Your pa wanted him to."

Elmer stepped away from the gentle pressure of Miss Charlotte's arm, and his voice was gruff in his own ears. "I been figuring," he said. "I can make out all right, but Varina—she needs looking after. Maybe we could make a deal."

"What kind of a deal, Elmer?" Miss Charlotte's voice was like rippling creek water.

"If you was to take her back East with you," he stumbled along, "I'd turn over our stock to your brother, and maybe it would bring enough to pay for raising her." He could not remind her that she owed him anything; he was suddenly a man, burdened with a man's gallantry. He was asking her for a favor. "If it ain't big enough," he offered, "I kin earn the rest after I git bigger."

She said, "Oh, Elmer!" as if she might cry any minute. "I—I might not go back East," she said. Lute, standing there black against the night, jerked his head.

"I don't want her raised out here!" Elmer cried out frantically. "Ma always said this ain't no country for women!"

"It will be," Miss Charlotte promised. "It's going to be, before long. Men like you and Mr. Kimball will make it so. This is going to be a good place to live."

He was not a man any more. He was eleven years old and had nothing more to do with problems that were too big for him. He put his hands up to his face and began to sob. He cried for a long time, and neither Lute nor Miss Charlotte said a word or made a move.

When he was through, Lute spoke as if nothing had happened. "Tomorrow," he said, "you can be a kid if you want to. If you haven't forgotten how. You got that coming to you. But tonight I need a partner."

Until dawn, Elmer stood in the doorway with his new gun in his hand—the Peacemaker that had been Buck Saddler's. Lute prowled around farther away with a rifle, listening and watching. Nobody came.

Twelve years later, Varina Merrick spent her double eagle to buy her wedding clothes. Elmer, stiff and solemn in a new suit, tall and sturdy, a good hand at anything he undertook, gave the bride away. He had almost forgotten how hard he tried to give Varina away once before.

Dorothy M. Johnson

Flame on the Frontier

ON Sunday morning, wearing white man's sober clothing, a Sioux chief named Little Crow attended the church service at the Lower Agency and afterward shook hands with the preacher. On Sunday afternoon, Little Crow's painted and feathered Santee Sioux swooped down on the settlers in bloody massacre. There was no warning....

Hannah Harris spoke sharply to her older daughter, Mary Amanda. "I've told you twice to get more butter from the spring. Now step! The men want to eat."

The men—Oscar Harris and his two sons, sixteen and eighteen—sat in stolid patience on a bench in front of the cabin, waiting to be called to the table.

Mary Amanda put down the book she had borrowed from a distant neighbor and went unwillingly out of the cabin. She liked to read and was proud that she knew how, but she never had another book in her hands as long as she lived. Mary Amanda Harris was, on that day in August in 1862, just barely thirteen years old.

Her little sister Sarah tagged along down to the spring for lack of anything better to do. She was healthily hungry, and the smell of frying chicken had made her fidget until her mother had warned, "Am I going to have to switch you?"

The two girls wrangled as they trotted down the accustomed path.

"Now what'd you come tagging for?" demanded Mary Amanda. She wanted to stay, undisturbed, in the world of the book she had been reading.

Sarah said, "I guess I got a right to walk here as good as you."

She shivered, not because of any premonition but simply because the air was cool in the brush by the spring. She glanced across the narrow creek and saw a paint-striped face. Before she could finish her scream, the Indian had leaped the creek and smothered her mouth.

At the cabin they heard that single, throat-tearing scream instantly muffled. They knew what had to be done; they had planned it, because this day might come to any frontier farm.

Hannah Harris scooped up the baby boy, Willie, and hesitated only to cry out, "The girls?"

The father, already inside the cabin, handed one rifle to his eldest son as he took the other for himself. To Jim, who was sixteen, he barked, "The axe, boy."

Hannah knew what she had to do—run and hide—but that part of the plan had included the little girls, too. She was to take the four younger children, including the dull boy, Johnny. She was too sick with the meaning of that brief scream to be able to change the plan and go without the girls.

But Oscar roared, "Run for the rushes! You crazy?" and broke her paralysis. With the baby under one arm she began to run down the hill to a place by the river where the rushes grew high.

The only reason Hannah was able to get to the rushes with her two youngest boys was that the men, Oscar and Jim and Zeke, delayed the Indians for a few minutes. The white men might have barricaded themselves in the cabin and stood off the attackers for a longer period, but the approaching Indians would have seen that frantic scuttling into the rushes.

Oscar and Jim and Zeke did not defend. They attacked. With the father going first, they ran toward the spring and met the Indians in the brush. Fighting there, they bought a little time for the three to hide down by the river, and they paid for it with their lives.

Hannah, the mother, chose another way of buying time. She heard the invaders chopping at whatever they found in the cabin. She heard their howls as they found clothing and kettles and food. She stayed in the rushes as long as she dared, but when she smelled the smoke of the cabin burning, she knew the Indians would be ranging out to see what else might be found.

Then she thrust the baby into Johnny's arms and said fiercely, "You take care of him and don't you let him go until they kill you."

She did not give him any instructions about how to get to a place of safety. There might be no such place.

She kissed Johnny on the forehead and she kissed the baby twice, because he was so helpless and because he was, blessedly, not crying.

She crawled to the left, far to the left of the children, so that she would not be seen coming directly from their hiding place. Then she came dripping up out of the rushes and went shrieking up the hill straight toward the Indians.

When they started down to meet her, she hesitated and turned. She ran, still screaming, toward the river, as if she were so crazed she did not know what she was doing. But she knew. She knew very well. She did exactly what a meadowlark will do if its nest in the grass is menaced—she came into the open, crying and frantic, and lured the pursuit away from her young.

But the meadowlark acts by instinct, not by plan. Hannah Harris had to fight down her instinct, which was to try to save her own life.

As the harsh hands seized her, she threw her arm across her eyes so as not to see death....

Of the two girls down at the spring, only Sarah screamed. Mary Amanda did not have time. A club, swung easily by a strong arm, cracked against her head.

Sarah Harris heard the brief battle and knew her father's voice, but she did not have to see the bodies, a few yards away on the path through the brush. One of the Indians held her without difficulty. She was a thin little girl, nine years old.

Mary Amanda was unconscious and would have drowned except that her guard pulled her out of the creek and laid her, face down, on the gravel bank.

The girls never saw their cabin again. Their captors tied their hands behind them and headed back the way they had come to rejoin the war party. The girls were too frightened to cry or speak. They stumbled through the brush.

Mary Amanda fell too many times. Finally she gave up and lay still, waiting to die, sobbing quietly. Her guard grunted and lifted his club.

Sarah flew at him shrieking. Her hands were tied, but her feet were free and she could still run.

"Don't you hurt my sister!" she scolded. "Don't you do it, I say!" She bowed her head and bunted him.

The Indian, who had never had anything to do with white people except at a distance, or in furious flurries of raiding, was astonished by her courage, and impressed. All he knew of white girls was that they ran away, screaming, and then were caught. This one had the desperate, savage fury of his own women. She chattered as angrily as a bluejay. (Bluejay was the name he gave her, the name everyone called her, in the years she lived and grew up among the Sioux.)

She had knocked the wind out of him, but he was amused. He jerked the older girl, Mary Amanda, to her feet.

The mother, Hannah, was taken along by the same route, about a mile behind them, but she did not know they were still alive. One of them she saw six years later. The other girl she never saw again.

For hours she went stumbling, praying, "Lord in thy mercy, make them kill me fast!"

When they did not, she let hope flicker, and when they camped that night, she began to ask timidly, "God, could you help me get away?"

She had no food that night, and no water. An Indian had tied her securely.

The following day her captors caught up with a larger party, carrying much loot and driving three other white women. They were younger than Hannah. That was what saved her.

When she was an old woman, she told the tale grimly: "I prayed to the Lord to let me go, and He turned the Indians' backs on me and I went into the woods, and that was how I got away."

She did not tell how she could still hear the piercing shrieks of the other white women, even when she was far enough into the woods so that she dared to run.

She blundered through the woods, hiding at every sound, praying to find a trail, but terrified when she came to one, for fear there might be Indians around the next bend. After she reached the trail and began to follow it, she had a companion, a shaggy yellow dog.

For food during two days she had berries. Then she came upon the dog eating a grouse he had killed, and she stooped, but he growled.

"Nice doggie," she crooned. "Nice old Sheppy!"

She abased herself with such praise until—probably because he had caught other game and was not hungry—he let her take the tooth-torn, dirt-smeared remnants. She picked off the feathers with fumbling fingers, washed the raw meat in the creek and ate it as she walked.

She smelled wood smoke the next morning and crawled through brush until she could see a clearing. She saw white people there in front of a cabin, and much bustling. She heard children crying and the authoritative voices of women. She stood up then and ran, screaming, toward the cabin, with the dog jumping and barking beside her.

One of the hysterical women there seized a rifle and fired a shot at Hannah before a man shouted, "She's white!" and ran out to meet her.

There were sixteen persons in the cramped cabin or near it—refugees from other farms. Hannah Harris kept demanding, while she wolfed down her food, "Ain't anybody seen two little girls? Ain't anybody seen a boy and a baby?"

Nobody had seen them.

The draggled-skirted women in the crowded cabin kept busy with their children, but Hannah Harris had no children any more—she who had had four sons and two daughters. She dodged among the refugees, beseeching, "Can't I help with something? Ain't there anything I can do?"

A busy old woman said with sharp sympathy, "Miz Harris, you go lay down some place. Git some sleep. All you been through!"

Hannah Harris understood that there was no room for her there. She stumbled outside and lay down in a grassy place in the shade. She slept, no longer hearing the squalling of babies and the wrangling of the women.

Hannah awoke to the crying of voices she knew and ran around to the front of the cabin. She saw two men carrying a stretcher made of two shirts buttoned around poles. A bundle sagged on the stretcher, and a woman was trying to lift it, but it cried with two voices.

Johnny lay there, clutching the baby, and both of them were screaming.

Kneeling, she saw blood on Johnny's feet and thought with horror. "Did the Injuns do that?" Then she remembered, "No, he was barefoot when we ran."

He would not release the baby, even for her. He was gaunt, his ribs showed under his tattered shirt. His eyes were partly open, and his lips were drawn back from his teeth. He was only half conscious, but he still had strength enough to clutch his baby brother, though the baby screamed with hunger and fear.

Hannah said in a strong voice, "Johnny, you can let go now. You can let Willie go. Johnny, this is your mother talking."

With a moan, he let his arms go slack.

For the rest of his life, and he lived another fifty years, he suffered from nightmares and often awoke screaming.

With two of her children there Hannah Harris was the equal of any woman. She pushed among the others to get to the food, to find cloth for Johnny's wounded feet. She wrangled with them, defending sleeping space for her children.

For a few months she made a home for her boys by keeping house for a widower named Lincoln Bartlett, whose two daughters had been killed at a neighbor's cabin. Then she married him.

The baby, Willie, did not live to grow up, in spite of the sacrifices that had been made for him. He died of diphtheria. While Link Bartlett dug a little grave, Hannah sat, stern but dry-eyed, on a slab bench, cradling the still body in her arms.

The dull boy, Johnny, burst out hoarsely, "It wasn't no use after all, was it?" and his mother understood.

She told him strongly, "Oh, yes, it was! It was worth while, all you did. He's dead now, but he died in my arms, with a roof over him. I'll know where he's buried. It ain't as if the Indians had butchered him some place that I'd never know."

She carried the body across the room and laid it tenderly in the box that had been Willie's bed and would be his coffin. She turned to her other son and said, "Johnny, come sit on my lap."

He was a big boy, twelve years old, and he was puzzled by this invitation, as he was puzzled about so many things. Awkwardly he sat on her knees, and awkwardly he permitted her to cuddle his head against her shoulder.

"How long since your mother kissed you?" she asked, and he mumbled back, "Don't know."

She kissed his forehead. "You're my big boy. You're my Johnny."

He lay in her arms for a while, tense and puzzled. After a while, not knowing why it was necessary to cry, he began to sob, and she rocked him back and forth. She had no tears left.

Johnny said something then that he had thought over many times, often enough to be sure about it. "It was him that mattered most, I guess."

Hannah looked down at him, shocked.

"He was my child and I loved him," she said. "It was him I worried about....But it was you I trusted."

The boy blinked and scowled. His mother bowed her head.

"I never said so. I thought you knowed that. When I give him to you that day, Johnny boy, I put more trust in you than I did in the Lord God."

That was a thing he always remembered—the time his mother made him understand that for a while he had been more important than God.

The Harris sisters were sold twice, the second time to a Sioux warrior named Runs Buffalo, whose people ranged far to the westward.

Bluejay never had to face defeat among the Indians. The little girl who had earned her name by scolding angrily had the privileges of a baby girl. She was fed and cared for like the Indian children, and she had more freedom and less scolding than she had had in the cabin that was burned. Like the other little girls, she was freer than the boys. Her responsibility would not begin for three or four years. When the time came, she would be taught to do the slow, patient work of the women, in preparation for being a useful wife. But while she was little, she could play.

While the boys learned to shoot straight and follow tracks, while they tested and increased their endurance and strength, the little girls played and laughed in the sun. Bluejay did not even have a baby to look after, because she was the youngest child in the lodge of Runs Buffalo. She was the petted one, the darling, and the only punishment she knew was what she deserved for profaning holy objects. Once at home she had been switched by her father for putting a dish on the great family Bible. In the Indian village, she learned to avoid touching medicine bundles or sacred shields and to keep silent in the presence of men who understood religious mysteries.

Mary Amanda, stooped over a raw buffalo hide, scraping it hour after hour with tools of iron and bone, because that was women's work and she was almost a woman, heard familiar shrill arguments among the younger girls, the same arguments that had sounded in the white settlement, and in the same language: "You're it! ... "I am not!"

That much the little Indian girls learned of English. Sarah learned Sioux so fast that she no longer needed English and would have stopped speaking it except that her older sister insisted.

Mary Amanda learned humility through blows. To her, everything about the Indians was contemptible. She learned their language simply to keep from being cuffed by the older women, who were less shocked at her ignorance of their skills than at her unwillingness to learn the work that was a woman's privilege to perform. She sickened at the business of softening hides with a mixture of clay and buffalo manure. If she had been more docile, she might have been an honored daughter in the household. Instead, she was a sullen slave. Mary Amanda remembered what Sarah often forgot: that she was white. Mary Amanda never stopped hoping that they would be rescued. The name the Indians gave her was The Foreigner.

When she tried to take Sarah aside to talk English, the old woman of the household scolded.

Mary Amanda spoke humbly in Sioux. "Bluejay forgets to talk like our own people. I want her to know how to talk."

The old woman growled, "You are Indians," and Mary Amanda answered, "It is good for Indians to be able to talk to white people."

The argument was sound. A woman interpreter would never be permitted in the councils of chiefs and captains, but who could tell when the skill might be useful? The girls were allowed to talk together, but Sarah preferred Sioux.

When The Foreigner was sixteen years old she had four suitors. She knew what a young man meant by sending a gift of meat to the lodge and later standing out in the front, blanket-wrapped and silent.

When the young man came, Mary Amanda pretended not to notice, and the old woman pretended with her, but there was chuckling in the lodge as everyone waited to see whether The Foreigner would go out, perhaps to bring in water from the creek.

Her little sister teased her. "Go on out. All you have to do is let him put his blanket around you and talk. Go on. Other girls do."

"Indian girls do," Mary Amanda answered sadly. "That ain't the way boys do their courting back home."

The tall young men were patient. Sometimes as many as three at once stood out there through twilight into darkness, silent and waiting. They were eligible, respected young men, skilled in hunting and taking horses, proved in courage, schooled in the mysteries of protective charms and chanted prayer. All of them had counted coup in battle.

Mary Amanda felt herself drawn toward the lodge opening. It would be so easy to go out!

She asked Sarah humbly, "Do you think it's right, the way they buy their wives? Of course, the girl's folks give presents to pay back."

Sarah shrugged. "What other way is there? ... If it was me, I'd go out fast enough. Just wait till I'm older!" She reminded her sister of something it was pleasanter to forget, "They don't have to wait for you to make up your mind. They could sell you to an old man for a third wife."

When Mary Amanda was seventeen, a man of forty, who had an aging wife, looked at her with favor, and she made her choice. On a sweet summer evening she arose from her place in the tepee and, without a word to anyone, stooped and passed through the lodge opening. She was trembling as she walked past Hawk and Grass Runner and eluded their reaching hands. She stopped before a young man named Snow Mountain.

He was as startled as the family back in the tepee. Courting The Foreigner had become almost a tradition with the young men, because she seemed unattainable and competition ruled their lives. He wrapped his blanket around her and felt her heart beating wildly.

He did not tell her she was pretty. He told her that he was brave and cunning. He told her he was a skilled hunter, his lodge never lacked for meat. He had many horses, most of them stolen from the Crows in quick, desperate raids.

Mary Amanda said, "You give horses to buy what you want. Will Runs Buffalo give presents to you in return?"

That was terribly important to her. The exchange of gifts was in itself the ceremony. If she went to him with no dowry, she went without honor.

"I cannot ask about that," he said. "My mother's brother will ask."

But Runs Buffalo refused.

"I will sell the white woman for horses," he announced. "She belongs to me. I paid for her."

Mary Amanda went without ceremony, on a day in autumn, to the new lodge of Snow Mountain. She went without pride, without dowry. The lodge was new and fine, she had the tools and kettles she needed, and enough robes to keep the household warm. But all the household things were from his people, not hers. When she cried, he comforted her.

For her there was no long honeymoon of lazy bliss. Her conscience made her keep working to pay Snow Mountain for the gifts no one had given him. But she was no longer a slave, she was queen in her own household. An old woman, a relative of his mother, lived with them to do heavy work. Snow Mountain's youngest brother lived with him, helping to hunt and butcher and learning the skills a man needed to know.

Mary Amanda was a contented bride—except when she remembered that she had not been born an Indian. And there was always in her mind the knowledge that many warriors had two wives, and that often the two wives were sisters.

"You work too hard," Snow Mountain told her. "Your little sister does not work hard enough."

"She is young," The Foreigner reminded him, feeling that she should apologize for Bluejay's shortcomings.

Snow Mountain said, "When she is older, maybe she will come here."

Afterward she knew he meant that in kindness. But thinking of Sarah as her rival in the tepee, as her sister-wife, froze Mary Amanda's heart. She answered only, "Bluejay is young."

Sarah Harris, known as Bluejay, already had two suitors when she was only fourteen. One of them was only two or three years older than she was, and not suitable for a husband; he had few war honors and was not very much respected by anyone except his own parents. The other was a grown man, a young warrior named Horse Ears, very suitable and, in fact, better than the flighty girl had any right to expect.

When Sarah visited in her sister's lodge, she boasted of the two young men.

Mary Amanda cried out, "Oh, no! You're too young to take a

man. You could wait two years yet, maybe three. Sarah, some day you will go back home."

Two years after the massacre, the first rumor that the Harris girls were alive reached the settlement, but it was nothing their mother could put much faith in. The rumor came in a roundabout way, to Link Bartlett, Hannah's second husband, from a soldier at the fort, who had it from another soldier, who had it from a white trader, who heard it from a Cheyenne. And all they heard was that two white sisters were with a Sioux village far to the westward. Rumors like that drifted in constantly. Two hundred women had been missing after that raid.

Two more years passed before they could be fairly sure that there were really two white sisters out there and that they were probably the Harrises.

After still another year, the major who commanded the army post nearest the settlement was himself convinced, and negotiations began for their ransom.

Link Bartlett raised every cent he could—he sold some of his best land—to buy the gifts for that ransom.

In the sixth year of the captivity, a cavalry detachment was ordered out on a delicate diplomatic mission—to find and buy the girls back, if possible.

Link Bartlett had his own horse saddled and was ready to leave the cabin, to go with the soldiers, when Hannah cried harshly, "Link, don't you go! Don't go away and leave me and the kids!"

The children were dull Johnny and a two-year-old boy, named Lincoln, after his father, the last child Hannah ever had.

Link tried to calm her. "Now, Hannah, you know we planned I should go along to see they got back all right—if we can find 'em at all."

"I ain't letting you go," she said. "If them soldiers can't make out without you, they're a poor lot." Then she jarred him to his heels. She said, almost gently, "Link, if I was to lose you, I'd die."

That was the only time she ever hinted that she loved him. He never asked for any more assurance. He stayed at home because she wanted him there.

Mary Amanda's son was half a year old when the girls first learned there was hope of their being ransomed.

The camp crier, walking among the lodges, wailed out the day's news so that everyone in the village would know what was planned: "Women, stay in the camp. Keep your children close to you where they will be safe. There is danger. Some white soldiers are camped on the other side of the hills. Three men will go out to talk to them. The three men are Runs Buffalo, Big Moon and Snow Mountain."

Mary Amanda did not dare ask Snow Mountain anything. She watched him ride out with the other men, and then she sat on the ground in front of his tepee, nursing her baby. Bluejay came to the lodge and the two girls sat together in silence as the hours passed.

The men from the Sioux camp did not come back until three days later. When Snow Mountain was ready to talk, he remarked, "The white soldiers came to find out about two white girls. They will bring presents to pay if the white girls want to go back."

Mary Amanda answered, "O-o-oh," in a sigh like a frail breeze in prairie grass.

There was no emotion in his dark, stern face. He looked at her for a long moment, and at the baby. Then he turned away without explanation. She called after him, but he did not answer. She felt the dark eyes staring, heard the low voices. She was a stranger again, as she had not been for a long time.

Nothing definite had been decided at the parley with the white soldiers, the girls learned. The soldiers would come back sometime, bringing presents for ransom, and if the presents were fine enough, there would be talk and perhaps a bargain. Mary Amanda felt suddenly the need to prepare Sarah for life in the settlement. She told her everything she could remember that might be useful.

"You'll cook over a fire in a fireplace," she said, "and sew with thread, and you'll have to learn to knit."

Bluejay whimpered, "I wish you could come, too."

"He wouldn't let me go, of course," Mary Amanda answered

complacently. "He wouldn't let me take the baby, and I wouldn't leave without *him*. You tell them I got a good man. Be sure to tell them that."

At night, remembering the lost heaven of the burned cabin, remembering the life that was far away and long ago, she cried a little. But she did not even consider begging Snow Mountain to let her go. She had offended him, but when he stopped brooding they would talk again. He had not said anything to her since he had tested her by telling her the ransom had been offered.

He did not even tell her that he was going away. He gave orders to the old woman in the lodge and discussed plans with his younger brother, but he ignored his wife. Five men were going out to take the horses from the Crows, he said. Mary Amanda shivered.

Before he rode away with his war party, he spent some time playing with the baby, bouncing the child on his knee, laughing when the baby laughed. But he said nothing to Mary Amanda, and the whole village knew that he was angry and that she deserved his anger.

Her hands and feet were cold as she watched him go, and her heart was gnawed by the fear that was part of every Indian woman's life: "Maybe he will never come back."

Not until the white soldiers had come back to parley again did she understand how cruelly she had hurt him.

She dreamed of home while they waited for news of the parley, and she tried to make Bluejay dream of it.

"You'll have to do some things different there, but Ma will remind you. I'll bet Ma will cry like everything when she sees you coming." Mary Amanda's eyes flooded with tears, seeing that meeting. "I don't remember she ever did cry," she added thoughtfully, "but I guess she must have sometimes....Ma must have got out of it all right. Who else would be sending the ransom? Oh, well, sometime I'll find out all about it from Snow Mountain....I wonder if she got Johnny and Willie away from the cabin safe. Tell her I talked about her lots. Be sure to tell Ma that, Sarah. Tell her how cute my baby is."

Bluejay, unnaturally silent, dreamed with her, wide-eyed, of the reunion, the half-forgotten heaven of the settlement.

"Tell her about Snow Mountain," Mary Amanda reminded her sister. "Be sure to do that. How he's a good hunter, so we have everything we want, and more. And everybody respects him. Tell her he's good to me and the baby....But, Sarah, don't ever say he steals horses. They wouldn't understand, back home....And don't ever let on a word about scalps. If they say anything about scalps, you say our people here don't do that."

"They do, though," Sarah reminded her flatly. "It takes a brave man to stop and take a scalp off when somebody's trying to kill him."

Looking at her, Mary Amanda realized that Sarah didn't even think taking scalps was bad, so long as your own people did it and didn't have it done to them.

"You're going to have to forget some things," she warned with a sigh.

While the parley was still on, Big Moon, the medicine priest, came to the lodge where The Foreigner bent over her endless work. He was carrying something wrapped in buckskin.

"Tell them the names of the people in your lodge before you came to the Sioux," he said shortly as he put down the buckskin bundle. "They are not sure you are the women they want."

In the bundle were sheets of paper and a black crayon.

Sarah came running. She sat fascinated as Mary Amanda wrote carefully on the paper: "Popa, Moma, Zeke, Jim, Johny, Wily."

Mary Amanda was breathless when she finished. She squeezed Sarah's arm. "Just think, you're going to go home!"

Sarah nodded, not speaking. Sarah was getting scared.

The following day, the ransom was paid and brought into camp. Then The Foreigner learned how much she had offended Snow Mountain.

Big Moon brought fine gifts to the lodge, and piled them inside—a gun, powder and percussion caps and bullets, bolts of cloth, mirrors and beads and tools and a copper kettle.

"The Foreigner can go now," he said.

Mary Amanda stared. "I cannot go back to the white people. I am Snow Mountain's woman. This is his baby."

"The gifts pay also for the baby," Big Moon growled. "Snow

Mountain will have another wife, more sons. He does not need The Foreigner. He has sold her to the white man."

Mary Amanda turned pale. "I will not go with the white men," she said angrily. "When Snow Mountain comes back, he will see how much The Foreigner's people cared for her. They have sent these gifts as her dowry."

Big Moon scowled. "Snow Mountain may not come back. He had a dream, and the dream was bad. His heart is sick, and he does not want to come back."

As a widow in the Sioux camp, her situation would be serious. She could not go back to her parents' home, for she had no parents. But neither could she leave the camp now to go back to the settlement and never know whether Snow Mountain was alive or dead. Sarah stood staring at her in horror.

"I will wait for him," Mary Amanda said, choking. "Will Big Moon pray and make medicine for him?"

The fierce old man stared at her, scowling. He knew courage when he saw it, and he admired one who dared to gamble for high stakes.

"All these gifts will belong to Big Moon," she promised, "if Snow Mountain comes back."

The medicine priest nodded and turned away. "Bluejay must come with me," he said briefly. "I will take her to the white soldiers and tell them The Foreigner does not want to come."

She watched Sarah walk away between the lodges after the medicine priest. She waved good-bye, and then went into the lodge. The old woman said, "Snow Mountain has a good wife. . . ."

Ten days passed before the war party came back. Mary Amanda waited, hardly breathing, as they brought Snow Mountain into camp tied on a travois, a pony drag.

Big Moon said, "His shadow is gone out of his body. I do not know whether it will come back to stay."

"I think it will come back to stay," said The Foreigner, "because I have prayed and made a sacrifice."

At the sound of her voice, Snow Mountain opened his eyes. He lay quiet in his pain, staring up at her, not believing. She saw tears on his dark cheeks.

Her name was always The Foreigner, but for the rest of her life she was a woman of the Santee Sioux.

Sarah Harris, who had been called Bluejay, was hard to tame, they said in the settlement. Her mother fretted over her heathen ways. The girl could not even make bread!

"I can tan hides," Sarah claimed angrily. "I can butcher a buffalo and make pemmican. I can pitch a tepee and pack it on a horse to move."

But those skills were not valued in a white woman, and Sarah found the settlement not quite heaven. She missed the constant talk and laughter of the close-pitched tepees. She had to learn a whole new system of polite behavior. There was dickering and trading and bargaining, instead of a proud exchanging of fine gifts. A neighbor boy slouching on a bench outside the cabin, talking to her stepfather while he got up courage to ask whether Sarah was at home, was less flattering as a suitor than a young warrior, painted and feathered, showing off on a spotted horse. Sometimes Sarah felt that she had left heaven behind her.

But she never went back to it. When she was seventeen, she married the blacksmith, Herman Schwartz, and their first baby was born six months later.

Sarah's oldest child was six and her second child was three when the Indian man appeared at the door of her cabin and stood silently peering in.

"Git out of here!" she cried, seizing the broom.

He answered in the Sioux tongue, "Bluejay has forgotten."

She gave Horse Ears a shrill welcome in his own language and the three-year-old started to cry. She lifted a hand for an accustomed slap but let it fall. Indian mothers did not slap their children.

But she was not Indian any more, she recollected. She welcomed Horse Ears in as a white woman does an invited guest. In her Sunday-company voice she chattered politely. It was her privilege because she was a white woman. No need any more for the meek silence of the Indian woman.

She brought out bread and butter and ate with him. That was her privilege, too.

"My sister?" she asked.

He had not seen The Foreigner for a long time. He had left that village.

"Does Bluejay's man make much meat?" Horse Ears asked. "Is he a man with many honors in war?"

She laughed shrilly. "He makes much meat. He has counted coup many times. We are rich."

"I came to find out those things," he answered. "In my lodge there is only one woman."

She understood, and her heart leaped with the flattery. He had traveled far, and in some danger, to find out that all was well with her. If it was not, there was refuge in his tepee. And not only now, she realized, but any time, forever.

A shadow fell across the threshold; a hoarse voice filled the room. "What's that bloody Injun doing here?" roared Sarah's husband. "Are you all right?"

"Sure, we're all right," she answered. "I don't know who he is. He was hungry."

His eyes narrowed with anger, "Is he one of them you used to know?"

Her body tensed with fear. "I don't know him, I told you!"

Her husband spoke to the Indian in halting Sioux, but Horse Ears was wise. He did not answer.

"Git out!" the blacksmith ordered, and the Indian obeyed without a word.

As Sarah watched him go down the path, without turning, she wished fervently that she could tell him good-bye, could thank him for coming. But she could not betray him by speaking.

Herman Schwartz strode toward her in silent, awesome, blazing fury. She did not cringe; she braced her body against the table. He gave her a blow across the face that rocked her and blinded her.

She picked up the heavy iron skillet.

"Don't you ever do that again, or I'll kill you," she warned.

He glared at her with fierce pride, knowing that she meant what she said.

"I don't reckon I'll have to do it again," he said complacently. "If I ever set eyes on that savage again, I'll kill him. You know that, don't you, you damn squaw?"

She shrugged. "Talk's cheap."

As she went down to the spring for a bucket of water, she was singing.

Her girlhood was gone, and her freedom was far behind her. She had two crying children and was pregnant again. But two men loved her, and both of them had just proved it.

Forty years later, her third child was elected to the state legislature, and she went, a frightened, white-haired widow, to see him there. She was proud, but never so proud as she had been on a summer day three months before he was born.

William Kittredge

The Waterfowl Tree

THEY ran into snow almost two hours before reaching
the valley, the storm at twilight whipping in gusts across the narrow asphalt. The station wagon moved slowly through the oncom-
ing darkness.

"A long haul," his father said. "Eva will be wondering."

The boy, tall and seventeen, his hands behind his neck, watched
out the glazed and crusted side windows at the indeterminate light.
This mention of the woman could be a signal, some special beginning.

"Is she pretty?" he asked.

"Pretty enough for me. And that's pretty enough."

The man laughed and kept his eyes on the road. He was massive, a widower in his late fifties. "I've got too old for worrying
about pretty," he said. "All I want is gentle. When that's all you
want, you got to be getting old."

In a little while, the man said, "I remember hunting when I was
a kid. It was different then, more birds for one thing, and you had
to kill something with every shot."

"How do you mean?" the boy asked.

"We were meat hunters. You spent money for shells, you brought home meat. I saw Teddy Spandau die on that account. Went off into open water chest deep, just trying to get some birds he shot. Cramped up and drowned. We hauled a boat down and fished him out that afternoon."

The snow began to thin and the man pushed the car faster and concentrated on his driving.

"It was like this then," he said. "Snowing, and ice a foot thick and below zero all day."

The boy wished his father would go on talking about these far-away and unsuspected things. But the man, long estranged from this remote and misted valley of his childhood, sat hunched over the wheel, absorbed in the road and grimacing.

"I guess it was different in those days," the boy said, wanting his father to keep talking.

"Quite a bit different," the man answered. "A different life altogether."

After this they drove in silence. It was completely dark when they came out of the storm, driving through the last drifting flakes into the light of a full moon and an intense and still cold that made the new snow crystallize and occasionally sparkle in the headlights.

"Freeze solid by morning," the man said. "Be some new birds coming in."

He stopped the car and switched off the headlights.

"Look there," he said, pointing.

The boy cranked down his window and looked across the distorted landscape of snow, blue and subdued in the moonlight. Far away he saw a high ridge shadowed in darkness.

"That's the rim," his father said. "We'll be home directly."

The boy looked again at the black vault. How could this be home, this place under that looming wall?

"All my life," the man said, "in strange places, I've caught myself looking up and expecting to see that rim."

The long attic room, unfinished, raftered under the peak roof, filled with soft darkness, illuminated by blue softness where moonlight shone through windows on either end. On the floor and inward sloping east wall he could see light reflected up from downstairs. The boy lay in the bundled warmth of a mummy bag on an iron cot and watched the light, imagined that he could see it slowly climb the wall as the moon dropped. The cold in this shed-like room above the barn was complete and still and frosted his breath when he moved.

"You're young and tough," his father had said. "You draw the outdoor room."

They'd unloaded the boy's suitcase and the new gear quickly in the darkness, tried to be quiet because the house across the road was completely dark. Then his father went ahead with a flashlight and they carried the gear up an old flight of stairs at the side of the barn and pushed through the ancient hanging door that opened into this long, barren room. After unrolling the sleeping bag on the cot, his father gripped him by the shoulder and shone the light in his face.

"You'll be warm inside the bag," the man said. "Take your coat in with you and sleep with your clothes on. That way they won't be frozen in the morning. Stick the boots under you. We'll get you up for breakfast."

Then he turned and took the light and left the boy standing in the cold. What would greet his father in that dark house across the road? They'd come upon the place after rounding a curve in the gravel road that crossed the upper part of the valley. A bunch of trees and a house and a barn and some corrals; just that in the midst of unending fields of fenced snow.

The boots made a comforting hump and the boy curled around them and tried to warm himself. Suddenly he was frantic and wished he were back in his bed at school, enduring the vacation, trying to guess tomorrow's movie.

"Goddamn," he said, clenched and shaking. "Damn, dirty son of a bitch."

But the warmth came and with it a quiet numbness. He felt himself drift and then he slept, surprised that he was not going to lie awake and search for a sense of how it would be in the morning.

And now, just as quickly, he was awake and watching the slow light on the far wall. Then he recognized, almost unnoticed among his thoughts, an ancient crying. Coyotes. He smiled and huddled deep in his warmth, secure against the night. The calls came fine and clear, and he struggled to get an arm out of the warmth. He looked at the illuminated face of his watch. It was almost three o'clock.

The wailing stopped and there was silence.

Geese were flying. He could hear, far away, but still clear and distinct, their wandering call. He felt himself slipping again into peaceful sleep. Then the coyotes began a long undulating wail and small yipping. He rested his head on his arm and slept, lulled by their noise and a small rhythm of his own.

A hand shook him, gently and firmly, and for a moment he was elsewhere and lost, then he was awake and remembering. He pushed up from the warmth of the sleeping bag and looked out at the morning, at the smile of this strange woman and the frosted windows, and the rough shingle and rafter roof. His breath swirled softly in the cold morning air. He smiled at the woman and stretched his arms. The woman stood next to his bed, leaning over, one hand touching him through the layers of the sleeping bag.

"Welcome," she said. "On the coldest day in a thousand years."

Really nothing but a fuzzy-headed woman. She was bundled in hunting clothes and wore a down cap tied under her chin with fringes and curls of hair protruding. Not the woman he'd expected. The face was heavier and older than he would have imagined, and he suddenly understood that his father was almost an old man.

"You must be Eva."

"The same," she said. "The famous Eva. Come on, breakfast is almost ready."

"I can't." He grinned, surprised at her easiness, taken in spite of himself. "I don't have any pants on."

"Come on. I won't look if I can help myself." She pulled on his arm and grinned.

He scrambled out of bed and was shocked at the cold. He jumped in dismay when she grabbed one of his bare ankles with her cold hands. He escaped and she dropped the mittens she had

tucked under one arm and began rummaging in the bed, fishing in
the warm darkness, finally pulling out his pants and coat while he
wrapped his arms around himself and watched. "Get 'em on," she
said.

The area between the house and the barn was ankle-deep in new
snow and marked only by the boot tracks of the night before and
her footprints of this morning. The trees around the house were
heaped with ice and snow. He had to squint against the glare.

The house was rough and worn and old, without any rugs to
cover the plank floor and with homemade wooden chairs and a
long table with benches on either side. The boy stood in the doorway and felt with pleasure the shock of warm air that softened his
face. In one corner of this main room was a big wood stove with
chopped wood and kindling in a box beside it. His father sat on a
stool beside the stove, filling shell belts. Open shell boxes were scattered around him on the floor.

"Come on in," the man said. "Close the door. Charlie will have
breakfast on in a minute."

Through an open doorway on the far side of the room came the
reflection of morning sunlight. Through the doorway he could see
another smaller man working over a woodburning cook stove. The
woman began pulling off her cap and coat, piling them on the far
end of the table. No one, not even the woman, paid attention to
the water and melting ice on the floor.

"Holy smokes," the woman said, brushing her hair back and
tucking her shirt in her pants. "It's so damned cold out there he
could have froze."

"Make you tough, won't it boy." His father looked up at him.

"It wasn't bad," the boy said. "I stayed warm."

"That's the spirit." The man stood up, dropping the finished
shell belts from his lap to the floor. "Come on."

The boy followed him into the next room where the other man
was tending a frying pan full of eggs and another pan with bacon.
"This is Charlie Anderson," his father said. "Me and Charlie are
hunting partners. From the old days."

Charlie turned and shook hands with the boy. "Glad to have

you, son," he said. "Eat in a minute." Charlie nodded and went back to his cooking.

"Come here." His father, massive in boots and khaki hunting gear, walked to the far end of the kitchen and opened a door to the outside. The boy followed him out, and the cold was at him again, hard and stiff.

"Look at that," his father said. Behind the house was a small orchard of six or seven trees. The tree nearest the house, gnarled and holding stiff winter limbs towards the thin sky, was hung with dead geese and ducks. They were in bunches of a dozen or more, strung together on short pieces of rope and suspended from heavy nails driven into limbs, crusted with ice and frozen and absolutely still, frosted and sparkling in the light.

"Deep freeze," the man said. "We hung them like that when we were kids."

The boy supposed that he should say something to please his father but was not sure what that would be. He turned away from the tree and looked to the west where the winter rim he had seen in the moonlight rose high over the far edge of the valley. Through the still air he could define individual trees among the groves of juniper along its upper edge. He heard the geese calling again and looked to see them flying, distant and wavering, and remembered the night before. "They sound so far away," he said.

"We'll get after them," his father said. "As soon as we eat."

The boy turned and looked again at the tree, hung with dead birds. He was unable to feel anything beyond his own chill.

"We hung them there when I was a kid," his father said. "A man named Basston owned this place, and my old man would bring me down here to help out on the weekends. There'd be a crowd all season. Guys from the city. Basston died. The guys stopped coming. Let's eat."

The boy watched his father turn and go in, surprised at the life that had been his father's. Maybe that's why he brought me here, he thought. To let me see what he was.

"Coming," he said.

The boy huddled lower in the blind of tules and reeds and wished the birds would hurry and come again. He and his father sat hidden only a few yards from a small patch of open water, on a neck of land in the tule swamps of the valley. They were alone and a long way from the warmth of the station wagon.

"I'll take you with me," the man said when they first spotted the birds with field glasses. He pointed far off from where they were parked above the frozen swamp, and the boy saw them, milling and keeping a stirred bit of water open and free of ice. A fantastic sight through the glasses—thousands of ducks crowding in the water and great bunches of Honkers and lesser Canadians walking the ice around them.

"Eva and Charlie can go over and wait at the decoys," his father said. "Give us two shots at them."

No one said anything, and after straightening the tangled gear in the back of the station wagon, the four of them walked off, two in each direction. The boy and his father walked in a long arc around the birds in order to come up on them from the sheltered land side and get as close as possible before they flushed. "Lots of time," his father said, after they'd walked a half mile or so. He was panting and sweating in the heavy gear. "Give Eva and Charlie time to get over to the decoys."

And their stalk was a good one. Between them, they had five greenhead Mallard drakes and two hens. "Pick the greenheads," his father whispered before they came up shooting. "Pick one each time before you shoot."

The geese had been too wise and flushed early, taking a few ducks with them, but the main flock of ducks was almost too easy, standing nearly still in the air during the long and suddenly clamorous second as they flushed, rising in waves, time to reload and shoot again before they were gone. The boy's first two shots had simply been pulled off into the rising mass. Then he remembered his father's words and aimed carefully and selectively.

After the first flush, the man and the boy dropped into the tules near the water's edge, leaving the dead birds on the ice. The thousands of ducks grouped and then turned in the distance and came back at them in long whirring masses, sensing something and veering off before getting into shooting range, but filling the air with the mounting rush of their wings. The boy, awed nearly to tears by the sight above him, and the sound of the wings, sat concealed beside his father and was unable and unready to shoot again.

"Charlie and I used to hunt here when we were kids," the man said after a time, during a lull. "This is the real coming back. I remember waking in the spring when the birds were flying north. I could hear them from my bed, and I'd go out and stand on the knoll behind the house and watch them leave and hear them calling and smell the corrals and just look at the valley where it had turned green and then over at the rim where a little snow lay near the top. I guess those were the best days I ever lived." The man spoke softly, and the boy half-listened to him and sucked in his breath, waiting for the birds to come wheeling at them again, thinking the sound of their flight the most beautiful thing he had ever heard.

Then the birds stopped coming, and he and his father went out on the ice and gathered the dead ones, five beautiful greenheads and the two hens and carried them back to the hiding place. "The dead ones scared them off," his father said. "Now we'll have to wait awhile on the honkers."

And so they waited, the boy trying to be comfortable in his heavy clothing as he listened to his father.

"We used to haul the birds back to the house in a wagon. There was ten times as many in those days and lots of Canvasbacks and Redheads. You don't see those birds any more." The man moved quietly and easily around their nest, pulling reeds together over them until they were completely hidden.

"I remember one afternoon when the wind was blowing and the clouds were below the rim and we sat in one place, Charlie and me, fourteen years old I guess, and we shot up over a case of old man Basston's 12-gauge shells. The birds kept coming and we just kept shooting. We killed a hundred and fifty birds that one afternoon. It was almost night when we got back to camp and we hung those birds in the dark and old man Basston came out and we stood under that tree and he gave each of us a couple of drinks of the best bourbon whiskey on earth and sent us to bed like men. I guess that was the best day, the tops in my life."

Had everything been downhill since? The boy understood, or hoped that he did, why he was here, that his father was trying to make up, to present a view of life before the time had completely passed. Was this only for himself, he wondered? He listened to his father and thought of this woman, Eva, and the others and the different man his father had become to him in this place.

Eventually the geese came, very high and veered out in their great formations. They dropped and started to wheel when they saw the water.

The flocks seemed endless, long flights coming one before the next, circling and wheeling and dropping. "I'll tell you when," the man said. "Just lay quiet."

The first flight had landed and was calming itself in the water and on the edge of the ice when the next, under a larger flight of ducks, came directly over them, settled on stiff wings, fell directly towards the water, unconscious and intent. "Now," the man said, and they rose, waist deep in the tules, and shot three times each and dropped six birds easily, the huge black and white geese thudding on the ice.

"That's it," his father said. "Beautiful shooting. Enough for this day. Let's go. They'll be back."

The geese scattered and wheeled above them while they went out on the ice again and began to pick up the dead birds. They were heavy and beautiful birds and the boy twisted their necks the way his father did and felt sorry that they could not have lived and yet was glad that they were dead. They were trophies of this world, soft and heavy and dead birds.

"We'll sit around this afternoon and play some fourhanded gin," his father said, after they had gathered the birds. "You ever play gin?"

"Sure," the boy said. "For pennies and buttons." They strung the ducks on a short piece of rope and the geese on another. "You carry the ducks," his father said. "I'll bring the geese. We'll go back across the ice."

It was a mile across to where the station wagon sat on a knoll. The going was slick and tricky with the new snow on the ice. The boy walked gingerly at first, then faster. Soon he was well out ahead of his father. The man came slowly and solidly, breathing heavily.

Far away the rim was a sharply defined edge. Between him and that high point, the boy watched the flocks of birds, some clearly visible against the flat sky, others almost indistinguishable against the snow-covered slopes.

From behind him he heard a distant, muffled cry.

He turned and saw that his father was gone, vanished from sight. Then the man reappeared on the surface of the snow, floundering in the water. The boy dropped the shotgun and the birds and ran towards his father.

While running he saw the man raise himself violently and wave, shout, then fall back again.

The cry, the boy understood, was a command to stay back; but he ran on, slipping and falling towards the hole in the ice. The man floundered through the chest-deep water, while the geese on their little rope floated beside him. The water steamed. The ice, incredibly, was soft and only a few inches thick.

The man waved him back and the boy stopped, yards short of the edge. He watched his father for some sign of what had happened, what to do.

The man stood quietly in the steaming and putrid water, gasping. He had been completely submerged and now the water was under his armpits. "Stay there," his father said, beginning to shake. "There's a hot spring and the ice is rotten."

"Let me rest a little," he said. "Then I'll try to work my way over to the solid ice."

The boy stood helpless. The edges of the broken and jagged water had begun to freeze again, solidifying as he watched. "Can you stand it?"

"It's not so bad here," the man said, composed now and shaking less, speaking quietly. "But it'll be cold out there."

Then the man began to move again, working slowly, pulling each leg out of the deep bottom mud and then moving forward another step. He made it almost to the edge of the ice and then stopped. "God Almighty," he said. "It's so goddamned cold."

And then the boy heard his father mutter something else, something subdued and private, saw his face begin to collapse and draw into itself and grow distant. The man began to thrash and move forward in lunges, reaching toward the edge of the ice, fighting and gasping, moving toward the boy.

Then, his eyes on the boy, the man simply turned onto his back, eyes rolling back and becoming blank. Then he sank, flailing his arms, the birds entangled in the rope going down with him. Then there was nothing but the water and some bubbling.

And then there were no no bubbles, nothing but the dead geese floating quietly, their heads pulled under the surface by the rope that still encircled his father's body.

The boy heard again the distant honking of the geese and the whirring of wings as a pair of ducks came directly at him and suddenly swung away.

The boy turned and began to rush across the ice, scrambling and slipping, sometimes falling as he ran across the open ice toward the station wagon.

Back in the station wagon with the engine going and the heater turned on, he began to shake. He stretched out on the seat and fell out of himself like a stone into what might have been taken for sleep.

He awoke fully in the warm darkness of a completely strange and unknown room, wondering what place this was. And then, with terrible swiftness, he was again in the moment of the inexplicable thing that had happened—he saw his father's eyes rolling backwards. He knew that it had happened, understood that this was one of the bedrooms in the strange house. He put his feet on the floor and was surprised to find himself in his underwear. A door slammed in another part of the house and he heard a voice, Eva's voice.

"I wonder if he's still sleeping?"

She appeared in the dim doorway.

"He's awake," she said over her shoulder.

She came into the room and turned on the light. Her hair was brushed away from her face and fell in waves to her shoulders. She looked younger, he thought, and somehow out of place here. He pulled the sheets over his bare legs.

"I'm all right now," he said. "Did they get him out?"

"He is out." The woman spoke formally and slowly, showing, the boy thought, that they were still really strangers, after all. "And now it is night. You slept a long time."

The boy turned away, beginning to cry, dissolving into the terror once more. The woman snapped off the light and came across the room to him. "Try to rest," she said, "I'm going to bed now."

"Your father loved this place," the woman said. "He told me it was the only surely happy place in his life. I'll be back in a minute," Eva said, and left the room.

The only surely happy place.

Presently the woman returned, wearing a brocade robe that reached the floor and with her hair pulled back and knotted behind her head. The boy turned and looked at her in the dim light, saw her drop the robe and pull back the covers on the other side of the bed and get under the covers, flinching when she touched the sheets. The boy started to get up.

"Stay and we'll talk," she said. She took him by the arm and pulled him towards her, and he was again surprised at the coldness of her hands.

"Why?" he said. "Why did it happen?" He began to cry again.

"His heart," she said. "He had been having trouble." The woman moved closer to him and put her arm around his shoulders. "I'm sorry," she said. "God," she said.

Presently he slept again, exhausted and calmed, slowly moving to huddle against the warmth of the woman. In the middle of the night he woke and felt the woman shuddering and crying beside him.

He woke to warmth and sunlight coming through the open doorway of the room. He was alone in the bed.

In the outer room the woman and Charlie Anderson were sitting quietly at the table. "Sit down," Charlie said. "I'll get you some food."

"Charlie doesn't trust my cooking," the woman said. The woman went into the kitchen and returned with a mug of coffee. She seemed self-conscious and almost shy.

Charlie Anderson came from the kitchen with eggs and a thick slice of fried ham. "Eat good," he said to the boy.

"He will." the woman said.

The boy wondered where the grief had gone and if his father had been so easily dismissed.

"We seen the end of a fine man," Charlie Anderson said and began to remove the dishes.

So the boy ate and watched them, these strangers. And then he walked through the house uneasily and went out through the kitchen door and stood beneath the heavily laden tree and shuffled in the snow and fingered the frozen bark while looking again to the far-off rim.

Eva came outside. The boy was conscious of her standing silently behind him. He blinked in the radiance and watched the high-flying birds, geese moving to feed and water. He heard the woman make a sound behind him, and he turned to see her face crumpling. She gasped slightly. She moved to him and pressed herself against him while she shook and wept. He stood with his arms at his sides and felt the softness of her breasts behind the sweater, and then nothing but the cold in her hair which was loose and open against his face.

Then she was quiet.

"Let's go in," she said. "I'm cold."

She moved away and he followed her, oblivious to everything and completely drawn into himself.

"It will make you tough," his father had said.

"Goddamn you for this," the boy thought.

He slammed the door behind him and went to stand before the fire. The woman stood at the window with her hands behind her while Charlie Anderson busied himself with the dishes. The house seemed filled with the musk of the dead birds. The boy's numb fingers throbbed and ached as he held them open to the radiant warmth of the fire. "Goddamn everything," the boy said.

David Long

Great Blue

PAUL'S grandfather cut the engine and the boat coasted
into a dark cove on the far side of the lake. It was a sweet late time
of the evening. Paul sat in the bow, his chin rubbing on the top of
the life preserver. He was happy his grandfather had picked him to
fish with tonight, and not let any of the other cousins come. They
were older, they'd gone out with their grandfather plenty—they already knew how the bats careening above the boat kept from striking your head, they knew about the ice age that gouged these lakes,
they knew the story of Father Marquette's trek through these
woods along Lake Superior, three-hundred-some years ago . . . not
that his grandfather acted obliged to improve every spare moment
with grandfatherly wisdom. No, he could be a stony quiet, the
cousins all knew, not to be budged by their best antics.

The other cousins lived downstate, no more than a day's drive
from camp, but Paul had flown back from Montana, alone. He'd
come just once before, a rushed pilgrimage he and his mother had
made at the tail end of last summer, a few clear days cool enough
for a jacket around suppertime. It was hardly long enough!

Everyone seemed lost in the work of closing things up for the year, and his mother was still coaching him on names by the time they left. Still, camp haunted him all winter: the lake, darker than Montana lakes, long and cinched in at the middle by two points overgrown with blueberries; the five cabins spaced along the edge of the pine woods; all the people kin to him in one fashion or another. And the grandfather he'd been named for. So this year his mother had set it up so he could stay at camp as long as he wanted, living with Aunt Hallie, her next-youngest sister, and Uncle Ray and their two girls. "Miss us, will you?" his mother had teased him in the car. Out on the water now, he did miss them a little, but it was a feeling he could bear.

"You put me in mind of your mother," his grandfather said after a while. "I'll tell you, Paulie, I see her best up here, your age or thereabouts."

His grandfather's voice wasn't loud like his uncles', but it seemed to roll and echo out from the middle of him.

"One summer," he said, "she wore long pants and a long flannel shirt with the cuffs snapped, a blue—I think it was a baseball cap, with her hair crammed up underneath it. All day everyday, hot or no. Not a one of us could talk her out of it. She was so serious, your mother . . . how we tried to get her into a swimsuit. No dice. I said, *Shirley, you afraid of poison ivy? Or yellowjackets? Something of that nature?* But no, it wasn't that."

Paul smiled and waited for his grandfather to finish, but he didn't.

"She swims a lot now," Paul offered finally.

"That summer feels like a hundred years ago," his grandfather said. "I think she just wanted to be *prepared*, set for things. You're a little that way, too, are you?"

Paul stared down at the fishing gear. He guessed maybe he was. He didn't much like surprises, he liked to know what he had to do—traveling by himself, for one thing. At the airport in Sperry they'd boarded him first, along with a woman strapped into a wheelchair; they'd let him take a window seat in the first row, and when the others walked on, there in Sperry, and in Great Falls and Billings, he tried to act like it was nothing to fly. He watched the mountains for a while, but out over the plains the clouds thickened and didn't break, so he brought out his book, *The Voyage of the "Dawn Treader"*. He'd read it straight through half a dozen times at least, but he'd given it to his mother to hide from him so he'd have it again now. He skipped ahead, reading certain pages at a crawl. He pictured the "Dawn Treader" in full sail crossing a sunny expanse of ocean—then out of nowhere they strike a patch of darkness . . . the crew pulls a raggedy man from the water, he screams for them to turn and fly back where they came from. *This is the island where dreams come true*, he tells them. *Not daydreams: dreams!* Paul closed his eyes, then stared out at the tops of the clouds, at the bright endless sky, considering what it would be like for his dreams to be real, and fighting off the squeeze of panic by turning from the window to another place in the book and making himself read.

He lifted the anchor over the side of the boat and ran the rope through his fingers until the weight settled on the silty bottom. There were no cabins on this side of the lake. The first reached the water's edge and the forest was heavily shadowed. The reeds at the shore rocked with the boat's last ripple.

Paul held his pole ready but waited for his grandfather to make the first cast.

"Your uncle had some luck over here last night," his grandfather said. "Not that it's ever the same two days running."

He sat in the stern, straight-backed, his eyes almost as drained of strong color as the sky. He wore a canvas cap with a long stained bill. Under it, Paul knew, he was bald as a hen's egg. His arm drew back, his lure skipped once and sank near the reeds. In a moment Paul made his own cast and began reeling in, trying to copy the even whirl of his grandfather's wrist. He hoped they'd get something, hoped actually that it would be his grandfather who did, so he could see what to do exactly—all he'd ever caught were little pan fish that jiggled in the air at the end of his pole. He wouldn't mind too much if they didn't, though. So far, the mosquitoes hadn't found them. He heard the hum of another boat far-off, but it was peaceful in the cove as the light began to pass from the lake.

Suddenly, just to one side of where he'd been staring, came an explosion of water and reeds and wingbeats, so startling him that his pole rang against the aluminum gunwale. A great bird rose and skirted the water, its wings dipping in long fluid strokes. He was transfixed.

"The great blue," his grandfather said. "Our heron. You've never seen it before?"

"I . . . no," Paul said. "I've heard them talk about it, I guess."

His grandfather spread out three spiny fingers and held them up to Paul. "Some morning before the others are up," he said, "you go down and look in the shallow water in front of the cabins, in the sand. You'll see where it's been."

The bird leveled off just above the treetops, tracing the outline of the lake, as if to mark off its territory before dark. The sharp beak jutted ahead, the legs trailed behind thin as pencil lines. Paul felt the goosebumps shoot down his legs and tried to wipe them away through his jeans. Minutes passed before he thought about fishing again. When he looked over at his grandfather, he saw that he'd been crying.

There were always secrets at camp. Some were even his: one afternoon last summer, walking along the bluff above the big lake, he'd spotted Aunt Leah's oldest girl—Lara, with the shiny black hair—down on the sand with a boy who was visiting another of the cousins. Paul had watched her suddenly jump up in front of him and strip off her t-shirt so he could look at her—even last year Paul knew she'd never do anything like that back at camp, but he kept it to himself, remembering all winter exactly how she'd stood with the waves curling behind her and how the boy didn't move at all except to run his hand through his hair over and over. Other secrets he glimpsed because the adults still felt free to talk in his presence—over a drink on the screened porch of his grandfather's cabin, called The Folly, or at the stove of Aunt Hallie's or Aunt Leah's: who'd broken her word, who Grampa Paul was going to have to lend money to, whose grown-up child was having mental problems. Sometimes he could tell they'd gauged him wrong, and that he shouldn't listen anymore, but those were the times he most wanted to hear it, the times he wished they'd say the parts they

never said out loud. Even so, it amazed him that he fit in as well as
he did, that all it took was having the mother he had. Only rarely
did the cousins ever draw back from him, making him feel there
remained a few things he hadn't a right to yet.

He slept on a pallet in the cabin's loft. Aunt Hallie and Uncle
Ray had the bedroom; the girls, Billie and Gwen, shared the
hide-a-bed below him in the front room. Curled in his bag, he'd
hear the soft-spoken tallying of the cribbage hands at the kitchen
table, then the sounds of the game ending, and the last relations
slipping off to their cabins. Someone would reach up and shut off
the gas lanterns and they'd gutter for a moment, then go quiet. In
the dark, he'd hear the two girls whispering, sometimes breaking
into talk or laughter loud enough to draw a muffled yell from Uncle Ray. Or he'd hear their bare feet slapping as one, then the other,
got up to use the pot. Tonight their voices were different,
though . . . hushed, pointed. He lay still, afraid to move his head
against the railing.

" . . . only because he's dying," the boy heard.

"It's pretty weird," Billie said.

"Uncle Duff said they'd have to build the cabin over. It's all rotten underneath, it's so *old*." She rolled over and the rest was
swallowed by her pillow.

After a long silence, the older girl said, "I think it's *creepy*."

Outside, pine boughs grated on the gable screen. He had no
trouble sleeping at home. He read as long as he wanted; next thing,
light would be speckling down through the horse chestnut leaves
and his book would be over on the bedstand, the page marked. But
the dark at camp brought raccoons with red-glowing eyes and
claws that scuttled across the porch boards, and it sent wind flying
down off Mt. Charles, whipping the lake up, leaving the shore
strewn with foam. Men didn't use the pot, so if he couldn't stand it
anymore, he'd talk himself down the stairs and back toward the
outhouse. He'd never make it the whole way. He'd stop beyond
the woodpile and go there, then find himself looking up through
the blowing limbs of the pines at the stars, so needle-bright and
endless that he imagined himself falling out into them . . . until he'd

look away and hurry back to the porch steps, hating himself for not being brave.

But now these worries vanished. He waited in the loft and thought: *Who's dying?* For a minute or two, his mind beat with wondering, then, just as suddenly, he was gone.

When he woke, the air in the loft was rich with cooking smells. At home, the mornings were frantic as his parents threw themselves together for work and prodded him to get his belt on, get his teeth brushed, get his lunchbox. At camp, they let him be, so he didn't get up yet, resting happily and listening to the breakfast talk. He couldn't hear his Uncle Ray and guessed he'd gone back to town early. Now and then he caught Aunt Hallie through the clatter of the girls' voices, nearly his mother's voice but without the hurry. He rolled over and peered down at her through the railing. They looked alike, too, except his aunt was a runner and kept her hair short as a boy's. She was looking off at the windows now, at the morning light coming in from the lake. She was wrapped in the same blue bathrobe his mother wore, and her arms were folded low at her waist, the way he'd see his mother standing sometimes when he looked up suddenly . . . .

Just then his grandfather came up the steps, stopped for a breath, and squinted through the screen door. Aunt Hallie and the girls looked up at once and their talk skipped a beat. As he made his way into the room, they seemed to part for him. Cousin Gwen got up, stuffing the last wedge of toast into her mouth, and gave him her chair at the dinette.

"How'd you sleep, Dad?" Aunt Hallie asked him.

He waived the question aside. Paul couldn't see his face, only the back of his head where wisps of hair stuck out from the cap and brushed the collar of his wool shirt, light as a dandelion gone to seed.

"Well, I see we have another good day," he said, not to any of them in particular.

"Yes, haven't we been lucky this year?" Aunt Hallie said.
Paul caught the change in her voice—his mother did that, too.

He could always tell how well she knew someone by how cheerful her voice got. She saved the plainer darker sound for her family. Funny that Aunt Hallie would talk like that to her own father. Maybe it was because of his hearing.

Then the room froze, as Paul remembered the words he'd overheard in the night, and knew what they meant. Daytime made it worse. Everything was plain to him and he couldn't say these were only terrible thoughts flung at him by the darkness. People died when they got old, he understood that. And afterward, he guessed, they went to heaven. *Your family'll all be waiting for you,* his friend Lynette told him over Monopoly one afternoon. *I mean everybody way way back.* She made it sound like a holiday dinner, all these relations arranged around a long table with candles and the best dishes and no empty chairs except the one he'd come to fill. Lynette acted comfortable with the idea, but Paul wasn't sure, not at all. He could only see himself as the boy he was now, and feel his legs squirming inside his good pants.

"You'd know all this if you went to Sunday school like you were supposed to," Lynette said.

Paul said they didn't do that in his family. Sundays they slept late. His father wore old clothes all day—he watched baseball or worked on the garden or split wood; once in a while he got up before anyone and went into the mountains with his friends. But sometimes Paul's mother took him inside one of the churches to hear a concert, and Paul saw right away that she knew how to act there. And the night the two of them walked through the snow to a candlelight service to sing carols, Paul studied her while everyone prayed, and saw how she looked, respectful and wide awake.

A few days after his talk with Lynette, he'd gone to his mother about what she'd said. They were out at the picnic table under the willow . . . she looked right into his face and told him: *No one knows.* And when she said it this way, she made it sound mysterious and not to be feared. "Don't you think there's more going on than we can see?" she said, and before Paul could wonder if he did, she went on, in another voice. "Besides, Paulie, look how young you are, I don't want to think of you worrying yourself about all that." He remembered how she sat with him, not growing impatient, and how the gold light struck her face and how her hair streamed down in harmony with the willow branches.

His grandfather *was* old, but not old like the old people he saw going in to eat at the cafe near his house, or like Lynette's great-grandmother who stayed with them next door part of the year, who was born in the 1800s. Paul felt his face burning. *His parents really didn't know*, he thought. He felt himself plummeting and grabbed the bars of the railing and squeezed them hard. He locked his eyes on his grandfather's figure below and imagined that he turned his face and smiled up at him, raising one of his freckled hands in a greeting. *Come along, Paulie, you're one of us.*

But no, the room was alive and loud again. His grandfather was stirring his coffee listlessly, and Aunt Hallie was saying, "Our girls are walking down to the barrens this morning . . . Paulie, too, I guess."

"No!" Paul burst out, though he'd only meant to think it.

Everyone turned and stared up at him. Aunt Hallie's mouth drooped open. "Paulie," she said. "Well, good morning." Her composure gathered again. "You don't have to go if you don't want to," she said. "But why don't you?"

Of course, Paul hadn't meant he wouldn't go walking with them, but now that he thought about it, he knew he didn't want to. He didn't want to do anything.

"There's nothing to be afraid of," Billie said.

"You can look for arrowheads," Gwen said.

Paul could hardly talk. He'd gone numb. He dug under the sleeping bag for his clothes and slipped back out of sight to put them on. In a moment, the talk below resumed, as though he'd never broken it.

Aunt Hallie lifted the big tea kettle two-handed and poured steaming water over the breakfast dishes. Everyone had gone. Paul sat by the Franklin stove, paging through old *Field and Streams*, waiting for a break in her work. But she moved from job to job so smoothly that Paul finally went and stood by her as she drove the fine sand from the rag rug to the linoleum and out the door.

"It's a wonder we have a beach anymore," she said, an old camp joke.

"What's wrong with Grampa Paul?" Paul asked.

He had no idea what she'd say. Some things, his mother reminded him constantly, weren't any of his business.

"Here, Paulie," Aunt Hallie said. "Give this a shake for me."

Paul took the mat she handed him and followed her to the porch. He held it over the edge and shook and the dirty sand showered the ivy below. As he finished, he saw she was watching him, so he gave it another little shake.

"That's good," she said, but didn't take it back from him. Her eyes had shifted to the lake. Through the pine branches, Paul saw the hazy sheen of the water and down by the lake's outlet the glint of a boat at anchor.

"Somebody said something, sounds like," Aunt Hallie said, back with him again. "Haven't they?" She walked to the edge of the porch and patted a plank beside her for him to sit, and he did.

"Honey," Aunt Hallie said, "Your grandfather has a kind of cancer. Do you know about that?"

Paul nodded, hoping desperately that she wouldn't ask him to say what he knew.

"Your mother didn't tell you anything?"

"No."

"Just as well," Aunt Hallie said. She was quiet for another moment. "The truth is," she said, "we just don't expect he'll be here when you come again next summer."

"Oh . . ."

"We'll miss him terribly, won't we?"

Paul felt that numbing in his chest again, but then Aunt Hallie put her hand to his forehead and smoothed back his hair, exactly what his mother would've done. He didn't know what in the world he should say.

"Be nice to him, Paulie," she said.

Everyone knew his grandfather's routine at camp—even now it wasn't much changed. He woke early and took the boat out, alone. The chug of a far-off motor was the first sound people would no- tice as they lay in bed. If he kept any fish—northerns or walleyes (rock bass he said ruined the lake and these he stuck through the gills with his pen knife and threw back to die)—he cleaned them on a board grown between two maples by the water, a few of the younger cousins crowding around. He took his time, now and then picking off one of the questions pitched at him, letting most of what they said fly past. But often he took no fish. After beaching the boat, he'd make the rounds of his children's cabins, then shut himself in the workroom, where he oiled and sharpened the tools, or fixed things that broke around camp, or where he just sat and read whatever newspaper he found in one of the outhouses, back to front, until he retired to The Folly and treated himself to deviled ham on Ry-Crisp, some black tea, and his medications, then shooed out any remaining cousins, drew the bamboo shades and slept.

After his aunt went back to her work, Paul drifted down the path toward Grampa Paul's. The day was getting hot. The lake was flat; nothing seemed to move. Someone called to him from inside Aunt Leah's, one of the girl cousins, but he skipped down the hill past the tangle of rosehips, as if he hadn't heard. A lantern was burning in the workroom. Paul veered off the trail and came around the shaded side and sat on the chopping block and waited for his grandfather to come outside. He didn't, though. After a while Paul climbed on the pile of birch rounds below the high screened window and tried to listen. All he heard were the jays fighting up in the hardwoods. He let himself down finally, then stood just to the side of the door, thinking how the others would barge straight in, until he couldn't stand it anymore and edged away.

It was too late to catch Gwen and Billie even if he wanted to. He crossed the strip of road behind the cabins and started running down the wide footpath through Uncle Mac's swath of thinned-out woods, called The Pinery, which lead a quarter mile to Lake Superior . . . and by the time the trail opened out above the rusty sandstone bluffs, he was crying and coughing and trying to get his breath. He went to his knees and covered his face from the glare of the bay, and before long the spasm began to ease. Leaning back into the roots of a cedar, he heard Aunt Hallie's voice again, and somehow the sound of it outweighed what she'd told him. He took a few deep breaths and gradually his hands unclenched. He sat up and stared out at the big lake. Miles out, an ore boat crept along the horizon, above it a wash of bright clouds, too far away to look like anything.

Before supper, everyone gathered on the porch of The Folly for happy hour—Uncle Ray and Aunt Hallie, Uncle Duff, Uncle Mac, and all the others. His grandfather sat in a high-backed wicker chair, and slats of light crossed his shirt, rippling down onto his folded hands. Paul walked through to the table and grabbed a handful of cashews and looked for a place to sit, but all the chairs and even the bench under the window were taken, so he backed against the wall and tried to be invisible.

"How's the boy?" Uncle Ray asked. Paul smiled blankly. It was all the answer his uncle seemed to want.

The talk was about electricity. One of the original land owners across the lake had brought in power and had a TV in his cabin. The road was still dug up in spots and even Uncle Ray complained.

Uncle Duff drank down the last of his beer and snapped the aluminum sharply between his fingers.

"What're you all afraid of?" he said. "What's going to happen is going to happen."

"It's better than listening to that god-awful generator of his," Aunt Leah said.

"I'll tell you, they don't even make gas iceboxes anymore," Uncle Duff added.

Uncle Mac gave them both a stare. He was oldest of the five, the most like Paul's grandfather, everyone said. "We all *agreed* about this, as I remember it," he said stiffly.

Uncle Duff was known as the family hothead, and Paul could see for himself he was itching to let loose with something more. But another look flew between the brothers, accompanied by the slightest nod toward their father. It was the same kind of thing that'd happened at breakfast that day. They *did* have an agreement . . . but it was about more than electricity, about more than not changing things at camp. They were all going to get along for a while, and they were all going to be nice to him.

The porch fell to silence.

Paul looked at his grandfather. He wondered how the sickness could be inside him and not show. Maybe everyone else knew what to look for, he thought. They acted as if they could see it, as if they felt it in the room with them, breathing and growing. Aunt Hallie came out from the kitchen and brought his glass back, filled mostly with ice, and fit it into his hand. "There now," she said. Paul saw his eyes flick from the glass up to her face, lingering just a second, then out to the rest of them fanned before him—all his family—and then saw the slow, tired-looking shake of his head.

After supper, Paul slipped away from his aunt and uncle and the cousins, and sat on the dock by The Folly. The evening birds came out, the swallows like scraps of shadow, then the loons and others he didn't know the names of. Far off, he heard a woman's voice calling, but it only made the lake seem quieter, farther from the rest of the world . . . then his grandfather was standing beside him. Without talking, they made the boat ready, loaded the cushions, the poles, the tacklebox. Paul dropped into the bow. His grandfather shoved them off and rowed out much farther than he had the night before, both of them looking back at the slice of cleared land where the cabins were, a few lights just now coming to the windows. Finally he primed the engine and started it. Paul turned and faced into the wind and watched the black choppy water separate before the bow, letting the rush of air scour his thoughts.

Near the far shore, his grandfather eased the engine back to a slow chug, then let it die, though they were still a ways out in deep water. From the corner of the sky, Paul saw the great heron again, just as it thrust down its long wings and braced itself to land.

"There!" he said, but his grandfather had already seen it.

Paul looked down at the fishing things and could barely think what they were for. He wanted to keep talking now, before his voice froze, though he couldn't think of what to say.

"I'll miss you terribly," he blurted—then gulped, felt his face flush. That was what Aunt Hallie had said, not his words at all. His grandfather was still watching the heron.

"After you go home?"

"Yes," Paul said. "And after that, I mean . . . ."

"Don't you think you'll be seeing me again?"

"No," Paul said. "Not really."

His grandfather thumbed up the bill of his cap and studied him, as if he hadn't taken a full reckoning of him until this instant. "Maybe you won't at that," he said.

His hands stirred on the oargrips, the callouses squeaking lightly. "Hardly seems fair, does it?"

Paul struggled to look straight across at him, but when he brought himself to do it, his grandfather was looking off, his eyes following the tree line around the lake, taking the same slow route the heron had.

"When I was a little older than you, twelve maybe," his grandfather said in a minute, "a couple of men my father knew drowned over there. In that water off the point."

Paul shot a look back over his shoulder, though he knew there'd be nothing to see.

"There wasn't any settlement up here yet, just an old homesteader's place where Uncle Mac's is now. It had pretty much gone to ruin and my father had decided it should come down—that's what we were busy with that day. I suppose your mother's told you that my father was a doctor . . ."

Paul shook his head.

"He and another doctor named Hollings had bought this land together and it was the two of them tearing down the cabin, and I was supposed to be helping, but I think I spent most of the day by the fire. It was early November, a Sunday . . . there was just a fringe of ice along in the cattails.

"These other men were older, people Dr. Hollings knew from Negaunee. They were going across to hunt deer in this part of the woods over where we are now. Big stocky men, all weighted down with wool, heavy lace-up boots . . ."

"What happened?" Paul asked.

His grandfather took a while to answer. "The weather wasn't so bad," he said. "Not a great deal of wind. The sun wasn't really out, still it wasn't a terribly dark day. Something must have happened in the boat, an argument maybe, or just . . . I don't know, Paulie. I really don't have any idea. Here my father and his friend were both doctors but it didn't make any difference at all. I was the first one to see the boat—it had drifted over toward the outlet, upside down.

"Dr. Hollings had to drive their truck back to town. We followed him in our car, my father and I. There wasn't much of a road then—some stretches of it were nothing more than grades the logging company had left years before. It was night now. My father stayed close behind the truck so our headlights shone on the bed where the men were, rolled up in a canvas tarp. But the road was so uneven, finally we had to stop and get out and tie them down with rope. I can remember them standing in the woods doing it, passing the rope back and forth."

Then his grandfather was quiet again.

Paul tried listening to the water against the side of the boat, but found himself thinking about those long-ago men trying to swim in the freezing water, about all the things in the boat falling out and sinking. He thought about the guns still lying at the bottom of the water, lost under generations of leaves.

His grandfather finally looked up again, offering Paul a brief smile in the creases of his eyes.

"You ever hear them call this God's Country," he said.

Paul couldn't tell if this was a question he had to answer, but he nodded.

"There's not another place so lovely, Paulie, so full of all of us, I know there isn't . . . *but God's country?*

His gaze came suddenly back and fixed hugely on Paul. "Paulie, can I tell you something? I'm not sure that God has a country."

"Me either," Paul murmured.

"*Nor anyone*," his grandfather said. He let go of the oars and let them drift back along the hull. "*Nor any living thing, Paulie.*"

The heron lifted its beak toward the sky. A harsh rattle escaped from its throat, echoing across the open water. The blue air deepened quickly, speckled by the dark shapes of insects, then by stars. A fish jumped near the boat, but neither Paul nor his grandfather made a move toward the tackle. They'd come out too late and pretty soon they'd need to turn around and go back, but for a few minutes more they sat in the boat together, watching the heron as it disappeared into the darkness of the reeds.

Norman Maclean

USFS 1919: The Ranger,

The Cook, and a Hole in the Sky

> *And then he thinks he knows*
> *The hills where his life rose. . .*
> —Matthew Arnold,
> "The Buried Life"

I was young and I thought I was tough and I knew it was beautiful and I was a little bit crazy but hadn't noticed it yet. Outside the ranger station there were more mountains in all directions than I was ever to see again—oceans of mountains—and inside the station at this particular moment I was ahead in a game of cribbage with the ranger of the Elk Summit District of the Selway Forest of the United States Forest Service (USFS), which was even younger than I was and enjoyed many of the same characteristics.

It was mid-August of 1919, so I was seventeen and the Forest Service was only fourteen, since, of several possible birthdays for the Forest Service, I pick 1905, when the Forest Division of the Department of the Interior was transferred to the Department of Agriculture and named the United States Forest Service.

In 1919 it was twenty-eight miles from the Elk Summit Ranger Station of the Selway Forest to the nearest road, fourteen miles to the top of the Bitterroot Divide and fourteen straight down Blodgett Canyon to the Bitterroot Valley only a few miles from Hamilton, Montana. The fourteen miles going down were as cruel as the fourteen going up, and far more dangerous, since Blodgett Canyon was medically famous for the tick that gave Rocky Mountain Fever, with one chance out of five for recovery. The twenty-eight-mile trail from Elk Summit to the mouth of Blodgett Canyon was a Forest Service trail and therefore marked by a blaze with a notch on top; only a few other trails in the vast Elk Summit district were so marked. Otherwise, there were only game trails and old trappers' trails that gave out on open ridges and meadows with no signs of where the game or trappers had vanished. It was a world of strings of pack horses or men who walked alone—a world of hoof and foot and the rest done by hand. Nineteen nineteen across the Bitterroot Divide in northern Idaho was just before the end of most of history that had had no four-wheel drives, no bull-dozers, no power saws and nothing pneumatic to take the place of jackhammers and nothing chemical or airborne to put out forest fires.

Nowadays you can scarcely be a lookout without a uniform and a college degree, but in 1919 not a man in our outfit, least of all the ranger himself, had been to college. They still picked rangers for the Forest Service by picking the toughest guy in town. Ours, Bill Bell, was the toughest in the Bitteroot Valley, and we thought he was the best ranger in the Forest Service. We were strengthened in this belief by the rumor that Bill had killed a sheepherder. We were a little disappointed that he had been acquitted of the charges, but nobody held it against him, for we all knew that being acquitted of killing a sheepherder in Montana isn't the same as being innocent.

As for uniform, our ranger always wore his .45 and most of our regular crew also packed revolvers, including me. The two old men in the outfit told the rest of us that "USFS" stood for "Use 'er Slow and Fuck 'er Fast." Being young and literal, I put up an argument at first, pointing out that the beginning letters in their motto didn't exactly fit USFS—that their last word "Fast" didn't begin with S as "Service" did. In fact, being thickheaded, I stuck with this argument quite a while, and could hear my voice rise. Each time, they spit through the parting in their moustaches and looked at me as if I were too young to say anything that would have any bearing on such a subject. As far as they were concerned, their motto fitted

the United States Forest Service exactly, and by the end of the summer I came to share their opinion.

Although our ranger, Bill Bell, was the best, he did not shine at
cribbage. He put down his cards and said, "Fifteen-two,
fifteen-four, fifteen-six, and a pair are eight." As usual, I spread out
his hand and counted after him. All he had was an eight and a pair
of sevens, a hand he always counted as eight. Maybe the eight card
gave him the idea. "Bill," I told him, "that's a six hand.
Fifteen-two, fifteen-four, and a pair are six." Being wrong always
made Bill Bell feel somebody was insulting him. "Damn it," he
said, "can't you see that eight card? Well, eight plus seven...." The
cook, still wiping dishes, looked over Bill's shoulder and said,
"That's a six hand." Bill folded up his cards and tossed them into
the pile—whatever the cook said was always right with Bill, which
didn't make me like the cook any better. It is always hard to like a
spoiled cook, and I disliked this one particularly.

Even so, I had no idea how much I was going to dislike him before the summer was over, or, for that matter, how big a thing
another card game was going to be. By the middle of that summer
when I was seventeen I had yet to see myself become part of a
story. I had as yet no notion that life every now and then becomes
literature—not for long, of course, but long enough to be what we
best remember, and often enough so that what we eventually come
to mean by life are those moments when life, instead of going
sideways, backwards, forward, or nowhere at all, lines out straight,
tense and inevitable, with a complication, climax, and, given some
luck, a purgation, as if life had been made and not happened. Right
then, though, I wasn't thinking of Bill as being the hero of any
story—I was just getting tired of waiting for him to make the next
deal. Before he did, he licked his fingers so he wouldn't deal two or
three cards at a time.

It was hard to figure out how Bill could be so different when he
had a rope in his hands—with a rope he was an artist, and he usually was doing something with one. Even when he was sitting in the
ranger station he would whirl little loops and "dab" them over a
chair; either that or tie knots, beautiful knots. While the crew
talked, he threw loops or tied knots. He was a sort of "Yeah" or

"No" guy to human beings—now and then he talked part of a sentence or a sentence or two—but to his horses and mules he talked all the time, and they understood him. He never talked loud to them, especially not to mules, which he knew are like elephants and never forget. If a mule got balky when he was shoeing him, he never reached for anything—he just led him out in the sun and tied up one front foot and let him stand there for a couple of hours. You can't imagine what a Christianizing effect it has, even on a mule, to stand for a couple of hours in the hot sun minus a foot.

Bill was built to fit his hands. He was big all over. Primarily he was a horseman, and he needed an extra large horse. He was not the slender cowboy of the movies and the plains. He was a horseman of the mountains. He could swing an ax or pull a saw, run a transit and build trail, walk all day if he had to, put on climbing spurs and string number nine telephone wire, and he wasn't a bad cook. In the mountains you work to live, and in the mountains you don't care much whether your horse can run fast. Where's he going to run? Bill's horse was big and long-striding, and could walk all day over mountain trails at five miles an hour. He was a mountain horse carrying a mountain man. Bill called him Big Moose. He was brown and walked with his head thrown back as if he wore horns.

Every profession has a pinnacle to its art. In the hospital it is the brain or heart surgeon, and in the sawmill it is the sawyer who with squinting eyes makes the first major cut that turns a log into boards. In the early Forest Service, our major artist was the packer, as it usually has been in worlds where there are no roads. Packing is an art as old as the first time man moved and had an animal to help him carry his belongings. As such, it came ultimately from Asia and from there across Northern Africa and Spain and then up from Mexico and to us probably from Indian squaws. You can't even talk to a packer unless you know what a cinch *(cincha)* is, a latigo, and a manty *(manta)*. With the coming of roads, this ancient art has become almost a lost art, but in the early part of this century there were still few roads across the mountains and none across the "Bitterroot Wall." From the mouth of Blodgett Canyon, near Hamilton, Montana, to our ranger station at Elk Summitt in Idaho nothing moved except on foot. When there was a big fire crew to be supplied, there could be as many as half a hundred mules and short-backed horses heaving and grunting up the narrow switchbacks and dropping extra large amounts of manure at the sharp turns. The ropes tying the animals together would jerk taut and stretch their connected necks into a straight line until they looked like dark gigantic swans circling and finally disappearing into a higher medium.

Bill was our head packer, and the Forest Service never had a better one. But right now he was having a hard time figuring out which of his three remaining cards he should play. He would like to have taken off his black Stetson and scratched his head, but the first thing he did when he dressed in the morning was to put on his black hat, and it was the last thing he took off when he went to bed. In between he did not like to remove it. Before he got around to pushing it back on his head and playing a card, I found myself thinking of some of the trips I had taken with him across the Bitterroot Divide.

As head packer, Bill rode in front of the string, a study in angles. With black Stetson hat at a slant, he rode with his head turned almost backward from his body so he could watch to see if any of the packs were working loose. Later in life I was to see Egyptian bas-reliefs where the heads of men are looking one way and their bodies are going another, and so it is with good packers. After all, packing is the art of balancing packs and then seeing that they ride evenly—otherwise the animals will have saddle sores in a day or two and be out of business for all or most of the summer.

Up there in front with Bill, you could see just about anything happen. A horse might slip or get kicked out of the string and roll frightened downhill until he got tangled around a tree trunk. You might even have to shoot him, collect the saddle, and forget the rest of what was scattered over the landscape. But mostly what you were watching for took Bill's trained eye to see—a saddle that had slipped back so far the animal couldn't breathe, or a saddle that had slipped sideways. In an outfit that large, there are always a few "shad bellies" that no cinch can hang on to and quite a few "bloaters" that blow up in the morning when the cinch touches them and then slowly deflate. Who knows what? The trouble may have started back in the warehouse where the load cargoer couldn't tell weight or didn't give a damn and now an animal was trying to keep steady across the Bitterroot Divide with lopsided packs. Or maybe the packs balanced, but some assistant packer had tied one higher than the other. Or had tied a sloppy diamond hitch and everything slipped. The Bitterroot Divide, with its many switchbacks, granite boulders, and bog holes, brought out every weakness in a packer, his equipment, and his animals. To take a pack string of nearly half a hundred across the Bitterroot Divide was to perform a masterpiece in that now almost lost art, and in 1919 I rode with Bill Bell and saw it done.

The divide was just as beautiful as the way up. In August it was blue with June lupine. Froth dropped off the jaws of the horses and mules, and, snorting through enlarged red nostrils, the animals shook their saddles, trying without hands to rearrange their loads. Not far to the south was El Capitan, always in snow and always living up to its name. Ahead and to the west was our ranger station—and the mountains of Idaho, poems of geology stretching beyond any boundaries and seemingly even beyond the world.

Six miles or so west of the divide is a lake, roughly two-thirds of the way between Hamilton and Elk Summit, that is the only place where there is water and enough grass to hold a big bunch of horses overnight. K. D. Swan, the fine photographer of the early Forest Service, should have been there to record the design of the divide—ascending in triangles to the sky and descending in ovals and circles to an oval meadow and an oval lake with a moose knee-deep beside lily pads. It was triangles going up and ovals coming down, and on the divide it was springtime in August.

The unpacking was just as beautiful—one wet satin back after another without saddle or saddle sore, and not a spot of white wet flesh where hair and hide had rubbed off. Perhaps one has to know something about keeping packs balanced on the backs of animals to think this beautiful, or to notice it at all, but to all those who work come moments of beauty unseen by the rest of the world.

So, to a horseman who has to start looking for horses before daybreak, nothing is so beautiful in darkness as the sound of a bell mare.

While I was sitting there thinking of how Bill was a major artist and how even the knots he tied were artistic, he had somehow got ahead of me in the cribbage game, at which he was a chump. At least, I was a lot better than he was at cribbage, once the favorite indoor pastime of the woods. We even played it outdoors, and often on the trail one of us would carry a deck of cards and a cribbage board in his pack sack, and in the middle of the morning and afternoon we would straddle a log and have a game.

Bill really wasn't ahead, but I was going to lose unless he played like a Chinaman. We both were in striking distance of 121, which is the end of the game in cribbage, and I had the advantage of counting first. I needed only eight points, which normally I should have been able to make with a decent hand plus the "pegging." But I had a lousy hand, just a pair of fours, and a pair is worth only two points, so I would have to peg six to make 121, and that's a lot. In case you don't know cribbage, about all Bill had to do to stop me from pegging six was not to pair anything I put down. I started the pegging by playing one of my fours, and so help me, he had a four in his hand and he slapped it down. "I'll take two for a pair of fours," he said. As I told you, all I had in my hand was a pair of fours. I put down the third four, and in cribbage three of a kind counts six, so I had 121 and the ball game, and a start toward discovering that somehow artists aren't sharp at cards.

Actually, I had heard rumors in Hamilton, which was Bill's headquarters in the Bitterroot Valley, that the local small-town gamblers could hardly wait for Bill to get his monthly check. Among the local housemen and shills he was supposedly noted for playing poker as if he breathed through gills. Knowing how Bill hated to lose, I was somewhat surprised that he hadn't also been acquitted of shooting a shill.

Knowing Bill, I also knew that he was sore at me, at least for the moment, so I thought, "Let's see if a change of games won't change the luck." Of course, three can play a lot more card games than two. As the cook was finishing dishes, I asked him, "Why don't you cut in on a nickel-and-dime game? Poker? Pinochle? You and Bill name it.''

I'll never forget that cook; in fact he was to become one of my longest memories. Even out in the woods, he wore low canvas shoes. He turned his shoes toward me and said, "I never play cards against the men I work with." This wasn't the first time the cook had made this stately speech to me, so I started disliking him all over again. His name may have been Hawkins, but I really think it was Hawks and in memory I made it into Hawkins because in some book there was a character I didn't like by the name of Hawkins.

Bill and I played one more game of cribbage trying to get over being sore, but we weren't successful. I picked up the cards and put them in their case and the case on the only shelf in the cabin. Before I reached the door the cook had picked them up and was sitting at the table shuffling. He dealt out four hands. Then he went around the first three hands again, quickly giving each hand one or two cards as if each hand had asked to draw. He paused, however, before giving himself cards. Then with one motion he picked them all up. After shuffling, he dealt out five hands, sometimes four, never three, lest I get the idea that he would play with Bill and me. I stood there watching him shuffling and dealing. It was worth watching. After about five minutes, he picked up all the cards with one swoop, stuck them in the case and the case on the shelf and started for bed. I closed the door and started for the tent where the crew slept. I liked him less than ever.

There were only four of us in the "regular crew," plus the lookouts who were stationed on the high peaks, plus the ranger and the cook. The regular crew was hired by the month (sixty dollars per) for the summer—the ranger was the only one in the district who was hired all year. Earlier in the season, there had been a big fire in the district and an emergency crew of over a hundred men had been hired on the streets of Butte and Spokane, but the fire had been put out and the emergency crew sent back to town. Our small regular crew now was building trail about three miles from the station—grade A trail, too, with about a twenty-foot right-of-way and no more than six-percent grade. A twenty-foot swath through the wilderness with no trees or brush left standing and, instead of going over an outcropping of rocks with a short steep pitch in the trail, we blasted through the rocks to keep the trail from gaining more than six feet of altitude every hundred feet. Tons of dynamite and we could have taken a hay wagon down our mountain boulevard. Of course, all we needed were trails wide enough to get pack horses through without the packs getting caught between trees, and in a few years the Forest Service revised the specifications and gave orders for the back country to be opened with as many trails as possible. Still, it is proper when young to strive for gigantic perfection that doesn't make sense, and today somewhere in the jungles of Idaho is a mile or two of overgrown boulevard leading nowhere, not even to a deserted Mayan temple.

Of the regular crew of four, two were old men and two were young punks. There was Mr. McBride and his red-headed son. Mr. McBride was a jack-of-all-trades who had worked at different ranches in the Bitteroot Valley and his son was trying to be like his father. Mr. Smith was the old man of the crew and was always worried about his bowels. He was addressed as "Mr. Smith." He was dignified and took small, aged steps on large legs that made his feet look tiny. He had been a miner and he naturally was our powder man, and a good one. Since there were four of us and Mr. McBride had a son, Mr. Smith looked upon me as his. That's how I was elected to the dynamite, which made me sick. Before I had started the job I had heard stories that if you touch dynamite and then your face you will get a headache. Maybe I was carried away by the story, because as long as I worked on the powder I always had headaches. Maybe, though, at seventeen I wasn't quite big enough to swing a double jackhammer all day.

When you are blasting, naturally you first make a hole in the rock for your powder. Nowadays it is done with a pneumatic drill; then it was done by hand and jackhammer. If you worked in a team of two it was called "double jacking." One man held the drill, and every time the other man hit the head of it with the jackhammer the man holding the drill would turn it slightly until the bit completed a circle. This was the outline for the hole, and the same thing went on until the hole was dug, stopping only when the man holding the drill said, "Mud." Then the hammer man gratefully rested while the man holding the drill took a very small dipper and cleaned out the hole. Otherwise, the man with the hammer kept swinging, and, if by chance just once he missed the small head of the drill and the hammer glanced off he would mutilate the hand or arm of the man holding the drill. Sometimes it seemed that Mr. Smith had forgotten how to say "Mud," and I would look down and see the heads of two or three drills, on each of which Mr. Smith had the same hand, the skin of which was already freckled by age. I no longer think that rubbing my face gave me the headaches.

This morning the headache started earlier than usual. I can't give you any very clear reason why I disliked the cook so much. I was honest enough with myself to say that I might be jealous of him. Although I was only seventeen, this was my third summer in the Forest Service, two of them working for Bill, and he had started to show me how to pack, and in return I would do him favors like coming back to camp in the morning to pack out lunch to the crew. I couldn't figure how this cook had moved into first place. Everything he said or did was just perfect, as far as Bill was concerned. Besides, I didn't like his looks—he looked like a bluejay, cocky, with his head on a slant and a tuft of hair on top of it. A bluejay with low canvas shoes. Mostly, though, I didn't need reasons to dislike him. When you get older, you become rational more or less, but when you are young you know. I knew this cook was a forty-cent piece.

It wasn't helping my headache either to think of the ranger being sore at me. I said to myself, "Take it easy, and keep your big mouth shut. It's nothing and it will blow over." Then I repeated to myself, "Keep your big mouth shut," but I knew I wouldn't. I had formed principles to compensate for having started work when I was fifteen. I had missed a lot, I knew—the swimming hole, summer girls, and a game called tennis which was played in white flannels with cuffs. I would say to myself, "You decided to go into the woods, so the least you can do is be tough." I hadn't felt this way at fifteen when I first worked for Bill, but that was the way I felt now at seventeen. Even though Bill was my model and an artist—maybe because he was—at seventeen something in me was half-looking for trouble with him.

Before noon who should come along but the cook packing our lunch. He said to me, "The ranger wants you to come back to camp after you eat."

When I got back to camp, Bill was in the cabin we used as a warehouse, building the packs for the string that was going to Hamilton soon. I didn't ask him why he had sent for me and he didn't say. I just started helping him build and balance the packs, and tried to keep my mind on what I was doing, partly because building packs is never a mechanical job. Not even when you're packing the simplest stuff like tin cans, which go into boxes called "panyards," made of rawhide, wood, or canvas, that are hung on the prongs of the saddle. You can't forget to wrap each can in toilet paper, or the labels on the cans will rub off and you won't be able to tell peaches from peas. And the heaviest cans have to go to the bottom, or the pack will shift. Then each of the two side packs has to weigh the same and together (with the top pack) they shouldn't weigh more than 175 pounds for a horse or 225 for a mule—at least, those were the Forest Service regulations then, but they were twenty-five pounds too heavy if the animals weren't to be bone heaps by the middle of the summer. I don't care who you are, I'll bet you that without a scale you can't build two packs weighing the same and together weighing 150 or 200 pounds when a top pack has been added.

After we had packed for a while, I forgot to wonder why the ranger had sent for me. Maybe it was just to help him box things up. Then, while we were working with our heads bent, I heard the cook come by jingling the knives and forks the crew had used for lunch.

Still working on a pack, I heard myself say, "I don't like that son of a bitch."

Bill lifted a pack and put it down. Inside I heard myself say, "Keep your big mouth shut." Outside, I heard myself add, "Some day I am going to punch the piss out of him." Bill stood up and said, "Not in this district you won't." He looked at me for a long time, and I looked back still crouched over my pack. I figured that at this moment crouching was a good position. Finally, we both went back to work.

Bending and lifting, he began to tell me about how the morning had gone. "The lookout on Grave Peak quit this morning." "Yeah?" I said. "Yeah," he said. "He came off that mountain in about three jumps." It was nearly twelve miles to the top of the peak. "Do you know what he said to me?" he asked. "No," I said. I wasn't happy about how this was going to end. "The lookout said, 'Give me my time. This is too tough a job for me, fighting fire in the day and sleeping with rattlesnakes at night.'" After lifting the pack again for weight, he went on, "Seems that he put his hand on the bed to pull back the blanket and he felt something shaped like a fire hose. Do you believe it?"

At Bear Creek, where I first worked for Bill, there had been a lot of rattlers on those bare mountainsides. On a steep sidehill trail, the up side can be as high as your hand, so you could almost brush those rattlesnakes as you swung along. And, being cold-blooded, they could be attracted to the warmth of a bed at night. But I hadn't seen a rattlesnake this summer in Elk Summit, although it was the adjoining district.

"No, I don't believe it," I said. "Why not?" he asked. "It's too high up there for rattlesnakes," I said. "Are you sure?" he asked, and I told him I wasn't sure but I thought so. Still working with the packs he said, "Why don't you go up on the lookout for a couple of weeks and find out?"

I didn't ask him when; I knew he meant now. I lifted the two packs until I thought they were balanced, and then started for the door. He added, "If you spot any fires, call them in. And, if there's a big rain or snow, close up camp and come back to the station."

I knew it would be dark before I got to Grave Peak, so I asked the cook to make me a sandwich. I had a big blue bandanna handkerchief, and I put the sandwich in the handkerchief and tied the handkerchief to my belt in the middle of my back. I picked up my razor, toothbrush, and comb, and my favorite ax and Carborundum stone. Then I strapped on my .32-20 and started up the high trail. I knew I had been sent into exile.

It was twelve miles and all up, but I never stopped to rest or eat the sandwich. Bill seemed to be watching all the time. By walking hard I kept even with daylight until near the end. Then darkness passed over me from below—just the dazzling peak above told me where I was going.

For the first few days, I was too tired to think about my troubles. I was still half-sick from the dynamite and I still dragged from that big fire we had fought in late July, so I spent most of my time just looking the place over and getting things squared away.

Modern lookouts live on top of their peaks in what are called "birdcages"—glass houses on towers with lightning rods twisted around them so that the lookouts are not afraid of lightning striking them, and for twenty-four hours a day can remain on the towers to watch for lightning to strike and smoke to appear. This, of course, is the way it should be, but in 1919 birdcages, as far as we knew, were only for birds. We watched from the open peak and lived in a tent in a basin close to the peak where usually there was a spring of water. From my camp to the lookout was a good half-hour climb, and I spent about twelve hours a day watching mountains.

Near the top there were few trees and nearly all of them had been struck by lightning. It had gone around them, like a snake of fire. But I was to discover that, on a high mountain, lightning does not seem to strike from the sky. On a high mountain, lightning seems to start somewhat below you and very close by, seemingly striking upward and outward. Once it was to knock me down, toss branches over me and leave me sick.

The basin where my tent was pitched was covered with chunks of cliff that had toppled from above. I did not see a rattlesnake, but I shared the basin with a grizzly bear who occasionally came along flipping over fallen pieces of disintegrated cliff as he looked for disproportionately small grubs. When I saw him coming, I climbed the highest rock and tried to figure out how many hundreds of grubs he had to eat for a square meal. When he saw me, he made noises in his mouth as if he were shifting his false teeth. In a thicket on top of a jack pine, I found the skeleton of a deer. Your guess is as good as mine. Mine is that the snow in the high basin was deep enough to cover the trees, and the deer was crossing the crust and broke through or was killed and eventually the snow melted. There was a tear in my tent so when it rained I could keep either my food or my bed dry, but not both.

Since this was not my first hitch as a lookout, I knew what to watch for—a little cloud coming up a big mountain, usually in the late afternoon when the dews had long dried and the winds were at their height. And usually it detached itself from the mountain and went on up into the sky and became just a little cloud. Once in a while it would disappear on the mountain, and then you didn't know what you had seen—probably a cloud but maybe a puff of smoke and the wind had changed and you couldn't see it now, so you marked it on your map to watch for several days. In a lightning storm you marked every strike to watch, and sometimes it was a week later before one of them became a little cloud again and then got bigger and began to boil. When a cloud began to boil, then it wasn't a cloud, especially if it reflected red on the bottom. It could mean fire even when the cloud was two or three miles down the canyon from where it was first seen, because, if there were no wind, smoke could drift a long way behind a ridge before rising again where it would show. So that's the way a fire first looks to a lookout: something—you don't know what—usually in late afternoon, that may go away and not come again and, if it comes back and is smoke, it may be quite a long way from the fire.

A possible late-afternoon cloud has no resemblance to what a fire looks like if it gets out of control, and it was often impossible in those early years to get men quickly on a fire when it was in the back country where there were no roads and sometimes not even trails, and of course long before there were planes stationed in Missoula ready to drop chemicals and smoke jumpers.

Instead, when a fire got out of control the Forest Service hired a hundred or so bindle stiffs off the streets of Butte or Spokane at thirty cents an hour (forty-five cents for straw bosses), shipped them to some rail station near the end of a branch line, and walked them the final thirty-five or forty miles over "the wall." By the time they reached the fire, it had spread all over the map, and had jumped into the crowns of trees, and for a lot of years a prospective ranger taking his exam had said the last word on crown fires. Even by my time he was a legend. When asked on his examination, "What do you do when a fire crowns?" he had answered, "Get out of the way and pray like hell for rain."

Our big fire that summer had been big enough so that I was still tired and my eyes still ached from smoke and no sleep, and big enough so that for years it crowned in my dreams, but it wasn't in the class of those fires of 1910 that burned out the Coeur d'Alene and great pieces of the Bitterroot. The smoke from those fires drifted seven hundred miles to Denver, and in my home town of Missoula the street lights had to be turned on in the middle of the afternoon, and curled ashes brushed softly against the lamps as if snow were falling heavily in the heat of August. Of course, no other fires on record were as big as those of 1910, but the one of 1919 was the biggest I was ever on.

It came in a rage and a crown to the top of the ridge. You may know, when a fire gets big enough it generates its own wind. The heat from the fire lightens the air, which rises in the sky, and the cooler air from above swoops down to replace it, and soon a great circular storm enrages the fire and the sky is a volcanic eruption of burning cones and branches descending in streamers of flames. The fire stands on the ridge, roaring for hell to arrive as reinforcement. While you are trying to peer through it to see the inferno on its way, suddenly somebody yells, "God, look behind. The son of a bitch has jumped the gulch." One hundred and eighty degrees from where you have been looking for the inferno and half-way up the opposite ravine a small smoke is growing big where one of those burning cones or branches dropped out of the sky and trapped you with a fire in your rear. Then what do you do?

Of course, the men who had been brought in from Butte or Spokane were dead tired and barefoot long before they reached the fire. At the hiring hall in Butte and Spokane each had to have a good pair of boots and a jacket to be employed, so they took turns in the alley changing the one good pair they had. Now all but one of them had marched across the Bitterroot wall in poor street shoes, and, not being able to keep ahead of the pack train, they ate twenty-eight miles of dust. They were buns off the street, miners out of the holes for the summer with the hope of avoiding tuberculosis, winos, and Industrial Workers of the World, who had been thick in Butte and Spokane during World War I. Since it was only the summer after the war, we ordinary working stiffs were still pretty suspicious of IWWs. Those of us who belonged to the regular crew (that is, who were paid sixty dollars a month instead of thirty cents an hour) said that IWW meant "I Won't Work," and we were also sure that they were happy to see our country burn. For whatever reason, we had to spend as much time patrolling them as we did the fire. First we had to get them to the top of the opposite ridge before the new fire arrived there, and a lot of them only wanted to lie down and go to sleep with the great fire coming from behind. It was the first time I ever saw that sometimes death has no meaning to men if they can lie down and sleep. We kicked them up the hill, while they begged to be left lying where they were, and we beat the new fire to the top. Then we made a "fire trench," just a scraping two or three feet wide to remove anything that would burn, like dry needles or duff. In front of the fire trench we built piles of dry twigs and then we waited for the wind to turn and blow back toward the new fire coming up the side of the ravine. We waited until the foreman gave us the signal before we lit the piles of twigs and sent fires burning back into the main one. This is known as "backfiring" and for once it worked, although if the wind had shifted again to its original direction, all we would have done was give the fire a head start on us. We did not sleep for three days. Some of us had to carry drinking water in warm canvas sacks up a thousand-foot ridge. The rest of us slowly extended the fire trench down the sides of the fire. The bottom of it we let go for a while—a fire doesn't go very far or fast downhill.

We had done a good job in heading off the fire. What you do in the first couple of hours after you hit a fire is what counts, and if it isn't right you had better take that young ranger's advice and give yourself over to prayer. Bill and the man he had made fire foreman had both experience and gift, and it takes gift as well as having been there before to know where to hit a fire hard enough to turn it in its tracks. When it's less than 110 degrees and nothing is about to burn you to death or roar at you and your lungs will still breathe

the heat and your eyes aren't closed with smoke, it's easy to state the simple principles of a science, if that's what it is. All you're trying to do is to force the fire into some opening at the top of the ridge that's covered with shale and rocks or, if such openings don't abound in your vicinity, to force it into a thin stand of alpine pine or something that doesn't burn very fast. But with the inferno having arrived and the smoke so thick you can see only two or three men ahead of you, it's gift and guts, not science, that tells you where the head of the fire is, and where an open ridge is that can't be seen, and where and when the wind will turn and whether your men have what it takes to stand and wait. Don't forget this last point when you place your men—it isn't just horses that panic when the barn burns. But we were placed right and either we had guts or we were too sick to care. Anyway, we stood and the wind stayed with us and we crowded the big fire with our backfires and turned it into the timberline.

But every time we got the fire under control, something strange would happen—the fire would jump our fire trench, usually at some fairly ordinary place, so we became sure that IWWs were rolling burning logs over the trench and starting the fire off again. If they were, it was probably just to keep their jobs going, but that wasn't what we thought, and anyway it didn't matter much what we thought—the fire kept jumping the line everywhere until I and the red-headed kid were picked to patrol the fire. The fire foreman told us to carry revolvers. That's all we were told. I still ask myself why the two youngest in the outfit were given this assignment. Did they think we were so young that we would make a big show of ourselves but would freeze in the clutch and wouldn't shoot? Or did they think we were so young we were crazy enough to shoot almost sight unseen? Or did they think that nobody, especially the IWWs, could answer these questions? Anyway we patrolled miles and miles through burning branches and feathered ashes so light they rose ahead of us as we approached. We didn't look for trouble and we didn't find any. Also, we didn't pray, but finally the rains came. The other kid being red-headed, I think he would have shot. That wouldn't have left me much choice.

I don't suppose Bill would have sent me up to the lookout if he knew how much I needed a couple of days of rest, a thought that gave me a good deal of pleasure. Still being sore at him, I reported by telephone to the ranger station the fewest number of times required—three times a day. The telephone, in a coffin-shaped box, was nailed to the tent pole and had a crank on it. Two longs rang the ranger station, and one long and a short was my call, but nobody called me from the station. There was one woman on a distant lookout and her call was two longs and a short, and I am sure the rest of us lookouts often stood poised ready to ring two longs and a short, but never did. Instead we looked at her mountain and thought it looked different from other mountains, and we took off our telephone receivers and listened to her voice when it was her turn to report to the station. She was married and talked every night to her husband in Kooskia, but we did not listen to avoid feeling sorry for ourselves.

After a few days of resting and not mending the tent, I started to feel tough again. I knew I had been sent up here as punishment. I was expected to sit still and watch mountains and long for company and something to do, like playing cribbage, I supposed. I was going to have to watch mountains for sure, that was my job, but I would not be without company. I already knew that mountains live and move. Long ago when I had had a child sickness and nobody could tell what it was or how to treat it, my mother put me outside in a bed with mosquito netting over it, and I lay there watching mountains until they made me well. I knew that, when needed, mountains would move for me.

About the same time, I began to have another feeling, although one related to the feeling that I wasn't going to let Bill punish me by making me watch mountains. Somewhere along here I first became conscious of the feeling I talked about earlier—the feeling that comes when you first notice your life turning into a story. I began to sense the difference between what I would feel if I were just nearing the end of a summer's work or were just beginning a story. If what were coming was going to be like life as it had been, a summer's job would be over soon and I would go home and tell my pals about the big fire and packing my .32-20 on the fire line and the dynamite. Looking down from Grave Peak, though, I was no longer sure that the big fire was of any importance in what was starting to happen to me. It was becoming more important that I didn't like the damn cook, who was nobody, not even a good or bad cook, and could do nothing well except shuffle cards. Faintly but nevertheless truly I was becoming part of a plot and being made the opponent of my hero, Bill Bell, in fact, mysteriously making myself his opponent. The cook began to look like the mysterious bad guy; even I became mysterious to myself—I was going to show a ranger and a cook that I couldn't be defeated by being made to watch mountains, which were childhood friends of mine.

It doesn't take much in the way of body and mind to be a lookout. It's mostly soul. It is surprising how much our souls are alike, at least in the presence of mountains. For all of us, mountains turn into images after a short time and the images turn true. Gold-tossed waves change into the purple backs of monsters, and so forth. Always something out of the moving deep, and nearly always oceanic. Never a lake, never the sky. But no matter what images I began with, when I watched long enough the mountains turned into dreams, and still do, and it works the other way around—often, waking from dreams, I know I have been in the mountains, and I know they have been moving—sometimes advancing threateningly, sometimes creeping hesitantly, sometimes receding endlessly. Both moutains and dreams.

In the late afternoon, of course, the mountains meant all business for the lookouts. The big winds were veering from the valleys toward the peaks, and smoke from little fires that had been secretly burning for several days might show up for the first time. New fires sprang out of thunder before it sounded. By three-thirty or four, the lightning would be flexing itself on the distant ridges like a fancy prizefighter, skipping sideways, ducking, showing off but not hitting anything. By four-thirty or five, it was another game. You could feel the difference in the air that had become hard to breathe. The lightning now came walking into you, delivering short smashing punches. With an alidade, you marked a line on the map toward where it struck and started counting, "Thousand-one, thousand-two," and so on, putting in the "thousand" to slow your count to a second each time. If the thunder reached you at "thousand-five," you figured the lightning had struck about a mile away. The punches became shorter and the count closer and you knew you were going to take punishment. Then the lightning and thunder struck together. There was no count.

But what I remember best is crawling out of the tent on summer nights when on high mountains autumn is always approaching. To a boy, it is something new and beautiful to piss among the stars. Not under the stars but among them. Even at night great winds seem always to blow on great mountains, and tops of trees bend, but, as the boy stands there with nothing to do but to watch, seemingly the sky itself bends and the stars blow down through the trees until the Milky Way becomes lost in some distant forest. As the cosmos brushes by the boy and disappears among the trees, the sky is continually replenished with stars. There would be stars enough to brush by him all night, but by now the boy is getting cold.

Then the shivering organic speck of steam itself disappears.

By figuring backward, I knew it was the twenty-fifth of August when an unusually hot electrical storm crashed into the peak and was followed by an unusually high wind. The wind kept up all night and the next day, and I tightened all the ropes on my tent. Cold rode in with the wind. The next night after I went to bed it began to snow. It was August 27, and the stuff was damp and heavy and came down by the pound. Most of it went through the tear in my tent but there was enough left over so that by morning you could track elk in the snow.

I didn't think much of the immediate prospects of building a fire and cooking breakfast, so first I climbed to the top of the peak. When I looked, I knew I might never again see so much of the earth so beautiful, the beautiful being something you know added to something you see, in a whole that is different from the sum of its parts. What I saw might have been just another winter scene, although an impressive one. But what I knew was that the earth underneath was alive and that by tomorrow, certainly by the day after, it would be all green again. So what I saw because of what I knew was a kind of death with the marvelous promise of less than a three-day resurrection. From where I stood to the Bitterroot wall, which could have been the end of the world, was all windrows of momentary white. Beyond the wall, it seemed likely, eternity went on in windrows of Bitterroot Mountains and summer snow.

Even before I got back to camp it had begun to melt. Hundreds of shrubs had been bent over like set snares, and now they sprang up in the air throwing small puffs of white as if hundreds of snowshoe rabbits were being caught at the same instant.

While I was making breakfast, I heard the ticktock of a clock repeating, "It's time to quit; it's time to quit." I heard it almost as soon as it began, and almost that soon I agreed. I said to myself, "You fought a big fire and packed a big gun," and I said, "You slit waxy sticks of dynamite and stuck detonation caps in them and jumped back to watch them sizzle," and then I said, "You helped Bill pack and you watched mountains by yourself. That's a summer's work. Get your time and quit." I said these things several times to impress them on myself. I knew, in addition, that the fire season was over; in fact, the last thing the ranger had told me was to come in if it snowed. So I rang two longs for the ranger station; I rang two longs until I almost pulled the crank off the telephone, but in my heart I knew that the storm had probably blown twenty trees across the line between the peak and the station. Finally, I told myself to stay there until tomorrow when most of the snow would be gone and then to walk to the station and get my time and start over the hill to Hamilton.

What I neglected to tell myself is that it is almost impossible to quit a ranger who is sore because you do not like his cook, or to quit a story once you have become a character in it. The rest of the day I straightened up the camp, finally mended the tent, and listened to the ticktock get louder. I put the boxes of tin cans in trees where the grizzly bear couldn't get them. I had seen him split them open with one snap to a can.

It was nearly ten o'clock the next morning before I started for the ranger station. There was no use starting until the sun had done some more melting. Besides, I had decided to take along the tree-climbing outfit with the faint hope that maybe the storm had blown only two or three trees across the telephone line, so in

addition to my ax and my own little odds and ends, I was walking
bow-legged with climbing spurs and climbing belt and was carrying
insulators and number nine telephone wire. I doubt if I had
dropped more than a thousand feet of altitude before I was out of
the snow. Also, by then I had chopped two trees that had fallen
across the line and had made one splice in the wire. I should have
known from the count that I would never clean out twelve miles of
telephone line in a day, but now that I was going to quit I
developed a pious feeling, wishing to end in the act of con-
scientiously performing my duty, so I kept the climbing spurs on
and followed the telephone right-of-way, watching the line dip
from tree to tree. When you are following line this way you lose all
sense of earth, and all that exists is this extended pencil line in your
eye. I wouldn't have seen a rattlesnake unless he had wings and was
flying south for the winter. As far as I was concerned, there were
no rattlesnakes in Elk Summit district, and, if there were any, they
would be holed up because it was late in the season and had just
snowed. You could have examined my thoughts clear to the bottom of the heap and never found a snake track.

I don't need to tell you how a rattlesnake sounds—you can't mistake one. Sometimes you can think that a big winged grasshopper is
a rattlesnake, but you can never think that a rattlesnake is anything
else. I stayed in the air long enough to observe him streaking for the
brush, an ugly bastard, short, not like a plains rattler, and much
thicker behind his head.

I don't know how far I jumped, but I was mad when I lit—mad
at myself for jumping so high. I took off my climbing spurs, picked
up my ax, and started into the brush after him. I remembered about
the crazy sheepherder in the valley who had been bitten that summer by a rattler and, instead of taking it easy and caring for the bite,
had chased the rattler until he killed him—and himself. I also
remembered the crew talking about it and saying that, even for a
sheepherder, he must have been crazy. I must have been crazier,
because after remembering I went into the brush after him. I went
in too fast and couldn't find him.

We talk nowadays about a "happening," which is a good term to
describe the next section of my life. In my mind it didn't occur

successively and can't be separated: the snake was coiled about four feet in front of me I stuck the ax down between him and me he hit the ax handle the ax handle rang like a bell that had been struck and there was no punctuation between any of this. Then time started again because it was after this happening that I felt my hands sting from holding the ax handle the way your hands sting when you are a kid holding a baseball bat and not paying any attention and another kid with a bat comes sneaking up and hits your bat with his.

The snake lay there as if he had never left his coil. He whirred and watched. He just barely left the next move up to me, and I made it fast. I almost set a record for a standing backward jump. It was getting so that I was doing most of my thinking in the air. I decided if I got to the ground again that I would try to take some of the sting out of my hands by chopping a few more fallen trees but instead when I lit I stood frozen trying to picture the snake as he struck because part of the picture was missing. All I could recall was about a foot and a half of his tail end lying on the ground. His head and all his upper part weren't in the picture. Where they should have been was just a vertical glaze. As I backed off farther, I came to the conclusion that about a foot and a half of him stayed on the ground as a platform to strike from and what struck was too fast to see. The bastard still whirred, so I backed off even farther before I strapped on my climbing spurs. This time when I started to follow the line, I kept one eye and a good part of another on where I was putting my feet.

If you have ever strung much wire, you know there is an important difference between the climbers used on telephone poles and on trees. Tree spurs are about two inches longer, because when you are climbing trees your spurs first have to penetrate the bark before they can start getting any hold in the wood, which is all fine and dandy as long as the trees have bark. But pretty soon the line crossed an old fire burn, maybe one of those 1910 burns, and the only trees standing were long dead and had no bark on them—and were as hard as ebony. I could get only about half an inch of spur in them and so I rocked around on the tips of my spurs and prayed the half inch would hold. The higher I climbed these petrified trees, the more I prayed. Before long, the line crossed a gulch 250 yards or more wide, and it was natural but tough luck that the line on one side of the gulch was down. A span of 250 yards of number nine line is a hell of a lot of weight for a dead tree to hold up in a storm, and one of the trees, rotted at the roots, had come down. I chopped out the line that had got wound around the tree when it fell and I spliced the line and added a few feet to it and picked a new tree to hang it on. Then I almost left the line lying there and started for the ranger station, because I didn't want to climb a dead tree while carrying that weight of line, but whenever I started to duck out like that the ranger was sure to be watching. So I put the wire over my climbing belt and the belt around the tree, and started up with my rear end sticking straight out to punch as much spur into that calcified tree as possible. You've seen linemen at work and know it's a job for rear ends that stick out and you should know why, even if you've never had climbers on. And when you're hanging line on trees instead of poles, you have an extra hazard to overcome—you have to lean even farther back on your rear end and swing a little ax to chop off the limbs as you go up, because your belt is around that tree and it has to go up if you are. Also going up with you are at least 250 yards of number nine wire, getting heavier and tauter every time you stick half an inch of spur into this totem pole of Carborundum. Below on the tree are the sharp stubs of branches you have chopped.

Less than half way up, the line had become so taut it would have pulled me out of the tree if I hadn't been strapped to it by the belt. The half inch of spur became less and less. Then I heard the splinter. Maybe I would have felt better if I had had no belt and the wire had just flipped me over the cliff into the gulch. Anyway, with my spurs torn out of the totem pole I came down about ten or twelve feet, and then my belt caught on something, and I dangled there and smelled smoke from the front of my shirt, my belly having passed over ten feet of the snag ends of chopped branches. I worked the belt loose and fell ten or twelve feet more, and so on. I never could push far enough away from the tree to jab my spurs into it again, and when I finally reached the ground I felt as if an Indian had started a fire by rubbing two stick together, using me for one of the stick.

I was afraid to look at my lower quarters to see what was still with me. Instead, I studied the snags of those branches to see which of my private parts were to hang there forever and slowly turn to stone. Finally, I could tell by the total distribution of pain that all of me was still on the same nervous system.

I was suddenly destitute of piety, and knew that I had done all the telephone repair work that I was going to do that day. I tried to tie my outfit into one pack, but all I was thinking about was how thick that mountain rattler was behind his head. And how warm I was in front.

It was downhill to the ranger station, and I arrived there late in the afternoon, still not altogether cooled off. As I expected, Bill was in the warehouse, and he didn't look up when I came in. He said, "Why did you leave the peak?" He knew damn well why I came in—he had told me to come in if it snowed. I said, "There are rattlers up there." He grinned and seemed pleased with himself and the snake. I didn't mention anything about tree climbing, although the front of my shirt was torn.

He wasn't building packs—he was just pulling things together at the end of the season. We didn't say much of anything to each other because I was sore about the snake and he was enjoying himself, but after a while we both got our minds on what we were doing and we both were enjoying ourselves. Maybe one of the chief reasons you become a packer is that you like to handle groceries—and tools. By this time in the season most of the slabs of bacon are moldy and a lot of the tools have broken handles or need their points or edges sharpened, but that's all right. It's a good feeling to pick up an honest mattock that's lost its edge from chopping roots and rocks while making a fire trench, and moldy bacon gives a feeling of having been more than ready to be of service. Finally Bill said, "Why do you go back with the trail crew? They've been doing without you, and I need somebody around camp to help me straighten out the stuff now that the season is over." Then he said, as if he had put the two things together in his mind, "How about a game of cribbage at the station tonight?" I said I would if he needed me and to myself I said I'd put off for a day or two telling him that I was going to quit. More and more, I sensed I was slipping out of life and being drawn into a story. I couldn't quit even when it was time to quit.

The cribbage I especially wasn't crazy about. Here he was, a big black hat and a blue shirt and a cold Bull Durham cigarette hanging on his lip and in his logging boots a double tongue with a fancy fringe cut in it; in addition to all this splendor, he was the best packer going and we thought the best ranger, and he could handle big crews of fire fighters as if he personally owned them and the Bitterroot Mountains, and maybe he had killed a sheepherder, and yet he couldn't play cribbage. And, if the rumors from Hamilton were true about his poker, he couldn't play cards and he couldn't keep away from them. But my immediate burden was this two-handed face-to-face cribbage, and I couldn't get anybody in the outfit to join and make a third so we could play something else. I've already told you about the cook turning me down, and you can bet I tried the crew before I tried him.

The crew was like nearly every other crew I ever worked with in the woods. They were misers on the job. They wouldn't buy shoelaces as long as they could tie more knots in the old ones; they wouldn't bet a nickel on a card game; they learned to sew great ugly patches on their shirts; they spent all Sunday darning their socks and patching the patches on their shirts; they hoarded and Christianized—all so they would have a bigger roll to lose the first night they hit town. The closer we got to quitting time, of course, the more they hoarded and Christianized. When I went to the crew's tent to find my bedroll and air it before night, I ran into the whole bunch, and it was good to see them, especially Mr. Smith, who gave me a thump on the back, but I didn't try to tempt them into any forms of sin like a dime-limit poker game. I knew I was stuck with cribbage, and I could hear Bill counting an eight and a pair of sevens: "fifteen-two, fifteen-four, fifteen-six, and a pair make eight."

That evening I learned never to quit hating a guy just because I hadn't seen him for a while. Bill and I were a little guarded with each other, but my two weeks in exile had cleaned away some of our bad feelings. Sending me to Siberia, though, hadn't given Bill

any greater insight into cards, and I knew that unless we changed
the game we would soon be in trouble again. I am sure that feeling
was right; where I was wrong was in forgetting to keep on hating
the cook. He was almost through wiping the dishes, the food had
tasted pretty good, especially after two weeks of my own cooking,
and three men seemed as if they should be friendly when we had
just been through an August snowstorm.

As one of those people who often are among the first to hear
what they are saying, I heard myself say, overloaded with friendship, "Here, give me a towel and let's finish the dishes. Then, how
about joining us in a game of something? The season is almost over
and the three of us have never sat down to a game."

He jerked away the towel I was reaching for. In his canvas shoes,
he rose on his toes, sank back on his heels, and rose again. Until this
time I hadn't been old enough to realize that you can't hate a guy
without expecting him to return the compliment. Up to now, I
thought you could hate somebody as if it were your own business.
"How many times do I have to tell you—I don't play cards against
guys I work with." The cards lay rejected in my hand. He rolled
the towel in a wad and threw it on the dishrack. "Here, give me
those cards," he said, and grabbed them out of my hand and sat
down at the table and began to shuffle. The cards seemed to burst
into flames. He said, "Sit down," and I obeyed, with my hand still
open where the cards had been.

Then he did two things.

First, he flashed through the cards and picked out the four aces.
Then he stuck them in the pack. Then he asked me to cut the deck.
Then he dealt out hands to Bill, me, and himself. "Turn them
over," he said to me. Mine was just a hand. So was Bill's. In his
hand were all four aces.

He started out the same way the next time—he picked out the
four aces, stuck them into the deck, shuffled, had me cut, and then
dealt out hands to the three of us. "Turn them over," he said, and
there wasn't a single ace in any hand. He slapped the deck of cards
in front of me. "Here," he said, "find the four aces." And he went
back to the dishes.

It wasn't like me to be obedient, but I was. I fumbled through the deck and never found an ace. Then I tried to conduct a more thorough search and then I gave up. As he spread his dish towel to dry, he said over his shoulder, "Look in your shirt pocket." They were there, all four of them. I spread them out to count them. I was to have plenty of reason to remember this trick.

"He's a cardshark," Bill said, with a smile on his face, something like the smile that was there when I had told him the rattler had almost bitten me.

After a while, Bill added, "He's an artist." Well, I was a little dazed, I admit, and there was no denying he was a cardshark, and in the center circle of male magic sits the cardshark, but Bill's calling him an artist was something I wouldn't accept. I said to myself—fortunately not out loud this time—"Still, there's something wrong with this guy. I still think he's a forty-cent piece."

He came over and sat down next to me at the table again and began to shuffle and deal. Now, he was only practicing by himself. Usually he dealt one round and said one sentence. If he wanted more emphasis, he would shuffle, cut, and deal four hands and then say one sentence. Something like this. "I'll tell you once and for all about my card playing ..." (one round). "I play cards for a living ..." (one round). "I have to get out in the summer for my health ..." (one round). "I can't do hard work because I have to keep my hands soft ..." (one round). "So I cook and wash dishes ..." (one round). "I practice every night before I go to bed." Then he played a whole poker game again before he finished, "I never play cards against men I work with."

With one movement he picked up the four hands, and we all started for bed.

"By the way," Bill said as I went out the door, "I have a scheme—I'll tell you about it tomorrow." Before I went to sleep I had the scheme fairly well figured out. Just fairly well.

The truth is that I don't think he had it figured out too well himself at the time—maybe never. It became obvious as we talked in the warehouse the next morning that he was talking to shape things in his own mind. From the beginning I was the one to pick up the money, and he would "cover me," whatever that meant. At the beginning, too, he thought he would need only two others, and he made what to me was a strange pick—Mr. Smith and a Canadian soldier who had been gassed and had been sent out to recover in the high mountains. Although he wore the first pair of hornrim glasses I ever saw, and with a braided cord attached, he turned out to be almost as gifted in communing with livestock as Bill himself. He could talk to all horses and mules and heal them, no matter what their trouble was. He must have had something for Bill to pick him for the rough work ahead, even though sometimes he coughed so bad that we would take the whiskey away from him and drink it ourselves on the theory that there was no use wasting fairly good moonshine on a dying man. Bill's picking him had to be a case of one horseman believing in another. At first, then, Bill was going to count on the three of us and himself, but before the morning was over he had decided on the whole crew. "It's a pretty good crew," he said. "We can't leave any of them out." As for the cook, I was warned again never to put a hand on him.

He estimated that it would take us another week or more to get the station in shape at the end of the season, and to load the pack string, mostly with surplus tools from the big fire. The cook, he said, would ride to Hamilton. The rest of us would walk. No wonder the cook wore low canvas shoes in the woods.

The first night in town we were to meet at the Oxford, a pool and card parlor that by report was Hamilton's best. He was betting all his roll on the cook. As for the rest of us, we could get in on a sure thing if we liked and just as much as we wanted to contribute. That was up to me and to them—me to tell them and all of us to contribute. I was told again—several times—that I was to pick up the money in case trouble started, and I was told again that he would "cover me."

"Wear your own gun, too," he said to me. "God," I said, "Bill, I can't do that. I've nothing but that .32-20 on a .45 frame. That's as big as horse artillery. I'd be arrested before I got to the bar." "Well," he said, "expect trouble." After a while I asked, "Bill, you don't have any side arm, do you, but the big .45? Do you think you can get into a gambling joint wearing that?" He said, "I said I'll cover you."

Early in the morning I had started putting pieces together by

remembering the rumors that in Hamilton Bill was regarded as nature's gift to the local gamblers. It was said that they even matched
to see which one would pluck him when he came to town. So now
we were going to have a big melodrama that might be called "The
Ranger's Revenge." I was to go out and invite the crew to make the
stake bigger so those Hamilton boys who had done Bill in would be
done in bigger themselves. And a couple of weeks ago I had been
sent into exile because I said I was going to take a punch at the
cook. And when the time came the cook was going to ride into
Hamilton, while we walked.

"Well," I said to myself, "it all fits." But I bet twenty dollars on
the son of a bitch myself, and normally I hoarded my money just
like the rest of them.

It took the crew some time to warm up to the idea of staking the
cook. To start with, they didn't like the cook much better than I
did. Then, too, in the struggle between instincts, it's hard to know
whether miserliness or greed will have the edge. The crew still
would rather darn their socks than lose a dime, but they couldn't
bear to miss a sure thing. Finally, I told them about finding the four
aces in my shirt pocket. "That's simple to explain but hard to do,"
Mr. Smith said. Since he had spent most of his life around mining
camps, he knew all about cards, but wasn't much good with them
himself and practically never played. "He palmed them," he said.
"What the hell is palming?" I asked. He got a card and showed us
how you hold the edges of a card between your first finger and
your little finger and then bend your fingers and reach with your
thumb and push or pull the card from your palm to the back of
your hand or vice versa, at the same time turning your wrist so the
card can't be seen by someone in front of you. "So what he did,"
Mr. Smith said, "was to have the cards in the back of his hand and
to show you the palm, and, as he went by your shirt pocket, he
bent his fingers and put the cards in it." He tried to show us but he
was clumsy and we could always see the card, though we got the
idea. We all tried to palm but we were clumsier than Mr. Smith. In
fact, I tried for several years to get fairly good, but never did. Mr.
Smith said to convince us, "You've seen this in vaudeville." In
those days the Pantages circuit made the rounds of Spokane, Butte,

and Missoula, so we had all seen a magician hold out a card in his palm and then toss it in the air where it disappeared. "Do you mean," Mr. McBride asked, "the cook is good enough to be in vaudeville?" "He might be," said Mr. Smith. "Here we're just trying to palm one card, but he may have palmed all those four aces at once." Someone reverently said, "Jesus!" and they all bet.

Besides, they too began to get the feeling that they were all to have parts in a sort of pulp-magazine plot, and they liked the feeling. If they seemed to feel a lot better than I did about having a part in a story, maybe that was because they liked their part better than I thought I was going to like mine. Anyway, when I collected the "hat pool," it turned out the average bet was more than what I had bet—even a little more than half a month's wages. Once their bets became official by my handing over their money to Bill, they gathered every night to see the cook shuffle, peering in a semicircle around the table like a bunch of rail birds at a race track watching their favorite horse work out. Now that they had bet on him, they even spoke of "having a piece of him."

Although, as Bill had suggested, I was working around the station and now with the trail crew, I knew that they weren't getting much done either. For them as for me, quitting time had come and we were all through for the season. It wasn't only because we felt carried away by being in our own story. Anyone who has done seasonal work knows that as regular as the seasons themselves is the return of this feeling at the end of each season, "It's time to quit. It's time to quit." Even Mr. Smith seemed to have lost his passion for dynamite.

We started trying to have some fun, more or less getting in practice for the first night in town. Now I know that it's common to picture loggers and cowboys as always whooping it up, full of bad whiskey and great jokes on greenhorns. I don't know much about cowboys—they come from my wife's country—but before I was through I worked a lot of crews in the woods, and day in and day out we weren't jokey, and jokes on greenhorns were pretty standardized. For one thing, we worked too hard and too long to be left bubbling over with the comic spirit. For another thing, we worked too often alone or in small groups to think it worth the time to be funny. It's no trouble at all to be tragic when you're tired and alone, but to be funny you have to be fresh and you have to have time on your hands and you have to have an audience—and you have to be funny. And, however much you may love the woods, you can't claim it is full of natural wits. Don't get me wrong—we had what we called our fun, but only on what seemed like state occasions, and often then our jokes were pretty much the same old jokes and often the laugh was on us at the end. A state occasion was when a big crew got together, especially if it was quitting time and no one was working hard any more.

Even so, we began very gently to throw off our workingman's puritanism and prepare for sin. We began with a crew from the Engineers that had camped at the ranger station for a few days. They were mapping the back country where, they said, "the government hadn't figured out yet what they had stolen from the Indians." I went over to see them right away, because I liked maps and what they stood for, but the rest of our bunch were slower to take an interest in this mapping crew. For one thing, they waited every night until the cook had finished shuffling cards. And for another, they had the practical woodsman's distrust of Forest Service maps. They were convinced that a lot of the back country was mapped in those early days by guys who sat in tents or in the Regional Office in Missoula in the winter and said, "No, it goes here." In fact, in those early days we never believed that a mountain was really there unless it had been located by the United States Geological Survey. So our bunch immediately got in an argument with the mapping crew. We pretended to ourselves that we were the Regional Office in Missoula. "Hell," we would say, "that creek doesn't go there. It goes here." Sometimes we were only trying to confuse them and sometimes we meant it.

At that time, though, the mapping crew was more troubled about the name of a creek than where it went. They had been over on the north fork of the Clearwater and of course had run into Wet Ass Creek. They had accurately located it, too. They may have compass-and-chained it; at least they had compass-and-paced it. But they were divided as to whether they should put down its real name on the map they were going to submit to the drafting room of the regional office. Well, the regional office has never cared much for jokes or poetry, so we sided loudly with those who were for its right name and argued that too much of the West had been named after some guy's home town in Minnesota or Massachusetts or even after the guy himself or after a bear or a deer. "There are only five thousand Deer Creeks in the country. Let's keep America's only Wet Ass Creek," we argued. The other bunch, who also would soon be spending a summer of money on a night with the whores of Hamilton, argued that many who worked in the Forest Service's drafting room in Missoula were women and would be offended by having to copy such language with their own pure hands.

We put it to a vote, and our side won, or, for the time being, we thought we had. Anyway, they all agreed to submitting its right name to the drafting room and we looked forward to its becoming a National Park—Wet Ass National Park, where all pilgrims from Brooklyn can stop their cars in the middle of the road to let their children feed the grizzlies and vice versa.

In the end, though, it turned out the joke was on us. On the next map of the Forest, it appeared all as one word and a final *e* had been added which henceforward was pronounced, and the *a* was made in Boston. Now, it doesn't mean anything but be sure you pronounce it right: Wĕ-tä´-sē Creek, just as if its headwaters were on Beacon Hill.

At the time, we liked our joke, and, on the temporary strength of it, tried others, but we were end-of-the-summer tired—for that matter, still tired from the big fire—and our jokes were tired, too. We even tried to take the Canadian on a snipe hunt and get him to hold the gunnysack open while we herded the snipe into it, but the Canadian hadn't been gassed in France just to get caught holding a gunnysack in Idaho. Besides, we were starting to get in practice for Hamilton, and we weren't thinking of making jokes when we got there. Instead, the crew had a still back in the woods and were making moonshine out of dried apricots, peaches, and prunes they stole from the warehouse. Old Mr. Smith had got hold of some Sterno and they would boil the pink stuff off the top and drink the rest and it would go right through them, sometimes before they could get to the toilet or to the brush. They were practicing up for Hamilton, and had a couple of days more to go. I'd decided I was going to leave next morning, and walk to Hamilton in one day and more or less set a record. So I wasn't drinking any of their stuff, not even their dried apricot brandy distilled in a lard pail. When I told them I was going to leave tomorrow, they said, "What the hell kind of a guy are you anyway? Aren't you going to stay with the crew and help us clean out the town? What about the cook winning all that money for us from those Hamilton tin-horn gamblers? What kind of a crew are we anyway if we don't clean out the town?"

All these were important matters, and you can be sure I'd thought about them. You just weren't a crew if you didn't "clean out the town" as your final act of the season. I don't know why, but it always happens if you're any good—and even if you're not much good—that when you work outside a town for a couple of months you get feeling a lot better than the town and very hostile toward it. The town doesn't even know about you, but you think and talk a lot about it. Old Mr. Smith would take another drink of that alcohol and other debris from the canned heat, and say, "We'll take that God damn town apart." Then with his dignity lost he would have to run for the toilet, yelling as he ran that we had to show them there were no guys as tough as those who worked for the USFS.

Besides, there was this big killing the cook was going to make for us. We spent part of every evening arguing about how much we'd win. The amounts varied depending upon whether we argued before or after we saw the cook deal, but we usually settled for a figure around what for each of us was a summer's wages. Secretly, we hoped for more.

But I was out to set a record. Ever since the ranger had realized that the cook was fancy with the cards and so had taken my place as his favorite, I'd felt a growing need to set a record. I wished that it could be in packing and that I could become known overnight as one of the Decker brothers, who had designed the latest packsaddle, but I couldn't live long in that pipe dream, and powder work made me sick, so it had to be walking. I knew I could outwalk anyone in our district, and at the moment I need a little local fame, and I needed it bad.

Twenty-eight miles from Elk Summit to the mouth of Blodgett Canyon plus a few more miles to Hamilton is not outstanding distance, just as distance, but still it is a damn tough walk. For one thing, those were Forest Service miles, and, in case you aren't familiar with a "Forest Service mile," I'll give you a modern well-marked example. Our family cabin is near the Mission Glaciers and naturally one of the many nearby lakes is named Glacier Lake, which is at the end of the Kraft Creek Road, except that the final pitch is so steep you have to make it on foot. Where the trail starts there is a Forest Service sign reading: "Glacier Lake—1 Mi." Then you climb quite a way on the trail toward Glacier Lake and you come to another Forest Service sign reading: "Glacier Lake—1.2 Mi." So a good working definition of a "Forest Service mile" is quite a way plus a mile and two-tenths, and I was going to walk over thirty Forest Service miles to Hamilton, about half of them up until I was above mountain goats and the other half down and down until my legs would beg to start climbing again and I wouldn't be able to comply. The trail was full of granite boulders, and I would manage somehow so that Bill would hear that I had walked it in a day.

I said to Bill while he was counting his cribbage hand with his lips, "When are you going to take the pack string and the men into town?"

He finished counting before he said, "You will wait till we get there." I didn't know whether he had asked or told me something.

I picked up his hand and counted it over again. "I need the whole crew," he said. I said, "Yes." "If you'll stay tomorrow," he said, "and help put the packs together, I'll try to get away by noon the next day and camp on the divide that night. You can start the same morning ahead of us."

It was Wednesday, and by his scheme we would work Thursday and I would start Friday morning and he and the men Friday noon.

"I'll meet you in town on Saturday," I said.

"Saturday night in Hamilton," he said, which was to become one of my walking tunes.

Long before daylight I was using my feet like beetle feelers to find my way across Horse Heaven Meadow. Don't look at me, look at the map, because I don't have the kind of a mind that could make up a name like that. Even if you want to drop the Horse Heaven business, you still have a high mountain meadow just before daybreak, full of snorts and spooks. There are lots of horses out there but also a lot of other big animals. Elk and deer for sure. Maybe bear. They wake in darkness and come down from the hills to drink, and then slowly feed toward higher ground until it gets hot and is time for them to lie down again. A clank in the darkness is the scariest of all sounds, but you know a second afterwards it has to be a hobbled horse. If you are listening for dainty sounds to signify deer, there is nothing daintier than a snort—but there are deer there. They snort, and then bound. Elk snort, and then crash. Bear bolt straight uphill in a landslide—no animal has such pistons for hindquarters.

I still walked in wonderland after daylight. Far ahead on gray cliffs I could see the white specks that were not spots in my eyes. The trail was already getting steep and I knew before noon I would be higher than the mountain goats and from experience I knew that there is nothing much higher on earth.

The first summer I worked in the Forest Service we had come out of Idaho over the Bitterroots by way of Lake Como, and the hunting season on mountain goats was open in Idaho but not in Montana, and also in those days we could buy a resident's license in Idaho if we worked for the Forest Service. So we all did, and camped for a few days near the divide to hunt. Bill said to me, "All you have to do is get above mountain goats. They never think anything is above them." So all I had to do was get above mountain goats, which is beyond where most men have been. But finally there was a goat standing below me near the edge of a cliff two hundred and fifty or so yards away. I knew that when you shoot downhill at such an angle, you have to shoot way under your target, but it was almost straight down and I didn't hold under him nearly enough. My bullet didn't even hit the cliff. It was just a loud sound bound for eternity. The goat only hightailed it behind a rock, and hid. Now nobody could see him from below but he was still in plain sight to me. So Bill had been right, and I thought afterwards it must be great to live believing that there is no danger from above. None of those goats could have been Presbyterians, or ever heard my father preach. This time, though, I held so far under him I was afraid I'd shoot my feet off and I still shot over him, but I did hit the rock, and I've often wondered where the bullet went from there. Likewise the goat, which may never again have been seen by man. I didn't get any more shots that season—man is evidently not entitled to miss a goat more than twice in the same year.

I walked head down because I wasn't getting anywhere when I watched, so I was aware of him first as a snort and then a stamp. He was in the trail in front of me and he was a big bull moose and he looked as if he had decided not to go any place. When you saw bull moose in Montana in those days you were probably near the Bitterroot Divide and close to one of those snowbank lakes left in the burrows of old glaciers.

This bull lowered his horns and then, possibly just for exercise, raised them. Some half-chewed marsh grass stuck out of his mouth. Finally, he reversed the order and stamped and then snorted. Reluctantly he turned and started down the trail, slowly at first but faster as he went along, as if the idea of retreating came very gradually to him. I watched those legs swinging those big feet that looked as if they had been shod, and I am almost sure he was a four-gaited animal, if you'll admit that for a short stretch I saw him single-foot. In wonderland, why shouldn't a moose single-foot as well as walk, trot, and pace?

Then I put my head down and started my one and only gait again. There was nothing but granite now and, as it became hard to climb and breathe, I needed somebody besides Bill to watch me. I began to think about my girl, and finally she appeared to me, as if her image had been resting in the woods with the deer.

Since my father was the Presbyterian minister in town, I had lived quite a few years under the impression that Roman Catholic girls were prettier than Protestant girls. About Jewish girls I was of a divided mind, probably because there were just two Jewish girls in my home town, one for each half of my mind. One was classy and played the piano and was several years older than I was and wouldn't even look my way. The other was younger than I was and ugly and would do anything to please me. She even made dates for me with other girls she thought I'd like. She had started me going with my present Irish Catholic girl, whose particular fascination was a deep scar in her forehead that half-closed a corner of her eye and made her look as if she was never quite looking at me. I discovered several years later that she had been screwing everybody in town, except me and possibly several other Protestants, and after that discovery I veered rapidly to red- (and black-) headed Protestant and Jewish girls, but at the time I conceived of her as my one and only. She watched me out of her deceptive eye, I thought admiringly, and I tore up the trail.

When I finally made the divide, I carefully studied the center of it, traced in my mind what I designated as the state line between Idaho and Montana and then made a small section of it real by pissing on it—a very short dehydrated state line. I always did this on big divides, especially on the Continental Divide where one is left wondering whether he is going to drain into the Atlantic or the Pacific. The divide here is not the Continental Divide, but it stirs the imagination.

Then I sat down and rested above the white goats. I looked back where I had worked three summers, and it looked strange. When you look back at where you have been, it often seems as if you have never been there or even as if there were no such place. Of the peaks in the sky, my old lookout, Grave Peak, of course, was the one I knew best. When I lived on it, it was a hard climb out of a basin full of big rocks and small grubs, a tent with a finally-mended hole, trees decapitated by lightning, no soft place to sit and one grizzly and one rattlesnake. But here from the divide, it was another reality. It was sculpture in the sky, devoid of any detail of life. There is a peak near my home town we call Squaw's Teat. It is not a great mountain but it has the right name for Grave Peak when viewed from the distance of the divide. From the divide the mountain I had lived on was bronze sculpture. It was all shape with nothing on it, just nothing. It was just color and shape and sky. It was as if some Indian beauty before falling asleep forever had decided to leave exposed what she thought was not quite her most beautiful part. So perhaps at a certain perspective what we leave behind is often wonderland, always different from what it was and generally more beautiful.

I was trying to keep from myself the fact that I had walked to the top too fast and was a lot tireder than I wanted to be. I had walked those fourteen miles to the rhythm of "It's time to quit. It's time to quit," but the tempo kept speeding up, especially after my girl began to watch me with a half-closed eye. Sitting there in the sun I began to feel chilled, so I crossed the divide and looked down Blodgett Canyon to see what it was like ahead.

You might never have heard the word geology and yet have known the instant you looked down Blodgett Canyon that you were looking at a gigantic, glacial classic. For thousands of years it must have been a monster of ice hissing in the cracks of the mountains. Coming at me from almost straight below was a Jacob's ladder of switchbacks, rising out of what I later discovered geologists call a cirque but what to me looked like the original nest of a green coiled glacier. When it struck for the valley, the mountains had split apart. At the top where it writhed out of its course and returned, it left a peak or a series of pinnacles. When it reached its own mouth, the partially digested remains of mountains rolled out of its gorge all the way to the river.

It was a big world and not a very big boy and I thought it was time he shoved off, even though he hadn't taken a long enough rest.

I shook myself to get warm and started down the switchbacks. I'd intended to take it easy in getting started again, but going down switchbacks doesn't give you much choice and when you're young and out to set a local record you aren't going to take the long way around each switchback. Wherever the face of the mountain was open, I cut straight down, omitting all six-percent grades. I descended in avalanches. Avalanches beside me, avalanches in the rear of me, avalanches in front of me. On the fly, I watched over my shoulder to duck the big boulders. When my legs felt torn in front and I had to stop, I could hear rivulets of granite particles pursuing me and then giving up and then making one more try. After I hit the bottom of the basin and had been standing there for some time to let the spasms in my legs quiet and even after all the avalanches behind had come to a rest, one big granite chunk dropped from nowhere beside me. I looked up and could find no likely place but the middle of the sky.

At the bottom of the basin I was already lower than the white specks on the cliffs. On the cliffs there was only an occasional tree where a bird had dropped a seed in a crevice. At the top of the divide I had felt chilled in the sun. Here, at the bottom of the glacial basin my face was tightened with heat. Accompanied by avalanches from the sky, I had descended into the pit. The heat made one gigantic bounce from the solar system to the granite cliffs to me personally. Besides, it rose from what I walked on and I could feel that I was turning black under my face like Dante descending into the Inferno.

I had also made myself into something of a medical problem by refusing to drink water. Since I'd never before walked this far in a day and didn't want anybody to know until I was sure I had, I took over all the thinking myself. I thought, when I go fishing on the Blackfoot River and it's hot and I start drinking from the river, pretty soon I can't stop drinking and pretty soon it doesn't even taste good and I end up waterlogged and half-sick. I reasoned, "You mustn't get sick, so you mustn't drink water." I can remember taking a sip when eating my sandwich, and although I can't remember, I must have taken a few other sips, but I stood pledged to some kind of youthful and lofty denial of the flesh. I walked suffering all afternoon down that chasm where mountains had cried for centuries as their structure cracked. At the end, I walked in semidarkness, medically dehydrated.

For irony, a plunging stream accompanied me to the divide and another one followed me down. Blodgett Creek had started at the bottom of the basin right beside where I and the big boulder lit—springs all over with green sponges around them. I took off my woolen socks and waded in one of them to restore firmness to the flesh I walked on. The water was so cold my heart did something funny, so I stepped back on the sponge. On my way down the canyon, I stopped several times to wade in the creek. I watched little black trout who lived and breathed in it, but I fought, nobly I judged, not to take a drink of it myself.

I tried to think of various things, but by the time I was half way down the canyon I could think of nothing but drinking. I had pictured myself reaching across the green table for all those dollars, but my pressure on the dollars weakened and I felt them slip slowly out of my hands. The man in the tall black Stetson that I wanted to be like, had from time to time said to me, "And I'll cover you," but I still didn't know what he meant. I couldn't even retain my girl as part of my mental life. She watched me until she was just her half-closed eye, and then, as some years later, she gave me the big wink and was gone.

From time to time, I thought I was on the fire line and that the sky was swirling with burning cones and that the universe was upside down, with hell above. The trail ahead seemed full of light ashes rising off the ground because I drew near them. At other times I felt sick and immediately afterwards thought I smelled dynamite.

But always I wanted a drink. I knew as a logger I should want a "boilermaker," a slug of whiskey with a bottle of beer as a chaser. Instead I wanted an ice-cream soda. I told myself that ice-cream sodas were for kids, but the image of a boilermaker left scars of dehydration. Besides, I liked ice-cream sodas and at seventeen was secretly curious how men could like the taste of whiskey. So I walked mile after mile with nothing in sight but ice-cream sodas that changed only to vary the color combinations—white vanilla, yellow lemon, and brown chocolate were my favorites, but once in a while I stuck in a strawberry flavor, just before chocolate. I filled the glasses nearly to the top with carbonated water, leaving not quite enough room for a dip of ice cream so that froth would run over. I drank all the ice-cream sodas I could make, always beginning by licking off the froth. I was a damn mess and childish a fact I tried to keep from myself.

When I finally saw the light from the canyon's mouth, the cliff on the north side looked tipped beyond ninety degrees.

Even so, I wouldn't have been in too bad shape when I reached Hamilton if Hamilton had been where I remembered it was, a mile

or two from the mouth of Blodgett Canyon. But after one good
look I had to stop to absorb my disbelief. Hamilton is way out in
the valley and upriver and must be five or six miles from the mouth
of the canyon. Five or six miles, all gently sloping to the river, may
be a breeze to you, but I sat by the side of the road and played
mumblety-peg to steady my hands. I thought of the Bible and
hoped that a pair of arms would enfold me and put me on a mule
and lead me into Hamilton without any more thorns. There it was
in plain view but farther away than seemed possible for a man to
walk. This was the first time I had ever been in a fight when I took
a terrible beating at the end. At seventeen I had been in a fair number of fights and had won most of them and naturally had lost some
too, but always before when I was losing some big friend who
maybe I hadn't seen before would step in and stop the fight. I had
never before taken a beating with nobody there to stop the beating.
When you're watching a fight and you see a guy's legs buckle and
his hands drop and he doesn't even back away, it's easy to say to
another bystander, "Look at that gutless son of a bitch. He won't
even put up his hands to fight." It's different, though, when you're
the guy with nothing left in your legs that will put up your hands,
or back away.

I didn't try any of the hard positions in mumblety-peg, nothing
harder than to the nose and to both ears. It helped, though, and
gradually I figured out why I was here and Hamilton was way out
there. In the spring our crew had been taken by truck from Hamilton to the mouth of Blodgett Canyon as a start on our way to Idaho—in a truck, what's the difference between a couple of miles and
five or six? In the spring, too, I hadn't looked back down Blodgett
Canyon to see how a glacier had made it and shoved its remains all
the way to the river. Hamilton was on the river, and now I understood why I had four or five miles yet to go.

With that out of the way, I got up and snapped my jackknife shut
and began to walk. Sometimes all you have left to win with is the
knowledge of why you're taking the beating and the realization
that nobody else is going to save you from it.

Since it never got closer while I watched, I didn't look until it was there. I have always been grateful to Hamilton for being, if not where I expected, at least where I could understand.

At the time I was also grateful to Hamilton for being an outwardly simple structure to comprehend after a long day. The road from Blodgett Canyon turns at right angles and joins the main street, and the main street of Hamilton is called Main Street, and the streets that cross it at right angles are named by number. I walked down Main Street to, I think, the block between Third and Second where there was a drugstore. I had two ice-cream sodas, a white vanilla and a yellow lemon, and ordered a third, a chocolate soda, to complete my favorite color sequence, but the drugstore clerk said, "Son, I don't think you should have another one now." I felt like going around behind the counter and shoving the drugstore clerk into his chocolate ice-cream freezer, especially for calling me "son," but I didn't and I can't claim to have thought better of it. I just felt strange all over.

Everything was going very fast, including the quitting time rhythm which I certainly had thought would slow and then stop when I got to town. Instead, everything I wanted to do all summer I wanted to do right now. I wanted to find the Chinese restaurant which all the Bitterrooters in the woods said was the best eating place in town, and I wanted to find this Oxford gambling joint and watch their shills at work and I more or less wanted to find a hotel and leave my pack and wash up and maybe lie down before going out on the town. This idea of lying down for a while interested me least of all, so I stopped somebody outside and asked where the Chinaman's was and I think it was in the same block, on Main between Third and Second.

The Chinaman behind the cash register wore a silky black coat, a white shirt, and a black string tie, and he studied me and my patches and pack and my hair that hadn't been cut in three months. He clearly didn't care for any Forest Service trade from Elk Summit, but without being asked I walked back near the kitchen and sat down at the smallest table in the room. I put my pack on the other chair for a guest. A white waitress came with a menu. Her voice was husky and she was the first woman I had smelled all summer, and she smelled like a woman. I couldn't read what was on the menu—maybe I didn't know the names of Chinese food or maybe I just couldn't see very well. The waitress came back several times and looked at me. I finally thought, "Probably I'm dirty," so I asked her where the men's room was and I washed in cold water and wiped myself with a cloth towel that came out about a foot at a time when I pushed a button. I wet my hair but my comb was in my pack so my hair was wet and stringy when I came back and, despite the cold water, I didn't feel any better. She returned soon and still looked troubled and finally asked, "Do you think you should order now? Why not wait another hour or so before you eat?"

I would never have got to Hamilton if I felt that way about things. I said, "No, I want to order now." She must have known that she would have to order for me. She would ask, "Wouldn't you like to try ...?" and then she would name something that ended with suey or mein. Each time I would say, "That would be just fine." I was overpolite in trying to show her that despite the way I looked I was really at home in such classy establishments as Chinese restaurants. I kept saying, "Yes, that would be just fine," until she stuck the pencil in her blouse and headed for the kitchen.

The moment I was alone I got very sick. I do not know whether I knew I was very sick. What I knew was that the world was made of two parts—inside and outside a Chinese restaurant—and that I was sure to feel better if only I could get to wherever I was not now. Later, I could look for the Oxford.

When the waitress finally came, I said, "Would you please give me my check?" She was frightened and said, "But you haven't even eaten yet." I said, "I know. Just bring me the check." She said, "Would you please wait a moment?" And she went, not to the kitchen, but to the cash register and talked to the Chinaman with the string tie.

Everything inside me was going sickeningly fast and everything outside was standing sickeningly still. I wondered how much longer I could wait for my check and then fresh air. I could even guess what they were whispering behind the cash register. Lumberjacks had pretty much the same joke that they played on Chinamen behind cash registers. Four or five jacks would finish eating together and then one would saunter to the front and say to the Chinaman, "He" (pointing in the general direction of the table) "is going to pay for mine. He" (pointing in the same general direction) "lost a bet to me." Then he would slide by, and this would go on until only one jack was left who would put down just enough money for his own dinner. "Hell, what do you mean me paying for those other guys? I don't even hardly know them." I was alone but clearly I was from the Forest Service and I had ordered dinner and now I was trying to get out of the restaurant before it was even served. It was a somewhat different lumberjack game, but it had to be a game between a lumberjack and a Chinaman that a Chinaman was supposed to lose. The waitress hurried past me to the kitchen, obviously not looking my way.

I couldn't wait any longer for anybody to talk to anybody else. I got up and thought I did pretty well to remember my pack. The kitchen door opened and I never knew before how many Chinamen work in the kitchen of a Chinese restaurant. Families of them, from children to old men, each outfitted with a butcher knife. They followed slowly behind me to the cash register. The waitress stood frightened by herself. She thought, Now I've done it.

I looked at the bill several times to be sure that it was not more than the silver dollar in my hand and then I put both on the counter next to the cash register and I remember thinking that my paying the bill was a kind of inscrutable joke on the Chinese. I reached out my hand for the change and knocked over the glass of toothpicks and then slid slowly to the floor in a cloud of toothpicks.

I do not remember hitting the floor.

The next thing I remember was a husky voice and the smell of woman, and when I opened my eyes I felt more than saw that the waitress was washing my face with a napkin and I immediately fell in love with her. Wherever I had been, I had been very lonely, and I immediately fell in love with her for bending over me. The Chinamen leaned forward in a circle, and were scared by what they saw. The Chinaman with the string tie was unhappy because it was happening in his place. The waitress made a big thing of smiling and said, "We've called the doctor."

I thought that would be quite a while, but when I opened my eyes next he had already listened to my chest and was lifting me up to listen to me through my back. When he saw I was awake, he asked questions. He was an old man, he wore a Stetson, and we all knew immediately that he was good. No one said a word unless the doctor asked him, and the doctor knew we all were scared and wanted to tell us not to be as soon as he could.

He pulled my shirt together and before he started to button it, he said, "It was those God damn ice-cream sodas."

He talked to all of us, not just to me. He said it was this way. I had walked too far; it was very hot; and I didn't drink anything. Then I drank two God damn ice-cream sodas. This is the way he explained to us what happened medically. He said my blood from "the exertion" (he said "exertion") was mostly in the outside of me—in my legs and arms and muscles. Then I drank the two God damn ice-cream sodas and they were cold and so the blood all rushed to the inside of me and left my head empty and I fainted. He said, don't worry, take it easy for a day or so, and you'll feel as good as ever. All of us thought we understood everything and were greatly relieved.

He was a small-town doctor, and I have never asked a big-town doctor for his opinion of the small-town doctor's medical explanation. I am sure, though, that no big-town doctor ever said what the small-town doctor said to me next. He said, "You come to see me late tomorrow morning in my office, do you hear? If you don't come tomorrow, I'll charge you for tonight. If you come tomorrow, I won't charge you for tomorrow or tonight. All I want is to know that you are well."

Then the circle began to break up, and people helped me to find the change that had slipped out of my hand when I'd fallen. The doctor said to the Chinaman with the silk coat, "Get him to a hotel." I don't remember anything for a long time after that. Either I fainted again or I just went to sleep.

Even while I was waking I knew I should be in a hotel. I got up and checked my clothes and they were on a chair and my pack was in a corner and about the amount of money I should have had was in a pocket. I knew I had been asleep for a while but I also knew it was a long time until daybreak. I went back to bed to check on myself and the surroundings.

At first I tried to find out about myself, but before long the surroundings forced themselves upon my attention—not, however, until I realized this must be early morning of Saturday night in Hamilton. It was still too early in the morning to know how I would feel about the night when it got here, but I felt very bad about the night before when I fell in front of the cash register with toothpicks in my hair. As far as I knew, no one ever before had fainted except women and then only in books. I had actually never known a person who had fainted. Suddenly, I felt one of those great waves of sadness that rarely come over me. I had made it clear from Elk Summit only to lie down on the floor of a Chinese restaurant. Now nothing was left that could be mentioned to Bill about a day fourteen miles up and fourteen miles down with five or six miles still left to go. The coming night would be the last night when the ranger and the cook and the crew and I would be together. I got hold of myself and said, "I'd better be good tonight and that damn cook had better faint." I explored myself a little further: "I wish I felt a little better—I'm not feeling bad, but I'd be afraid to get up and walk down the hall and find out."

About here the surroundings took over. A big ass pushed the wall next to my bed and gave me a nudge. As the books would say, I sat bolt upright. It had to be an ass, but how the hell did it come through the wall? It was half-light in my room and I studied the wall. So help me, it was made of canvas. Likewise the other wall, but once in a while the wall beside my bed bulged as if the glacier that had made Blodgett Canyon was at work next door. Suddenly, I remembered things that aged Mr. Smith and Mr. McBride had told me. "This is just like an old-time western whorehouse," I thought, "with canvas partitions between the cribs." I watched and listened, and, after I saw and heard what was happening in the next room and was extending into part of mine, I said, "What the hell do I mean, like an old-time western whorehouse? This is the thing itself."

At first I thought that there had to be several people in the crib

next door, but I finally added up everything and settled for a pimp
and a whore screwing up and down the bed, occasionally swerving
out of their course and then returning to leave peaks and pinnacles
on my wall. It was only his ass that took the scenic route, unfortunately; hers must have kept on a straight course, and never
nudged me, and I eventually came to understand why. She talked
all the time in a monotone, and while they screwed she talked
about how he had been out screwing other whores. I happened to
be very sensitive to rhythm that year and I finally realized that I
could scan what she was saying. If I allowed for understandable ca-
esuras, she was speaking blank verse.

That year I had taken an English course from the most famous
teacher in our high school. She was very good, but perhaps was a
little overwrought about poetry and students. Anyway, by early
winter she decided her juniors could write a sonnet, so she assigned
one. At that time, high school juniors in Montana could tell where
a cinch ended and a latigo began, but had no such knowledge about
an octave and a sestet, so after feeling steadily worse for several
days I approached my mother with my problem, who looked at me
carefully to be sure I had a problem, and then said, "After dishes, I
will help you." So we sat down at a table and I held her left hand
and she wrote the sonnet with her right hand, while her left hand
trembled. Her sonnet was "On Milton's Blindness," something I
had never heard of before. The poem was regarded as very good by
the English teachers of Missoula County High School, and in May
received the prize as the best poem of the year and was published in
the school annual with a sterilized photograph of me adjoining it.
My mother was very proud of me, but quietly insisted that I stay in
after supper until I at least learned to scan, so again we sat at the
table, this time with Milton or Shakespeare between us, and again I
held her left hand and with her right hand she would beat out the
accented syllables. Then we would write lines of our own iambic
pentameter, and our blank verse, unlike Milton's or Shakespeare's,
never had any little odds or ends left over. We wrote: "Immortal
Milton, builder of my soul," and other such lines that all Montana
high school juniors could scan and tell was poetry. At least, if they
could count to five.

At first I hadn't picked up the rhythm next door. Evidently she was just warming up and she spoke in just ordinary irritable profanity. "You lousy bastard," and so on. But then she started to dedicate a stave to each time he had double-crossed her, and each stave she ended with: "Yŏu áre ăs cróokĕd as ă túb ŏf gúts." She liked this line and used it as a kind of refrain, and from it I picked up the scansion and realized for the first time that she was speaking iambic pentameter, but with skips and jumps here and there, more like Milton and Shakespeare than mother or me. Evidently her man not only had done her wrong but had gone around talking about it, because she had another set of staves she always ended with, "Yŏu're like ă bábў crów, ăll móuth ănd áss." I couldn't verify what she said about his mouth, because he was too busy ever to open it, but all you had to do to check his big ass was to watch my wall. It went down my wall like a wave, and back up it like a Rainbow trout.

I was about to consider her imagery when I must have fallen asleep, possibly lulled by her rhythms, and when I woke up, certainly much later, there was not a stir next door. I was nervous for having fallen asleep and wondered whether this business about a pimp and a whore and especially iambic pentameter wasn't a dream, a distorted continuation of my rhythm in my sickness. Outside in the hall a kind of marching was going on that faded and returned. I waited until it was in a fading cycle before sticking out my head, and, sure enough, it had to be him, though all that could be seen clearly was a hairy ass that could be recognized even by gaslight. When he turned at the end of the hall, there she was in his arms, with her little ass and knees draped in a V. Evidently, they were out for a stroll, taking a breather before the real work of the night began. They came up the hall toward me, and somehow I couldn't pull my neck in. They went right by my immovable nose and then made for their room. He was a man with his toes turned up and too much in love with his work to notice me, but she was just as nasty-looking a little whore as you will ever see, and whatever she and this big ape were doing, clearly she could think of two or three other things at the same time, including me. She half twisted her neck off her shoulders just to give me the once over.

Then, adding a twist to the twist, she said, "Go fuck yourself," so she still scanned, although no one will give her grade points in originality for declaiming one of the most famous lines in the English language.

The old lumberjacks used to talk about "a walking whorehouse," and now what they meant became clearer. I was about to say next, "All night whores flitted around the hotel," but I remembered in time that whores don't flit. One whore almost came through the other side of my wall. She came so close to coming through that somebody must have tried to throw her through.

You know, I wasn't very well while all this was happening, and eventually I fell asleep, not to waken until late in the morning, when, I thought, I was much refreshed. Anyway, I was all full of rhythms. To my quitting-time rhythm were permanently added those of my next-door neighbor. These were all iambic. But the one that now was pounding loudest was "Saturday night in Hamilton." I didn't know the name of this rhythm but it sounded something like "This is the forest primeval."

After dressing a little more shakily than expected, I took a tryout down the hall, and lay down again. Finally, I went out for breakfast and looked for some place that wasn't the Chinese restaurant for fear the waitress I fell in love with last night might not look any better in the daylight than I felt. I found a Greek restaurant, and never again went back to the Chinese restaurant in order to preserve my first feelings about the waitress there. With a menu in front of me, I thought for a long time and finally ordered tea and toast. The expression on this new waitress's face suggested that she hadn't fallen in love with me at first sight and that this workmen's restaurant didn't welcome short orders, especially when they included tea instead of coffee. To make matters worse, I managed to put away the tea but not the toast.

Then I went looking for the doctor's office and found it in a building a block off Main Street where the rents were lower. The office was small and crowded and the air around which it had been built must have been the air which was still there. People sat on the exposed springs of couches, and the name of the doctor was Charles Richey, M.D., spelled backward on the window.

Dr. Richey did not practice a complicated branch of medicine. He wore his black Stetson in the office and spent about five minutes with each patient. He would stick his Stetson out of the inner office, point his finger at a patient and wiggle his finger. When it came my turn, he had his earphones on before I got through his door. He never said a word and he worried me when he went back to listen to the same spot on my chest. Finally, he jerked the phones out of his ears, and, like the night before, he tried to say something cheerful as soon as he was sure. He said, "You're all right." Then he asked me where I lived, and I told him Missoula and he told me I had better stay in Hamilton for another night. "Take it easy a little longer," he said, "and don't get in any fights."

I was an especially uncomplicated case and he had only one more thing to say to me. He said, "It was those God damn ice-cream sodas. After this, never drink anything but good whiskey."

It seemed like good advice and besides it came free, so, by way of expressing my gratitude, I have followed it ever since.

I tried to thank him but he was already wiggling his finger at another patient.

On the way back to my room, I kept an eye open for a different hotel, and saw one that said it was Deluxe at 25¢ per night (double that with bath). Just as I was to enter my old room to pack up, I noted that my neighbor's room was wide open and she was standing naked in front of a mirror trying on a hat. She was adding to her stature by wearing high-heeled shoes and tilting a very large hat this way and that, but when she saw me, she took off her hat so as not to impede her vision. What she said to me she had said once before, and so of course it still scanned. After I got into my own room, I had to lie down again. I lay there hoping that some day my next-door neighbor and the cook would meet socially. Concerning the outcome, I didn't care which one lost.

Later, I collected myself and my stuff, went downstairs and couldn't find anybody to pay. In that hotel they probably didn't charge by the room. I don't remember whether it was from the exertion of moving, but when I got to my new room I had to stretch out again. I rolled over and for the first time since I'd left home in the spring I felt the security of rubbing shoulders with a plaster wall and for the first time in several days I almost overslept. As I woke I knew I'd no time to enjoy in waking. I knew, even before looking at my watch, that Bill and the crew should be arriving or already had arrived from what should have been the camp on Big Sand Lake near the divide. I washed my face from a pitcher, but the water was stale, just like the knowledge that I would have nothing to say about walking from Elk Summit in a day.

By the time I got to the corral on the road to Blodgett Canyon that the Forest Service used to hold the stock, Bill was already unloading the string, and the cook and the Canadian were sitting in the shade of a deserted cabin that the Service had turned into a warehouse. Since the rest of the crew hadn't arrived, it was clear that the cook and the Canadian had ridden in and the rest of the crew, including Mr. Smith with tiny aged steps, were somewhere behind on foot. No one could kick about the Canadian riding and then just sitting there and not helping Bill unload—he was lucky to be alive after a horse had brought him down that canyon. As for the cook, you might feel like kicking him on to his feet but you'd restrain yourself if you knew anything about the woods. In the woods, the cooks are known as the kings of the camps, and they sit on the throne, because in the woods eating is what counts most in life. In the woods you work so damn hard you have to spend most of the rest of the time taking on fuel, and besides, if you're looking for your just rewards in the Forest Service, which has never been noted for wages, you'd better eat all you can while you're there and enjoy it, if possible.

So in the woods the rest of us do everything that has to be done, but the damn cook only cooks, and talks to the boss.

Without saying a word, Bill and I unloaded and unsaddled the string, and carried the packs, saddles, and drenched saddle blankets into the warehouse, right past the cook who sat in the shade swatting flies.

Finally, Bill and I had a conversation. In the Forest Service very few sentences are completed, either because you have to grunt or catch your breath or because guys who work in the woods aren't the kind who go running around finishing sentences. Bill was taking off the pack on one side of a mule and I was taking off the other.

He asked, "How did you ...?"

And, as the pack slipped on my shoulders, I grunted, "I made ..."

Which, if we had the air and inclination to finish, would probably have sounded something like this. Question: "How did you make it walking from Elk Summit?" Answer: "I made it, but don't ask anything more."

We must have understood each other without finishing, because nothing further was said until the crew came straggling into the corral. They crawled through the corral bars and sat down in the shade near the cook and Canadian; then all of them together said nothing. I especially cared for Mr. Smith who cared for me, and it was painful to see how short his steps were and how white with perspiration his neck was above his bandanna handkerchief where it was usually dark with old veins.

While the crew rested, Bill and I fed the stock oats. It was September, and you can't pack animals all summer over the Bitterroot Divide and expect them to survive on the grass they pass on the way. Bill didn't say he was proud of them, but he slapped each one on its rump as it snorted into its feed. At the end of the summer, they looked fine.

After he finished with the animals, he turned to the men. He and Mr. Smith did all the talking, although I don't think they'd worked things out beforehand. Bill said, "We're one crew, but don't let's hang together in one bunch until we get to the Oxford. It would look bad."

Mr. Smith asked, "When do you want us, Bill?"

Bill said, "Drift into this Oxford place between nine-thirty and ten."

Mr. Smith was showing remarkable recuperative powers for his age. He took off the bandanna handkerchief and wiped his neck. He seemed to be talking always to Bill and not to us. "Bill," he said, "you take charge of the inside of that poker room and I'll stand at the door and take care of whatever tries to get in from the poolroom."

Bill said to me, "You're to get the money if anything goes

wrong." And then he added, as he always did, "I'll cover you."

Mr. McBride had something to say to Bill, and he had a point. "Be sure we play for money and not for chips. We may not be able to cash in any chips on the way out."

Bill said, "The rest of you help where we're hurting. You're a good crew and we don't want too many plans."

Mr. Smith agreed, "That's right. For what we're doing, we don't want too many plans."

Then the cook spoke up and added one of his stately speeches. "You must realize," he said, "that I rarely make a tricky deal. If I won only when I dealt I would have been dead long ago. Except for one or two hands a night I am a percentage player" (which was the first time I had ever heard this phrase). "I'm a very good percentage player, and I should be ahead. But, if I am not, don't lose patience. There will come one big hand and be ready."

So the cook had the last word, as I am sure he had planned. He liked being the center of the drama, and he liked being Bill's favorite. Mr. Smith and I exchanged our dislike of him by a glance. Then we soon broke up, as directed, and on the way back to my room I stopped at my new restaurant where I was not well liked and asked the waitress if they had a small flour sack they could spare. She seemed to like me better and came back from the kitchen and said, no, they didn't have a flour sack but they had a ten-pound sugar sack and she showed it to me and the word SUGAR had not yet faded from being washed. I said, "That's fine. That's better than flour." In fact, SUGAR seemed just right, since I wanted the sack to put our big winnings in. It's funny how many non-funny jokes we make to ourselves.

I had been gone from my room for a long time, so when I got back I lay down on the bed and was still amused by my sugar sack when all of a sudden things fell apart. I say "all of a sudden," but for a long time I had only been pretending not to know that I was going to take a hell of a beating when I reached across the table to pick up the money. I always suspected that Bill was looking for trouble more than for money, but from time to time I would cheer myself up by underestimating the crew and thinking they were just greedy, not fighty, and would take their winnings and go off and get drunk. I had not fully realized how I was doomed until I had seen that the oldest men in the crew, Mr. Smith and Mr. McBride, were counting on a fight just as much as Bill was and, independently, had worked out an almost identical plan. In fact, when I said a temporary good-bye to Mr. Smith at the corral I discovered that the crew's fighting plans didn't stop with the tin-horn gamblers. He said, "We're going to clean out the town. First we'll take those tin-horn gamblers, then the ranch hands, and then the whores."

If we did all that we sure as hell would clean out the town as we knew it. As we knew the town, there were houses in it, but we weren't sure what if anything was inside them. The establishments open to us were inhabited by gamblers, ranch hands, and whores. Add a Chinese and a Greek restaurant and you have what the town was to us. You will note that Mr. Smith and I both said "ranch hands" and not "cowboys"—in the Forest Service we called cowboys ranch hands to show what we thought of them. I said to Mr. Smith, "The whores may be the toughest of all." He laughed through his moustache that was darker than his white hair; he was hoping this would be the case.

There shouldn't have been any doubt in my mind, though, that we were in for big trouble. After all I was finishing up my third summer in the Forest Service, so twice before I had gone through this autumn rite at quitting time. Twice before I had seen a catch-as-catch-can bunch of working stiffs transformed into blood brothers by the act of Cleaning Out the Town. Everybody got cleaned in this autumn rite of the early Forest Service—we cleaned up on the town and the town cleaned us out. When the rite was completed, all of it thereafter could be solemnized and capitalized—the Crew, Quitting Time, and Cleaning Out the Town. Everything about us was bigger than before, except our cash.

At the time, I thought the Big Fire was no longer important, but before all this became a story I realized the Big Fire is the Summer Festival and Cleaning Out the Town is the way it all ends in the autumn. It's as simple as this—you never forget the guys who helped you fight the big fire or clean out the town.

Lying on the bed, though, I couldn't see how I was going to avoid a beating. There's bound to be a fight, I knew now, and I'll have to reach over the table for the money. I'll need both hands to pick it up and put it in the sugar sack, which didn't seem funny now, and there will be my jaw sticking out for anybody to bruise with brass knuckles. I lay on the bed for some hours and couldn't think of any way to protect myself, and, worse still, I knew I'd thought often of this problem before and had kept burying it, because even in half-dreams no way came to me of defending myself. Now was my last chance to think, but after it became dark I still had no thoughts. Just sensations. Always I felt that in reaching for the money I was hit on the jaw from the side and couldn't see who had hit me. Next, I felt blood from inside my head slide down my throat.

I don't pretend I liked the beating or the blood, but it was not being able to lift a hand that sickened me most. It was like being a child again and being sent to a dark room and waiting for your father to come and whip you. It was a place of no ideas. Finally I said to myself, "At least don't lie here in the dark. Go over and take a look at the joint." I don't know whether I expected to get any new ideas, but at least I went to see.

The Oxford was the combination billiard, pool, and card parlor which for many westerners was the home away from home. The entering door led past the bar and tobacco stand; the guy behind the bar looked like he was trying to look like the owner. I bought a bottle of homebrew beer, but if I'd asked for a shot of moonshine I probably could have got it. Then I sauntered through the big door into the game room. It retreated to the rear in geometric patterns. The farther back it went the higher the stakes, the deeper the sin and the lower the social order. The large rectangles of billiard and pool tables in front become shortened by distance into round card tables. The ceilings were concealed in darkness; each green cloth-covered table glared under its own light shade. The big room narrowed into one small, slightly raised room in which was one glaring green table surrounded almost by darkness. Here at the end of space was the poker table.

I worked slowly to the rear, pretending to walk casually and trying to drink the flat beer. The billiard table was for the sporting elite who could pay twenty-five cents an hour. The table was in good shape and the two players were good and were playing three-cushion billiards. The spectator next to me clapped when they made a hard shot and in a whisper told me that one of the players was the best barber in town and the other was vice-president of the bank. Then, in an even lower whisper and in greater awe, he told me that by common agreement they quit playing every night at nine because each had a woman he spent a couple of hours with before going home to his wife.

The pool players and tables were so bad nobody was watching. The balls must have been made of concrete and the rubber in the cushions was dead, so the players, to get any bounce, shot too hard. If you fired a rifle and jerked up your head and shoulder the way they did when they shot their cue ball, you'd have missed Grave Peak at a hundred yards. When they miscued, they said, "God damn it," and chalked the tips of their cues. You can tell poor pool players anywhere—they're the ones who are always saying, "God damn it," and are always chalking their cues and always jerking their heads when they shoot—something chalk won't cure. On the rifle range, it's called "flinching." I kept moving, and came to the first card tables.

The Oxford was no exception. The first card tables are always for the regular local players—not the gamblers but the clothing-store clerks and delivery men who married when they were young and can't afford to lose but can't stay away from cards. So they pretend with the help of the house that they're not gambling and certainly not losing. They play slow games in which they lose steadily but never, as in poker, lose a bundle of cash on a turn of a card. The ones I watched were playing "pan" and pinochle, and they were playing for "chits," not chips. They had paid real money for their chits, as if they were chips, but when they traded them back the house would give them only trade tokens that would allow them to buy homebrew beer or play pool. The house was even pretending that it wasn't charging them for using the table, but while I stood there a houseman came by and picked a chit out of the pot. If you count the number of times the houseman picks a chit out of a pot in a year, you'll probably find that it's not the gamblers but the deliverymen pretending they aren't gambling who keep small town gambling joints going financially.

I pretended to be drinking from my bottle of beer when I passed the poker room so that they couldn't get a good look at me. There were three of them, also engaged in pretending. They were pretending to play poker against each other, and they were studying their cards and stroking their piles of chips with their left hands. It was a cinch they were all housemen and were just keeping a game going as a decoy for some working stiff with a pay check from the Forest Service on a sheep ranch. They were all dressed alike, and were all dressed like Bill Bell—black Stetson hats, blue shirts, and yellow strings from sacks of Bull Durham hanging out of their shirt pockets. I wondered if all the guys in the Bitterroot who thought they were tough wore some kind of uniform, because even the doctor wore a small black Stetson. They pretended that no one was standing in the doorway, as, faceless, they studied their cards under their hat brims; then almost as one the hat brims raised slightly and they peered from underneath. What made it a cinch they were all shills working for the house was that nobody watched them play. Any westerner knows that when nobody watches the poker game, the poker game isn't real. The poker game is Magnetic North, and when even a sheepherder with his summer's pay is drawn into the magnetic field, a circle forms around it.

Not wanting them to get a good look at me, I kept moving. But then I didn't get a good look at them either—mostly what I saw down the sides of my tipped beer bottle were the brims of their hats and their hunched shoulders shielding their cards. Their black hats were black but not like Bill's black hat, gray with dust. Hunched shoulders always look big, but one pair looked at least as big as Bill's. I began to think of him as Biggest Brim, and the other two as Big Brim and Bigger Brim, just like olives, the smallest grade always being marked Large. Not much else of them was allowed to show except their hands, which looked as if they were trying to be clumsy to get me into the game.

Something had made me crawl out of bed and go spying, although I hadn't learned much. My first view of the tin-horn gamblers in the flesh wasn't a great deal different from my mental image of tin-horn gamblers—they were faceless but had an eye on me. I had learned just one thing for sure—that it was a long way from the poker room in the rear to the front door, and I made a note, if we had to back out fighting, to watch sideways for anybody who might be swinging the butt of a pool cue.

I was nervous and much too early and, although still not feeling well, I began to realize I hadn't eaten much of anything since leaving Elk Summit. I crossed the street to the Greek restaurant with the waitress who didn't like me. The waitress was on shift, gave my table a swish with her apron and said, as if there'd always been complete understanding between us, "You're going to eat something tonight. You haven't eaten anything since you came to town."

I said, "I was thinking the same thing myself."

"I'll get some soup while you're looking the menu over," she said. "Be sure to order meat. It'll make you strong again."

I thought about her all the time she was in the kitchen. I wasn't exactly prepared for this sudden motherly change in events, and when you're hurt you don't forgive quickly. Looking at the soup, as she put it down, she said, "I think I know where Bill Bell's dog is."

The soup came up in steam and I was glad it smelled good because that meant I was better, so for a moment I really didn't hear what she said. When I did, I asked, "Do you know Bill Bell?" Then she didn't hear. "You must order something with a lot of meat." She helped me think things over, and after a lot of thought we decided on what anyone probably would have—a hamburger, rare and with onions, on a theory we both shared, that rare and onions make you strong. When she came back from the kitchen after ordering, she said, "I don't know Bill Bell but I know where his dog is. Did you like your soup?" "It was good and hot," I said, and left it up to her to go on.

As she lifted the soup bowl and brushed off the bits of crackers from the table, she said, "I come from a sheep ranch near Darby, and I've heard his dog is on a sheep ranch near Hamiliton. I can sell you where."

This time she was gone quite a while, waiting for the hamburger to get done. I knew that she was probably right about Bill's dog. Like Bill himself, the dog was one of the legends of the Bitterroot Valley. He had a name, but everybody called him "Bill's Dog." He liked Bill best among humans but he had an even higher commitment—he was committed to sheep. He would follow Bill into the woods in the spring and he liked especially to be around Bill when he was working with livestock or twirling his rope in the evening, but by the middle of July he would get an inner call and be gone, and when autumn came Bill would find him at some sheep camp.

As a sheep dog he specialized on coyotes. Coyotes are wily animals, but wily animals including ourselves and coyotes have more set patterns than we think. The sheep camp is usually on a creek bottom or near a spring, and one coyote usually appears on top of a nearby ridge and barks like hell and makes a big show of himself, and the sheep dog, following his usual pattern, takes out after the coyote and the coyote of course disappears over the hill. Then it so happens that when the dog comes sailing over the ridge with his tongue hanging out, there are three or four coyotes waiting to meet him. The first coyote didn't know that just what Bill's Dog was looking for was three or four coyotes.

Bill's Dog looked as if he were divided into two parts, his head and shoulders being pit bull and the remaining half with which he ran being greyhound. Probably nothing in the valley touched him for speed and ferocity. Actually, he wasn't so much committed to sheep as he was to sheep camps where he could kill coyotes. Every sheep camp in the valley regarded it a privilege to entertain him.

The waitress came back and asked, "When is Bill going to leave tomorrow for Elk Summit?" "It's a guess," I told her, "but I'd guess around noon." "I'll try to get his dog to him in the morning," she said, "but if I don't make it, here's a piece of paper that tells the ranch where he is and how to get there. Will you give the note to Bill?"

I nodded and put it in my shirt pocket. "So you don't know Bill?" I asked. I cut the hamburger sandwich into four pieces and even then it was big and I had to open my mouth wide. She said, "No, I come from Darby and I ran away to go to Missoula." Missoula was my town. It is the biggest town around, and is near the mouth of the Bitterroot River. Darby is a small town about seventy miles up the Bitterroot River, and Hamilton is in between in both distance and size, but closer to Darby than to Missoula. "But," she said, "I got a job here in Hamilton slinging hash, and somehow I never got as far as Missoula."

Since I was still trying to open my mouth wide, she went on. "I'm a Bitterrooter, so even if I don't know Bill Bell I know all about him and his dog."

She had dark red hair and perhaps her teeth were a little too far apart but she looked good and she looked strong and it was not hard to imagine her on a sheep ranch. Her face and neck were covered with outdoor freckles and they got even thicker as they disappeared toward her breasts.

"I know you work for Bill," she said, and then she said as if she'd tried to say it before, "and I know you're in for big trouble tonight."

I put down the remaining quarter of the sandwich. "How do you know that?" I asked.

"Men eat here," she said. I looked at the clock and told her, "I have to be going." She said, "You haven't finished your sandwich." I assured her, "It was good, but I have to be on my way."

"All right," she said, "but don't forget about Bill's Dog." "I won't," I told her.

"Be sure now," she said, "not to forget about Bill's Dog. I want you to think about him tonight."

"You sound smart," I told her.

"No," she said. "I haven't been to Missoula yet."

The Bitterroot girl who followed me to the door was about my age, and we both felt it. "So long and good luck," she said. Then she called after me, "Don't forget to tell Bill that I gave him the slip of paper, but you're not supposed to look at it."

"I'll tell him," I called back, and then I put all my life out of my mind except around a poker table.

I focused so intensely I still remember all that happened as if it were last night.

There was no one in the barroom except the guy behind the bar, who looked as if he were about to lose the place he may have owned. For a moment I thought there was no sound at all in the next room. Then suddenly a crash was followed by several thuds as the life went out of concrete pool balls when they hit dead cushions. Evidently one pair of pool players was left.

"Hey, punk," the barkeep snarled, "where do you think you're going?"

I was late and worried because there was just one set of sounds in the next room, so I tried to slide past by being polite.

"I'm supposed to meet with some friends in there," I said.

"Come over here," he said. Then I got really worried, because I should have been standing right behind the cook, but I went part way to the bar, close enough to see a Smith & Wesson .38 on the lower counter where he washed the glasses. No revolver had been there when I bought my homemade beer. He stopped looking at me long enough to take a drink from a shot glass sitting by the revolver.

"Have a shot of moonshine," he said to me. "Thanks," I said, and shook my head. "It's on the house," he said, and I said "Thanks" again.

He said, actually pointing at me, "You're with Bill Bell, aren't you? You were in here not long ago."

I said, "I work for him."

"He's in there," he told me. "What's he doing in there?" I asked.

"Why don't you look in there and tell me?" he asked.

I could see that I would be here forever if I kept on being polite. I said, "Why don't you look in there yourself? You've got a gun and it's only twenty feet to the door where you can look."

He said, "I'm afraid to leave the front of the place alone. Somebody might come in and steal something." I took another look and when I saw it actually wasn't twenty feet to the door, I realized he was scared. I don't like guys who look big and tough but aren't and also happen to have a gun. When they're tough all the way through, it's easier to figure out what the gun will do.

I walked those less than twenty feet softly and looked.

Just as sound had said, in all the big room there were only two pool players, probably a couple of ranch hands who had worked with cattle so long they didn't notice any more what went on among humans. Otherwise, it was as if the earth had tilted and everybody had slid into the back room. You could hardly see the poker table, but everybody was peering at it and watching in silence.

You know, watching a poker game isn't like watching most other card games where all is silent while the hand is played and there's a round of relaxation and comment after the cards have been thrown into a pile. In this usual kind of card game everybody sees all the cards by the time the cards are thrown in, so nobody's giving anything away by talking when the game's over. But in draw poker half or more of the game is psychology, and you toss your hand face down into the pile so no one can see what cards you held unless you're willing to stay in the game and bet that you're the winner. Hand after hand in poker is played with nothing showing at the end but a pair of whatever it took to open the betting, and nobody would be allowed to watch the game if he gave an indication of what the cards were that had been tossed face down into the pile. In draw poker, you pay for every card you see.

As I stood at the door of the pool room looking back at the poker table, a moment of my life came back to me and I was a child watching a pageant of big boys dressed as sheepherders trying to be statues bent over something mystic in a shining light.

Turning to the barkeeper nursing his shot of moonshine, I said, "It looks like Sunday school at Christmas," and I walked rapidly toward the back room, nervous that I was making any noise at all and nervous also about that .38 I was leaving in my back.

Although Mr. Smith was standing at the door of the poker room where he should be, he wasn't happy. According to the plan, he was to be the palace guard and keep out all except our guys, but when the earth had tilted he obviously had been covered by a landslide. I told him, "The barkeeper has a .38." He didn't say a thing to me, but he shoved people aside until he got me to a spot right behind the cook. Before I really looked at the cook I looked at the pile in front of him. It was a pile all right, not big but forty dollars anyway. The other three at the table had big hat brims but small piles of money. Bill Bell was standing right behind Biggest Brim. The light shade over the table almost cut Bill in half. In the semi-darkness above the light his shoulders and hat were gigantic; then suddenly beneath the light his hands glared on his hips, as if he had a gun. My attention stopped jumping while I studied him for a bulge around the waist or a shoulder strap, and I knew finally for sure it was going to be just a plain fight. As I was studying Bill, Biggest Brim moved his chair to the right and, when he moved a second time, I guessed that Biggest didn't like Bill directly behind him. Just as he took a look at Bill, Bill pushed a bystander to the right and got behind Biggest again. I thought, "If they go on doing this they'll be in front of me before long." Just then, the red-headed kid developed out of the shadows and became a form on one side of Biggest Brim. The red-headed kid was about my size, but he didn't budge an inch when Biggest tried to make another move to get another look at Bill. I didn't have to guess any longer about whether he would have shot on the fireline.

Then who appeared on the other side of Biggest Brim but the gassed Canadian. He coughed but he didn't move either.

In front of me, the cook looked just as cocky as ever. In fact, standing over him, I could look down on that bluejay tuft sticking up from the back of his head. Being the only player not hidden by a hat and being the only player with a fair-sized pile in front of him, he was the one we all watched most.

He stood out even more when it was his turn to deal, and it was clear to me after a couple of rounds that the strategy of the Faceless Three when it came to dealing cards had changed completely since early evening when they had tried to draw me into the game by looking clumsy. Now every player knew the other was a gambling man, so the psychology had changed to shaking the other guy's confidence in his game. The three Brims were pretty handy with cards, but no better than that. I was just beginning to find out that there were quite a few differences between my picture of a gambling man and a small-town shill who lies in wait for working stiffs with monthly checks. The cook, though, was a flash. The cards leaped out of the messy pile into his hands, and then darted out of his hands around the circle of the table. For my money he was too flashy and was showing off, but our crew was proud of him, and, standing right over him as if I owned him, I guess I was, too, although never completely losing the feeling that something was missing in him somewhere.

By what he had said earlier, he was playing percentage poker, although I wouldn't have called it that. It was a lot more daring than just sitting there counting the spots and playing the odds. For instance, twice in a short time he had a chance to open the betting on a pair of jacks (jacks were the lowest openers) and twice he passed and twice somebody else opened and then both times he raised the opening bet. But from there on he played each hand differently. To the first hand, he drew only one card, as if to suggest that he was holding two pairs and hadn't opened the betting on them because of the difficulties you can get into with two pairs if you have to bet on them before getting an idea of what anybody else has. The smallest of the Faceless Three, who was sitting to the cook's left, opened the betting, and he drew an honest three, which meant, since jacks were openers, that he could be holding any one of three pairs that would beat the cook—and, at worst, he couldn't be holding less than a pair of jacks, which was all the cook was holding after he drew his one card.

Bigger Brim and Biggest Brim dropped out after the raise. Since Big Brim had opened, it was his turn to bet first after the draw and, thinking a long time about the raise the cook had given him, he passed. The cook had done his thinking long before. He bet two dollars. Two dollars at that stage of the game was a pretty good-sized bet—not staggering as if you were betting big because you weren't holding much but big enough to look as if you had what you thought could win and you wanted to get the other guys to stay in the betting. This time Big Brim had done all his thinking. He showed a pair of queens for openers, and the cook lowered his elbows and embraced the pile of money. Biggest Brim grunted. If I had been playing against him I would have figured he didn't like to be bluffed.

The second time that the cook didn't open the pot on a pair of jacks but instead raised, he drew not one but two cards, as if to suggest he had three of a kind, and damned if one of the two cards he drew wasn't another jack, so he ended with three of a kind. Of course, when you're that lucky, you don't have to be Nick the Greek to play them. This time Big Brim and Biggest Brim both stayed in the game, and it cost Biggest Brim nearly five dollars to think he discovered that the cook didn't bluff because he ended up with three jacks.

As the cook's winnings increased, he became cockier and he began to talk and his game got even better. He was the only one who talked, and he talked all the time about his cards. One of the best poker players I ever saw was a punch-drunk prizefighter who, like the cook, talked all the time about what he was holding. You couldn't tell what to believe about anything he said, but you couldn't stop listening. The cook would say, "I'm going to raise you on a pair of jacks," and he'd have three kings, and then later he'd say, "I'm going to try to raise you again on a pair of jacks," and this time that's just what he had. Always he talked about his hand, and generally he lied but every now and then what he said was what he held, and only I who was behind him could tell the difference. I was glad I wasn't playing against him. Obviously, it was also the flashiest poker the three Brims from Hamilton had seen in some time. Biggest Brim twisted around in his chair until he could pull out his purse from his hip pocket. It was a little black purse that snapped shut and he unsnapped it and unfolded several bills. Then he untwisted, traded bills for silver dollars, started a new pile with the dollars and went on losing.

Although only the cook talked, there was an audible relaxation of muscles between deals except for Bill who never moved unless to keep Biggest Brim in front of him. Otherwise, Bill was a giant hat and pair of shoulders in shadows, and in light a pair of hands resting on hips that by now everyone besides me had studied. Mr. Smith was a full-time giant beside the door, ocasionally looking back in the direction of the .38 Smith & Wesson.

My left arm was slightly brushed, and looking down on me but pretending to look at the card game was Mr. McBride. He was standing so much over me that if it had been raining he would have dripped off the corners of his moustache on to my head. I was glad to have that feeling over me, and I reached inside my shirt and touched the sugar sack. Still, I didn't like it that nearly all our crew were standing in the rim of light around the table, except Mr. Smith and the two lookouts, whose names and locations I can't remember. I wasn't much worried about the three Faceless Wonders at the table. After all, we had them outnumbered, and, if they were fighty, they'd been sitting soft all summer around a green table while we'd been getting case-hardened climbing the high hills. I was worried about the extra help that might come out of nowhere. I'd seen at least two housemen working the poolroom earlier in the evening. Then, some of those clumsy pool players had to be housemen who were only faking and would take you to the cleaners if you dropped in from another town and thought you were good. There was also that .38 behind the bar. Still another question: How many of the customers would stick with the house in a fight? There was no way of answering that now. It could depend on who was winning or on how the Oxford treated its customers or on how many friends Bill had in the house. At present, they were standing back in the shadows, but probably were all for war up in front. As for me personally, I knew I'd take a beating. It was getting so that every few minutes I'd feel the sugar sack.

Evidently, the barkeeper hadn't yet dared come as far as the door to look.

The cook kept on winning—not big but steadily—and I began to think he would go on playing his so-called percentage game for the rest of the night as it would have been percentage to do, but I kept forgetting that one thing you can be sure about a show-off is that he will show off.

When it happened, there was a good-sized pot, not big enough to risk your shirt on and certainly not big enough to risk getting shot over, but still a fair-sized pot. Three or four deals in a row had been passed without an opening bet and of course each time everybody had to ante so the pot got to be a pretty good one. Actually, the cook had made the last deal and, when nobody had an opening bet, I knew he was still dealing honest. Everybody chipped into the pot again and the cook passed the cards to Big Brim, who was sitting to his left. Big Brim handled the cards better than anyone in the game except the cook, and was even slightly ahead, but by now I was sure that none of the Brims was a great card player. I asked myself, "Anyway, what the hell ever made you think a great card player would be staying in Hamilton?" Now I had them cased as pretty good card players who probably had a few two-bit tricks up their sleeves to fool the ranch hands and us Forest Service stiffs from the high brush.

Big Brim dealt out the hands and the cook picked his up and had just started to sort it when he put his cards face down on the table, leaned over and slightly raised Big Brim's hat.

"I beg your pardon," he said with a little stately speech, "I always like to see a man's face when I play cards with him."

I saw something flash and disappear as the cook withdrew his hand from the hat, like the tail of a rabbit into the brush, but even though I stretched my neck I couldn't get sight of it again. I knew, though, that something had happened to Big Brim from the sudden stir among people across the table who could get a front view of him. Biggest Brim closed his cards in one fist and half pushed himself up from the table. Bill stepped from behind him for a better view and perhaps a better shot. Bigger Brim, who had done little more in the game than lose, raked in his little pile of money, whereupon I reached in my shirt and got a fist on the sugar sack.

Big Brim himself, though, didn't seem to notice that a rabbit had ducked into his hat or something like that. With his hat now tilted away from me, he leaned back and started to sort his cards. He had his move timed perfectly, just when the cook had finished sorting his hand and had definitely assumed possession of it.

"Sorry, pardner," he said to the cook, "but you'll have to throw in your hand. You've an extra card."

"Who? Me?" asked the cook.

"Yes, you," said Big Brim. "You have six cards in your hand.

You must have had that extra card up your sleeve just for a big pot like this one."

"Count 'em," said the cook, and he spread them face down in a small fan in front of Big Brim.

Big Brim spread them even further apart and counted. "How many?" asked the cook. Big Brim went back over the cards, spread them even further apart, felt each one, and gave them another count.

From across the table, Bill asked, "How many?"

Big Brim looked at the cook and not at Bill. "Five," he said, still feeling the cards.

The cook said, blown wide open with pride, "If you're looking for that extra card you dealt me to get my hand thrown out of the game, you'll find it in your hatband."

Big Brim took off his hat and rested it on the table while he tried to believe it. There in his hatband was the deuce of clubs, the lowest card in the deck, but if it had still been in the cook's hand it would have put him out of the game.

The aces the cook had palmed into my shirt pocket at Elk Summit jumped out of my mind like rabbits and arranged themselves around the band of Big Brim's hat. Nobody needed to tell me how the deuce of clubs got there or where the rabbit had gone.

I went for the money.

First for the pot on the table, figuring that the cook should be able to protect his pile until I got there. I don't know who started the fight. I heard a chair crash. Either somebody got hit with a chair or was knocked off one.

Somebody slugged me as I reached for the pot, and it happened just as I had imagined it would—somebody from the side slugged me high on the jaw, and I never saw him. I guess it was Big Brim, and it must have been Mr. McBride who flattened him. Anyway, while I was still reaching for the pot Big Brim lit on top of me and didn't move until I heaved up straight and let him slide off. There was still some money left in the pot that hadn't spilled or been taken but, when I reached over to pick up the remains, somebody grabbed my arm and somebody else stretched out and helped him twist it. I could also feel things hurt in my ear where I was hit on the side of my head.

When I finally got my arm loose it was so weak I couldn't pick up the rest of the pot, but I didn't miss much, maybe a couple of dollars of change that were hard to pick up with numb fingers. Instead, I went for the pile of money in front of the cook, who, so help me, was just sitting there. You would think that somebody would have flattened him right off, but there he sat with the tuft on his head and nobody had laid a hand on him, probably because, as I said earlier, among men the cardshark is a sorcerer in everyone's eyes, and this one had just performed magic. Maybe they were afraid they'd go up in smoke if they touched him. So there he sat, untouched and maybe untouchable. The son of a bitch didn't even help me stuff his money into the sack, although I think I got it all.

Then somebody hit me between the eyes harder than I was ever able to remember. I just stood there and my clothes felt like a potato sack and my body felt like potatoes, and the sack sank to the floor with me inside it. I tried to remain conscious. I tried to think, knowing I was nodding at the fringe of reality. I tried to think big thoughts, as if I were having thoughts about life. I even started sentences that began, "Life is ...," but I never finished them, because I never had any thoughts to put in them.

At first, everything corresponded exactly with my foresight. I reached across the table for the money, and there was no way I could protect myself. Next, as in anticipation, I felt actual blood from inside my head slip down my throat.

But, as I folded on the floor, everything became unexpected. Suddenly, as if from nowhere, I got not one but two ideas of how I could have protected myself when I reached across the table, whereas for weeks before, when an idea would have done some good, I couldn't get a single one. I struggled to my elbows to see if it was too late to act, but, once on the tripod of my elbows, I could tell the ideas weren't worth a damn. And in another moment they disappeared, never to be remembered again.

While my body was still raised off the floor, though, I managed twist it. I could also feel things hurt in my ear where I was hit on to shove the sugar sack into my shirt. In the process, I realized I recognized some of the feet under and around the table.

Lying again on the floor on the side of my face, I wondered, since I couldn't think believable thoughts, whether, by watching feet, I could figure out some of what was going on. I lifted my face again from the sawdust and stained Bull Durham butts, and again put it on the tripod of elbows. This was to be the biggest fight I ever viewed almost entirely from the prone position. And under a poker table.

Right off the bat I could tell us guys from those guys. They were the cowboy boots and we were the logging boots, and I remembered with a sickly feeling that later this night we were going to clean out all the ranch hands in town. It took me time to sort out this fight between men up to their knees. But things got clearer, and first there was the biggest pair of cowboy boots right across from me. The knees were spread wide apart and the boots were turned up at the toes. Bill, the redhead, and the Canadian must have nailed him to his chair before he ever moved. Then suddenly a pair of cowboy boots went straight up in the air and then just dangled there—one of our boys must have draped this body across the poker table and left his head and feet hanging over. To check, I looked on the opposite side and, sure enough, there was his head with saliva stringing out of his mouth. I looked back real quick to see who of our guys had stretched out the body, and, just as expected, there were Bill's big loggers spread out. Bill's loggers, you remember, had that fringed extra tongue, you couldn't miss them, and they were working slowly toward me.

Suddenly, a pair of city shoes jumped into the front ring, belonging, I guessed, to one of the housemen who racked up the pool balls. His legs danced once and disappeared rhythmically into the blue. I don't know what happened to him, but he left so suddenly that Bill must have taken him, too.

A faded pair of Levi's went bowlegged and kept on spreading until Mr. McBride sank down beside me. I didn't have strength to move out of his way, so he just leaned against me. The pair of loggers that skipped in and out across the table had to belong to his red-headed son. He could make those loggers move, and I could see that it helped him and our guys to be wearing loggers and not cowboy boots. Everybody in town yelled at us stiffs from the Forest Service when we walked indoors, because admittedly the sharp caulks in the soles of our loggers left little holes in the floors, but when that fast red-headed kid jumped back to duck and counterpunch, those loggers held on the wood floor and the slick high-heeled cowboy boots trying to sidestep his counter-punches slipped and then skidded.

It's hard to believe, but the Canadian puttees were standing most of the time, only once in a while bending at the knee and coughing.

All the time, sitting flat-footed next to me, was a pair of low canvas shoes with rubber soles, like a pair of girl's basketball shoes. They just sat there flat-footed. I started to climb to my feet even before I determined to. It took me a couple of pushes and I wobbled on the way up. It was funny, but right there I thought of my Presbyterian father, and I quit wobbling.

The cook picked up the cards and strained them through his hands. Just keeping his hands soft, I suppose.

I hit him on the side of the head about where I thought I'd been hit. He bounced to the floor, and I went down softly. I knew that I hadn't hit him hard. I didn't have the strength. Mr. McBride must have been coming to, because he rolled over slightly to make room for me. I was fairly sure that the cook, who was curled up, was playing possum. I saw one of his eyes open and study me. Then, when he became sure that I was pretty much beyond recall, he jumped up and started kicking me. Among lumberjacks, this is known as "giving the guy the leather" and you not only put the boots to him when he's down but you also rake him with the sharp caulks bristling from your soles and what you leave behind is full of dirt and takes a long time to heal. Only I wasn't being kicked by loggers, but by girl's basketball shoes. Even so, the bastard managed to kick me once on the side of the head just about where I'd been hit and I could feel blood start down my throat again. I tried to catch one of his feet and trip him and I caught one but I couldn't hold it.

Then suddenly both canvas shoes went straight up in the air and I heard something crash and later I was to have it confirmed that the cook hit the wall and that Bill threw him there. Anyway, spread in front of me was a pair of loggers with a fringed double tongue. Then Bill reached over and picked me up with one arm, and before he had fully straightened he reached down again and picked up Mr. McBride with his other arm.

He shook both arms and said, "How are you?" and we both said, as if we'd talked it over together, "Oh, we're all right." We both started sliding out of his arms, and he took a fast new hold on us and said, "Now, wait a minute." Then, with his arms around us, he made us walk a few steps, and just a few steps helped to clear things up, and both of us, feeling embarrassed by being held, muttered, "Thanks, Bill," and tried to push free, and he grinned to see us better, but he still held us tight. This time he walked us five or six steps and back again, and this time we pushed free of him and regained our manhood and tried to appear as if we were looking for more fight.

But the fight was nearly over. Off to one side the redhead was fighting with some town guy in a buttoned shirt. Mr. McBride wobbled over and broke it up just as his son absorbed a roundhouse punch to his belly, but the old man wouldn't let him go on, and the town guy was glad to quit on the strength of getting in the last punch. His son walked off with bowed head thinking deep thoughts, and then he whirled and ran after the town guy to start the fight over again but now the crowd came out of the shadows and held him back. The crowd that was all for war when I disappeared under the table and they disappeared into the shadows was now all for peace.

As my brain cleared, I began to feel like the redhead, and was surprised and disappointed to see that the fight was over. This was the first fight I was ever in where there were a lot of other guys, and I hadn't learned yet that when there are a lot of guys in a fight it usually doesn't last long, for the simple reason that a lot of guys don't like to fight. Only a few like to fight and know how. Most guys take a couple of punches on the nose and swallow blood and suddenly grow weak with sisterly feelings about brotherly love. All that was left of the war now that the redhead had retired was old Mr. Smith standing by the door with a bear hug on the barkeeper.

This was probably the first and last time in his life that the bar-keeper would walk into the arms of a man who swung a jackham-mer for a living. The head of the barkeeper, which was the only part of him that could move, moved wildly. Finally his arms must have run short of blood, because the revolver dropped from his hand. Bill picked up the .38, flipped open the chamber, shook out the shells, and the war was officially over.

My head hurt and so did my feelings. I was still trying to figure out how the war could have been won without me. Mr. McBride had been out of business most of the time, too, and Mr. Smith had been standing at the door with a bear hug on the barkeeper. As in a lot of big fights, most of the fighting had been done by one fine fighter and a kid who might grow up to be one. Together they got at least two of the Hat Brims and all the housemen who racked up the pool balls and whatever customers were overcome by loyalty to the Oxford. The Canadian was sitting bent over in one of the poker chairs. He was doubled up as if he had to cough but couldn't. Whatever he'd done was done nobly but it couldn't have counted for much.

The three Brims sat by themselves, with their brims pulled lower than ever, but they didn't look badly hurt. They were showing each other their fingers. Then they went around the spectators trying to explain that they didn't get into the fight much because they were card players and were afraid to break the bones in their hands. Probably all three of the tin-horn gamblers pimped on the side for a living. I even suspected one of them was my next-door neighbor last night, but I never got a good enough look to be sure. Mostly, I was trying to get used to the fact that no one seemed real-ly hurt except me—and probably Mr. McBride. Even the place, which looked torn apart when Bill had pulled me from under the table, was being quickly straightened out by the barkeeper and the housemen. Customers helped set up the chairs. The rest of the regular customers started talking, and then one pair started playing pool with a loud bang of the balls. Others followed. Everyone was acting as if nothing had happened, and nothing looked as if it had.

I spit out a clot of blood and went over and sat down by the

Canadian to find out how he was. He put an arm around me and I put an arm around him, and that had to be the answer.

It seemed suddenly like everybody in the house was Bill's friend and they all came over to shake his hand or feel how hard his arm was. The cook got up from the floor where he had been leaning against the wall and tried to be near Bill while Bill was accepting congratulations, and clearly Bill was pleased with everything. The redhead held on to his father, but his eyes still smoldered.

Otherwise, all was peace. I couldn't get over it. For at least two weeks we had been building up steam, and each of us was going to win a summer's wages by some sweep of a black cape and then we were going to clean out the town. Well, the black cape had swept and I reached inside my shirt to feel my ten-pound sugar sack, and all the money that was in it could have been put in a Bull Durham sack. We had cleaned out the town and I already knew that I'd always talk about it, but everything already was running normally again at the Oxford. Even the three tin-horn gamblers had moved back to the poker table and had started an innocent-looking game among themselves, hoping all over that some sheepherder with his summer check would saunter by and they could deal him a sixth card. All the tables were being played on but the billiard table, but it was the time of night that barbers and vice-presidents of banks spend with their women before going home to their wives.

It's lucky for towns that good fighters first have to be fighters and that there aren't many of those to start with. Otherwise, towns would be destroyed overnight, because in late summer every town is going to be cleaned out every night by some crew and usually is, and then the town straightens up the chairs and goes on taking the crew's money as before.

Bill rounded up his bunch, and herded us out like sheep. The barkeeper raised his head and said good-bye to us directly. He was selling chits to two married men who were going to get into the pinochle game.

Mr. McBride and I were holding each other by the arm, and we felt better when we got outside. But I was hurt and everyone in the bunch knew it. They also knew I had the money. They helped me around the block and we stopped at a street corner under an arc light. I sat down on the curbing near the light and rested a few minutes before taking the sack out of my shirt. Everybody gathered close. They gathered so close Bill finally said, "Get back a bit. We can't get enough light to see." Then he and Mr. Smith went back to counting. I didn't try to help them count. I didn't think I could.

First, they gave each of us the money he had bet. Then Bill asked, "Any objection if we split our winnings even nine ways, no matter what each of the nine bet? We are one crew, aren't we?" Heads nodded, and he started to sit down again. Then he got up and made what was a speech for him. "And a pretty damn good crew. We always did what we had to." Besides, none of us could do the arithmetic to figure out exactly each one's share.

Bill sat down to finish counting our winnings, and we stood around and didn't know what to do but to admire ourselves. I suppose factually we were probably not much to brag about. We were fairly representative of early Forest Service crews as I came to know them—maybe not even that good, because the war had ended less than a year before and many of the best men had not yet returned to the woods, and the earth was still pretty much in the care of the old with corrugated skin and tiny steps and young punks looking for a fight and gassed Canadians and anonymous lookouts who had to be there but can't be remembered. Not one had ever seen the inside or the outside of a school of forestry. But, as Bill said, we were a pretty good crew and we did what we had to do and loved the woods without thinking we owned them, and each of us liked to do at least one thing especially well—liked to swing a jackhammer and feel the earth overpowered by dynamite, liked to fight, liked to heal the injuries of horses, liked to handle groceries and tools and tie knots. And nearly all of us liked to work. When you think about it, that's a lot to say about a bunch of men.

At the moment, in our hearts we felt indissoluble, although in our heads we knew that after tonight we might never see one another again. We were summer workers. We belonged to no union, no lodge, and most of us had no families and no church. In late spring, we had landed jobs in a new outfit called the United States Forest Service which we vaguely knew Teddy Roosevelt had helped to get going and which somehow made us feel proud and tough and always looking for trouble of some sort, like fires, dynamite, and rattlesnakes on mountains too high to have any. Besides doing what we had to, we did a few other things, like playing practical jokes and distilling dried apricots and having some troubles among ourselves. And at the end we banded together to clean out the town—probably something also that had to be done for us to become a crew. For most of us, this momentary social unit the crew was the only association we had ever belonged to, although somehow it must have been for more time than a moment. Here I am over half a century later trying to tell you about it.

While the ranger and Mr. Smith finished counting, the moths fried on the arc light over us and the blood again slid inside my head.

Bill said to Mr. Smith, "You announce it." Mr. Smith stood up and announced, "The total is $64.80. Split nine ways, that's $7.20 apiece." Everybody said "Wow" and forgot all about $7.20 being several hundred dollars short of summer expectations.

Bill divided the money and Mr. Smith said, "Now for the ranch hands and the whores." Some wanted to reverse the order, and then, since we were a crew, they suddenly got solicitous about me, but in succession. "How you feeling, kid?" "You sure took a beating but you got the dough." "Good going, kid." And then Bill said, "We'll walk you back to your hotel."

"Hell, no," I said, "The night is but a pup."

Bill said, "You've had a big night. Now take it easy. But I want you to come to the corral before noon tomorrow and help me saddle up."

Then everybody said, again not together but one after another, "We'll walk you back to your hotel."

So they walked me back, and when we got in front of my twenty-five-cent lodging for the night, we all put our arms around each other but none of us tried to sing because none of us could carry a tune. Instead, we stood in a circle with heads bowed like a college glee club just before beginning to hum. Then I suddenly felt weak and turned away and started up an uncarpeted stair and was too tired and disappointed in myself to say, "So long."

I rolled over against the plaster wall for comfort. In the center of my brain the pain from the side of my head met the pain from the front of my head. Never before had I taken two beatings in two days. I felt especially sensitive to pain, being young and used to winning. Though it was dark in the room, I squeezed my eyes extra tight hoping to keep out the sight of my lying on the Chinaman's floor with toothpicks in my hair. And I tried to squeeze out the sight of my head leaning over the table ready to be punched. My head shook in revulsion and tried to back away from what it did not see coming. I thought, it was the biggest fight I was ever in, and I swung only one punch. Thoughts came slowly, so it was some time before I followed up with the next thought, "But if a man had only one punch to give for his country, I sure picked a good target." When I quit pulling my head back from my thoughts, I could feel the muscles in my neck relax and I fell asleep.

It was late in the morning when I woke, and I felt just a little better and, while I washed from the pitcher, I was glad there was no mirror. As I awoke, I wanted to take one step from the bed and be with Bill at the corral, but when I jumped into my clothes I looked again at my watch and asked myself, "What's your rush?" Also I realized that some of the sickness might go from my stomach if I had "a little something for breakfast," as my mother would say. It was ten when I got to the Greek restaurant, and the girl from Darby was on shift.

She seated me at a table in a dark corner, started to the front counter to get me a menu and then came back. "I knew you were in for big trouble last night," she said. "You'd better come and let me wash you off." Then she led me into the ladies' room and locked the door and made me sit down on the cover of the toilet, which to my surprise looked the same as the men's toilet. From there I could lean my head over the basin, and she washed all my head, including my hair. "Don't argue," she said. "You must have rolled in the dirt."

"Sawdust," I said.

"Oh," she said. I was becoming embarrassed by getting the motherly treatment and also by the prospect of being seen coming out of a ladies' toilet with my hair dripping, but she wouldn't let loose of me. She opened her purse and took out a little tube of something—cold cream, probably—and dabbed some of whatever it was on the cut in my forehead. Then she took a comb from her purse and parted my dripping hair, using her apron to dry my face. When she leaned over I could see that her freckles enlarged as they went down her neck and that her breasts were all brown. "There you are," she said, and let loose of my neck and I tried not to be seen with her as I came out of the ladies' toilet, but she didn't seem to give a damn.

She acted as if it was all business until I finished breakfast. Then she said, looking down at me the way waitresses do while pretending they are looking for dirty dishes, "There's a friend of yours sitting in the alley. I think you had better go out to see him."

"Who?" I asked. "I don't know," she said. "But he's one of your crew." Knowing she didn't have to say any more, she picked up the dishes and I paid the check and then she led me through the kitchen and opened the door to the alley.

He was sitting on a cardboard box full of old newspapers. Although his head was bowed, without doubt it was the cook's because in a world of men with black hats he was always bare-headed with a tuft at the top. One of the old newspapers was on the ground between his feet and he was bent over as if he were reading it except that blood dropped on it from his unseen face. I walked over slowly toward him to be sure about the blood.

"What happened?" I asked. "I'm broke," he said, never raising his head. "But are you hurt?" I asked. "I'm broke," he repeated.

"How come?" I asked. "I'm broke. They rolled me," he replied. "Who?" I asked. He looked up at me and when his head was lifted the blood ran down his lip into his mouth.

Finally he said, "She was as crooked as a tub of guts."

Having scanned that line before, I didn't wait to ask, "Was she just a little whore?" He replied, "I don't feel hurt. I feel broke. I need money to get to Butte." I repeated, "Was it a little whore who rolled you?" He replied, "She had a big guy with her. They beat hell out of me and took my money." I asked, "Did he have a hairy ass?" He replied, "I didn't see his ass." "Well," I told him, "it is hairy."

Then I said to myself, "don't be such a wise guy," and a great shame swept over me for asking him a show-off question that he couldn't possibly answer. By this time blood had spread into the corners of his mouth. Then I think it was my father who spoke out of the whirlwind of my mind, and said unto me, as if he had just written the Bible, "Be ye compassionate." My father reserved the right to speak to me on any occasion and on any subject, even if he knew nothing about it. It was his voice that went on to talk to me about card playing, and in summary he said I should not rejoice because someone with great gifts in handling cards turned out not to be even a good card player on account of something little (so he said) inside him. Although my father knew absolutely nothing about cards, what he said sounded like him, including his not knowing anything about cards or the cook.

"How much do you want?" I asked. "Would you lend me ten bucks? I'll pay it back."

As I remembered, it was about 170 miles to Butte and the coach fare then was three cents a mile.

I told him, "No, I won't lend you anything. But I'll give you enough to get to Butte. I'll give you $7.20. It's all yours and I don't want it back."

He lowered his head and reached out his hand, and the blood began dripping on the newspaper again.

I went into the restaurant and, since it was still a long time before lunch, Miss Brown Breasts was alone. I said to her, "It is the cook." "Yes?" she said. I said, "It is the cook." She said, "Yes?" I knew I must say something else. I said, "He is hurt. Would you wash him and give him something to eat?" She asked, "Has he any money?" And I said, "Yes," and she said, "He didn't have any money before and the boss threw him out," and I said, "He has money now," and she looked at me and said, "Bring him in."

So I went outside and brought the cook in and gave him to the girl from Darby who took him into the ladies' room and locked the door.

Then I started for the road to the corral where I knew Bill would be saddling up.

Bill's Dog was there and saw me when I was still a long way off.

He got up and started toward me. I heard Bill speak to him from the corral, and he quit growling, but he kept coming. He walked around me as if I were a pole, sniffed me once and then went back and lay in the trail watching the horses. He lay flat on his long belly. His neck, too, was outstretched and he looped his front paws over his nose. About all you could see of him from the front were his big eyes and bulldog ears. Along the side of one eye was an open cut, and where it was still draining was a fly that he kept trying to blink off. The dog lay there watching over us as if we were sheep.

Bill said, "A girl brought him this morning."

"Did she have freckles?" I asked. "Lots," he said.

"She's nice," I volunteered. "She's a hasher down at the Greek's joint. Here's a note she sent you when she thought maybe she couldn't get the dog here in time. She wanted me to be sure you got it."

"Thanks," he said, and stuck the letter in his shirt pocket beside the Bull Durham sack. The dog knew we were talking about him, so he got up and came over and stood by us, ready to be obedient.

Bill was taking only five horses back with him, counting his own saddle horse, Big Moose, and all but one of them, a pack horse, were saddled. I went into the warehouse and got the blanket and saddle and I spent an extra amount of time smoothing the blanket on the horse's back. Finally I said, "She is real nice," and pointed at his shirt pocket.

Bill looked over the saddle and down at me. "She's just a kid," he said. "Why don't you take her out?"

He evidently thought I was wasting time fussing around with the blanket. He picked up the saddle which I had dropped at my feet and he put it on the horse himself.

"How many horses are you packing on the way back?" I asked. He said, "They're all going empty but the 'original.'" I knew then he was going to go fast.

"The original" was a big iron-gray that was faster and tougher than any of the mules. And meaner. Everybody said the reason they called him an original was that one of his testicles had been missed when he was castrated so he wasn't either a gelding or a stallion. You would have thought, though, that he had two or three complete sets. He started chasing mares the moment you took the saddle off him at night, and it didn't seem to make much difference if you hobbled him. He was the only horse I ever saw that could catch and screw a mare with two front feet tied together and only one testicle. After he finished with the mares, he started chasing the geldings. If you were the one to wrangle the horses in the morning, you had to start long before daybreak, because by then you would be lucky to find even one of your string in the state of Idaho.

I went slowly to the warehouse to haul out his packs. I went slowly because I wished I were going back with Bill. Here on the valley floor it was late summer and hot noon. Tonight, they would camp on the divide at Big Sand where it would be deep in autumn. There the needles of the tamaracks had already turned yellow. A delicacy of ice would fringe the lake in the morning. I would be willing to get up and wrangle the horses myself, provided Bill had let me picket the original to a two-ton log the night before. If so, perhaps I might hear again the most beautiful sound that comes through darkness—the sound of a bell mare. Perhaps, too, at daybreak I might see my four-gaited moose steaming beside a lilypad. It is certain that for an hour or two in life I would again be higher than the mountain goats and above nearly all men. And it is certain that, if I weren't dehydrated, I would piss on the state line and wonder where in the world I had flowed.

I set a pack on each side of the original. I don't care what anybody says, it is a great advantage to be a big man if you are a packer. I admit I have seen some fine packers who were middle-sized and some even who were small, but a big man picks up a pack and just pushes it away from him and it's about where he wants it on the saddle and he can work with everything in plain view in front of him. At seventeen I was probably about five foot nine, and had to hoist the pack up on my shoulders and work from underneath, sometimes not seeing the hitches I was tying and also sometimes not finishing my sentences.

"The cook ...," I said, and the pack slipped as I tried to hoist it up on the saddle, and besides I didn't know how to go on.

"He didn't look good this morning," I said, even though I hadn't got a good hold on the pack yet.

"What was the matter?" Bill asked. Bill didn't look too good himself. When he leaned his head back to push the pack up, I could see dried blood in his nose, and his hands were swollen and we packed slowly.

"They rolled him and beat hell out of him," I said. "Did they get all his dough?" Bill asked. "I had to give him money to get to Butte," I told him.

The dog figured we weren't talking about him anymore, so he went back to watching the horses.

"Seven dollars and twenty cents," I said. You could almost hear Bill from the other side of the horse multiplying 170 miles by three cents. "That's enough," he said.

I wanted bad to say one more thing about the cook, but the dog was uncomfortable and got up and circled stiffly and then lay down again. He looked a lot older than when I had seen him last spring. Besides the open cut near his eyes, he had several fresh scars that were also close to his eyes. I thought to myself, "What can you expect if you fight coyotes for a living?" so I didn't say this other thing about the cook for fear I might end up in the same trouble as the dog.

Although Bill was putting a light load on the original, we started to tie it tight together with a diamond hitch, because clearly he was going to travel fast. Bill threw the canvas manty over the load and each of us smoothed out his side of it. Bill asked, tossing the cinch to me under the horse, "What'r you going to do next summer?" Until I heard my answer tremble, I did not know how long I had been waiting for the question. "Nothing yet," I answered.

"Let's tie a double diamond on this last load," he suggested. "Fine," I said. "How would you like to work for me next summer?" he asked.

I went looking for words like "privilege" and "honor" and ended with, "It's a deal."

"It's a deal," he replied. "I'll write you early in the spring."

"When I get here next spring," I said, hidden by my side of the horse, "I'll date that girl with all the freckles."

"She's nice," he said, "real nice."

"I know," I said.

Suddenly I realized I had been scared for a long time, because suddenly I wasn't scared any more. I had been scared ever since I had started getting in trouble with Bill, but didn't dare admit it to myself. I don't believe I was ever afraid he would take a punch at me, because I don't believe I ever thought he would. I was scared because I had to lose something I wanted to be like and yet wanted to keep when the trouble was over.

On our last load of the summer, we threw the double diamond, and Bill was ready to go. He didn't tie his string together—he had picked his best horses, and they would trail each other.

We stood beside Big Moose, his giant saddle horse. We stood close together and never said a word. Then he turned slightly, twisted his stirrup, and with his back to me started a 180-degree swing into the saddle. When he completed his semicircle, he was looking down at me from the sky. From my angle below I could see right up the barrel of his .45 and up his nostrils rimmed with dry blood.

"I'll be seein' you," he said.

"Me, too," I answered, but didn't quite know what I meant.

I let down the bars of the corral, and the moment the outfit was on the road each assumed his own character and collectively all became Bill's string. Big Moose immediately hit his five-mile-an-hour stride; dark brown and mooselike, with head thrown back, he coasted on slipperlike feet. You wouldn't realize he was covering five miles an hour until you noticed that the other horses, except the original, would drop behind when they walked and every now and then had to trot to catch up. The original kicked a horse that got too close. The dog trotted to one side, stopping now and then with raised paw and in his mind clearly protecting the string from all possible attack and any combination of coyotes.

Bill sat twisted in his saddle like the Egyptian bas-relief.

Collectively, Bill's outfit—Bill himself, his favorite saddle horse, his favorite pack horse, and his dog—were about the finest the early Forest Service had to offer.

For a while the road went mostly down the valley and only slightly toward the mountains, and then it took a sudden turn to the left and headed nearly straight for Blodgett Canyon. Bill studied his horses almost to the turn. Then he must have stood up in his stirrups, for suddenly he took off his hat and gave me a big wave, and I stood on the middle rail of the corral and gave him a big wave back. He must have been feeling great. Why not? Maybe for the first time in years the Ranger had got out of a card game while he was still ahead—by $7.20. Although I still was not well, I felt great, too.

I had the promise that I could work for him again. I was only seventeen, and I hoped more than ever that someday I would become a packer.

Then the string swung to the left and trotted in a line toward Blodgett Canyon, with a speck of a dog to the side faithfully keeping always the same distance from the horses. Gradually, the trotting dog and horses became generalized into creeping animals and the one to the side became a speck and those in a line became just a line. Slowly the line disintegrated into pieces and everything floated up and away in dust and all that settled out was one dot, like Morse code. The dot must have been Morse code for a broad back and a black hat. After a while, the sunlight itself became disembodied. There was just nothing at all to sunlight, and the mouth of Blodgett Canyon was just nothing but a gigantic hole in the sky.

"The Big Sky," as we say in Montana.

Although I had no way of knowing it at the time, I was never to cross the Bitterroot Mountains again. When early spring came, I was offered a job for the summer with the engineering department of the Forest Service on a mapping crew that was going to work in the Kootenai Forest. For a long time I wondered why by the spring of 1920 it seemed to me that having a different and more professional job in a different part of the woods was better than working again for Bill Bell, and I think the answer has something to do about my becoming eighteen. I was very conscious of becoming eighteen.

So I was never to see Bill Bell or any of the other men again. Or the girl my age from Darby. When the dot of Morse code disappeared into the sky, another Summer Crew of the United States Forest Service had come and gone forever.

Everything that was to happen had happened and everything that was to be seen had gone. It was now one of those moments when nothing remains but an opening in the sky and a story—and maybe something of a poem. Anyway, as you possibly remember, there are these lines in front of the story:

And then he thinks he knows
The hills where his life rose ...

These words are now part of the story.

David Quammen

Walking Out

As the train rocked dead at Livingston he saw the man, in a worn khaki shirt with button flaps buttoned, arms crossed. The boy's hand sprang up by reflex, and his face broke into a smile. The man smiled back gravely, and nodded. He did not otherwise move. The boy turned from the window and, with the awesome deliberateness of a fat child harboring reluctance, began struggling to pull down his bag. His father would wait on the platform. First sight of him had reminded the boy that nothing was simple enough now for hurrying.

They drove in the old open Willys toward the cabin beyond town. The windshield of the Willys was up, but the fine cold sharp rain came into their faces, and the boy could not raise his eyes to look at the road. He wore a rain parka his father had handed him at the station. The man, protected by only the khaki, held his lips strung in a firm silent line that seemed more grin than wince. Riding through town in the cold rain, open topped and jaunty, getting drenched as though by necessity, was—the boy understood vaguely—somehow in the spirit of this season.

"We have a moose tag," his father shouted.

The boy said nothing. He refused to care what it meant, that they had a moose tag.

"I've got one picked out. A bull. I've stalked him for two weeks. Up in the Crazies. When we get to the cabin, we'll build a good roaring fire." With only the charade of a pause, he added, "Your mother." It was said like a question. The boy waited. "How is she?"

"All right, I guess." Over the jeep's howl, with the wind stealing his voice, the boy too had to shout.

"Are you friends with her?"

"I guess so."

"Is she still a beautiful lady?"

"I don't know. I guess so. I don't know that."

"You must know that. Is she starting to get wrinkled like me? Does she seem worried and sad? Or is she just still a fine beautiful lady? You must know that."

"She's still a beautiful lady, I guess."

"Did she tell you any messages for me?"

"She said . . . she said I should give you her love," the boy lied, impulsively and clumsily. He was at once embarrassed that he had done it.

"Oh," his father said. "Thank you, David."

They reached the cabin on a mile of dirt road winding through meadow to a spruce grove. Inside, the boy was enwrapped in the strong syncretic smell of all seasonal mountain cabins: pine resin and insect repellent and a mustiness suggesting damp bathing trunks stored in a drawer. There were yellow pine floors and rope-work throw rugs and a bead curtain to the bedroom and a cast-iron cook stove with none of the lids or handles missing and a pump in the kitchen sink and old issues of *Field and Stream*, and on the mantel above where a fire now finally burned was a picture of the boy's grandfather, the railroad telegrapher, who had once owned the cabin. The boy's father cooked a dinner of fried ham, and though the boy did not like ham he had expected his father to cook canned stew or Spam, so he said nothing. His father asked him about school and the boy talked and his father seemed to be interested. Warm and dry, the boy began to feel safe from his own anguish. Then his father said:

"We'll leave tomorrow around ten."

Last year on the boy's visit they had hunted birds. They had lived in the cabin for six nights, and each day they had hunted pheasant in the wheat stubble, or blue grouse in the woods, or ducks along the irrigation sloughs. The boy had been wet and cold and miserable at times, but each evening they returned to the cabin and to the boy's suitcase of dry clothes. They had eaten hot food cooked on a stove, and had smelled the cabin smell, and had slept together in a bed. In six days of hunting, the boy had not managed to kill a single bird. Yet last year he had known that, at least once a day, he would be comfortable, if not happy. This year his father planned that he should not even be comfortable. He had said in his last letter to Evergreen Park, before the boy left Chicago but when it was too late for him not to leave, that he would take the boy camping in the mountains, after big game. He had pretended to believe that the boy would be glad.

Last year his father had given him a 16-gauge over-and-under, and on the first morning they had practiced until the boy's shoulder was bruised. He had never before fired a gun. He hit a few coffee cans. Then they walked in the woods after blue grouse, and his father turned quickly, and the boy heard a rustle, and his father fired, and a blue grouse was dead in the bushes.

"Like that," his father said. "They're stupid, and slow. Not like a duck."

His father killed four blue grouse in five shots before he began to touch the boy's elbow and whisper, "There, David," instead of shooting. But the woods were thick and confused with bare alder bushes and everything was the same color and the blue grouse were faster than the boy could lift the gun. The ducks and pheasants were faster than the blue grouse. The boy's aim was not good. Sometimes he fired with his eyes closed, to see if it made any difference. It did not. So he gave up. Long before his father let him stop shooting, the boy had given up.

"It's hard, I know," his father said. "And then it gets easier. Eventually, you'll hit your first bird. You will. Then all of a sudden it gets very easy. But you have to keep trying. Don't close your eyes, David." The boy knew his father was lying. His father often said things were easy, when the boy knew they were not.

Then the boy hit his first grouse. The boy did not know whether he had hit it or not, but his father said that he had. He had hit it in the wing, and it faltered, and dropped. They went to the spot and searched the brush and the ground for an hour. Even his father could not find the crippled grouse, and they did not have a dog. The boy's father would not own a hunting dog. He had said that, since he was already alone, he did not want to give that much love to a creature who would only live fourteen or fifteen years. The bird must have run off and hidden itself to die, his father said.

The boy was disappointed at not finding the grouse. But his father, the boy could see, was even more disappointed. An hour seemed a very long time to keep looking.

"Just too bad we couldn't find that blue grouse you killed," his father had said at the station, when the boy left, and the boy was embarrassed. He understood how his father felt. So he had agreed to come back for hunting this year. His father did not mean to make everything difficult for the boy. He couldn't help it.

Now a deer or a moose would be a much bigger target than a blue grouse. But a deer is not slow, the boy knew, and is probably not stupid, he thought. He knew nothing about a moose except that it was stupid-looking. The boy wished again that they could have found the blue grouse he may have wounded last year, found it dead, and eaten it roasted in butter as they had the birds his father killed. That would have made a great difference to the boy now.

They would leave around ten the next day for the Crazy Mountains. The boy slept on the far edge of the bed, and did not let himself touch up against his father's warm body.

Then there was nothing, then more cold, and then the faint steady gray light of November dawn. The boy's father was up, and the stove was already making its warm noises. After breakfast they sighted in the boy's gun. They set up coffee cans on a fence in the meadow, and the boy hit a few. The rain had paused, so the boy was only drenched from the thighs down.

This year his father gave him a different gun. It was a lever-action

Winchester .30-30, with open sights. It was a simple gun. It was older than the over-and-under, and it was probably a better gun, the boy could see, and it was certainly heavier and more powerful. This was just like the rifle with which he had killed his own first moose, when he was thirteen, the boy's father said. This was not the same rifle, but it was just like it. The boy's grandfather, the railroad telegrapher, had given him that gun. A boy should learn how to shoot with open sights, his father said, before he learns to depend on a telescope.

The Willys was loaded and moving by ten minutes to ten. For three hours they drove, through Big Timber, and then north on the highway, and then back west again on a logging road that took them winding and bouncing higher into the mountains. Thick cottony streaks of white cloud hung in among the mountain-top trees, light and dense dollops against the bulking sharp dark olive, as though in a black-and-white photograph. They followed the gravel road for an hour, and the boy thought they would soon have a flat tire or break an axle. If they had a flat, the boy knew, his father would only change it and drive on until they had the second, farther from the highway. Finally they crossed a creek and his father plunged the Willys off into a bed of weeds.

His father said, "Here."

The boy said, "Where?"

"Up that little drainage. At the head of the creek."

"How far is it?"

"Two or three miles."

"Is that where you saw the moose?"

"No. That's where I saw the sheepman's hut. The moose is farther. On top."

"Are we going to sleep in a hut? I thought we were going to sleep in a tent."

"No. Why should we carry a tent up there when we have a perfectly good hut?"

The boy couldn't answer that question. He thought now that this might be the time when he would cry. He had known it was coming.

"I don't much want to sleep in a hut," he said, and his voice broke with the simple honesty of it, and his eyes glazed. He held his mouth tight against the trembling.

As though something had broken in him too, the boy's father laid his forehead down on the steering wheel, against his knuckles. For a moment he remained bowed, breathing exhaustedly. But he looked up again before speaking.

"Well, we don't have to, David."

The boy said nothing.

"It's an old sheepman's hut made of logs, and it's near where we're going to hunt, and we can fix it dry and good. I thought you might like that. I thought it might be more fun then a tent. But we don't have to do it. We can drive back to Big Timber and buy a tent, or we can drive back to the cabin and hunt birds, like last year. Whatever you want to do. You have to forgive me the kind of ideas I get. I hope you will. We don't have to do anything that you don't want to do."

"No," the boy said. "I want to."

"Are you sure?"

"No," the boy said. "But I just want to."

They bushwhacked along the creek, treading a thick soft mixture of moss and humus and needles, climbing upward through brush. Then the brush thinned and they were ascending an open creek bottom, thirty yards wide, darkened by fir and cedar. Farther, and they struck a trail, which led them upward along the creek. Farther still, and the trail received a branch, then another, then forked.

"Who made this trail? Did the sheepman?"

"No," his father said. "Deer and elk."

Gradually the creek's little canyon narrowed, steep wooded shoulders funneling closer on each side. For a while the game trails forked and converged like a maze, but soon again there were only two branches, and finally one, heavily worn. It dodged through alder and willow, skirting tangles of browned raspberry, so that the boy and his father could never see more than twenty feet ahead. When they stopped to rest, the boy's father unstrapped the .270 from his pack and loaded it.

"We have to be careful now," he explained. "We may surprise a bear."

Under the cedars, the creek bottom held a cool dampness that seemed to be stored from one winter to the next. The boy began at once to feel chilled. He put on his jacket, and they continued climbing. Soon he was sweating again in the cold.

On a small flat where the alder drew back from the creek, the hut was built into one bank of the canyon, with the sod of the hillside lapping out over its roof. The door was a low dark opening. Forty or fifty years ago, the boy's father explained, this hut had been built and used by a Basque shepherd. At that time there had been many Basques in Montana, and they had run sheep all across this ridge of the Crazies. His father forgot to explain what a Basque was, and the boy didn't remind him.

They built a fire. His father had brought sirloin steaks and an onion for dinner, and the boy was happy with him about that. As they ate, it grew dark, but the boy and his father had stocked a large comforting pile of naked deadfall. In the darkness, by firelight, his father made chocolate pudding. The pudding had been his father's surprise. The boy sat on a piece of canvas and added logs to the fire while his father drank coffee. Sparks rose on the heat and the boy watched them climb toward the cedar limbs and the black pools of sky. The pudding did not set.

"Do you remember your grandfather, David?"

"Yes," the boy said, and wished it were true. He remembered a funeral when he was three.

"Your grandfather brought me up on this mountain when I was seventeen. That was the last year he hunted." The boy knew what sort of thoughts his father was having. But he knew also that his own home was in Evergreen Park, and that he was another man's boy now, with another man's name, though this indeed was his father. "Your grandfather was fifty years older than me."

The boy said nothing.

"And I'm thirty-four years older than you."

"And I'm only eleven," the boy cautioned him.

"Yes," said his father. "And someday you'll have a son and you'll be forty years older than him, and you'll want so badly for him to know who you are that you could cry."

The boy was embarrassed.

"And that's called the cycle of life's infinite wisdom," his father said, and laughed at himself unpleasantly.

"Why didn't he?" the boy asked, to escape the focus of his father's rumination.

"Why didn't who what?"

"Why was it the last year he hunted?"

"He was sixty-seven years old," his father said. "But that wasn't the reason. Because he was still walking to work at the railroad office in Big Timber when he was seventy-five. I don't know. We took a bull elk and a goat that year, I remember. The goat was during spring season and every inch of its hide was covered with ticks. I carried it down whole and after a mile I was covered with ticks too. I never shot another goat. I don't know why he quit. He still went out after birds in the wheat stubble, by himself. So it's not true that he stopped hunting completely. He stopped hunting with me. And he stopped killing. Once in every five or six times he would bring back a pheasant, if it seemed like a particularly good autumn night to have pheasant for supper. Usually he just went out and missed every shot on purpose. There were plenty of birds in the fields where he was walking, and your grandmother or I would hear his gun fire, at least once. But I guess when a man feels himself getting old, almost as old as he thinks he will ever be, he doesn't much want to be killing things anymore. I guess you might have to kill one bird in every ten or twenty, or the pheasants might lose their respect for you. They might tame out. Your grandfather had no desire to live among tame pheasants, I'm sure. But I suppose you would get a little reluctant, when you came to be seventy, about doing your duty toward keeping them wild. And he would not hunt with me anymore then, not even pheasants, not even to miss them. He said it was because he didn't trust himself with a partner, now that his hands were unsteady. But his hands were still steady. He said it was because I was too good. That he had taught me as well as he knew how, and that all I could learn from him now would be the bad habits of age, and those I would find for myself, in my turn. He never did tell me the real reason."

"What did he die of?"

"He was eighty-seven then," said his father. "Christ. He was tired."

The boy's question had been a disruption. His father was silent. Then he shook his head, and poured himself the remaining coffee. He did not like to think of the boy's grandfather as an eighty-seven-year-old man, the boy understood. As long as his grandfather was dead anyway, his father preferred thinking of him younger.

"I remember when I got my first moose," he said. "I was thirteen. I had never shot anything bigger than an owl. And I caught holy hell for killing that owl. I had my Winchester .30-30, like the one you're using. He gave it to me that year, at the start of the season. It was an old-looking gun even then. I don't know where he got it. We had a moose that he had stalked the year before, in a long swampy cottonwood flat along the Yellowstone River. It was a big cow, and this year she had a calf.

"We went there on the first day of the season and every hunting day for a week, and hunted down the length of that river flat, spaced apart about twenty yards, and came out at the bottom end. We saw fresh tracks every day, but we never got a look at that moose and the calf. It was only a matter of time, my father told me, before we would jump her. Then that Sunday we drove out and before he had the truck parked my hands were shaking. I knew it was that day. There was no reason why, yet I had such a sure feeling it was that day, my hands had begun shaking. He noticed, and he said: 'Don't worry.'

"I said: 'I'm fine.' And my voice was steady. It was just my hands.

"'I can see that,' he said. 'But you'll do what you need to do.'

"'Yessir,' I said. 'Let's go hunting.'

"That day he put me up at the head end of our cottonwood flat and said he would walk down along the river bank to the bottom, and then turn in. We would come at the moose from both ends and meet in the middle and I should please not shoot my father when he came in sight. I should try to remember, he said, that he was the uglier one, in the orange hat. The shaking had left me as soon as we started walking, holding our guns. I remember it all. Before he went off I said: 'What does a moose look like?'

"'What the hell do you mean, what does a moose look like?'

"'Yes, I know,' I said. 'I mean, what is he gonna do when I see him? When he sees me. What color is he? What kind of thing is he gonna do?'

"And he said: 'All right. She will be black. She will be almost pitch black. She will not look to you very much bigger than our pickup. She is going to be stupid. She will let you get close. Slide right up to within thirty or forty yards if you can and set yourself up for a good shot. She will probably not see you, and if she does, she will probably not care. If you miss the first time, which you have every right to do, I don't care how close you get, if you miss the first time, she may even give you another. If you catch her attention, she may bolt off to me or she may charge you. Watch out for the calf when you come up on her. Worry her over the calf, and she will be mad. If she charges you, stand where you are and squeeze off another and then jump the hell out of the way. We probably won't even see her. All right?'

"I had walked about three hundred yards before I saw what I thought was a Holstein. It was off to my left, away from the river, and I looked over there and saw black and white and kept walking til I was just about past it. There were cattle pastured along in that flat but they would have been beef cattle, Herefords, brown and white like a deer. I didn't think about that. I went on looking everywhere else until I glanced over again when I was abreast and saw I was walking along sixty yards from a grazing moose. I stopped. My heart started pumping so hard that it seemed like I might black out, and I didn't know what was going to happen. I thought the moose would take care of that. Nothing happened.

"Next thing I was running. Running flat out as fast as I could, bent over double like a soldier would do in the field, running as fast but as quietly as I could. Running right at that moose. I remember clearly that I was not thinking anything at all, not for those first seconds. My body just started to run. I never thought, Now I'll scoot up to within thirty yards of her. I was just charging blind, like a moose or a sow grizzly is liable to charge you if you get her mad or confused. Who knows what I would have done. I wanted a moose pretty badly, I thought. I might have galloped right up to within five yards before I leveled, if it hadn't been for that spring creek.

"I didn't see it till I was in the air. I came up a little hillock and jumped, and then it was too late. The hillock turned out to be one bank of a spring-fed pasture seepage, about fifteen feet wide. I landed up to my thighs in mud. It was a prime cattle wallow, right where I had jumped. I must have spent five minutes sweating my legs out of that muck, I was furious with myself, and I was sure the moose would be gone. But the moose was still grazing the same three feet of grass. And by that time I had some of my sense back.

"I climbed the far bank of the mudhole and lay up along the rise where I could steady my aim on the ground. From there I had an open shot of less than forty yards, but the moose was now facing me head on, so I would probably either kill her clean or miss her altogether. My hands started shaking again. I tried to line up the bead and it was ridiculous. My rifle was waving all over that end of the woods. For ten minutes I lay there struggling to control my aim, squeezing the rifle tighter and tighter and taking deeper breaths and holding them longer. Finally I did a smart thing. I set the rifle down. I rolled over on my back and rubbed my eyes and discovered that I was exhausted. I got my breath settled back down in rhythm again. If I could just take that moose, I thought, I was not going to want anything else for a year. But I knew I was not going to do it unless I could get my hands to obey me, no matter how close I was. I tried it again. I remembered to keep breathing easy and low and it was a little better but the rifle was still moving everywhere. When it seemed like the trembling was about to start getting worse all over again I waited till the sights next crossed the moose and jerked off a shot. I missed. The moose didn't even look up.

"Now I was calmer. I had heard the gun fire once, and I knew my father had heard it, and I knew the moose would only give me one more. I realized that there was a good chance I would not get this moose at all, so I was more serious, and humble. This time I squeezed. I knocked a piece off her right antler and before I thought to wonder why a female should have any antlers to get shot at she raised her head up and gave a honk like eleven elephants in a circus-train fire. She started to run.

"I got off my belly and dropped the gun and turned around and jumped right back down into that mud. I was still stuck there when I heard her crash by on her way to the river, and then my father's shot.

"But I had wallowed myself out again, and got my rifle up off the ground, by the time he found me, thank God. He took a look at my clothes and said:

"'Tried to burrow up under him, did you?'

"'No sir. I heard you fire once. Did you get her?'

"'Him. That was no cow and calf. That was a bull. No. No more than you.'

"He had been at the river edge about a hundred yards down-stream from where the bull broke out. He took his shot while the bull was crossing the gravel bed and the shallows. The moose clambered right out into midstream of the Yellowstone and started swimming for his life. But the current along there was heavy. So the moose was swept down abreast with my father before he got halfway across toward the opposite shore. My father sighted on him as he rafted by, dog-paddling frantically and staying afloat and inching slowly away. The moose turned and looked at him, my father said. He had a chunk broken out of one antler and it was dangling down by a few fibers and he looked terrified. He was not more than twenty yards off shore by then and he could see my father and the raised rifle. My father said he had never seen more personality come into the face of a wild animal. All right, my father said the moose told him, Do what you will do. They both knew the moose was helpless. They both also knew this: my father could kill the moose, but he couldn't have him. The Yellowstone River would have him. My father lowered the gun. When he did, my father claimed, the moose turned his head forward again and went on swimming harder than ever. So that wasn't the day I shot mine.

"I shot mine the next Saturday. We went back to the cotton-wood flat and split again and I walked up to within thirty yards of

the cow and her calf. I made a standing shot, and killed the cow
with one bullet breaking her spine. She was drinking, broadside to
me. She dropped dead on the spot. The calf didn't move. He stood
over the dead cow, stupid, wondering what in the world to do.

"The calf was big as a four-point buck. When my father came
up, he found me with tears flooding all over my face, screaming at
the calf and trying to shoo him away. I was pushing against his
flanks and swatting him and shouting at him to run off. At the sight
of my father, he finally bolted.

"I had shot down the cow while she stood in the same spring
seep where I had been stuck. Her quarters weighed out to eight
hundred pounds and we couldn't budge her. We had to clean her
and quarter her right there in the water and mud."

His father checked the tin pot again, to be sure there was no
more coffee.

"Why did you tell me that story?" the boy said. "Now I don't
want to shoot a moose either."

"I know," said his father. "And when you do, I hope you'll be
sad too. But the other thing about a moose is, she makes eight
hundred pounds of delicious meat. In fact, David, that's what we
had for supper."

Through that night the boy was never quite warm. He slept on
his side with his knees drawn up, and this was uncomfortable but
his body seemed to demand it for warmth. The hard cold
mountain earth pressed upward through the mat of fir boughs his
father had laid, and drew heat from the boy's body like a pallet of
leeches. He clutched the bedroll around his neck and folded the
empty part at the bottom back under his legs. Once he woke to a
noise. Though his father was sleeping between him and the door of
the hut, for a while the boy lay awake, listening worriedly, and
then woke again on his back to realize time had passed. He heard
droplets begin to hit the canvas his father had spread over the sod
roof of the hut. But he remained dry.

He rose to the smell of a fire. The tarp was rigid with sleet and
frost. The firewood and knapsacks were frosted. It was that gray
time of dawn before any blue and, through the branches above, the
boy was unable to tell whether the sky was murky or clear.

Delicate sheet ice hung on everything, but there was no wetness. The rain seemed to have been hushed by the cold.

"What time is it?"

"Early yet."

"How early?" The boy was thinking about the cold at home as he waited outside on 96th Street for his school bus. That was the cruelest moment of his day, but it seemed a benign and familiar part of him compared to this.

"Early. I don't have a watch. What difference does it make, David?"

"Not any."

After breakfast they began walking up the valley. His father had the .270 and the boy carried the old Winchester .30-30. The walking was not hard, and with this gentle exercise in the cold morning the boy soon felt fresh and fine. Now I'm hunting for moose with my father, he told himself. That's just what I'm doing. Few boys in Evergreen Park had ever been moose hunting with their fathers in Montana, he knew. I'm doing it now, the boy told himself.

Reaching the lip of a high meadow, a mile above the shepherd's hut, they had not seen so much as a magpie.

Before them, across hundreds of yards, opened a smooth lake of tall lifeless grass, browned by September drought and killed by the frosts and beginning to rot with November's rain. The creek was here a deep quiet channel of smooth curves overhung by the grass, with a dark surface like heavy oil. When they had come fifty yards into the meadow, his father turned and pointed out to the boy a large ponderosa pine with a forked crown that marked the head of their creek valley. He showed the boy a small aspen grove midway across the meadow, toward which they were aligning themselves.

"Near the far woods is a beaver pond. The moose waters there. We can wait in the aspens and watch the whole meadow without being seen. If he doesn't come, we'll go up another canyon, and check again on the way back."

For an hour, and another, they waited. The boy sat, and his buttocks drew cold moisture from the ground. He bunched his jacket around him with hands in the pockets. He was patient. His father squatted on his heels like a country man. Periodically, his father rose and inspected the meadow in all directions.

"He comes once in the morning, and again in the evening, I think. It looked from the tracks like he comes at least twice a day. But he may not show up for hours. You can't tell. If you could, it wouldn't be hunting. It would be shopping.

"He may even know that this is the last week of season. He may remember. So he'll be especially on his guard, and go somewhere else to drink. Somewhere less open." They waited in silence.

"But he may not be all that clever," his father added. "He may make a mistake."

The morning passed, and it was noon.

His father stood. He fixed his stare on the distant meadow, and like a retriever did not move. His said: "David."

The boy stood beside him. He father placed a hand on the boy's shoulder. The boy saw a large dark form rolling toward them like a great slug in the grass.

"Is it the moose?"

"No," said his father. "That is a grizzly bear, David. An old male grizzly."

The boy was impressed. He sensed an aura of power and terror and authority about the husky shape, even at two hundred yards.

"Are we going to shoot him?"

"No."

"Why not?"

"We don't have a permit," his father whispered. "And because we don't want to."

The bear plowed on toward the beaver pond for a while, then stopped. It froze in the grass and seemed to be listening. The boy's father added: "That's not hunting for the meat. That's hunting for the fear. I don't need the fear. I've got enough in my life already."

The bear turned and moiled off quickly through the grass. It disappeared back into the far woods.

"He heard us."

"Maybe," the boy's father said. "Let's go have a look at that beaver pond."

A sleek furred body lay low in the water. The boy thought at first it was a large beaver. It was too large. His father moved quickly ahead off the trail and said nothing. The boy saw that his father was not concerned to surprise it.

The carcass was swollen grotesquely with water and putrescence, and coated with glistening blowflies. His father did not touch it. Four days, his father guessed. He stood up to his knees in the sump. The moose had been shot at least eighteen times with a .22 pistol. One of its eyes had been shot out, and it had been shot twice in the jaw. Both of the quarters on the side that lay upward had been ruined with shots. The boy's father took the trouble of counting the holes in that side of the carcass, and probing one of the slugs out with his knife. It only made him angrier. He flung the lead away.

Nearby in the fresh mud was the lid from a can of wintergreen chewing tobacco.

For the next three hours, with his father withdrawn into a solitary and characteristic bitterness, the boy felt abandoned. He did not understand why a moose would be slaughtered with a light pistol and left to rot. His father did not bother to explain; like the bear, he seemed to understand it as well as he needed to. They walked on, but they did not really hunt.

They left the meadow for more pine, and now tamarack, naked tamarack, the yellow needles nearly all down and going ginger where they coated the trail. The boy and his father hiked along a level path into another canyon, this one vast at the mouth and narrowing between high ridges of bare rock. They crossed and re-crossed the shepherd's creek, which in this canyon was a tumbling free-stone brook. The boy was miserably uneasy because his father had grown so quiet.

The boy's father tortured him when he spoke at the boy obscurely, both of them knowing that the boy could not hope to understand him, and that his father did not really care whether he did. But the boy preferred even that to his silences.

They wandered forward, deeper into the rock canyon, the boy following five yards behind his father, watching the cold, unapproachable rage that shaped the line of his father's shoulders. They climbed over deadfalls blocking the trail, skirted one boulder large as a cabin, and blundered into a garden of nettles that stung them fiercely through their trousers. They saw fresh elk scat, and bear, diarrhetic with late berries. The boy's father eventually grew bored with brooding. He showed the boy how to stalk. Before dusk that day they had shot an elk.

An open and gently sloped hillside, almost a meadow, ran for a quarter mile in quaking aspen, none over fifteen feet tall. The elk was above. The boy's father had the boy brace his gun in the notch of an aspen and gave him the first shot. The boy missed. The elk reeled and bolted down and his father killed it before it made cover. It was a five-point bull.

His father showed the boy how to approach a downed animal: from behind, so he could not lash out with his hooves. Get hold of his rack, in case he's not dead, the boy's father explained; reach forward and hook your fingers into the nostrils, he said; and then, suddenly, to the boy's utter shock, his father slit the elk's throat. The boy gagged.

They dressed the elk out and dragged it down the hill to the cover of large pines, near the stream. When they quartered the animal tomorrow, his father said, they would want water. They covered the body with fresh branches, and returned to the hut under twilight. The boy's father was satisfied and the boy was relieved. Again that evening, his father talked.

He talked about the former railroad telegrapher of Big Timber, Montana. He told of going to the station at 6:00 a.m. on school days to find the boy's grandfather bent forward and dozing over the key. He told of walking the old man back home for breakfast, and of his predictable insistence, against all fact, that the night had been busy, full of transmissions. He described how the boy's grandfather became subject to chronic, almost narcoleptic drowsiness after the boy's grandmother, still a young middle-aged woman, checked into the hospital for the last time and began dying. Then, until it faded to embers and the embers went gray, the boy's father stared at his memories, in the fire.

That night even the fetal position could not keep the boy warm. He shivered wakefully for hours. He was glad that the following day, though full of walking and butchery and oppressive burdens, would be their last in the woods. He heard nothing. When he woke, through the door of the hut he saw whiteness like bone.

Six inches had fallen, and it was still snowing. The boy stood about in the campsite, amazed. When it snowed three inches in Evergreen Park, the boy would wake before dawn to the hiss of sand trucks and the ratchet of chains. Here there had been no warning. The boy was not much colder than he had been yesterday, and the transformation of the woods seemed mysterious and benign and somehow comic. He thought of Christmas. Then his father barked at him.

His father's mood had also changed, but in a different way; he seemed serious and hurried. As he wiped the breakfast pots clean with snow, he gave the boy orders for other chores. They left camp with two empty pack frames, both rifles, and a handsaw and rope. The boy soon understood why his father felt pressure of time: it took them an hour to climb the mile to the meadow. The snow continued. They did not rest until they reached the aspens.

"I had half a mind at breakfast to let the bull lie and pack us straight down out of here," his father admitted. "Probably smarter and less trouble in the long run. I could have come back on snow-shoes next week. But by then it might be three feet deep and starting to drift. We can get two quarters out today. That will make it easier for me later." The boy was surprised by two things: that his father would be so wary in the face of a gentle snowfall and that he himself would have felt disappointed to be taken out of the woods that morning. The air of the meadow teemed with white.

"If it stops soon, we're fine," said his father.

It continued.

The path up the far canyon was hard climbing in eight inches of snow. The boy fell once, filling his collar and sleeves, and the gun-sight put a small gouge in his chin. But he was not discouraged. That night they would be warm and dry at the cabin. A half mile on and he came up beside his father, who had stopped to stare down at dark splashes of blood.

Heavy tracks and a dragging belly mark led up to the scramble of deepening red, and away. The tracks were nine inches long and showed claws. The boy's father knelt. As the boy watched, one shining maroon splotch the size of a saucer sank slowly beyond sight into the snow. The blood was warm.

Inspecting the tracks carefully, his father said, "She's got a cub with her."

"What happened?"

"Just a kill. Seems to have been a bird. That's too much blood for a grouse, but I don't see any signs of any four-footed creature. Maybe a turkey." He frowned thoughtfully. "A turkey without feathers. I don't know. What I dislike is coming up on her with a cub." He drove a round into the chamber of the .270.

Trailing red smears, the tracks preceded them. Within fifty feet they found the body. It was half-buried. The top of its head had been shorn away, and the cub's brains had been licked out.

His father said, "Christ," and plunged off the trail. He snapped at the boy to follow closely.

They made a wide crescent through brush and struck back after a quarter mile. His Father slogged ahead in the snow, stopping often to stand holding his gun ready and glancing around while the boy caught up and passed him. The boy was confused. He knew his father was worried, but he did not feel any danger himself. They met the trail again, and went on to the aspen hillside before his father allowed them to rest. The boy spat on the snow. His lungs ached badly.

"Why did she do that?"

"She didn't. Another bear got her cub. A male. Maybe the one we saw yesterday. Then she fought him for the body, and she won. We didn't miss them by much. She may even have been watching. Nothing could put her in a worse frame of mind."

He added: "If we so much as see her, I want you to pick the nearest big tree and start climbing. Don't stop till you're twenty feet off the ground. I'll stay down and decide whether we have to shoot her. Is your rifle cocked?"

"No."

"Cock it, and put on the safety. She may be a black bear and black bears can climb. If she comes up after you, lean down and stick your gun in her mouth and fire. You can't miss."

He cocked the Winchester, as his father had said.

They angled downhill to the stream, and on to the mound of their dead elk. Snow filtered down steadily in purposeful silence. The boy was thirsty. It could not be much below freezing, he was aware, because with the exercise his bare hands were comfortable, even sweating between the fingers.

"Can I get a drink?"

"Yes. Be careful you don't wet your feet. And don't wander anywhere. We're going to get this done quickly."

He walked the few yards, ducked through the brush at streamside, and knelt in the snow to drink. The water was painful to his sinuses and bitterly cold on his hands. Standing again, he noticed an animal body ahead near the stream bank. For a moment he felt sure it was another dead cub. During that moment his father called:

"David! Get up here right now!"

The boy meant to call back. First he stepped closer to turn the cub with his foot. The touch brought it alive. It rose suddenly with a high squealing growl and whirled its head like a snake and snapped. The boy shrieked. The cub had his right hand in its jaws. It would not release.

It thrashed senselessly, working its teeth deeper and tearing flesh with each movement. The boy felt no pain. He knew his hand was being damaged and that realization terrified him and he was desperate to get the hand back before it was ruined. But he was helpless. He sensed the same furious terror racking the cub that he felt in himself, and he screamed at the cub almost reasoningly to let him go. His screams scared the cub more. Its head snatched back and forth. The boy did not think to shout for his father. He did not see him or hear him coming.

His father moved at full stride in a slowed laboring run through the snow, saying nothing and holding the rifle he did not use, crossed the last six feet still gathering speed, and brought his right boot up into the cub's belly. That kick seemed to lift the cub clear of the snow. It opened its jaws to another shrill piggish squeal, and the boy felt dull relief on his hand, as though his father had pressed open the blades of a spring trap with his foot. The cub tumbled once and disappeared over the stream bank, then surfaced downstream, squalling and paddling. The boy looked at his hand and was horrified. He still had no pain, but the hand was unrecognizable. His fingers had been peeled down through the palm like flaps on a banana. Glands at the sides of his jaw threatened that he would vomit, and he might have stood stupidly watching the hand bleed if his father had not grabbed him.

He snatched the boy by the arm and dragged him toward a tree without even looking at the boy's hand. The boy jerked back in angry resistance as though he had been struck. He screamed at his father. He screamed that his hand was cut, believing his father did not know, and as he screamed he began to cry. He began to feel hot throbbing pain. He began to worry about the blood he was losing. He could imagine his blood melting red holes in the snow behind him and he did not want to look. He did not want to do anything until he had taken care of his hand. At that instant he hated his father. But his father was stronger. He all but carried the boy to a tree.

He lifted the boy. In a voice that was quiet and hurried and very unlike the harsh grip with which he had taken the boy's arm, he said:

"Grab hold and climb up a few branches as best you can. Sit on a limb and hold tight and clamp the hand under your other armpit, if you can do that. I'll be right back to you. Hold tight because you're going to get dizzy." The boy groped desperately for a branch. His father supported him from beneath, and waited. The boy clambered. His feet scraped at the trunk. Then he was in the tree. Bark flakes and resin were stuck to the raw naked meat of his right hand. His father said:

"Now here, take this. Hurry."

The boy never knew whether his father himself had been frightened enough to forget for that moment about the boy's hand or whether his father was still thinking quite clearly. His father may have expected that much. By the merciless clarity of his own standards, he may have expected that the boy should be able to hold onto a tree, and a wound, and a rifle, all with one hand. He extended the stock of the Winchester toward the boy.

The boy wanted to say something, but his tears and his fright would not let him gather a breath. He shuddered, and could not speak. "David," his father urged. The boy reached for the stock and faltered and clutched at the trunk with his good arm. He was crying and gasping, and he wanted to speak. He was afraid he would fall out of the tree. He released his grip once again, and felt himself tip. His father extended the gun higher, holding the barrel. The boy swung out his injured hand, spraying his father's face with blood. He reached and he tried to close torn dangling fingers around the stock and he pulled the trigger.

The bullet entered low on his father's thigh and shattered the knee and traveled down the shin bone and into the ground through his father's heel.

His father fell, and the rifle fell with him. He lay in the snow without moving. The boy thought he was dead. Then the boy saw him grope for the rifle. He found it and rolled onto his stomach, taking aim at the sow grizzly. Forty feet up the hill, towering on hind legs, she canted her head to one side, indecisive. When the cub pulled itself up a snowbank from the stream, she coughed at it sternly. The cub trotted straight to her with its head low. She knocked it off its feet with a huge paw, and it yelped. Then she turned quickly. The cub followed.

The woods were silent. The gunshot still echoed awesomely back to the boy but it was an echo of memory, not sound. He felt nothing. He saw his father's body stretched on the snow and he did not really believe he was where he was. He did not want to move: he wanted to wake. He sat in the tree and waited. The snow fell as gracefully as before.

His father rolled onto his back. The boy saw him raise himself to a sitting position and look down at the leg and betray no expression, and then slump back. He blinked slowly and lifted his eyes to meet the boy's eyes. The boy waited. He expected his father to speak. He expected his father to say *Shinny down using your elbows and knees and get the first-aid kit and boil water and phone the doctor. The number is taped to the dial.* His father stared. The boy could see the flicker of thoughts behind his father's eyes. His father said nothing. He raised his arms slowly and crossed them over his face, as though to nap in the sun.

The boy jumped. He landed hard on his feet and fell onto his back. He stood over his father. His hand dripped quietly onto the snow. He was afraid that his father was deciding to die. He wanted to beg him to reconsider. The boy had never before seen his father hopeless. He was afraid.

But he was no longer afraid of his father.

Then his father uncovered his face and said, "Let me see it."

They bandaged the boy's hand with a sleeve cut from the other arm of his shirt. His father wrapped the hand firmly and split the sleeve end with his deer knife and tied it neatly in two places. The boy now felt searing pain in his torn palm, and his stomach lifted when he thought of the damage, but at least he did not have to look at it. Quickly the plaid flannel bandage began to soak through maroon. They cut a sleeve from his father's shirt to tie over the wound in his thigh. They raised the trouser leg to see the long swelling bruise down the calf where he was hemorrhaging into the bullet's tunnel. Only then did his father realize that he was bleeding also from the heel. The boy took off his father's boot and placed a half-clean handkerchief on the insole where the bullet had exited, as his father instructed him. Then his father laced the boot on again tightly. The boy helped his father to stand. His father tried a step, then collapsed in the snow with a blasphemous howl of pain. They had not known that the knee was shattered.

The boy watched his father's chest heave with the forced sighs of suffocating frustration, and heard the air wheeze through his nostrils. His father relaxed himself with the breathing, and seemed to be thinking. He said,

"You can find your way back to the hut."

The boy held his own breath and did not move.

"You can, can't you?"

"But I'm not. I'm not going alone. I'm only going with you."

"All right, David, listen carefully," his father said. "We don't have to worry about freezing. I'm not worried about either of us freezing to death. No one is going to freeze in the woods in November, if he looks after himself. Not even in Montana. It just isn't that cold. I have matches and I have a fresh elk. And I don't think this weather is going to get any worse. It may be raining again by morning. What I'm concerned about is the bleeding. If I spend too much time and effort trying to walk out of here, I could bleed to death.

"I think your hand is going to be all right. It's a bad wound, but the doctors will be able to fix it as good as new. I can see that. I promise you that. You'll be bleeding some too, but if you take care of that hand, it won't bleed any more walking than if you were standing still. Then you'll be at the doctor's tonight. But if I try to walk out on this leg it's going to bleed and keep bleeding and I'll lose too much blood. So I'm staying here and bundling up warm and you're walking out to get help. I'm sorry about this. It's what we have to do.

"You can't possibly get lost. You'll just follow this trail straight down the canyon the way we came up, and then you'll come to the meadow. Point yourself toward the big pine tree with the forked crown. When you get to that tree you'll find the creek again. You may not be able to see it, but make yourself quiet and listen for it. You'll hear it. Follow that down off the mountain and past the hut till you get to the jeep."

He struggled a hand into his pocket. "You've never driven a car, have you?"

The boy's lips were pinched. Muscles in his cheeks ached from clenching his jaws. He shook his head.

"You can do it. It isn't difficult." His father held up a single key and began telling the boy how to start the jeep, how to work the clutch, how to find reverse and then first and then second. As his father described the positions on the floor shift the boy raised his swaddled right hand. His father stopped. He rubbed at his eye sockets, like a man waking.

"Of course," he said. "All right. You'll have to help me."

Using the saw with his left hand, the boy cut a small forked aspen. His father showed the boy where to trim it so that the fork would reach just to his armpit. Then they lifted him to his feet. But the crutch was useless on a steep hillside of deep grass and snow. His father leaned over the boy's shoulders and they fought the slope for an hour.

When the boy stepped in a hole and they fell, his father made no exclamation of pain. The boy wondered whether his father's knee hurt as badly as his own hand. He suspected it hurt worse. He said nothing about his hand, though several times in their climb it was twisted or crushed. They reached the trail. The snow had not stopped, and their tracks were veiled. His father said:

"We need one of the guns. I forgot. It's my fault. But you'll have to go back down and get it."

The boy could not find the tree against which his father said he had leaned the .270, so he went toward the stream and looked for blood. He saw none. The imprint of his father's body was already softened beneath an inch of fresh silence. He scooped his good hand through the snowy depression and was startled by cool slimy blood, smearing his fingers like phlegm. Nearby he found the Winchester.

"The lucky one," his father said. "That's all right. Here." He snapped open the breach and a shell flew and he caught it in the air. He glanced dourly at the casing, then cast it aside in the snow. He held the gun out for the boy to see, and with his thumb let the hammer down one notch.

"Remember?" he said. "The safety."

The boy knew he was supposed to feel great shame, but he felt little. His father could no longer hurt him as he once could, because the boy was coming to understand him. His father could not help himself. He did not want the boy to feel contemptible, but he needed him to, because of the loneliness and the bitterness and the boy's mother; and he could not help himself.

After another hour they had barely traversed the aspen hillside. Pushing the crutch away in angry frustration, his father sat in the snow. The boy did not know whether he was thinking carefully of how they might get him out, or still laboring with the choice against despair. The light had wilted to something more like moonlight than afternoon. The sweep of snow had gone gray, depthless, flat, and the sky warned sullenly of night. The boy grew restless. Then it was decided. His father hung himself piggyback over the boy's shoulders, holding the rifle. The boy supported him with elbows crooked under his father's knees. The boy was tall for eleven years old, and heavy. The boy's father weighed 164 pounds.

The boy walked.

He moved as slowly as drifting snow: a step, then time, then another step. The burden at first seemed to him overwhelming. He did not think he would be able to carry his father far.

He took the first few paces expecting to fall. He did not fall, so he kept walking. His arms and shoulders were not exhausted as quickly as he thought they would be, so he kept walking. Shuffling ahead in the deep powder was like carrying one end of an oak bureau up stairs. But for a surprisingly long time the burden did not grow any worse. He found balance. He found rhythm. He was moving.

Dark blurred the woods, but the snow was luminous. He could see the trail well. He walked.

"How are you, David? How are you holding up?"

"All right."

"We'll stop for a while and let you rest. You can set me down here." The boy kept walking. He moved so ponderously, it seemed after each step that he had stopped. But he kept walking.

"You can set me down. Don't you want to rest?"

The boy did not answer. He wished that his father would not make him talk. At the start he had gulped for air. Now he was breathing low and regularly. He was watching his thighs slice through the snow. He did not want to be disturbed. After a moment he said, "No."

He walked. He came to the dead cub, shrouded beneath new snow, and did not see it, and fell over it. His face was smashed deep into the snow by his father's weight. He could not move. But he could breathe. He rested. When he felt his father's thigh roll across his right hand, he remembered the wound. He was lucky his arms had been pinned to his sides, or the hand might have taken the force of their fall. As he waited for his father to roll himself clear, the boy noticed the change in temperature. His sweat chilled him quickly. He began shivering.

His father had again fallen in silence. The boy knew that his father would not call out or even mention the pain in his leg. The boy realized that he did not want to mention his hand. The blood soaking the outside of his flannel bandage had grown sticky. He did not want to think of the alien tangle of flesh and tendons and bones wrapped inside. There was pain, but he kept the pain at a distance. It was not *his* hand any more. He was not counting on ever having it back. If he was resolved about that, then the pain was not his either. It was merely pain of which he was aware. His good hand was numb.

"We'll rest now."

"I'm not tired," the boy said. "I'm just getting cold."

"We'll rest," said his father. "I'm tired."

Under his father's knee, the boy noticed, was a cavity in the snow, already melted away by fresh blood. The dark flannel around his father's thigh did not appear sticky. It gleamed.

His father instructed the boy how to open the cub with the deer knife. His father stood on one leg against a deadfall, holding the Winchester ready, and glanced around on all sides as he spoke. The boy used his left hand and both his knees. He punctured the cub low in the belly, to a soft squirting sound, and sliced upward easily. He did not gut the cub. He merely cut out a large square of belly meat. He handed it to his father, in exchange for the rifle.

His father peeled off the hide and left the fat. He sawed the meat in half. One piece he rolled up and put in his jacket pocket. The other he divided again. He gave the boy a square thick with glistening raw fat.

"Eat it. The fat too. Especially the fat. We'll cook the rest farther on. I don't want to build a fire here and taunt Momma."

The meat was chewy. The boy did not find it disgusting. He was hungry.

His father sat back on the ground and unlaced the boot from his good foot. Before the boy understood what he was doing, he had relaced the boot. He was holding a damp wool sock.

"Give me your left hand." The boy held out his good hand, and his father pulled the sock down over it. "It's getting a lot colder. And we need that hand."

"What about yours? We need your hands too. I'll give you my—"

"No, you won't. We need your feet more than anything. It's all right. I'll put mine inside your shirt."

He lifted his father, and they went on. The boy walked.

He moved steadily through cold darkness. Soon he was sweating again, down his ribs and inside his boots. Only his hands and ears felt as though crushed in a cold metal vise. But his father was shuddering. The boy stopped.

His father did not put down his legs. The boy stood on the trail and waited. Slowly he released his wrist holds. His father's thighs slumped. The boy was careful about the wounded leg. His father's grip over the boy's neck did not loosen. His fingers were cold against the boy's bare skin.

"Are we at the hut?"

"No. We're not even to the meadow."

"Why did you stop?" his father asked.

"It's so cold. You're shivering. Can we build a fire?"

"Yes," his father said hazily. "We'll rest. What time is it?"

"We don't know," the boy said. "We don't have a watch."

The boy gathered small deadwood. His father used the Winchester stock to scoop snow away from a boulder, and they placed the fire at the boulder's base. His father broke up pine twigs and fumbled dry toilet paper from his breast pocket and arranged the wood, but by then his fingers were shaking too badly to strike a match. The boy lit the fire. The boy stamped down the snow, as his father instructed, to make a small ovenlike recess before the fire boulder. He cut fir boughs to floor the recess. He added more deadwood. Beyond the invisible clouds there seemed to be part of a moon.

"It stopped snowing," the boy said.

"Why?"

The boy did not speak. His father's voice had sounded unnatural. After a moment his father said:

"Yes, indeed. It stopped."

They roasted pieces of cub meat skewered on a green stick. Dripping fat made the fire spatter and flare. The meat was scorched on the outside and raw within. It tasted as good as any meat the boy had ever eaten. They burned their palates on hot fat. The second stick smoldered through before they had noticed, and that batch of meat fell in the fire. The boy's father cursed once and reached into the flame for it and dropped it and clawed it out, and then put his hand in the snow. He did not look at the blistered fingers. They ate. The boy saw that both his father's hands had gone clumsy and almost useless.

The boy went for more wood. He found a bleached deadfall not far off the trail, but with one arm he could only break up and carry small loads. They lay down in the recess together like spoons, the boy nearer the fire. They pulled fir boughs into place above them, resting across the snow. They pressed close together. The boy's father was shivering spastically now, and he clenched the boy in a fierce hug. The boy put his father's hands back inside his own shirt. The boy slept. He woke when the fire faded and added more wood and slept. He woke again and tended the fire and changed places with his father and slept. He slept less soundly with his father between him and the fire. He woke again when his father began to vomit.

The boy was terrified. His father wrenched with sudden vomiting that brought up cub meat and yellow liquid and blood and sprayed them across the snow by the grayish-red glow of the fire and emptied his stomach dry and then would not release him. He heaved on pathetically. The boy pleaded to be told what was wrong. His father could not or would not answer. The spasms seized him at the stomach and twisted the rest of his body taut in ugly jerks. Between the attacks he breathed with a wet rumbling sound deep in his chest, and did not speak. When the vomiting subsided, his breathing stretched itself out into long bubbling sighs, then shallow gasps, then more liquidy sighs. His breath caught and froth rose in his throat and into his mouth and he gagged on it and began vomiting again. The boy thought his father would choke. He knelt beside him and held him and cried. He could not see his father's face well and he did not want to look closely while the sounds that were coming from inside his father's body seemed so inhuman. The boy had never been more frightened. He wept for himself, and for his father. He knew from the noises and movements that his father must die. He did not think his father could ever be human again.

When his father was quiet, he went for more wood. He broke limbs from the deadfall with fanatic persistence and brought them back in bundles and built the fire up bigger. He nestled his father close to it and held him from behind. He did not sleep, though he was not awake. He waited. Finally he opened his eyes on the beginnings of dawn. His father sat up and began to spit.

"One more load of wood and you keep me warm from behind and then we'll go."

The boy obeyed. He was surprised that his father could speak. He thought it strange now that his father was so concerned for himself and so little concerned for the boy. His father had not even asked how he was.

The boy lifted his father, and walked.

Sometime while dawn was completing itself, the snow had resumed. It did not filter down soundlessly. It came on a slight wind at the boy's back, blowing down the canyon. He felt as though he were tumbling forward with the snow into a long vertical shaft. He tumbled slowly. His father's body protected the boy's back from being chilled by the wind. They were both soaked through their clothes. His father was soon shuddering again.

The boy walked. Muscles down the back of his neck were sore from yesterday. His arms ached, and his shoulders and thighs, but his neck hurt him most. He bent his head forward against the weight and the pain, and he watched his legs surge through the snow. At his stomach he felt the dull ache of hunger, not as an appetite but as an affliction. He thought of the jeep. He walked.

He recognized the edge of the meadow but through the snow-laden wind he could not see the cluster of aspens. The snow became deeper where he left the wooded trail. The direction of the wind was now variable, sometimes driving snow into his face, sometimes whipping across him from the right. The grass and snow dragged at his thighs, and he moved by stumbling forward and then catching himself back. Twice he stepped into small overhung fingerlets of the stream, and fell violently, shocking the air from his lungs and once nearly spraining an ankle. Farther out into the meadow, he saw the aspens. They were a hundred yards off to his right. He did not turn directly toward them. He was afraid of crossing more hidden creeks on the intervening ground. He was not certain now whether the main channel was between him and the aspen grove or behind him to the left. He tried to project from the canyon trail to the aspens and on to the forked pine on the far side of the meadow, along what he remembered as almost a straight line. He pointed himself toward the far edge, where the pine should have been. He could not see a forked crown. He could not even see trees. He could see only a vague darker corona above the curve of white. He walked.

He passed the aspens and left them behind. He stopped several times with the wind rasping against him in the open meadow, and rested. He did not set his father down. His father was trembling uncontrollably. He had not spoken for a long time. The boy wanted badly to reach the far side of the meadow. His socks were soaked and his boots and cuffs were glazed with ice. The wind was chafing his face and making him dizzy. His thighs felt as if they had been bruised with a club. The boy wanted to give up and set his father down and whimper that this had gotten to be very unfair; and he wanted to reach the far trees. He did not doubt which he would do. He walked.

He saw trees. Raising his head painfully, he squinted against the rushing flakes. He did not see the forked crown. He went on, and stopped again, and craned his neck, and squinted. He scanned a wide angle of pines, back and forth. He did not see it. He turned his body and his burden to look back. The snow blew across the meadow and seemed, whichever way he turned, to be streaking into his face. He pinched his eyes tighter. He could still see the aspens. But he could not judge where the canyon trail met the meadow. He did not know from just where he had come. He looked again at the aspens, and then ahead to the pines. He considered the problem carefully. He was irritated that the forked ponderosa did not show itself yet, but not worried. He was forced to estimate. He estimated, and went on in that direction.

When he saw a forked pine it was far off to the left of his course. He turned and marched toward it gratefully. As he came nearer, he bent his head up to look. He stopped. The boy was not sure that this was the right tree. Nothing about it looked different, except the thick cakes of snow weighting its limbs, and nothing about it looked especially familiar. He had seen thousands of pine trees in the last few days. This was one like the others. It definitely had a forked crown. He entered the woods at its base.

He had vaguely expected to join a trail. There was no trail. After two hundred yards he was still picking his way among trees and deadfalls and brush. He remembered the shepherd's creek that fell off the lip of the meadow and led down the first canyon. He turned and retraced his tracks to the forked pine.

He looked for the creek. He did not see it anywhere near the tree. He made himself quiet, and listened. He heard nothing but wind, and his father's tremulous breathing.

"Where is the creek?"

His father did not respond. The boy bounced gently up and down, hoping to jar him alert.

"Where is the creek? I can't find it."

"What?"

"We crossed the meadow and I found the tree but I can't find the creek. I need you to help."

"The compass is in my pocket," his father said.

He lowered his father into the snow. He found the compass in his father's breast pocket, and opened the flap, and held it level. The boy noticed with a flinch that his right thigh was smeared with fresh blood. For an instant he thought he had a new wound. Then he realized that the blood was his father's. The compass needle quieted.

"What do I do?"

His father did not respond. The boy asked again. His father said nothing. He sat in the snow and shivered.

The boy left his father and made random arcs within sight of the forked tree until he found a creek. They followed it onward along the flat and then where it gradually began sloping away. The boy did not see what else he could do. He knew that this was the wrong creek. He hoped that it would flow into the shepherd's creek, or at least bring them out on the same road where they had left the jeep. He was very tired. He did not want to stop. He did not care any more about being warm. He wanted only to reach the jeep, and to save his father's life.

He wondered whether his father would love him more

generously for having done it. He wondered whether his father would ever forgive him for having done it.

If he failed, his father could never again make him feel shame, the boy thought naively. So he did not worry about failing. He did not worry about dying. His hand was not bleeding, and he felt strong. The creek swung off and down to the left. He followed it, knowing that he was lost. He did not want to reverse himself. He knew that turning back would make him feel confused and desperate and frightened. As long as he was following some pathway, walking, going down, he felt strong.

That afternoon he killed a grouse. He knocked it off a low branch with a heavy short stick that he threw like a boomerang. The grouse fell in the snow and floundered and the boy ran up and plunged on it. He felt it thrashing against his chest. He reached in and it nipped him and he caught it by the neck and squeezed and wrenched mercilessly until long after it stopped writhing. He cleaned it as he had seen his father clean grouse and built a small fire with matches from his father's breast pocket and seared the grouse on a stick. He fed his father. His father could not chew. The boy chewed mouthfuls of grouse, and took the chewed gobbets in his hand, and put them into his father's mouth. His father could swallow. His father could no longer speak.

The boy walked. He thought of his mother in Evergreen Park, and at once he felt queasy and weak. He thought of his mother's face and her voice as she was told that her son was lost in the woods in Montana with a damaged hand that would never be right, and with his father, who had been shot and was unconscious and dying. He pictured his mother receiving the news that her son might die himself, unless he could carry his father out of the woods and find his way to the jeep. He saw her face change. He heard her voice. The boy had to stop. He was crying. He could not control the shape of his mouth. He was not crying with true sorrow, as he had in the night when he held his father and thought his father would die; he was crying in sentimental self-pity. He sensed the difference. Still he cried.

He must not think of his mother, the boy realized. Thinking of her could only weaken him. If she knew where he was, what he had to do, she could only make it impossible for him to do it. He was lucky that she knew nothing, the boy thought.

No one knew what the boy was doing, or what he had yet to do. Even the boy's father no longer knew. The boy was lucky. No one was watching, no one knew, and he was free to be capable.

The boy imagined himself alone at his father's grave. The grave was open. His father's casket had already been lowered. The boy stood at the foot in his black Christmas suit, and his hands were crossed at his groin, and he was not crying. Men with shovels stood back from the grave, waiting for the boy's order for them to begin filling it. The boy felt a horrible swelling sense of joy. The men watched him, and he stared down into the hole. He knew it was a lie. If his father died, the boy's mother would rush out to Livingston and have him buried and stand at the grave in a black dress and veil squeezing the boy to her side like he was a child. There was nothing the boy could do about that. All the more reason he must keep walking.

Then she would tow the boy back with her to Evergreen Park. And he would be standing on 96th Street in the morning dark before his father's cold body had even begun to grow alien and decayed in the buried box. She would drag him back, and there would be nothing the boy could do. And he realized that if he returned with his mother after the burial, he would never again see the cabin outside Livingston. He would have no more summers and no more Novembers anywhere but in Evergreen Park.

The cabin now seemed to be at the center of the boy's life. It seemed to stand halfway between this snowbound creek valley and the train station in Chicago. It would be his cabin soon.

The boy knew nothing about his father's will, and he had never been told that legal ownership of the cabin was destined for him. Legal ownership did not matter. The cabin might be owned by his mother, or sold to pay his father's debts, or taken away by the state, but it would still be the boy's cabin. It could only forever belong to him. His father had been telling him *Here, this is yours. Prepare to receive it.* The boy had sensed that much. But he had been threatened, and unwilling. The boy realized now that he might be resting warm in the cabin in a matter of hours, or he might never see it again. He could appreciate the justice of that. He walked.

He thought of his father as though his father were far away from him. He saw himself in the black suit at the grave, and he heard his father speak to him from aside: *That's good. Now raise your eyes and tell them in a man's voice to begin shoveling. Then turn away and walk slowly back down the hill. Be sure you don't cry. That's good.* The boy stopped. He felt his glands quiver, full of new tears. He knew that it was a lie. His father would never be there to congratulate him. His father would never know how well the boy had done.

He took deep breaths. He settled himself. Yes, his father would know somehow, the boy believed. His father had known all along. His father knew.

He built the recess just as they had the night before, except this time he found flat space between a stone bank and a large fallen cottonwood trunk. He scooped out the snow, he laid boughs, and he made a fire against each reflector. At first the bed was quite warm. Then the melt from the fires began to run down and collect in the middle, forming a puddle of wet boughs under them. The boy got up and carved runnels across the packed snow to drain the fires. He went back to sleep and slept warm, holding his father. He rose again each half hour to feed the fires.

The snow stopped in the night, and did not resume. The woods seemed to grow quieter, settling, sighing beneath the new weight. What was going to come had come.

The boy grew tired of breaking deadwood and began walking again before dawn and walked for five more hours. He did not try to kill the grouse that he saw because he did not want to spend time cleaning and cooking it. He was hurrying now. He drank from the creek. At one point he found small black insects like winged ants crawling in great numbers across the snow near the creek. He stopped to pinch up and eat thirty or forty of them. They were tasteless. He did not bother to feed any to his father. He felt he had come a long way down the mountain. He thought he was reaching the level now where there might be roads. He followed the creek, which had received other branches and grown to a stream. The

ground was flattening again and the drainage was widening, opening to daylight. As he carried his father, his head ached. He had
stopped noticing most of his other pains. About noon of that day
he came to the fence.

It startled him. He glanced around, his pulse drumming suddenly, preparing himself at once to see the long empty sweep of snow
and broken fence posts and thinking of Basque shepherds fifty years
gone. He saw the cabin and the smoke. He relaxed, trembling hel-
plessly into laughter. He relaxed, and was unable to move. Then he
cried, still laughing. He cried shamelessly with relief and dull joy
and wonder, for as long as he wanted. He held his father, and cried.
But he set his father down and washed his own face with snow before he went to the door.

He crossed the lot walking slowly, carrying his father. He did not
now feel tired.

The young woman's face was drawn down in shock and revealed
at first nothing of friendliness.

"We had a jeep parked somewhere, but I can't find it," the boy
said. "This is my father."

They would not talk to him. They stripped him and put him before the fire wrapped in blankets and started tea and made him
wait. He wanted to talk. He wished they would ask him a lot of
questions. But they went about quickly and quietly, making things
warm. His father was in the bedroom.

The man with the face full of dark beard had used the radio to
call for a doctor. He went back into the bedroom with more
blankets, and stayed. His wife went from room to room with hot
tea. She rubbed the boy's naked shoulders through the blanket, and
held a cup to his mouth, but she would not talk to him. He did not
know what to say to her, and he could not move his lips very well.
But he wished she would ask him some questions. He was restless,
thawing in silence before the hearth.

He thought about going back to their own cabin soon. In his
mind he gave the bearded man directions to take him and his father
home. It wasn't far. It would not require much of the man's time.
They would thank him, and give him an elk steak. Later he and his

father would come back for the jeep. He could keep his father warm at the cabin as well as they were doing here, the boy knew.

While the woman was in the bedroom, the boy overheard the bearded man raise his voice:

"He what?"

"He carried him out," the woman whispered.

"What do you mean, carried him?"

"Carried him. On his back. I saw."

"Carried him from where?"

"Where it happened. Somewhere on Sheep Creek, maybe."

"Eight miles?"

"I know."

"Eight miles? How could he do that?"

"I don't know. I suppose he couldn't. But he did."

The doctor arrived in half an hour, as the boy was just starting to shiver. The doctor went into the bedroom and stayed five minutes. The woman poured the boy more tea and knelt beside him and hugged him around the shoulders.

When the doctor came out, he examined the boy without speaking. The boy wished the doctor would ask him some questions, but he was afraid he might be shivering too hard to answer in a man's voice. While the doctor touched him and probed him and took his temperature, the boy looked the doctor directly in the eye, as though to show him he was really all right.

The doctor said:

"David, your father is dead. He has been dead for a long time. Probably since yesterday."

"I know that," the boy said.

Wallace Stegner

The Colt

IT was the swift coming of spring that let things happen. It was spring, and the opening of the roads, that took his father out of town. It was spring that clogged the river with floodwater and ice pans, sent the dogs racing in wild aimless packs, ripped the railroad bridge out and scattered it down the river for exuberant townspeople to fish out piecemeal. It was spring that drove the whole town to the riverbank with pikepoles and coffeepots and boxes of sandwiches for an impromptu picnic, lifting their sober responsibilities out of them and making them whoop blessings on the C.P.R. for a winter's firewood. Nothing might have gone wrong except for the coming of spring. Some of the neighbors might have noticed and let them know; Bruce might not have forgotten; his mother might have remembered and sent him out again after dark.

But the spring came, and the ice went out, and that night Bruce went to bed drunk and exhausted with excitement. In the restless sleep just before waking he dreamed of wolves and wild hunts, but when he awoke finally he realized that he had not been dreaming the noise. The window, wide open for the first time in months, let in a shivery draught of fresh, damp air, and he heard the faint yelping far down in the bend of the river.

He dressed and went downstairs, crowding his bottom into the warm oven, not because he was cold but because it had been a ritual for so long that not even the sight of the sun outside could convince him it wasn't necessary. The dogs were still yapping; he heard them through the open door.

"What's the matter with all the pooches?" he said. "Where's Spot?"

"He's out with them," his mother said. "They've probably got a porcupine treed. Dogs go crazy in the spring."

"It's dog days they go crazy."

"They go crazy in the spring, too." She hummed a little as she set the table. "You'd better go feed the horses. Breakfast won't be for 10 minutes. And see if Daisy is all right."

Bruce stood perfectly still in the middle of the kitchen. "Oh my gosh!" he said. "I left Daisy picketed out all night!"

His mother's head jerked around. "Where?"

"Down in the bend."

"Where those dogs are?"

"Yes," he said, sick and afraid. "Maybe she's had her colt."

"She shouldn't for two or three days," his mother said. But just looking at her he knew that it might be bad, that there was something to be afraid of. In another moment they were both out the door, both running.

But it couldn't be Daisy they were barking at, he thought as he raced around Chance's barn. He'd picketed her higher up, not clear down in the U where the dogs were. His eyes swept the brown, wet, close-cropped meadow, the edge of the brush where the river ran close under the north bench. The mare wasn't there! He opened his mouth and half turned, running, to shout at his mother coming behind him, and then sprinted for the deep curve of the bend.

As soon as he rounded the little clump of brush that fringed the cutbank behind Chance's he saw them. The mare stood planted, a bay spot against the gray brush, and in front of her, on the ground, was another smaller spot. Six or eight dogs were leaping around, barking, sitting. Even at that distance he recognized Spot and the Chapmans' Airedale.

He shouted and pumped on. At a gravelly patch he stooped and clawed and straightened, still running, with a handful of pebbles. In one pausing, straddling, aiming motion he let fly a rock at the distant pack. It fell far short, but they turned their heads, sat on their haunches and let out defiant short barks. Their tongues lolled as if they had run far.

Bruce yelled and threw again, one eye on the dogs and the other on the chestnut colt in front of the mare's feet. The mare's ears were back, and as he ran Bruce saw the colt's head bob up and down. It was all right then. The colt was alive. He slowed and came up quietly. Never move fast or speak loud around an animal, Pa said.

The colt struggled again, raised its head with white eyeballs rolling, spraddled its white-stockinged legs and tried to stand. "Easy, boy," Bruce said. "Take it easy, old fella." His mother arrived, getting her breath, her hair half down, and he turned to her gleefully. "It's all right, Ma. They didn't hurt anything. Isn't he a beauty, Ma?"

He stroked Daisy's nose. She was heaving, her ears pricking forward and back; her flanks were lathered, and she trembled. Patting her gently, he watched the colt, sitting now like a dog on its haunches, and his happiness that nothing had really been hurt bubbled out of him. "Lookit, Ma," he said. "He's got four white socks. Can I call him Socks, Ma? He sure is a nice colt, isn't he? Aren't you, Socks, old boy?" He reached down to touch the chestnut's forelock, and the colt struggled, pulling away.

Then Bruce saw his mother's face. It was quiet, too quiet. She hadn't answered a word to all his jabber. Instead she knelt down, about ten feet from the squatting colt, and stared at it. The boy's eyes followed hers. There was something funny about . . .

"Ma!" he said. "What's the matter with its front feet?"

He left Daisy's head and came around, staring. The colt's pasterns looked bent - *were* bent, so that they flattened clear to the ground under its weight. Frightened by Bruce's movement, the chestnut flopped and floundered to its feet, pressing close to its mother. And it walked, Bruce saw, flat on its fetlocks, its hooves sticking out in front like a movie comedian's too-large shoes.

Bruce's mother pressed her lips together, shaking her head. She moved so gently that she got her hand on the colt's poll, and he bobbed against the pleasant scratching. "You poor broken-legged thing," she said with tears in her eyes. "You poor little friendly ruined thing!"

Still quietly, she turned toward the dogs, and for the first time in his life Bruce heard her curse. Quietly, almost in a whisper, she cursed them as they sat with hanging tongues just out of reach. "God damn you," she said. "God damn your wild hearts, chasing a mother and a poor little colt."

To Bruce, standing with trembling lip, she said, "Go get Jim Enich. Tell him to bring a wagon. And don't cry. It's not your fault."

His mouth tightened, a sob jerked in his chest. He bit his lip and drew his face down tight to keep from crying, but his eyes filled and ran over.

"It is too my fault!" he said, and turned and ran.

Later, as they came in the wagon along the cutbank, the colt tied down in the wagon box with his head sometimes lifting, sometimes bumping on the boards, the mare trotting after with chuckling vibrations of solicitude in her throat, Bruce leaned far over and tried to touch the colt's haunch. "Gee whiz!" he said. "Poor old Socks."

His mother's arm was around him, keeping him from leaning over too far. He didn't watch where they were until he heard his mother say in surprise and relief, "Why, there's Pa!"

Instantly he was terrified. He had forgotten and left Daisy staked out all night. It was his fault, the whole thing. He slid back into the seat and crouched between Enich and his mother, watching from that narrow space like a gopher from its hole. He saw the Ford against the barn and his father's big body leaning into it pulling out gunny sacks and straw. There was mud all over the car, mud on his father's pants. He crouched deeper into his crevice and watched his father's face while his mother was telling what had happened.

Then Pa and Jim Enich lifted and slid the colt down to the ground, and Pa stooped to feel its fetlocks. His face was still, red from windburn, and his big square hands were muddy. After a long examination he straighted up.

"Would've been a nice colt," he said. "Damn a pack of mangy mongrels, anyway." He brushed his pants and looked at Bruce's mother. "How come Daisy was out?"

"I told Bruce to take her out. The barn seems so cramped for her, and I thought it would do her good to stretch her legs. And then the ice went out, and the bridge with it, and there was a lot of excitement. . . ." She spoke very fast, and in her voice Bruce heard the echo of his own fear and guilt. She was trying to protect him, but in his mind he knew he was to blame.

"I didn't mean to leave her out, Pa," he said. His voice squeaked, and he swallowed. "I was going to bring her in before supper, only when the bridge . . ."

His father's somber eyes rested on him, and he stopped. But his father didn't fly into a rage. He just seemed tired. He looked at the colt and then at Enich. "Total loss?" he said.

Enich had a leathery, withered face, with two deep creases from beside his nose to the corner of his mouth. A brown mole hid in the left one, and it emerged and disappeared as he chewed a dry grass stem. "Hide," he said.

Bruce closed his dry mouth, swallowed. "Pa!" he said. "It won't have to be shot, will it?"

"What else can you do with it?" his father said. "A crippled horse is no good. It's just plain mercy to shoot it."

"Give it to me, Pa. I'll keep it lying down and heal it up."

"Yeah," his father said, without sarcasm and without mirth. "You could keep it lying down about one hour."

Bruce's mother came up next to him, as if the two of them were standing against the others. "Jim," she said quickly, "isn't there some kind of brace you could put on it? I remember my dad had a horse once that broke a leg below the knee, and he saved it that way."

"Not much chance," Enich said. "Both legs, like that." He plucked a weed and stripped the dry branches from the stalk.

"You can't make a horse understand he has to keep still."

"But wouldn't it be worth trying?" she said. "Children's bones heal so fast, I should think a colt's would too."

"I don't know. There's an outside chance, maybe."

"Bo," she said to her husband, "why don't we try it? It seems such a shame, a lovely colt like that."

"I know it's a shame!" he said. "I don't like shooting colts any better than you do. But I never saw a broken-legged colt get well. It'd just be a lot of worry and trouble, and then you'd have to shoot it finally anyway."

"Please," she said. She nodded at him slightly, and then the eyes of both were on Bruce. He felt the tears coming up again, and turned to grope for the colt's ears. It tried to struggle to its feet, and Enich put his foot on its neck. The mare chuckled anxiously.

"How much this hobble brace kind of thing cost?" the father said finally. Bruce turned again, his mouth open with hope.

"Two-three dollars, is all," Enich said.

"You think it's got a chance?"

"One in a thousand, maybe."

"All right. Let's go see MacDonald."

"Oh, good!" Bruce's mother said, and put her arm around him tight.

"I don't know whether it's good or not," the father said. "We might wish we never did it." To Bruce he said, "It's your responsibility. You got to take complete care of it."

"I will!" Bruce said. He took his hand out of his pocket and rubbed below his eye with his knuckles. "I'll take care of it every day."

Big with contrition and shame and gratitude and the sudden sense of immense responsibility, he watched his father and Enich start for the house to get a tape measure. When they were thirty feet away he said loudly, "Thanks, Pa. Thanks an awful lot."

His father half turned, said something to Enich. Bruce stooped to stroke the colt, looked at his mother, started to laugh and felt it turn horribly into a sob. When he turned away so that his mother wouldn't notice he saw his dog Spot looking inquiringly around the corner of the barn. Spot took three or four tentative steps and paused, wagging his tail. Very slowly (never speak loud or move fast around an animal) the boy bent and found a good-sized stone. He straightened casually, brought his arm back, and threw with all his might. The rock caught Spot squarely in the ribs. He yiped, tucked his tail, and scuttled around the barn, and Bruce chased him, throwing clods and stones and gravel, yelling, "Get out! Go on, get out of here or I'll kick you apart. Get out! Go on!"

So all that spring, while the world dried in the sun and the willows emerged from the floodwater and the mud left by the freshet hardened and caked among their roots, and the grass of the meadow greened and the river brush grew misty with tiny leaves and the dandelions spread yellow among the flats, Bruce tended his colt. While the other boys roamed the bench hills with .22's looking for gophers or rabbits or sage hens, he anxiously superintended the colt's nursing and watched it learn to nibble the grass. While his gang built a darkly secret hide-out in the deep brush beyond Hazard's, he was currying and brushing and trimming the chestnut mane. When packs of boys ran hare and hounds through the town and around the river's slow bends, he perched on the front porch with his sling-shot and a can full of small round stones, waiting for stray dogs to appear. He waged a holy war on the dogs until they learned to detour widely around his house, and he never did completely forgive his own dog, Spot. His whole life was wrapped up in the hobbled, leg-ironed chestnut colt with the slow-motion lunging walk and the affectionate nibbling lips.

Every week or so Enich, who was now working out of town at the Half Diamond Bar, rode in and stopped. Always, with that expressionless quiet that was terrible to the boy, he stood and looked the colt over, bent to feel pastern and fetlock, stood back to watch the plunging walk when the boy held out a handful of grass. His expression said nothing; whatever he thought was hidden back of his leathery face as the dark mole was hidden in the crease beside his mouth. Bruce found himself watching that mole sometimes, as if revelation might lie there. But when he pressed Enich to tell him, when he said, "He's getting better, isn't he? He walks better, doesn't he, Mr. Enich? His ankles don't bend so much, do they?" the wrangler gave him little encouragement.

"Let him be a while. He's growin', sure enough. Maybe give him another month."

May passed. The river was slow and clear again, and some of the boys were already swimming. School was almost over. And still Bruce paid attention to nothing but Socks. He willed so strongly that the colt should get well that he grew furious even at Daisy when she sometimes wouldn't let the colt suck as much as he wanted. He took a butcher knife and cut the long tender grass in the fence corners, where Socks could not reach, and fed it to his pet by the handful. He trained him to nuzzle for sugar-lumps in his pockets. And back in his mind was a fear: in the middle of June they would be going out to the homestead again, and if Socks weren't well by that time he might not be able to go.

"Pa," he said, a week before they planned to leave. "How much of a load are we going to have, going out to the homestead?"

"I don't know, wagonful, I suppose. Why?"

"I just wondered." He ran his fingers in a walking motion along the round edge of the dining table, and strayed into the other room. If they had a wagon load, then there was no way Socks could be loaded in and taken along. And he couldn't walk thirty miles. He'd get left behind before they got up on the bench, hobbling along like the little crippled boy in the Pied Piper, and they'd look back and see him trying to run, trying to keep up.

That picture was so painful that he cried over it in bed that night. But in the morning he dared to ask his father if they couldn't take Socks along to the farm. His father turned on him eyes as sober as Jim Enich's, and when he spoke it was with a kind of tired impatience. "How can he go? He couldn't walk it."

"But I want him to go, Pa!"

"Brucie," his mother said, "don't get your hopes up. You know we'd do it if we could, if it was possible."

"But Ma . . ."

His father said, "What you want us to do, haul a broken-legged colt thirty miles?"

"He'd be well by the end of the summer, and he could walk back."

"Look," his father said. "Why can't you make up your mind to it? He isn't getting well. He isn't going to get well."

"He is too getting well!" Bruce shouted. He half stood up at the table, and his father looked at his mother and shrugged.

"Please, Bo," she said.

"Well, he's got to make up his mind to it sometime," he said.

Jim Enich's wagon pulled up on Saturday morning, and Bruce was out the door before his father could rise from his chair. "Hi, Mr. Enich," he said.

"Hello, Bub. How's your pony?"

"He's fine," Bruce said. "I think he's got a lot better since you saw him last."

"Uh-huh." Enich wrapped the lines around the whip-stock and climbed down. "Tell me you're leaving next week."

"Yes," Bruce said. "Socks is in the back."

When they got into the back yard Bruce's father was there with his hands behind his back, studying the colt as it hobbled around. He looked at Enich. "What do you think?" he said. "The kid here thinks his colt can walk out to the homestead."

"Uh-huh," Enich said. "Well, I wouldn't say that." He inspected the chestnut, scratched between his ears. Socks bobbed, and snuffled at his pockets. "Kid's made quite a pet of him."

Bruce's father grunted. "That's just the damned trouble."

"I didn't think he could walk out," Bruce said. "I thought we could take him in the wagon, and then he'd be well enough to walk back in the fall."

"Uh," Enich said. "Let's take his braces off for a minute."

He unbuckled the triple straps on each leg, pulled the braces off, and stood back. The colt stood almost as flat on his fetlocks as he had the morning he was born. Even Bruce, watching with his whole mind tight and apprehensive, could see that. Enich shook his head.

"You see, Bruce?" his father said. "It's too bad, but he isn't getting better. You'll have to make up your mind. . . ."

"He will get better though!" Bruce said. "It just takes a long time, is all." He looked at his father's face, at Enich's, and neither one had any hope in it. But when Bruce opened his mouth to say-something else his father's eyebrows drew down in sudden, unaccountable anger, and his hand made an impatient sawing motion in the air.

"We shouldn't have tried this in the first place," he said. "It just tangles everything up." He patted his coat pockets, felt in his vest. "Run in and get me a couple cigars."

Bruce hesitated, his eyes on Enich. "Run!" his father said harshly.

Reluctantly he released the colt's halter rope and started for the house. At the door he looked back, and his father and Enich were talking together, so low that their words didn't carry to where he stood. He saw his father shake his head, and Enich bend to pluck a grass stem. They were both against him, they both were sure Socks would never get well. Well, he would! There was some way.

He found the cigars, came out, watched them both light up. Disappointment was a sickness in him, and mixed with the disappointment was a question. When he could stand their silence no more he burst out with it. "But what are we going to *do?* He's got to have some place to stay."

"Look, kiddo." His father sat down on a sawhorse and took him by the arm. His face was serious and his voice gentle. "We can't take him out there. He isn't well enough to walk, and we can't haul him. So Jim here has offered to buy him. He'll give you three dollars for him, and when you come back, if you want, you might be able to buy him back. That is if he's well. It'll be better to leave him with Jim."

"Well . . ." Bruce studied the mole on Enich's cheek. "Can you get him better by fall, Mr. Enich?"

"I wouldn't expect it," Enich said. "He ain't got much of a show."

"If anybody can get him better, Jim can," his father said. "How's that deal sound to you?"

"Maybe when I come back he'll be all off his braces and running around like a house afire," Bruce said. "Maybe next time I see him I can ride him." The mole disappeared as Enich tongued his cigar.

"Well, all right then," Bruce said, bothered by their stony-eyed silence. "But I sure hate to leave you behind, Socks, old boy."

"It's the best way all around," his father said. He talked fast, as if he were in a hurry. "Can you take him along now?"

"Oh, gee!" Bruce said. "Today?"

"Come on," his father said. "Let's get it over with."

Bruce stood by while they trussed the colt and hoisted him into the wagon box, and when Jim climbed in he cried out, "Hey, we forgot to put his hobbles back on." Jim and his father looked at each other. His father shrugged. "All right," he said, and started putting the braces back on the trussed front legs. "He might hurt himself if they weren't on," Bruce said. He leaned over the endgate stroking the white blazed face, and as the wagon pulled away he stood with tears in his eyes and the three dollars in his hand, watching the terrified straining of the colt's neck, the bony head raised above the endgate and one white eye rolling.

Five days later, in the sun-slanting, dew-wet spring morning, they stood for the last time that summer on the front porch, the loaded wagon against the front fence. The father tossed the key in his hand and kicked the door-jamb. "Well, good-bye, Old Paint," he said. "See you in the fall."

As they went to the wagon Bruce sang loudly,
Good-bye, Old Paint, I'm leavin' Cheyenne,
I'm leavin' Cheyenne, I'm goin' to Montana,
Good-bye, Old Paint, I'm leavin' Cheyenne.

"Turn it off," his father said. "You want to wake up the whole town?" He boosted Bruce into the back end, where he squirmed and wiggled his way neck-deep into the luggage. His mother, turning to see how he was settled, laughed at him. "You look like a baby owl in a nest," she said.

His father turned and winked at him. "Open your mouth and I'll drop in a mouse."

It was good to be leaving; the thought of the homestead was exciting. If he could have taken Socks along it would have been perfect, but he had to admit, looking around at the jammed wagon box, that there sure wasn't any room for him. He continued to sing

softly as they rocked out into the road and turned east toward
MacKenna's house, where they were leaving the keys.

At the low, sloughlike spot that had become the town's dump
ground the road split, leaving the dump like an island in the middle.
The boy sniffed at the old familiar smells of rust and tar-paper and
ashes and refuse. He had collected a lot of old iron and tea lead and
bottles and broken machinery and clocks, and once a perfectly
good amberheaded cane, in that old dumpground. His father
turned up the right fork, and as they passed the central part of the
dump the wind, coming in from the northeast, brought a rotten,
unbearable stench across them.

"Pee-you!" his mother said, and held her nose. Bruce echoed
her. "Pee-you! Pee-you-willy!" He clamped his nose shut and
pretended to fall dead.

"Guess I better get to windward of that coming back," said his
father.

They woke MacKenna up and left the key and started back. The
things they passed were very sharp and clear to the boy. He was
seeing them for the last time all summer. He noticed things he had
never noticed so clearly before: how the hills came down into the
river from the north like three folds in a blanket, how the stovepipe
on the Chinaman's shack east of town had a little conical hat on it.
He chanted at the things he saw. "Good-bye, old Chinaman.
Good-bye, old Frenchman River. Good-bye, old Dumpground,
good-bye."

"Hold your noses," his father said. He eased the wagon into the
other fork around the dump. "Somebody sure dumped something
rotten."

He stared ahead, bending a little, and Bruce heard him swear. He
slapped the reins on the team till they trotted. "What?" the mother
said. Bruce, half rising to see what caused the speed, saw her lips go
flat over her teeth, and a look on her face like the woman he had
seen in the traveling dentist's chair, when the dentist dug a living
nerve out of her tooth and then got down on his knees to hunt for
it, and she sat there half raised in her seat, her face lifted.

"For gosh sakes," he said. And then he saw.

He screamed at them. "Ma, it's Socks! Stop, Pa! It's Socks!"

His father drove grimly ahead, not turning, not speaking, and his mother shook her head without looking around. He screamed again, but neither of them turned. And when he dug down into the load, burrowing   in and shaking with long smothered sobs, they still said nothing.

So they left town, and as they wound up the dugway to the south bench there was not a word among them except his father's low, "For Christ sakes, I thought he was going to take it out of town." None of them looked back at the view they had always admired, the flat river bottom green with spring, its village snuggled in the loops of river. Bruce's eyes, pressed against the coats and blankets under him until his sight was a red haze, could still see through it the bloated, skinned body of the colt, the chestnut hair left a little way above the hooves, the iron braces still on the broken front legs.

Wallace Stegner

Chip Off the Old Block

SITTING alone looking at the red eyes of the parlor heater, Chet thought how fast things happened. One day the flu hit. Two days after that his father left for Montana to get a load of whiskey to sell for medicine. The next night he got back in the midst of a blizzard with his hands and feet frozen, bringing a sick homesteader he had picked up on the road; and now this morning all of them, the homesteader, his father, his mother, his brother Bruce, were loaded in a sled and hauled to the school-house-hospital. It was scary how fast they all got it, even his father, who seldom got anything and was tougher than boiled owl. Everybody, he thought with some pride, but him. His mother's words as she left were a solemn burden on his mind. "You'll have to hold the fort, Chet. You'll have to be the man of the house." And his father, sweat on his face even in the cold, his frozen hands held tenderly in his lap, saying, "Better let the whiskey alone. Put it away somewhere till we get back."

So he was holding the fort. He accepted the duty soberly. In the two hours since his family had left he had swept the floors, milked old Red and thrown down hay for her, brought in scuttles of lignite. And sitting now in the parlor he knew he was scared. He heard the walls tick and the floors creak. Every thirty seconds he looked up from his book, and finally he yawned, stretched, laid the book down, and took a stroll through the whole house, cellar to upstairs, as if for exercise. But his eyes were sharp, and he stepped back a little as he threw open the doors of bedrooms and closets. He whistled a little between his teeth and looked at the calendar in the hall to see what day it was. November 4, 1918.

A knock on the back door sent him running. It was the young man named Vickers who had taken his family away. He was after beds and blankets for the schoolhouse. Chet helped him knock the beds down and load them on the sled. He would sleep on the couch in the parlor; it was warmer there, anyway; no cold floors to worry about.

In the kitchen, making a list of things he had taken, Vickers saw the keg, the sacked cases of bottles, the pile of whiskey-soaked straw sheaths from the bottles that had been broken on the trip. "Your dad doesn't want to sell any of that, does he?" he said.

Chet thought briefly of his father's injunction to put the stuff away. But gee, the old man had frozen his hands and feet and caught the flu getting it, and now when people came around asking . . . "Sure," he said. "That's what he bought it for, flu medicine."

"What've you got?"

"Rye and bourbon," Chet said. "There's some Irish, but I think he brought that special for somebody." He rummaged among the sacks. "Four dollars a bottle, I think it is," he said, and looked at Vickers to see if that was too much. Vickers didn't blink. "Or is it four-fifty?" Chet said.

Vickers's face was expressionless. "Sure it isn't five? I wouldn't want to cheat you." He took out his wallet, and under his eyes Chet retreated. "I'll go look," he said. "I think there's a list."

He stood in the front hall for a minute or two before he came back. "Four-fifty," he said casually. "I thought probably it was."

Vickers counted out twenty-seven dollars. "Give me six rye," he said. With the sack in his hand he stood in the back door and looked at Chet and laughed. "What are you going to do with that extra three dollars?"

Chet felt his heart stop while he might have counted ten. His face began to burn. "What three dollars?"

"Never mind," Vickers said. "I was just ragging you. Got all you need to eat here?"

"I got crocks of milk," Chet said. He grinned at Vickers in relief, and Vickers grinned back. "There's bread Ma baked the other day, and spuds. If I need any meat I can go shoot a rabbit."

"Oh." Vickers's eyebrows went up. "You're a hunter, eh?"

"I shot rabbits all last fall for Mrs. Rieger," Chet said. "She's 'nemic and has to eat rabbits and prairie chickens and stuff. She lent me the shotgun and bought the shells."

"Mmm," Vickers said. "I guess you can take care of yourself. How old are you?"

"Twelve."

"That's old enough," said Vickers. "That's pretty old, in fact. Well, Mervin, if you need anything you call the school and I'll see that you get it."

"My name isn't Mervin," Chet said. "It's Chet."

"Okay," Vickers said. "Don't get careless with the fires."

"What do you think I am?" Chet said in scorn. He raised his hand stiffly as Vickers went out. A little tongue of triumph licked up in him. That three bucks would look all right, all right. Next time he'd know better than to change the price, too. He took the bills out of his pocket and counted them. Twenty-seven dollars was a lot of dough. He'd show Ma and Pa whether he could hold the fort or not.

But holding the fort was tiresome. By two o'clock he was bored stiff, and the floors were creaking again in the silence. Then he remembered suddenly that he was the boss of the place. He could go or come as he pleased, as long the cow was milked and the house kept warm. He thought of the two traps he had set in muskrat holes under the river bank. The blizzard and the flu had made him forget to see to them. And he might take Pa's gun and do a little hunting.

"Well," he said in the middle of the parlor rug, "I guess I will."
For an hour and a half he prowled the river brush. Over on the
path toward Heathcliff's he shot a snowshoe rabbit, and the second
of his traps yielded a stiffly frozen muskrat. The weight of his game
was a solid satisfaction as he came up the dugway swinging the rabbit by its feet, the muskrat by its plated tail.

Coming up past the barn, he looked over towards Van Dam's,
then the other way, toward Chapman's, half hoping that someone
might be out, and see him. He whistled loudly, sang a little into the
cold afternoon air, but the desertion of the whole street, the un-
broken fields of snow where ordinarily there would have been do-
zens of sled tracks and fox-and-goose paths, let a chill in upon his
pride. He came up the back steps soberly and opened the door.

The muskrat's slippery tail slid out of his mitten and the frozen
body thumped on the floor. Chet opened his mouth, shut it again,
speechless with surprise and shock. Two men were in the kitchen.
His eyes jumped from the one by the whiskey keg to the other, sitting at the table drinking whiskey from a cup. The one drinking he
didn't know. The other was Louis Treat, a halfbreed who hung out
down at the stable and sometimes worked a little for the
Half-Diamond Bar. All Chet knew about him was that he could
braid horsehair ropes and sing a lot of dirty songs.

"Aha!" said Louis Treat. He smiled at Chet and made a rubbing
motion with his hands. "We 'ave to stop to get warm. You 'ave
been hunting?"

"Yuh," Chet said automatically. He stood where he was, his
eyes swinging between the two men. The man at the table raised
his eyebrows at Louis Treat.

"Ees nice rabbit there," Louis said. His bright black button eyes
went over the boy. Chet lifted the rabbit and looked at the frozen
beads of blood on the white fur. "Yuh," he said. He was thinking
about what his father always said. You could trust an Indian, if he
was your friend, and you could trust a white man sometimes, if
money wasn't involved, and you could trust a Chink more than
either, but you couldn't trust a halfbreed.

Louis' voice went on, caressingly. "You 'ave mushrat too, eh?
You lak me to 'elp you peel thees mushrat?" His hand, dipping

under the sheepskin and into his pants pocket, produced a long-bladed knife that jumped open with the pressure of his thumb on a button.

Chet dropped the rabbit and took off his mitts. "No thanks," he said. "I can peel him."

Shrugging, Louis put the knife away. He turned to thump the bung hard into the keg, and nodded at the other man, who rose. "Ees tam we go," Louis said. "We 'ave been told to breeng thees wiskey to the 'ospital."

"Who told you?" Chet's insides grew tight, and his mind was setting like plaster of Paris. If Pa was here he'd scatter these thieves all the way to Chapman's. But Pa wasn't here. He watched Louis Treat. You could never trust a halfbreed.

"The doctor, O'Malley," Louis said. Keeping his eye on Chet, he jerked his head at the other man. "'Ere, you tak the other end."

His companion, pulling up his sheepskin collar, stooped and took hold of the keg. Chet, with no blood in his face and no breath in his lungs, hesitated a split second and then jumped. Around the table, in the dining room door, he was out of their reach, and the shotgun was pointed straight at their chests. With his thumb he cocked both barrels, click, click.

Louis Treat swore. "Put down that gun!"

"No, sir!" Chet said. "I won't put it down till you drop that keg and get out of here!"

The two men looked at each other. Louis set his end gently back on the chair, and the other did the same. "We 'ave been sent," Louis said. "You do not understan' w'at I mean."

"I understand all right," Chet said. "If Doctor O'Malley had wanted that, he'd've sent Mr. Vickers for it this morning."

The second man ran his tongue over his teeth and spat on the floor. "Think he knows how to shoot that thing?"

Chet's chest expanded. The gun trembled so that he braced it against the frame of the door. "I shot that rabbit, didn't I?" he said.

The halfbreed's teeth were bared in a bitter grin. "You are a fool," he said.

"And you're a thief!" Chet said. He covered the two carefully as they backed out, and when they were down the steps he slammed and bolted the door. Then he raced for the front hall, made sure that door was locked, and peeked out the front window. The two were walking side by side up the irrigation ditch toward town, pulling an empty box sled. Louis was talking furiously with his hands.

Slowly and carefully Chet uncocked the gun. Ordinarily he would have unloaded, but not now, not with thieves like those around. He put the gun above the mantel, looked in the door of the stove, threw in a half-scuttle of lignite, went to the window again to see if he could still see the two men. Then he looked at his hands. They were shaking. So were his knees. He sat down suddenly on the couch, unable to stand.

For days the only people he saw were those who came to buy whiskey. They generally sat a while in the kitchen and talked about the flu and the war, but they weren't much company. Once Miss Landis, his schoolteacher, came apologetically and furtively with a two-quart fruit jar under her coat, and he charged her four dollars a quart for bulk rye out of the keg. His secret hoard of money mounted to eighty-five dollars, to a hundred and eight.

When there was none of that business (he had even forgotten by now that his father had told him not to meddle with it), he moped around the house, milked the cow, telephoned to the hospital to see how his folks were. One day his dad was pretty sick. Two days later he was better, but his mother had had a relapse because they were so short of beds they had had to put Brucie in with her. The milk crocks piled up in the cellarway, staying miraculously sweet, until he told the schoolhouse nurse over the phone about all the milk he had, and then Doctor O'Malley sent down old Gundar Moe to pick it up for the sick people.

Sometimes he stood on the porch on sunny, cold mornings and watched Lars Poulsen's sled go out along the road on the way to the graveyard, and the thought that maybe Mom or Bruce or Pa might die and be buried out there on the knoll by the sandhills made him swallow and go back inside where he couldn't see how deserted the street looked, and where he couldn't see the sled and the streaming gray horses move out toward the south bend of the river. He resolved to be a son his parents could be proud of, and sat down at the piano determined to learn a piece letter-perfect. But the dry silence of the house weighed on him; before long he would be lying with his forehead on the keyboard, his finger picking on one monotonous note. That way he could concentrate on how different it sounded with his head down, and forget to be afraid.

And at night, when he lay on the couch and stared into the sleepy red eyes of the heater, he heard noises that walked the house, and there were crosses in the lamp chimneys when he lighted them, and he knew that someone would die.

On the fifth day he sat down at the dining-room table determined to write a book. In an old atlas he hunted up a promising locale. He found a tributary of the Amazon called the Tapajos, and firmly, his lips together in concentration, he wrote his title across the top of a school tablet: "The Curse of the Tapajos." All that afternoon he wrote enthusiastically. He created a tall, handsome young explorer and a halfbreed guide very like Louis Treat. He plowed through steaming jungles, he wrestled pythons and other giant serpents which he spelled boy constructors. All this time he was looking for the Lost City of Gold. And when the snakes got too thick even for his taste, and when he was beginning to wonder himself why the explorer didn't shoot the guide, who was constantly trying to poison the flour or stab his employer in his tent at midnight, he let the party come out on a broad pampa and see in the distance, crowning a golden hill, the lost city for which they searched. And then suddenly the explorer reeled and fell, mysteriously stricken, and the halfbreed guide, smiling with sinister satisfaction, disappeared quietly into the jungle. The curse of the Tapajos, which struck everyone who found that lost city, had struck again. But the young hero was not dead. . . .

Chet gnawed his pencil and stared across the room. It was going to be hard to figure out how his hero escaped. Maybe he was just stunned, not killed. Maybe a girl could find him there, and nurse him back to health. . . .

He rose, thinking, and wandered over to the window. A sled came across the irrigation ditch and pulled on over to Chance's house. Out of it got Mr. Chance and Mrs. Chance and Ed and

Harvey Chance. They were well, then. People were starting to
come home cured. He rushed to the telephone and called the hospital. No, the nurse said, his family weren't well yet; they wouldn't
be home for three or four days at least. But they were all better.
How was he doing? Did he need anything?

No, Chet said, he didn't need anything.

But at least he wasn't the only person on the street any more.
That night after milking he took a syrup pail of milk to the
Chances. They were all weak, all smiling. Mrs. Chance cried every
time she spoke, and they were awfully grateful for the milk. He
promised them, over their protests, that he would bring them some
every day, and chop wood and haul water for them until they got
really strong. Mr. Chance, who had the nickname of Dictionary
because he strung off such jaw-breaking words, told him he was a
benefactor and a Samaritan, and called upon his own sons to witness this neighborly kindness and be edified and enlarged. Chet
went home in the dark, wondering if it might not be a good idea,
later in his book somewhere, to have his explorer find a bunch of
people, or maybe just a beautiful and ragged girl, kept in durance
vile by some tribe of pigmies or spider men or something, and have
him rescue them and confound their captors.

On the afternoon of the eighth day Chet sat in the kitchen at
Chance's. His own house had got heavier and heavier to bear, and
there wasn't much to eat there but milk and potatoes, and both
stores were closed because of the flu. So he went a good deal to
Chance's, doing their chores and talking about the hospital, and
listening to Mr. Chance tell about the Death Ward where they put
people who weren't going to get well. The Death Ward was the
eighth-grade room, his own room, and he and Ed Chance
speculated on what it would be like to go back to that room where
so many people had died—Mrs. Rieger, and old Gypsy Davy from
Poverty Flat, and John Chapman, and a lot of people. Mrs. Chance
sat by the stove and when anyone looked at her or spoke to her she
shook her head and smiled and the tears ran down. She didn't seem
unhappy about anything; she just couldn't help crying.

Mr. Chance said over and over that there were certainly going to be a multitude of familiar faces missing after this thing was over. The town would never be the same. He wouldn't be surprised if the destitute and friendless were found in every home in town, adopted and cared for by friends. They might have to build an institution to house the derelict and the bereaved.

He pulled his sagging cheeks and said to Chet, "Mark my words, son, you are one of the fortunate. In that hospital I said to myself a dozen times, 'Those poor Mason boys are going to lose their father.' I lay there—myself in pain, mind you—and the first thing I'd hear some old and valued friend would be moved into the Death Ward. I thought your father was a goner when they moved him in."

Chet's throat was suddenly dry as dust. "Pa isn't in there!"

"Ira," said Mrs. Chance, and shook her head and smiled and wiped the tears away. "Now you've got the child all worked up."

"He isn't in there now," said Mr. Chance. "By the grace of the Almighty"—he bent his head and his lips moved—"he came out again. He's a hard man to kill. Hands and feet frozen, double pneumonia, and still he came out."

"Is he all right now?" Chet said.

"Convalescing," Mr. Chance said. "Convalescing beautifully." He raised a finger under Chet's nose. "Some people are just hard to kill. But on the other hand, you take a person like that George Valet. I hesitate to say before the young what went on in that ward. Shameful, even though the man was sick." His tongue ticked against his teeth, and his eyebrows raised at Chet. "They cleaned his bed six times a day," he said, and pressed his lips together. "It makes a man wonder about God's wisdom," he said. "A man like that, his morals are as loose as his bowels."

"Ira!" Mrs. Chance said.

"I would offer you a wager," Mr. Chance said. "I wager that a man as loose and discombobulated as that doesn't live through this epidemic."

"I wouldn't bet on a person's life that way," she said.

"Ma," Harvey called from the next room, where he was lying down. "What's all the noise about?"

They stopped talking and listened. The church bell was ringing madly. In a minute the bell in the firehouse joined it. The heavy bellow of a shotgun, both barrels, rolled over the snowflats between their street and the main part of town. A six-shooter went off, bang-bang-bang-bang-bang-bang, and there was the sound of distant yelling.

"Fire?" Mr. Chance said, stooping to the window.

"Here comes somebody," Ed said. The figure of a boy was streaking across the flat. Mr. Chance opened the door and shouted at him. The boy ran closer, yelling something unintelligible. It was Spot Orullian.

"What?" Mr. Chance yelled.

Spot cupped his hands to his mouth, standing in the road in front of Chet's as if unwilling to waste a moment's time. "War's over!" he shouted, and wheeled and was gone up the street toward Van Dam's.

Mr. Chance closed the door slowly. Mrs. Chance looked at him, and her lips jutted and trembled, her weak eyes ran over with tears, and she fell into his arms. The three boys, not quite sure how one acted when a war ended, but knowing it called for celebration, stood around uneasily. They shot furtive grins at one another, looked with furrowed brows at Mrs. Chance's shaking back.

"Now Uncle Joe can come home," Ed said. "That's what she's bawling about."

Chet bolted out the door, raced over to his own house, pulled the loaded shotgun from the mantel, and burst out into the yard again. He blew the lid off the silence in their end of town, and followed the shooting with a wild yell. Ed and Harvey, leaning out their windows, answered him, and the heavy boom-boom of a shotgun came from the downtown district.

Carrying the gun, Chet went back to Chance's. He felt grown-up, a householder. The end of the war had to be celebrated; neighbors had to get together and raise cain. He watched Mrs. Chance, still incoherent, rush to the calendar and put a circle around the date, November 11. "I don't ever want to forget what day it happened on," she said.

"Everyone in the world will remember this day," said Mr.

Chance, solemnly, like a preacher. Chet looked at him, his mind clicking.

"Mr. Chance," he said, "would you like a drink, to celebrate?"

Mr. Chance looked startled. "What?"

"Pa's got some whiskey. He'd throw a big party if he was home."

"I don't think we should," said Mrs. Chance dubiously. "Your father might . . ."

"Oh, Mama," Mr. Chance said, and laid his arm across her back like a log. "One bumper to honor the day. One leetle stirrup-cup to those boys of the Allies. Chester here is carrying on his father's tradition like a man." He bowed and shook Chet's hand formally. "We'd be delighted, Sir," he said, and they all laughed.

Somehow, nobody knew just how, the party achieved proportions. Mr. Chance suggested, after one drink, that it would be pleasant to have a neighbor or two, snatched from the terrors of the plague, come and join in the thanksgiving; and Chet, full of hospitality, said sure, that would be a keen idea. So Mr. Chance called Jewel King, and when Jewel came he brought Chubby Klein with him, and a few minutes later three more came, knocked, looked in to see the gathering with cups in their hands, and came in with alacrity when Chet held the door wide. Within an hour there were eight men, three women, and two Chance boys, besides Chet. Mr. Chance wouldn't let the boys have any whiskey, but Chet, playing bartender, sneaked a cup into the dining room and all sipped it and smacked their lips.

"Hey, look, I'm drunk," Harvey said. He staggered, hiccoughed, caught himself, bowed low and apologized, staggered again. "Hic," he said. "I had a drop too much." The three laughed together secretly while loud voices went up in the kitchen.

"Gentlemen," Mr. Chance was saying, "I give you those heroic laddies in khaki who looked undaunted into the eyes of death and saved this ga-lorious empire from the rapacious Huns."

"Yay!" the others said, banging cups on the table. "Give her the other barrel, Dictionary."

"I crave your indulgence for a moment," Mr. Chance said. "For one leetle moment, while I imbibe a few swallows of this delectable amber fluid."

The noise went up and up. Chet went among them stiff with pride at having done all this, at being accepted here as host, at having men pat him on the back and shake his hand and tell him, "You're all right, kid, you're a chip off the old block. What's the word from the folks?" He guggled liquor out of the sloshing cask into a milk crock, and the men dipped largely and frequently. About four o'clock, two more families arrived and were welcomed with roars. People bulged the big kitchen; their laughter rattled the window frames. Occasionally Dictionary Chance rose to propose a toast to "those gems of purest ray serene, those unfailing companions on life's bitter pilgrimage, the ladies, God bless 'em!" Every so often he suggested that it might be an idea worth serious consideration that some liquid refreshments be decanted from the aperture in the receptacle.

The more liquid refreshments Chet decanted from the aperture in the receptacle, the louder and more eloquent Mr. Chance became. He dominated the kitchen like an evangelist. He swung and swayed and stamped, he led a rendition of "God Save the King," he thundred denunciations on the Beast of Berlin, he thrust a large fist into the lapels of new arrivals and demanded detailed news of the war's end. Nobody knew more than that it was over.

But Dictionary didn't forget to be grateful, either. At least five times during the afternoon he caught Chet up in a long arm and publicly blessed him. Once he rose and cleared his throat for silence. Chubby Klein and Jewel King booed and hissed, but he bore their insults with dignity. "Siddown!" they said. "Speech!" said others. Mr. Chance waved his hands abroad, begging for quiet. Finally they gave it to him, snickering.

"Ladies and gen'lemen," he said, "we have come together on this auspicious occasion . . ."

"What's suspicious about it?" Jewel King said.

". . . on this auspicious occasion, to do honor to our boys in Flander's field, to celebrate the passing of the dread incubus of Spanish Influenza . . ."

"Siddown!" said Chubby Klein.

". . . and last, but not least, we are gathered here to honor our friendship with the owners of this good and hospitable house, Bo Mason and Sis, may their lives be long and strewn with flowers, and this noble scion of a noble stock, this tender youth who kept the home fires burning through shock and shell and who opened his house and his keg to us as his father would have done. Ladies and gen'lemen, the Right Honorable Chester Mason, may he live to bung many a barrel."

Embarrassed and squirming and unsure of what to do with so many faces laughing at him, so many mouths cheering him, Chet crowded into the dining-room door and tried to act casual, tried to pretend he didn't feel proud and excited and a man among men. And while he stood there with the noise beating at him in raucous approbation, the back door opened and the utterly flabbergasted face of his father looked in.

There was a moment of complete silence. Voices dropped away to nothing, cups hung at lips. Then in a concerted rush they were helping Bo Mason in. He limped heavily on bandaged and slippered feet, his hands wrapped in gauze, his face drawn and hollow-eyed and noticeably thinner than it had been ten days ago. After him came Chet's mother, half carrying Bruce, and staggering under his weight. Hands took Bruce away from her, sat him on the open oven door, and led her to a chair. All three of them, hospital-pale, rested and looked around the room. And Chet's father did not look pleased.

"What the devil is this?" he said.

From his station in the doorway Chet squeaked, "The war's over!"

"I know the war's over, but what's this?" He jerked a bandaged hand at the uncomfortable ring of people. Chet swallowed and looked at Dictionary Chance.

Dictionary's suspended talents came back to him. He strode to lay a friendly hand on his host's back; he swung and shook his hostess' hand; he twinkled at the white-faced, big-eyed Bruce on the oven door.

"This, Sir," he boomed, "is a welcoming committee of your

friends and neighbors, met here to rejoice over your escape from
the dread sickness which has swept to untimely death so many of
our good friends, God rest their souls! On the invitation of your
manly young son here we have been celebrating not only that
emancipation, but the emancipation of the entire world from the
dread plague of war." With the cup in his hand he bent and
twinkled at Bo Mason. "How's it feel to get back, old

Bo grunted. He looked across at his wife and laughed a short,
choppy laugh. The way his eyes came around and rested on Chet
made Chet stop breathing. But his father's voice was hearty enough
when it came. "You got a snootful," he said. "Looks like you've all
got a snootful."

"Sir," said Dictionary Chance, "I haven't had such a delightful
snootful since the misguided government of this province suspended the God-given right of its free people to purchase and imbibe and ingest intoxicating beverages."

He drained his cup and set it on the table. "And now," he said,
"It is clear that our hosts are not completely recovered in their
strength. I suggest that we do whatever small tasks our ingenuity
and gratitude can suggest, and silently steal away."

"Yeah," the others said. "Sure. Sure thing." They brought in
the one bed from the sled and set it up, swooped together blankets
and mattresses and turned them over to the women. Before the
beds were made people began to leave. Dictionary Chance, voluble
to the last, stopped to praise the excellent medicinal waters he had
imbibed, and to say a word for Chet, before Mrs. Chance, with a
quick pleading smile, led him away. The door had not even closed
before Chet felt his father's cold eye on him.

"All right," his father said. "Will you please tell me why in the
name of Christ you invited that God-damned windbag and all the
rest of those sponges over here to drink up my whiskey?"

Chet stood sullenly in the door, boiling with sulky resentment.
He had held the fort, milked the cow, kept the house, sold all that
whiskey for all it was worth, run Louis Treat and the other man
out with a gun. Everybody else praised him, but you could depend
on Pa to think more of that whiskey the neighbors had drunk than
of anything else. He wasn't going to explain or defend himself. If

the old man was going to be that stingy, he could take a flying leap in the river.

"The war was over," he said. "I asked them over to celebrate."

His father's head wagged. He looked incredulous and at his wits' end. "You asked them over!" he said. "You said, 'Come right on over and drink up all the whiskey my dad almost killed himself bringing in.'" He stuck his bandaged hands out. "Do you think I got these and damned near died in that hospital just to let a bunch of blotters . . . Why, God damn you," he said. "Leave the house for ten days, tell you exactly what to do, and by Jesus everything goes wrong. How long have they been here?"

"Since about two."

"How much did they drink?"

"I don't know. Three crocks full, I guess."

His father's head weaved back and forth, he looked at his wife and then at the ceiling . . . "Three crocks. At least a gallon, twelve dollars' worth. Oh Jesus Christ, if you had the sense of a pissant . . . ."

Laboriously, swearing with the pain, he hobbled to the keg. When he put his hand down to shake it, his whole body stiffened.

"It's half empty!" he said. He swung on Chet, and Chet met his furious look. Now! his mind said. Now let him say I didn't hold the fort.

"I sold some," he said, and held his father's eyes for a minute before he marched out stiff-backed into the living room, dug the wad of bills from the vase on the mantel, and came back. He laid the money in his father's hand. "I sold a hundred and twenty-four dollars' worth," he said.

The muscles in his father's jaw moved. He glanced at Chet's mother, let the breath out hard through his nose. "So you've been selling whiskey," he said. "I thought I told you to leave that alone?"

"People wanted it for medicine," Chet said. "Should I've let them die with the flu? They came here wanting to buy it and I sold it. I thought that was what it was for."

The triumph that had been growing in him ever since he went for the money was hot in his blood now. He saw the uncertainty in his fathers's face, and he almost beat down his father's eyes.

"I suppose," his father said finally, "you sold it for a dollar a bottle, or something."

"I sold it for plenty," Chet said. "Four-fifty for bottles and four for quarts out of the keg. That's more than you were going to get, because I heard you tell Ma."

His father sat down on the chair and fingered the bills, looking at him. "You didn't have any business selling anything," he said. "And then you overcharge people."

"Yeah!" Chet said, defying him now. "If it hadn't been for me there wouldn't't've been any to sell. Louis Treat and another man came and tried to steal that whole keg, and I run 'em out with a shotgun."

"What?" his mother said.

"I did!" Chet said. "I made 'em put it down and get out."

Standing in the doorway still facing his father, he felt the tears hot in his eyes and was furious at himself for crying. He hoped his father would try thrashing him. He just hoped he would. He wouldn't make a sound; he'd grit his teeth and show him whether he was man enough to stand it. . . . He looked at his father's gray expressionless face and shouted, "I wish I'd let them take it! I just wish I had!"

And suddenly his father was laughing. He reared back in the chair and threw back his head and roared, his bandaged hands held tenderly before him like helpless paws. He stopped, caught his breath, looked at Chet again, and shook with a deep internal rumbling. "Okay," he said. "Okay, kid. You're a man. I wouldn't take it away from you."

"Well, there's no need to laugh," Chet said. "I don't see anything to laugh about."

He watched his father twist in his chair and look at his mother. "Look at him," his father said. "By God, he'd eat me if I made a pass at him."

"Well, don't laugh!" Chet said. He turned and went into the living room, where he sat on the couch and looked at his hands the way he had when Louis Treat and the other man were walking up the ditch. His hands were trembling, the same way. But there was no need to laugh, any more than there was need to get sore over a little whiskey given to the neighbors.

His mother came in and sat down beside him, laid a hand on his head. "Don't be mad at Pa," she said. "He didn't understand. He's proud of you. We all are."

"Yeah?" said Chet. "Why doesn't *he* come and tell me that?"

His mother's smile was gentle and a little amused. "Because he's ashamed of himself for losing his temper, I suppose," she said. "He never did know how to admit he was wrong."

Chet set his jaw and looked at the shotgun above the mantel. He guessed he had looked pretty tough himself when he had the drop on Louis Treat and his thieving friend. He stiffened his shoulders under his mother's arm. "Just let him start anything," he said. "Just let him try to get hard."

His mother's smile broadened, but he glowered at her.

"And there's no need to laugh!" he said.

Wallace Stegner

The Chink

IT is an odd trick of memory that after almost a quarter of a century I still remember Mah Li better than I can remember anyone else in that town. The people I grew up among, many of the children I played with every day, are vague names without faces, or faces without names. Maybe I remember him well because he was so ambiguous a figure in the town's life. He and his brother Mah Jim, who ran the restaurant, were the only Chinese in town, and though Mah Li did our laundry, worked for us, delivered our vegetables punctually at seven in the morning three days a week, he was as much outside human society as an animal would have been. Sometimes I catch myself remembering him in the same way I remember the black colt my father gave me when I was nine. I loved Mah Li as I loved the colt, but neither was part of the life that seemed meaningful at the time.

He called me O-Fi', because O-5, our laundry mark, was easier for him to say than Lederer. Every Monday morning he appeared at the back door with his basket, got the laundry, grinned and bobbed so that his pigtail twitched like a limber black snake, and said, "Velly good, O-Fi'. Leddy Fliday." I have a picture of him in my mind, shuffling up the worn path along the irrigation ditch, dogtrotting in his hurry as if daylight were going out on him while he still had a lot to do, and his black baggy pants and loose blouse blowing against his body.

I have other pictures, too. Whenever I think of him a swarm of things come up: Mah Li and Mah Jim sitting in the bare kitchen of the restaurant, a candle between them on the table with its flame as straight as a blade, playing fan-tan in intent, serious, interminable silence. Somehow that picture seems sad now, like a symbol of their homelessness. They had no women, no friends, no intercourse with the townspeople except when men kidded them along in the way they kid half-wits, condescendingly, with an edge of malice in their jokes.

I remember Mah Li meeting someone on the street in winter, the white man stopping him to say hello, rubbing his stomach and saying, "Belly cold today," and Mah Li beaming his wide smile, jabbering, and the white man saying, "Put your shirt inside your pants and your belly won't be cold," and slapping Mah Li on the back and guffawing. Old jokes like that, always the same ones. And the kids who hung around Mah Jim's restaurant jerking the Chinks' pigtails and asking them if it was true that they kneaded their bread in big tubs with their bare feet, or if they really spit in the soup of people they didn't like.

The town accepted them, worked them like slaves for little pay, I suppose even liked them after a fashion, but it never adopted them, just as Mah Jim and Mah Li never adopted white man's clothes, but always wore their black baggy pants and blouses. They never got the white man's habit of loafing, either. Mah Li, for instance, when he worked for us in summers down at the potato field, tended his own garden from daylight till about seven, worked our potatoes till almost dark, and then came into town to wash and iron till midnight on the laundry Mah Jim had taken in for him during the day. Maybe they liked to work that hard; maybe it helped them against their loneliness. My father always said that a Chinaman would outwork a white man two to one, and do it on a cupful of rice a day.

It is around the potato field and the garden that most of my recollections of the Chink center. The second year he worked for us he asked my father if he could rent a little piece of land to put in vegetables, and father let him have the ground free. Mah Li never thanked him—I don't think he ever knew what the word for thanks was. He just looked at him a minute with impassive slant eyes, bobbed his pigtail, and went dogtrotting down to go to work. But in July of that summer he appeared at our back door one morning just after I'd brought the milk in from the barn. He had a basket over his arm.

"Nice day, O-Fi'," he said. "Velly fine day!"

"It's a swell day," I said, "but you've got your dates mixed. It isn't laundry day."

"No laundly," he said, grinning, and passed me the basket. It was full of leaf lettuce and carrots and string beans and green peas, with two bunches of white icicle radishes sticking up in it like bouquets.

After that he came three times a week, regular as sunrise, with vegetables that were the envy of every gardener in town. And when Mother tried to pay him for them he beamed and bobbed and shook his head. I remember her saying finally, in a kind of despair, that she wouldn't take his baskets free any more, but he always came, and we always took them. It would have hurt his feelings if we hadn't.

It was Mother who suggested that I give the Chinese the suckers I caught in the river. We never ate them, because suckers are full of little needle-bones and don't taste very good. I just fished for the fun of it. So one afternoon I went down to the potato field in the river bottom, near the flume, with four big suckers on a willow crotch. Mah Li was moving down the field with a hoe, loosening the ground around the vines. When I gave him the fish he looked surprised, beamed, nodded, trotted down to the riverbank and packed them in grass, and rolled them up in a big handkerchief.

"Nice, O-Fi'," he said. I guess that was the way he said thanks.

That afternoon I hung around and helped him a little in the field, and went over with him to see his own garden. I remember him stooping among his tomato vines feeling the fruit till he found a big, red, firm one, and rubbing it off on his blouse and handing it to me. And I remember how heavy and sun-warmed that tomato was, and how I had to jump backward and stick out my face because the juice spurted and ran down my chin when I bit into it. We stood in the plant-smelling garden, under the yellow summer hills, with the sun heavy and hot on our heads, and laughed at each other, and I think that's where I first found out the Mah Li was human.

After that I was around the field a good deal. Whenever I didn't have anything else to do I'd go down and help him, or sit on the riverbank and fish while he worked. Just to watch him in a garden made you know he loved it. I used to watch him to see how long he'd swing the hoe without taking a rest, and sometimes I'd fish for two hours before he'd pause. Then he'd sit down on his heels, the way I've seen Chinese squat on the rails when they work on a section gang, and stay perfectly still for about ten minutes. He was so quiet then that bumblebees would blunder into him and crawl around and fly away again, and butterflies would light on his face. He let them sit there with their wings breathing in and out, and never made so much as the flicker of an eyelash that would disturb them. When he was ready to go to work again his hand would come up slowly, to pick them off so gently that they never knew he touched them.

His yellow hands were very gentle with everything they touched, even with the potato bugs we picked into tin cans and burned. Many afternoons in August I worked down the rows with him while he went bent-kneed along, his face placid and contented and his eyes sharp for bugs. He could do it three times as fast as I could, and cleaner too. We'd meet at the ends of rows every now and again, and dump the striped bugs out into piles, and Mah Li would pour kerosene over them and touch a match to it. Then we'd go down the rows again while stinking smudge went up behind.

And then there was the magpie that I ran across in the brush one day when I was coming up from fishing. It was a young one, with a hurt wing so that it couldn't fly, but it ran like a pheasant with that one wing trailing, and I had a chase before I caught it. It was still pecking at my fingers and flapping to get away when I brought it up to show Mah Li.

The Chink's face looked as if a lamp had gone on behind it. He chirped with his lips, quietly, and put out a dry hand to stroke the feathers on the bird's head. After a minute he lifted it out of my hands and held its body cradled in his palm, stroking its head, chirping at it. And it lay in his hand quietly as if it were on a nest; it made no attempt to peck him or to get away.

"He likes you," I said.

Mah Li's shaved head nodded very slowly, his lips going in a singsong lullaby and his finger moving gently on the magpie's head.

"Think his wing is broken?"

He nodded again; his pigtail crawled up his back with the bend of his head, and then crawled down.

"You better keep him," I said. "Maybe you can fix his wing."

Mah Li fixed his narrow black eyes on me. I was always being surprised by his eyes, because just talking to him, working with him, I though of him as another person, like anybody else. Then every once in a while I'd see those eyes, flat on his face, with scarcely any sockets for them to sink back into, and so narrow that it looked as if the skin had grown over and almost covered them.

"Slicee tongue," Mah Li said. "Talkee."

That night he carried the magpie home. A month later, when I saw it perched on the back of a chair in Mah Jim's kitchen, glossy and full of life, it opened its mouth and made squawking noises that sounded almost like words. By the middle of October he had it so tame that it rode around on his shoulder, balancing with its tail and squawking if he moved too fast and disturbed its footing, and whenever he chirped at it it squawked and jabbered. I laughed like anything when I heard what it said. It said "O-Fi'! O-Fi'! Nice, O-Fi'!"

So that's the way we were, friends — very good friends, in a way — even though Mah Li touched my life only on one of its outside edges. He was like a book I went back to read when there was nothing else doing. And I suppose it was that quality of unreality about our friendship, the strange and foreign things about him — pigtail and singsong and slant eyes — that made me think of him always in a special way, and forced me into the wrong loyalty that night at the end of October in 1918.

I came downtown that night about eight o'clock to join the gang and pull off some Hallowe'en tricks. You were everybody's enemy on Hallowe'en. You hauled your own father's buggy up on somebody's barn, and pushed over your own outhouse along with everybody else's. I say that to explain, in a way, how I came to be lined up against the Chinks that night. Things like that were automatic on Hallowe'en.

We had planned to meet at Mah Jim's, but I found the crowd gathered a block up the street. They were all sore. I didn't understand very clearly then, but I gathered that they'd been fooling in the restaurant and Tad McGovern had hooked a handful of bars from the candy counter. Mah Jim saw him, and raised a fuss, but Tad wouldn't give them back. He challenged Mah Jim to wrestle for them. The Chink got excited, and jabbered, and the kids all ragged him, and finally Mah Jim got really mad. I never saw him that way, but he must have been, because he jumped on Tad and took the bars away from him, and when three or four other kids took hold of him to put him down he shook them off and grabbed up the poker from the stove and ran the whole crowd out. So now they were just on the verge of getting even. They were going to tip over the Chinks' privy first, and then put the hospital sign on their front door, and then pour water down their chimney and put their fire out, and some other things.

I joined in and we went sneaking back through the alley toward Mah Jim's. It was a cold night, with a light snow that didn't quite cover the ground. In the dark it was just possible to see the pale patches where the snow lay. We crept up behind the laundry, just a couple of rods from the outhouse. Mah Jim must have closed up his restaurant after the ruckus with the gang, because there wasn't a light. The privy was just a vague blob of shadow in the dark.

We gathered behind Tad, waiting for the signal. Sometimes people stood guard on their privies, and we had developed a raiding technique that didn't give them a chance to do anything. When

Tad whistled we rushed out pell-mell, about a dozen of us. Our hands found the front of the privy and we heaved hard, all in one hard running push. There was a startled yelp from inside, a yelp almost like a dog's, as the privy lifted and tottered and went over with a crash.

Tad let out a whoop. "Gee, the Chink's in here!"

"Let's lock him in!" somebody said, and a half-dozen boys dived for the door to hold it down. Someone found a nail, and they hammered it in with a rock.

I stood back, because I didn't quite like the idea of the Chink's being locked in there in the cold, and because I was a little scared at the silence from inside. After that one yelp there hadn't been a sound. Even when Tad put his face down close to the boards and said, "Hey there, you Chink Mah Jim!" there was no answer. Tad laughed right out loud. "Gee, he's so mad he can't speak," he said. He put his face down again. "When you get tired you can come out the hole," her said.

Then one of the scouts stationed at the back of the laundry jiggered us and we scattered. I ducked behind a shed in the back lot and listened. Someone was calling from the side of the restaurant. "Boys!" he said. "Boys, come out. I want to talk to you."

In the dark somebody made a spluttering noise with his mouth. "Try and catch us," he said. But the voice went right on. I recognized it as belonging to Mr. Menefee, the principal of the school. "I don't want to catch you. I want to talk to you."

"What do you want to talk about?" I yelled, and felt big and brave for coming right back at Mr. Menefee that way. But Tad McGovern, over behind the hardware store, shouted at me: "Shut up! It's a trick."

"No, it isn't a trick," Mr. Menefee said. "Word of honor, boys. I just want to speak to you a minute.

There was such an anxious, worried tone in his voice that I stepped out from behind the shed and into the open. I could hear others coming too, cautiously, ready to break and run, but Mr. Menefee didn't make a move, and soon we were all around him where he stood in the faint light from the street with his overcoat up around his ears and his hands in his pockets.

"I just wanted to tell you," he said, "that it wouldn't be quite decent to pull any pranks tonight. Three people are down sick and Doctor Carroll says it's the flu."

His voice was so solemn, and the thought of the flu was so awful, that we stood there shuffling our feet without being able to say anything. We'd heard plenty about the flu. It killed you off in twenty-four hours, and you died in delirium, and after you were dead you turned black and shriveled. I felt it then like a great shadowy Fear in the dark all around me, while Mr. Menefee stood and looked at us and waited for his words to sink in.

"We're all going to have to help," he said finally. "I hate to take you away from your fun. You're entitled to it on Hallowe'en. But this is a time when everybody has to pitch in. Are you willing to help?"

That gave us our tongues, like a chorus of dogs after a porcupine. "Sure," we said. "Sure, Mr. Menefee!"

He lined it up for us. We were to go to the drugstore and get bundles of flu masks and bottles of eucalyptus oil, which we were to distribute to every house in town, warning people not to come out without their masks, and not to come out at all except when they had to. The town was going to be quarantined and nobody could leave it.

It was like being Paul Revere, and in the excitement of hearing all that I forgot for a minute about Mah Jim locked in the over turned privy. Then I caught myself listening, and all at once I remembered what I was listening for. I was expecting the Chink to hammer on the door and yell to get out. But there wasn't a sound from out in the back.

Mr. Menefee snapped to attention the way he did when we were having fire drill in school. "All right, men! What are we standing around for?"

The crowd shuffled their feet, and I knew most of them were thinking, just as I was, of the privy out behind with the Chink in it.

"Mr. Menefee," I said, and stopped.

"What?" I could see him bend over and stare around at us sharply. "You haven't started anything already, have you?" he said.

The silence came down again. Every one of us was ashamed of

what we'd just done, I imagine, except Tad McGovern. But none
of us dared admit we'd done anything. It would have been a kind of
treason. We were soldiers in the army, helping protect the town
against the plague. We couldn't just stand there and admit we'd
done something pretty raw, something we shouldn't have dared do
to a white man. It made us look small and mean and vicious, and
we wanted to look heroic.

Tad McGovern was right at my elbow. "Naw," he said. "We
were just getting ready to start."

Mr. Menefee snapped to attention again. "Good!" he said. "All
right, on the jump now. Divide up into squads, half of you into
each end of town. And remember to put on your own masks and
keep them on."

Some of the boys jumped and ran, and in a second we were all
running for the drugstore. All the time I wanted to turn around and
go back and say, "Mr. Menefee, we pushed over the Chink's privy
and Mah Jim's in there." But I kept on running, and got my bundle
of masks in the drugstore, and my package of eucalyptus oil bottles,
and opened one and soused a mask with it and put it on, and
gathered with the others outside, where we split.

The eucalyptus oil smelled so bad, and came so strong into my
mouth and nose through the mask, that I almost gagged, and that
made me think about myself for a while. But while we were running from door to door up in the Poverty Lane end of town I got
thinking more and more about how the Chinks didn't ever wear
very heavy clothes, and how Mah Jim might be freezing out there,
catching the flu, and how he'd be too big to crawl out through the
hole. I mentioned it to the boy I was with, but he said he was sure a
grown man could kick that nail loose with one kick. The Chink
was already out, he said. He'd be sitting by his fire right now, cussing us in Chinese.

Still I wasn't satisfied. Suppose he was hurt? Everything had been
dark when we pushed the privy over. That meant that if Mah Li
had gone to bed in his laundry room he wouldn't know Mah Jim
was still out. And if Mah Jim was hurt he'd lie there all night.

It gnawed at me until, after we had raised Orullian's house, I was
ready to quit the army and go back to see if the Chink was all right.

The excitement had worn off completely. I was cold, my nose was running into my mask, the stink of the oil made my stomach roll every time I took a breath. And so the first chance I got I stuck the remaining masks and bottles into my mackinaw pocket and cut out across the irrigation ditch toward town.

Everything was quiet when I slipped into the black back yard. Probably everything's all right, I thought. Probably he did kick the door out and get loose. But when I felt for the door and tried to open it, it was still nailed down.

"Mah Jim!" I said. I knocked on the boards and listened. Not a sound. I could feel sweat start out all over me, and my hands shook as I groped around in the dark for a stone. What if he was dead? What if we'd killed him?

With the rock I hammered and pulped the edge of the board where the nail was, until I could spring the door past. And when I scratched a match and looked down inside, into the overturned privy that looked like a big coffin, I saw not Mah Jim, but Mah Li, and he was sprawled back against the downward wall with his legs across the seat, absolutely quiet, and his pigtail hanging across the bend of his arm.

It took me five minutes to rouse Mah Jim. I could hear moving inside, and I yelled and cried that Mah Li was hurt, but he didn't open the door for a long time, and then only a crack. I suppose he thought it was another trick. My flu mask slipped down over my chin, and I was crying. "Help me get him out," I said. "He's back here. He's hurt. Come on."

Finally he came, and we got Mah Li out and carried him into the kitchen. He lay perfectly still, his face like a mask, every line smoothed out of it and his eyes shut. His breathing sounded too loud in the bare room. I couldn't take my eyes off his face, and while Mah Jim was squatting and feeling over his body I thought of the butter flies that used to crawl on Mah Li's face when he was resting. This was a different kind of stillness, and it scared me.

For five minutes Mah Jim squatted there, his pigtail hanging, and didn't say a word. I could feel the silence in the kitchen swell up around me; the only audible sound was the slow loud breathing of Mah Li, each breath coming with a hard finality, as if it were the last one he'd ever breathe. My nose kept running, and I'd lost my handkerchief, so that I had to sniffle every minute or so. I hated it, because it sounded as if I were crying, and I didn't want to seem to cry.

I kept thinking how I could have done something when the privy went over and I heard the yell from inside, how I'd had the chance to tell Mr. Menefee and get Mah Li out, but hadn't taken it. And I stood there thinking, What if I'd hauled off and socked Tad McGovern when he first jumped on that door to hold it down? I had just come up, not knowing anything about the privy-tipping, and I said loudly, What's going on here? and then I hit Tad and he fell down and I felt the jar in my wrist from the blow, and then three or four others jumped me, and I tossed them off and punched them in the nose until they all stood around me in an amazed ring, and I stood there with my fists up and said, "Come on, you cowards! You're so brave, picking on a poor harmless old Chink. Come on and get a taste of knuckles, any three of you at a time!"

But all the time while I was doing that in my mind I heard that rough slow breathing, and saw Mah Jim in the lamplight squatting by Mah Li's body, and I was sick with shame, and sniffled, and hated the smell of eucalyptus hanging under my nose.

"Is he hurt bad?" I said. "Can you tell what's the matter?"

I almost whispered it, afraid to talk right out loud. Mah Jim rose, and his eyes glittered. His face, like a slotted mask the color of dry lemon peel, made me swallow. I began to remember all the stories I'd heard about Chinks—how if they ever got it in for you, or if you did them an injustice, they'd slice your eyeballs and cut off your ears and split your nostrils and pierce your eardrums and pull out your toenails by the roots. Staring into his glittering slit eyes, I thought sure he was going for me, and my knees went weak. A kind of black fog came up in front of me; I lost Mah Jim's face, the room rocked, I could feel myself falling. Then the fog cleared again, and I was still on my feet, Mah Jim was staring at me, Mah Li was unconscious on the floor.

My shame was greater than my fear, and I didn't run, but I couldn't meet Mah Jim's eyes. I looked away to where the magpie was sitting on a chair back, with his white wing feathers almost hidden and his eyes as black and glittering as Mah Jim's.

"I better get the doctor," I said, and swallowed. The moment I said it I wondered why I hadn't done it already. I was starting for the door, full of relief at being able to do something, glad to get away, when I took a last look at Mah Jim, hoping he'd look kinder, hoping perhaps that he'd give me a word that would make me feel better about my own shame. And I stood there, half turned, staring at him. He hadn't moved, hadn't raised a hand, hadn't spoken, but I knew exactly what he meant. He meant no. He didn't want the doctor, even to save Mah Li's life. He didn't want any white man around, didn't want anything to do with us any more. There was bitterness, and anger, and a strange unreachable patience in his look that stopped me cold in the doorway.

And after a minute, in the face of Mah Jim's bitter dignity, I mumbled that I hoped Mah Li would be all right, that I'd come to see him tomorrow, and sneaked out. As I shut the door and stood shivering on the step I heard the magpie croaking and jawing inside. "Nice!" it said. "Nice, O-Fi'!"

Later, when I lay in bed at home with my head under the covers, shivering between the cold sheets and breathing hard with my mouth open to warm the bed, I resolved that next morning I would take the doctor down, Mah Jim or no Mah Jim. "You can't just lock the doors when somebody's sick or hurt," I'd tell him. "You have to have help, and I'm the one that's going to see you get it."

But I never did wake up to do what I planned. My sleep was haunted by wild dreams, flashes, streamers of insane color that went like northern lights across my nightmares. Once I woke up and discovered that I had been vomiting in my bed, but before I could do more than gag and gasp for somebody to come I was out again. I remember a hand on my head, and face over me, and once a feeling of floating. I opened my eyes then, to see the stair rails writhing by me like snakes, and I shut my eyes again to keep from dying. When I woke up it was a week later; I was in bed with my mother in the sixth grade room of the schoolhouse, and my nose was bleeding.

They kept us in the schoolhouse ten more days. After I was home, lying in bed in the dining room where it was warm, I felt good, full of the tired quietness that comes after sickness, and sleepy all the time, and pleased that I was getting well. Once or twice a day I got up in a bathrobe and tottered a few steps on crazy knees so that everybody laughed at me as if I were a child just taking his first steps.

On the fourth morning at home I felt perfectly well. When I woke up the sun was shining in the dining-room windows, and outside I could see the clean snow and the tracked path that led up past Shawn's house. Then I realized that something had awakened me, and listened. There was a mild, light tapping on the kitchen door. For a minute I forgot I was still weak, and jumped out of bed so fast that I sprawled on hands and knees, but laughing at myself, still feeling well and full of life. I got up and found my slippers and tottered into the kitchen, hanging to walls and doorjambs. On the back step Mah Jim was standing, with a basket on his arm.

"Nice day, O-Fi," he said, just the way Mah Li used to say it when he brought the vegetables. All in a rush the memory of that Hallowe'en night came back to me. I'd forgotten it completely during my sickness. I pulled Mah Jim inside and shut the door. "How's Mah Li?" I said.

His face perfectly blank, Mah Jim passed me the basket, covered with a clean dish towel. I lifted the cover and there was the magpie, looking ruffled and mad. I didn't understand. "You mean he's giving me the magpie?" I said.

Mah Jim nodded.

"Is he all right now?"

Like a wooden man, full of ancient and inscrutable patience, Mah Jim stood with his hands in the sleeves of his blouse. "All lightee now," he said.

The magpie shook its feathers, snapped its long tail, opened its beak, and its harsh squawk cut in. "O-Fi'! O-Fi'! Nice, O-Fi'!" I put out a finger to stroke its head the way Mah Li did, and it pecked me a sharp dig on the hand. I was so relieved about Mah Li, and so bursting with the feeling of being well, that I laughed out loud.

"That's swell," I said. "Tell him thanks very much. Tell him I

sure appreciate having it, Mah Jim. And tell him I'm glad he's well
again."

He stood silently, and I began to remember how sinister he'd
looked in the kitchen that night, and how he'd scared me then. To
keep the silence from getting too thick I kept on talking. "I've been
sick myself," I said. "I got sick that same night, or I'd have been
over to see him." The sunlight flashed on the windshield of a car
turning around in the road, and the light was so bright and gay that
I wanted to yell for just feeling good. I bragged. "They thought I
was going to die. I had a fever of a hundred and five, and was unconscious for a week, and my nose bled like anything."

I stopped. Mah Jim had not moved; his face was yellow parch-
ment with the slit eyes bright and still in it. "So you tell Mah Li I'll
be down to see him soon as I get on my feet," I said.

Something in the way he looked stopped me. Why did Mah Li
send him with the magpie? I wondered. Why didn't he come himself? Mah Jim took his hands out of his sleeves and made a short,
stiff little bow.

"Mah Li dead," he said. "We go back China. Bye, O-Fi'. Nice
day."

He opened the door and shuffled out, and I sat still in the kitchen
chair too shocked to feel anything really, except just the things
around me. I felt the cold draft on my bare ankles, and I felt the sun
warm on my arm and shoulder, but I couldn't feel anything about
Mah Li. I didn't really feel anything yet when I started to cry. The
tears just came up slowly the way a spring fills, and hung, and
brimmed over, and the first ones ran down my face and splashed
warm on the back of my hand.

About the Authors

MARY CLEARMAN BLEW 1939-

Mary Blew was born in Lewistown, Montana, and grew up on the family ranch on the Judith River. The ranch was homesteaded by her grandfather in 1882. Not surprisingly, she identifies the traditions evolving from the early 20th century experiences of homesteading, ranching, and the one-room schoolhouse as perhaps the most influential in her own writing. Blew financed her first years of college by breaking horses in Lewistown. She holds B.A. and M.A. degrees in English from the University of Montana (1962, 1963) and a Ph.D. (with a specialization in the English Renaissance) from the University of Missouri at Columbia (1969). Her first story, "Lambing Out," was written for a campus fiction contest at Missouri. She used the award money to buy a typewriter so she could type her dissertation. Public education has been her primary professional commitment since starting out as an elementary school teacher in Winnett—"a part of Montana," she says, "where even the jackrabbits packed a lunch." She taught at both Montana and Missouri while in graduate school. Returning to Montana in 1969, she served as Chair of the Department of Languages and Literature (1969-79) and Dean of the School of Arts and Sciences (1979-87) at Northern Montana College in Havre. She currently teaches English and creative writing at Lewis-Clark State College in Lewiston, Idaho, where she lives with the youngest of her three children. Her short stories have appeared in numerous literary journals (among them, *The Georgia Review, The North American Review, Four Quarters, The Iowa Review*) and won a prize for Best American Short Stories. To date, she has published two collections of stories, *Lambing Out and Other Stories* (1977) and *Runaway* (1990). She is now at work on a series of essays, tentatively entitled, *Leaving Montana, Essays of Place*, which will be published by Viking in 1991.

RAYMOND CARVER 1938-1988

Carver's first collection of short stories, *Will You Please Be Quiet, Please?* (1976), stunned critics and readers with the economy of its prose and the unrelenting honesty of its vision. The volume also earned him a nomination for the National Book Award. His next two collections, *What We Talk About When We Talk About Love* (1981) and *Cathedral* (1983), established Carver as one of America's most widely read and universally acclaimed practitioners of the short story. ("A true contemporary master," according to critic Robert Towers.) Carver was born in Oregon and grew up with a younger brother in Yakima,

About the Authors

Washington. His father was a saw-filer at a lumber mill and his mother worked off-and-on as a waitress and clerk. Carver indicated that his father, who told him family stories and read to him from the Bible and Zane Grey's works, initiated his interest in writing; but his love of hunting and fishing was what he first attempted to write about, when he was still in high school. At the age of eighteen, he married sixteen-year-old Maryann Burk, who was pregnant with the first of their two children. "We didn't have any youth," Carver said. "Years of working at crap jobs and raising kids and trying to write" also forced him to work on poems and stories, pieces he "could finish and be done with in a hurry." Carver stated that his two children were the most fundamental influence upon his writing during these apprenticeship years; but John Gardner, his teacher at Chico State College, and Gordon Lish, his editor at *Esquire*, also played substantial roles. In 1963, Carver earned an A.B. degree in English from Humboldt State College in California. Ironically, his literary success in the seventies was paralleled by deepening alcoholism, the collapse of his marriage, and the near destruction of his health, before he managed to stop drinking in 1977. Carver's awards are numerous: a Wallace Stegner Fellowship (1972), two NEA fellowships (1971, 1980), a Guggenheim (1979), and three O. Henry's (1974, 1975, 1980). In 1983, he was a first recipient of the Strauss Livings Award, a three-year, tax-free stipend from the American Academy and Institute of Arts and Letters. This award required him to resign a professorship in English at Syracuse University. From the late seventies until his death from cancer, he shared a home with poet Tess Gallagher, most recently in Port Angeles, Washington. Carver published six volumes of poems and six volumes of stories, as well as *Fires*, a 1983 collection of essays, poems, stories, and an interview. A reading of *Fires* is essential to any full understanding of his achievement.

WALTER VAN TILBURG CLARK 1909-1971

Clark came from distinguished academic parents. His father, an economist, was president of the University of Nevada for twenty years (1917-37) and his mother, a pianist, was a graduate of Cornell who pursued advanced study in music at Columbia. The first of four children, Clark took both B.A. and M.A. degrees from the University of Nevada (1927, 1931), where he was apparently a model student. In addition to his study of English and American literature, philosophy, and drama, he played varsity tennis and basketball, contributed to campus publications, and immersed himself in a wide range of artistic and social interests. He later received a second Master's degree from the University of Vermont

(1934). His thesis at Vermont was a defense of Robinson Jeffers' science-based philosophy. Clark married in 1933, fathered two sons, and taught high school English for ten years in Cazenovia, New York, before he began a peripatetic life of writing and teaching creative writing in various colleges and universities throughout the West. These included Reed College, the Universities of Oregon, Washington, and Montana, San Francisco State, and the University of Nevada. At Nevada, he resigned in protest against the administration in 1953 but returned to teach (and settle permanently in nearby Virginia City) in 1962. Clark's poetry of the thirties reveals a youthful romantic idealism which was clearly outgrown by the decade of the forties, the period of his major works of fiction — *The Oxbow Incident* (1940), *The City of Trembling Leaves* (1945), *The Track of the Cat* (1949), and *The Watchful Gods and Other Stories* (1950). As a writer, Clark was mysteriously silent the last twenty years of his life. His reputation as one of the West's most accomplished authors, however, is secured by what he published before that.

H. L. DAVIS 1894-1960

The oldest of four sons, Harold Lenoir Davis spent his early youth in various small communities between the Coast Range and the Cascade Mountains in the vicinity of Roseburg, Oregon. His father was a country school teacher, horse trainer, marksman, and amateur poet, who moved from job to job almost yearly. When Davis was twelve, the family settled for two years in Antelope, a dryland farming town in central Oregon. There young Davis dabbled at cowboying and sheepherding, and apparently initiated his career as a writer working for the *Antelope Herald* during the summer of 1907. The family soon moved on to The Dalles, the hub of railroad and riverboat commerce on the Columbia River. Though Davis called The Dalles home for the next twenty years, his experiences at Antelope were more influential, judging from their recurrence in his poetry, fiction, and essays. Davis began publishing poems in Harriet Monroe's *Poetry* in 1919. At H. L. Mencken's urging, he also began writing fiction and published his first story in *American Mercury* ten years later. His first novel, *Honey in the Horn*, won the Harper Novel Prize (1935) and the Pulitzer Prize (1936). The next decade was marred by publisher disputes and a broken marriage. Davis' best fiction emerged in the fifties—two novels, *Winds of Morning* (1952) and *The Distant Music* (1957), and two collections of stories and essays, *Team Bells Woke Me* (1953) and *Kettle of Fire* (1959). Davis married happily in 1953. Unfortunately, he was soon stricken with severe arteriosclerosis. His left leg had to be amputated while he was on a trip to Mexico in 1956, and four years later, he suffered a fatal heart attack in San Antonio. When he died, he was at work on a new novel with the manuscript title, "Exit, Pursued by a Bear." Davis' published work includes twenty-four short stories, five novels, over twenty essays, and forty-two poems.

IVAN DOIG 1939-

Doig burst into western literature in 1976, with the publication of his Montana autobiography, *This House of Sky*. He gives substantial credit for the success of the book to Carol Hill, the book's editor at Harcourt. "She was the thirteenth person to see that manuscript, and she brought it into being with loving care." But he says his father and his grandmother—his mother died when he was six—were even more fundamental influences upon his commitment to writing. Listening to the "dance of language" in their stories and conversation impressed on him the fact that westerners were "rich in language, even if they didn't have much else." Working with this "dance," making it tell stories on paper, was to become his life work. Doig was born in White Sulpher Springs, a small ranching town near Helena. He was raised by his father, a ranch hand and crew foreman, and his grandmother, a ranch cook. A "bookish" boy, he was an exceptional student throughout his public school years. At sixteen, he became disillusioned with his father's "dream" of sheep ranching and turned instead to a career in journalism. He took both B.S. and M.S. degrees from Northwestern University (1961, 1962) and began working for Lindsay-Schaub newspapers in Decatur. The next year he moved on to the assistant editorship of *The Rotarian*, a magazine with a circulation of 400,000. He married Carol Muller, a former classmate at Northwestern and a magazine editor herself, in 1965. He soon tired of "mid-way-up-the-mast-head jobs" requiring "automatic skills" and entered the Ph.D. program in western American history at the University of Washington, set on becoming a professor. Though Doig did complete the Ph.D. (1968), he realized in the process that he was "hopelessly a writer" and not cut out for the academic life. He consequently took up full-time free-lancing for magazines. In the next few years, he also published four textbook anthologies, one a joint effort with his wife Carol. Since *This House of Sky* appeared, he has authored a second work of nonfiction and five novels. Among the latter is the McCaskill family trilogy, a trio of novels probing Doig's roots in Montana history. The triology includes:

English Creek (1984), *Dancing at the Rascal Fair* (1987), and *Ride With Me, Mariah, Montana*, (1990). Doig believes "we've had too damn much of the cowboy West" and frankly admits to writing against the grain of what he calls "Wisterns" in these novels.

VARDIS FISHER 1895-1968

Fisher is the first major American novelist to emerge from the Mountain West. When his historical novel about the Mormons, *Children of God*, won the Harper Prize in 1939, he had already published eight novels. Four of these were set in the Antelope Hills country of eastern Idaho—*Toilers of the Hills* (1928), *Dark Bridwell* (1931), *In Tragic Life* (1932), and *April* (1937). These early works are now generally recognized as his crowning achievement, together with the Harper Prize winner, fictional treatments of the Donner Party (*The Mothers*, 1943) and the Lewis and Clark expedition (*Tale of Valor, 1958*), and his collected stories (*Love and Death*, 1959). (Fisher's prodigious energy resulted in six more historical novels as well as an eleven-volume series of novels dealing with the evolution of civilization, *Testament of Man*.) Born in Annis, Idaho, Fisher spent his early years on the family homestead in the bottomlands of the Snake River's South Fork, thirty miles from the nearest town. His autobiographical novel, *In Tragic Life*, depicts a youth marred by neurotic fears of social and sexual relations which are caused by an overly strict Morman mother. Ultimately, Fisher rejected his parent's religion, enrolled at the University of Utah, and married his teenage sweetheart (Leona McMurtrey). While at Utah, he became a regular contributor to the *University Pen*. The Fishers had one son while in Salt Lake and a second after he went on to complete M.A. and Ph.D. degrees in English at the University of Chicago (1922 and 1925). Tragically, his first wife committed suicide in 1924. Fisher returned to Utah to teach English the next year, but his strong views against Mormonism attenuated this venture into academe. After an unsuccessful second marriage (and a third son), Fisher married Opal Laurel Holmes in 1940. This marriage endured.

RICHARD FORD 1944-

Ford says his interest in writing came from a love of reading that dates from the time of his late teens. Also, like any native of Jackson, Mississippi, he considered writing an "entirely legitimate vocation" because of the local prominence of two literary figures, Eudora Welty and William Faulkner. Ford, however, initially "put all of his chips on law school," after graduating with a B.A. in English from Michigan State University in 1966. He hated law school, though, and quit halfway through his first year. With these plans dashed, he applied for a job with a bank, and then for another with the CIA. He even thought of joining the state police. Though he was accepted by both the bank and the CIA, neither offer finally interested him: "I simply found myself with nothing else to do, so I decided I would write stories." He had little success with publishing his early efforts, though. After completing an M.A. in English at the University of California at Irvine (1970), he ceased writing stories altogether and began work on a novel. "Failure at publishing stories where I wanted to publish them turned me back to my work . . . and I somehow was encouraged," he explained in a 1988 *Harper's* essay, "First Things First." Ford consequently considers his novel, *A Piece of My Heart* (1976), his first real publication. Since then, he has published two novels, *The Ultimate Good Luck* (1981) and *The Sportswriter* (1986), and a collection of stories, *Rock Springs* (1988). His stories have also appeared in *Esquire* and *The New Yorker*. Ford has received a Guggenheim Fellowship (1978) and the American Academy and Institute of Arts and Letters' Award for Literature (1988). His wife, Kristina, is a former Director of the Montana Public Policy Research Institute and author of *Planning Small Town America* (1990). They currently reside in both Montana and Louisiana, summering near Great Falls and wintering in New Orleans. Ford's fourth novel, *Wildlife* (1990), is set in Great Falls during the sixties. He plans to write more about Montana in the future.

A. B. GUTHRIE, JR. 1901-

Alfred Bertram Guthrie, Jr., was born in Indiana and raised from an early age in Choteau, Montana, where his father became principal of the county high school. As a teenager, he worked for the local weekly, the *Choteau Acantha*. He majored in journalism at both the Universities of Washington and Montana, before receiving a degree from the latter in 1923. Soon after, he took a reporter's job at the *Lexington Leader* in Kentucky, remaining there for twenty years and eventually rising to the rank of Executive Editor. In 1944 he won a Nieman Fellowship at Harvard University, which freed him to pursue an abiding interest in western history as well as cultivate relationships with influential figures such as Bernard DeVoto, Arthur Schlesinger, Sr., and Theodore Morrison. He followed his year in Cambridge with a stint at the Bread Loaf Writers' conference in Vermont. Both experiences were critical to the genesis of his first and best novel, *The Big Sky* (1947). His second novel, *The Way West* (1949), won him the Pulitzer Prize and enabled him to leave newspaper work, return to Choteau, and write fiction full-time. He has since published four additional, interrelated novels on the theme of developing the West, one juvenile fable, and four detective novels set in Montana small towns. He also wrote the screenplay for the film version of Jack Schaefer's *Shane*. By far his most admired work since the first two novels is a volume of short stories, *The Big It and Other Stories* (1960), and a memorable autobiography of his early life, *The Blue Hen's Chick* (1965).

DOROTHY M. JOHNSON 1905-1984

Though her birthplace was Iowa, home for Dorothy Marie Johnson was the railroad town of Whitefish in northwestern Montana, from the age of six until she went off to Missoula to college. She began writing as a girl, publishing poetry and a collaborative farce about a classmate ("The Lively Life of Leon") in her high school yearbook. At the University of Montana, she took up writing seriously and majored in English. More poems and her first short stories appeared in the campus literary magazine (*Frontier*), under the editorship of Professor Harold Merriam. Merriam's own interest in western literature may have been a strong influence on Johnson, as she later dedicated her first volume of stories to him. After graduating, Johnson worked as a secretary and continued to write stories, perfecting a form of which she was eventually to become a consummate master. She sold her first short story to the *Saturday Evening Post* when she was twenty-five, but did not sell another story until she was thirty-six. Johnson moved to New York in 1935, where she worked as a staff writer for Gregg Publishing Company. She ultimately became managing editor for *The Woman*, a digest magazine. During the forties, she published widely in popular magazines such as *The Post, Collier's,* and *Cosmopolitan.* Her stories from that time reflect a definite shift from contemporary to western subject matter, a shift brought on by an admitted "homesickness" for the West which moved her to immerse herself in a study of western history. After returning permanently to Montana in 1953, Johnson published her most outstanding collection of stories about the pre- and post-frontier West, *Indian Country*. An equally important collection, *The Hanging Tree*, came out in 1957. Stories from both collections have been made into films. With the decline of popular magazines in the sixties, Johnson reluctantly turned to writing juvenile fiction. All in all, she published seventeen titles of fiction, history, and personal reminiscence, almost all of which are currently out-of-print—a situation especially unfortunate because her fiction so often centers on a scarce commodity in western fiction, the female protagonist.

WILLIAM KITTREDGE 1932-

Kittredge grew up with a younger brother and sister on the family ranch in Warner Valley, near the town of Lakeview, in southeastern Oregon. The ranch was purchased by his grandfather during the Depression years. After receiving a B.S. degree in agriculture from Oregon State University (1953), he married and served in the Air Force for three years before returning to the Warner Valley to manage the ranch and raise a son and daughter. For the next ten years, he presided over the conversion of the ranch into a model of modern agri-business. At the same time, unfortunately, he came to feel the ranch had turned into "a landscape organized like a machine for growing crops and fattening cattle, a machine that creaked a little louder each year, a dreamland gone wrong." The family sold the ranch in 1967 and Kittredge immediately entered the University of Iowa's Writer's Workshop, taking an M.F.A. degree in 1969. That same year he joined the University of Montana's Creative Writing faculty, under the Directorship of Richard Hugo. In a 1987 volume of autobiographical essays, *Owning It All*, Kittredge depicts his last years on the ranch as a time when one dream died and another awakened. He credits his mother with passing on to him the "notion that there was more to life than cattle ranching" and describes his own lonely "yearning" for books and ideas during these years. Although he did not attempt to write until he was thirty-three, his stories and essays have since appeared in *Atlantic, Harper's, Rolling Stone, Outside,* and *Triquarterly*, as well as many other periodicals. Kittredge has been honored with a Stegner Fellowship at Stanford University (1973) and two NEA Fellowships (1974, 1981). He has published two collections of stories, *The Van Gogh Field* (1979) and *We Are Not in This Together* (1984).

DAVID LONG 1948-

Long has made Kalispell, Montana, his home since graduating from the University of Montana's M.F.A. program in Creative Writing in 1974. Long and his wife Suzy, a medical librarian, have two sons. Long initially attended Montana to study poetry with Richard Hugo and Madeline DeFrees, but switched to writing short stories under the influence of Bill Kittredge. (Long says Kittredge helped him "zero in on writing stories where something significant is at stake.") Long was born in Boston, grew up in Lunenburg, Massachusetts, and holds a bachelor's degree in English from Albion College in Michigan. He indicates that his move to Missoula in 1972 marked a major transformation in his life—from adolescence to adulthood as well as from east to west. Long's stories have appeared in *Anteus* and *The Sewanee Review*. He has published two collections, *Home Fires* (1982) and *The Flood of '64* (1987), and is currently working on a third. Montana history and small town life are the predominant subject matter in his recent fiction.

NORMAN MACLEAN 1902-

Maclean's parents were Canadian immigrants, his mother, English, his father, Scotch. Maclean was born in Iowa and his family settled permanently in Missoula, Montana, when he was seven. He was tutored at home by his father, a Presbyterian minister, until he was almost eleven. His intensely patriotic father insisted that Maclean learn American language and American speech idioms. Maclean indicates that his father particularly admired the prose of Mark Twain and "an odd combination" of Woodrow Wilson, Franklin Roosevelt, and Walt Whitman. Maclean was saturated as well, from an early age, with the rhythms of the "great King James translation" of the Bible. Maclean says he was also raised to view the family as the "center of the universe and the center of America." Maclean took an A.B. degree from Dartmouth College (1924) and a Ph.D. in English from the University of Chicago (1940). He taught at Dartmouth for two years and at Chicago from the time he began graduate work until he retired in 1973. His teaching career at Chicago was exceptionally distinguished. He received three Quantrell Awards for Excellence in Undergraduate Teaching and served for ten years as William Rainey Harper Professor of English Literature. The most startling facts about Norman Maclean are that he did not begin writing fiction until after his retirement at the age of 70, and then, at 73, he published a phenomenal first work, *A River Runs Through It and Other Stories*. This book was nominated for the Pulitzer Prize and has since become a best-seller and an American classic. Maclean is currently in the last stages of completing a long work on the 1949 forest fire at Mann Gulch near Helena.

DAVID QUAMMEN 1948-

According to Quammen, he began writing "juvenalia" at the age of eight; he has also been a "natural history fanatic" from the same age. Throughout his youth, consequently, he assumed that he would become a biologist, but Tom Savage, his Jesuit English teacher at St. Xavier High School in Cincinnati, changed all of that. Savage encouraged him to pursue a degree in English at Yale University because Robert Penn Warren was teaching there. During his junior year at Yale, Quammen enrolled in Penn Warren's criticism seminar and wrote a long essay on the "epistemology" of William Faulkner. All three men, in Quammen's view, were determining influences upon his decision to make his way as a free-lance writer. Quammen's formal education includes a B.A. from Yale (1970) and a B. Litt. from Oxford University (1973), where he was a Rhodes Scholar. After moving to Montana in 1973, he worked as a bartender in Missoula and as a fishing guide in Ennis, among other jobs—"paying dues" as a writer. He married Kris Ellingsen, a biological illustrator, in 1982, and settled permanently in Bozeman two years later. His stories have appeared in *TriQuarterly* and his essays in *Audubon, Harper's, Esquire, Rolling Stone,* and *The New York Times Book Review.* He has written a regular natural science column ("Natural Acts") for *Outside* magazine since 1983. Quammen's science and nature essays have been collected in two books, *Natural Acts* (1985) and *The Flight of the Iguana* (1988). He has published three novels, the most notable being *The Soul of Victor Tronko* (1987), an espionage story which has thematic linkages with his most recent work of fiction, *Blood Line* (1988), a collection of three stories about fathers and sons. The version of "Walking Out" which appears in this volume is from *Blood Line*, and has not been previously anthologized.

WALLACE STEGNER 1909-

The most prolific, versatile, and widely admired author in the collection, Stegner has published thirty-one works of fiction, biography, history, autobiography, and literary and cultural criticism, since his first stories appeared in 1934. Stegner was born in Lake Mills, Iowa, the second son of parents of German and Norwegian descent. He recounts the story of his childhood and youth in the novel, *The Big Rock Candy Mountain* (1943), as well as in a later work of fiction, history, and autobiography, *Wolf Willow* (1962). In both accounts, he depicts parents with contrasting roles: the father, restless, hardworking, punitive, always moving the family on to greener pastures in his tireless quest for financial success; the mother, understanding, loving, forgiving, stabilizing the family throughout almost constant vicissitude. Family settling points ranged from Puget Sound and southern Saskatchewan to Reno and Los Angeles. Stegner has said he believes a writer is most influenced by his pre-adolescent years, a time he himself spent in East End, a small Saskatchewan town fifty miles north of the U. S. border. The family did remain in Salt Lake City for fifteen years, permitting Stegner to finish public school and complete a B.A. degree at the University of Utah (1930). While at Utah, he was a student of Vardis Fisher, the man Stegner credits for stearing him towards a career in writing. During the next decade, Stegner lost his entire family. His brother died from pneumonia in 1931; his mother, from a protracted fight with cancer in 1933; and his father, by suicide in 1940. While still at Utah, Stegner began a parallel career in teaching; he soon moved on to complete a Ph.D. in English at the University of Iowa (1935). He later taught at several universities, most notably Harvard (1939-45) and Stanford (1945-71). At Harvard, he made a number of influential academic friends, including Robert Frost and Bernard DeVoto. At Stanford, he became director of the prestigious Stanford Writing Program, a position he held until his retirement. Stegner has published two collections of stories, *The Women on the Wall* (1950) and *The City of the Living, and Other Stories* (1956), His *Collected Stories* appeared in 1990. In addition to *Wolf Willow*, Stegner's most distinguished works of nonfiction are: a biography of John Wesley Powell, *Beyond the Hundredth Meridian* (1954); a collection of essays, *The Sound of Mountain Water* (1969); and a biography of Bernard DeVoto, *The Uneasy Chair* (1974). Two essays in the above collection—"Born a Square" and "History, Myth, and the Western Writer"—outline an important early theory of western fiction. Stegner's singular achievement in the two novels, *Angle of Repose* (the Pulitzer Prize winner in 1972) and *The Spectator Bird* (the National Book Award winner in 1976), unequivocally places him among those in the forefront of modern realist fiction in America, as well as explains his well-known objection to narrowing "regional" labels on his fiction.